A mother to five sons, **Fiona M**[obscured] wife who loves to write. Med[obscured] scope to write about all the w[obscured] romance, medicine and midwi[obscured] about—as well as an excuse to travel! Now that her boys are older, Fiona and her husband Ian are off to meet new people, see new places, and have wonderful adventures. Fiona's website is at www.fionamcarthur.com

Award-winning author **Jennifer Faye** pens fun, heart-warming romances. Jennifer has won the RT Reviewers' Choice Award, is a TOP PICK author, and has been nominated for numerous awards. Now living her dream, she resides with her patient husband, one amazing daughter (the other remarkable daughter is off chasing her own dreams) and two spoiled cats. She'd love to hear from you via her website: www.JenniferFaye.com

Margaret McDonagh says of herself: 'I began losing myself in the magical world of books from a very young age, and I always knew that I had to write, pursuing the dream for over twenty years, often with cussed stubbornness in the face of rejection letters! Despite having numerous romance novellas, short stories and serials published, the news that my first "proper book" had been accepted by Mills & Boon for their Medical Romance line brought indescribable joy! Having a passion for learning makes researching an involving pleasure, and I love developing new characters, getting to know them, setting them challenges to overcome. The hardest part is saying goodbye to them, because they become so real to me. And I always fall in love with my heroes! Writing and reading books, keeping in touch with friends, watching sport and meeting the demands of my four-legged companions keeps me well occupied. I hope you enjoy reading this book as much as I loved writing it.'

www.margaretmcdonagh.com margaret.mcdonagh@yahoo.co.uk

A Taste of Italy

FIONA McARTHUR
JENNIFER FAYE
MARGARET McDONAGH

MILLS & BOON

All rights reserved including the right of reproduction in whole or in part in any form. This edition is published by arrangement with Harlequin Books S.A.

This is a work of fiction. Names, characters, places, locations and incidents are purely fictional and bear no relationship to any real life individuals, living or dead, or to any actual places, business establishments, locations, events or incidents. Any resemblance is entirely coincidental.

This book is sold subject to the condition that it shall not, by way of trade or otherwise, be lent, resold, hired out or otherwise circulated without the prior consent of the publisher in any form of binding or cover other than that in which it is published and without a similar condition including this condition being imposed on the subsequent purchaser.

® and ™ are trademarks owned and used by the trademark owner and/or its licensee. Trademarks marked with ® are registered with the United Kingdom Patent Office and/or the Office for Harmonisation in the Internal Market and in other countries.

First Published in Great Britain 2018
by Mills & Boon, an imprint of HarperCollins*Publishers*
1 London Bridge Street, London, SE1 9GF

A TASTE OF ITALY © 2018 Harlequin Books S. A.

Midwife, Mother...Italian's Wife © 2011 Fiona McArthur
The Playboy Of Rome © 2015 Jennifer F. Stroka
St Piran's: Italian Surgeon, Forbidden Bride © 2011 Harlequin Books S.A.

ISBN: 978-0-263-26718-1

05-0518

MIX
Paper from
responsible sources
FSC™ C007454

This book is produced from independently certified FSC™ paper to ensure responsible forest management.

For more information visit: www.harpercollins.co.uk/green

Printed and bound in Spain
by CPI, Barcelona

MIDWIFE, MOTHER...
ITALIAN'S WIFE

FIONA McARTHUR

For Rosie and Carol, my fabulous friends,
who put up with those phone calls when I'm stuck.

CHAPTER ONE

As a reluctant best man, Leonardo Durante Bonmarito caught the unashamed adoration on the groom's face as he circled the room with his new bride, and knew his own earlier arrival in Australia would have made no difference.

Leon's intention of stopping this wedding had faltered at the first sight of Gianni at the airport because nothing would have prevented his brother from marrying this woman.

Such happiness made Leon's chest hurt and he'd never liked wedding feasts. It was even harder when he felt insulated from the joy and gaiety around him by the fact he still hadn't had a chance to talk to Gianni properly since arriving.

'Not a big fan of weddings?' The words were mild enough but the tone held a hint of quiet rebuke. Tammy Moore, chief bridesmaid and for tonight his partner, spoke at his shoulder and Leon returned to the present with a jolt. She went on, 'We're supposed to join them on the floor now.'

'*Sì*. Of course. My apologies.' Automatically he glanced around and down and unexpectedly his vision was filled with the delightful valley between her breasts.

He swept his eyes upwards and her dark brows tilted at the flicker of a smile he couldn't help.

It was a problem but what was a man to do with a bodice just under eye level? It would be strange dancing with a woman willow-slim in body and almost as tall as himself. She felt twice the height of his late wife.

He wondered if others might think they looked good together. Little did observers know their rapport had been anything but cordial, because he feared he hadn't endeared himself to her.

Leon repressed a sigh. He'd barely talked, in fact, it seemed he'd forgotten how to be at ease with a young woman, but in his defence, his mind had been torn between the recent danger to Paulo and when he could discuss it with his brother.

Tammy tapped her foot with the music, surely not with impatience, as she waited for them to join the bride and groom on the floor and he'd best concentrate. He hoped it would not be too much of a disaster because his heart wasn't in it. 'You are very good to remind me,' he said by way of apology, but she didn't comment, just held out one slender hand for him to take so the guests could join in after the official party was on the floor.

The music wheezed around them with great gusto if not great skill, like a jolly asthmatic between inhaler puffs, and Leon took her fingers in his and held them. Her hand lay small and slim, and somehow vulnerable, in his clasp, and suddenly he wasn't thinking of much except the way she unexpectedly fitted perfectly into his arms, her small breasts soft against his chest, and her hair smooth against his face.

In fact, her hip swung against his in seamless timing as if they'd danced together to a breathless piano accordion since birth.

Such precision and magical cadence took him from this place—and his swirling, painful thoughts—to a strange mist of curative tranquillity he'd craved since not just yesterday but from the haze of time in his youth.

Where was the awkwardness that'd always seemed to dog him and his late wife whenever they'd danced? The concept deepened the guilt in his heart and also the frown across his brows.

'You sway like a reed in my arms.' He tilted his head in reluctant approval. 'You must dance often.'

He thought he heard, 'Nearly as often as you frown, you great thundercloud.' The unexpected words were quiet, spoken to his feet, and he must have heard wrong because she followed that with, 'Yes, we love dancing here.'

He decided he was mistaken, but the humility in

her expression had a certain facade of mock innocence, and made his suspicions deepen with amused insight. Then he caught his son's eye as they swept past, and Leon raised his eyebrows at the flower girl standing beside him.

Paulo glanced at the young girl and then back at his father, nodded and took her hand to lead her into the dance. Tammy followed his gaze and smiled stiffly, something, he realised guiltily, she'd been doing for a couple of hours now.

She slanted a glance at him. 'Does your son dance as well as his father?'

They both turned their heads to watch the children waltz and Leon felt the warmth of pride. Paulo did well and it had not been an easy few days for him. 'I hope so. He has been taught. A man must be able to lead.'

'Emma's daughter can hold her own,' she murmured, and he bent his head closer to catch her words. Did the woman talk to him or to herself? An elusive scent, perfectly heated by the satin skin of her ridiculously long neck, curled around his senses with an unexpectedly potent assault. Without thought he closed his eyes and inhaled more deeply. This scent was a siren's weapon, yet she portrayed none of the siren's tricks.

He realised with delay that she'd continued the conversation. 'We have a bring-a-plate country dance once a month in the old hall. The children enjoy it as much as the adults.'

Leon eased back, he hoped unobtrusively, to clear the opulent fog from his mind but his voice came out deeper than he expected—deeper, lower, almost a caress. 'So dance nights are common in Australia?' What was happening? His brain seemed to have slowed to half speed as if he'd been drugged. Perhaps she did have tricks he was unaware of.

He lifted his head higher and sought out his son. The most important reason he needed his wits about him. Whatever spell she'd cast over him, he did not want it.

No doubt she'd sensed the change in him. He could only hope he'd left her as confused as she'd left him. 'To hold a dance is not unusual in a country town.' Her dark brows drew together in a glower such as she'd accused him of.

'Of course.' Thankfully, this time, his voice emerged normally, though he wondered if she could hear the ironic twist under the words. 'My brother is full of the virtues of your Lyrebird Lake.' And its incredibly fertile qualities, but he wouldn't go there.

She lifted her chin high and stared into his eyes as if suspicious of his tone and the implication he might disparage her hometown. Her irises were a startling blue and reminded him of the glorious sea on the Amalfi Coast, disturbingly attractive, yet with little waves of tempest not quite concealed and a danger that could not be underestimated. He knew all about that.

She went on in that confident voice of hers that managed to raise the dominant side of him like hairs on his neck. 'Lyrebird Lake has everything I need,' she stated, almost a dare to contradict.

He bit back the bitter laugh he felt churn in his chest. A fortunate woman. 'To have everything you want is a rarity. You are to be congratulated. Even if it seems a little unrealistic for such a young woman with no husband.'

Tammy smiled between gritted teeth. This man had created havoc in her usual calm state since the first moment she'd seen him. Too tall, too darkly handsome with sensually heavy features and so arrogant, so sure of his international power. Fancifully she'd decided he'd surveyed them all as if they were bush flies under an empty Vegemite jar.

One more dance and she was done. She felt like tapping her foot impatiently as she waited for the music to start again now the guests and not just the wedding party filled the floor.

It had been as if he'd barely got time for this frivolity of weddings, such an imposition to him, but she'd stayed civil because of Emma, and Gianni, obviously the much nicer brother of the two. But soon this last dance would be over, then everyone else would not notice her slip away. The official responsibilities she'd held would be complete apart from helping the bride to change.

No more being nice to Leonardo Bonmarito.

Though Tammy did feel sorry for Paulo Bonmarito, a handsome but quiet and no doubt downtrodden child, and she'd asked her own son to look after him. Nobody could call her Jack downtrodden.

As if conjured by the thought, eight-year-old Jack Moore, another young man resplendent in his miniature wedding tuxedo, walked up to Paulo. They looked almost like brothers, both dark-haired, olive-skinned boys with the occasional awkwardness of prepubescence. Then Jack tapped the young Italian boy on the shoulder as he and Grace waited to begin again. 'My dance now, I think.'

That wasn't what she'd envisaged when she'd said watch out for Paulo. Leon's back was to the children and Tammy frowned as she strained to hear as they stood waiting.

'You said you weren't dancing,' she heard Grace say, and the girl looked unimpressed with swapping for a boy she always danced with.

Jack shrugged as he waited for Paulo to relinquish his partner. 'Changed my mind.'

Without looking at Jack, Paulo bowed over Grace's hand, kissed her fingers in the continental way with practised ease and shrugged. *'Non importo. Grazie,'* he said, and turned with head high and walked away.

The music started and the dance floor shifted

like a sleepy animal awakening. Leon's son leaned with seeming nonchalance against a flower-decked pole and watched Grace being swung around easily by Jack. Like his father, his face remained expressionless and Tammy wondered if Paulo was used to disappointment.

When the dance was over, Tammy eased her hand out of Leon's firm grip as unobtrusively as she could and stepped back. She only just prevented herself from wiping her hand down the side of her bridesmaid dress to try and diffuse the stupid buzz of connection she could still feel.

The contact hadn't been what she expected and the dancing had increased her need to distance herself from this haughty stranger even more. It had been ridiculous the way they'd danced together as if they'd spent years, not seconds, training to synchronise. Not a common occurrence with her local partners but maybe she was imagining it just because he was taller and stronger, and decidedly more masterful, than most men she danced with.

Or maybe the strength of her disquiet about him had made her more aware. Either way she wasn't interested and needed to get away from him to her friends.

'Thank you.' She didn't meet his eyes and instead glanced around at the crowded dance floor. 'Everyone seems to be up now. If you'll excuse me?'

Leon raised one sardonic eyebrow at her apparent haste. 'You have somewhere you need to run off to?'

She opened her mouth to fabricate an excuse when the glowing bride, her best friend, Emma, dragged her smiling new husband across to his brother. 'Tammy! You and Leon dance wonderfully together.' She beamed at her husband, and the look that passed between them made Tammy glance away with a twist of ridiculous wistfulness.

'Almost as good as us,' Emma went on. 'Isn't my wedding beautiful?'

'Truly magnificent,' Leon said, and glanced at Gianni. 'Your organisational skills exceed even what I expected.'

'Nothing is too perfect for my wife.' Gianni, tall and solid like his brother, stroked Emma's cheek, and then looked across at Tammy. He smiled. 'And your partner for tonight?' He kissed his fingers. *'Bellissimo.* You, too, are blessed, brother. Tammy is another of the midwives here. Has she told you?'

'We've had little time for discussion.' Leon leaned forward and unexpectedly took Tammy's hand in his large one again. He held it firmly and the wicked glint in his eyes when he looked at her said he knew she wouldn't quibble in front of her friend. 'I was just going to find us a drink and sit down for a chat.'

Dear Emma looked so delighted Tammy didn't have the heart to snatch her fingers free, so she smiled, ignored the restart of the buzz in her fingers and wondered bitterly if her teeth would ache tonight from all the clenching she'd done today.

The music started and Gianni held out his hand to his wife. Emma nodded. 'I'll see you back at the bridal table, Tammy, after this dance. I want to tell you something.' Then Emma smiled blithely at them, sighed into her husband's arms and danced away.

Tammy looked around for escape but there was none. Trapped by her friend. Great. Leon held firmly on to her hand and steered her off the floor towards the official table. Unobtrusively Tammy tugged at her fingers and finally he let her hand free. She leaned towards him with a grim smile and, barely moving her lips, let him have it. 'Don't ever do that again or you will get more than you bargained for.'

'Tut. Temper.' He glanced down at her, amused rather than chastened by her warning, which made her more cross.

She grimaced a smile again and muttered, 'You have no idea,' as he pulled her chair out. She slipped into the chair and shifted it slightly so that it faced towards the dance floor and her shoulder tilted away from him.

When he returned with two tiny champagne flutes Leon was fairly sure she didn't realise the angle she gave him lent a delightful view of her long neck and the cleft below the hollow of her throat...and there was that incredible drift of scent again.

He controlled his urge to move closer. This woman

had invaded his senses on many unexpected levels and here he was toying with games he hadn't played since his amorous youth.

'Drink your wine,' he said.

She turned to him and her eyes narrowed blue fire at him. 'Were you born this arrogant or did you grow into it?'

So, her temper remained unimproved. She amused him. He shrugged and baited her. 'Bonmaritos have been in Portofino for six generations. My family are very wealthy.'

She lifted one elegant shoulder in imitation. 'Big deal. So were mine and my childhood was less than ideal.'

'And you are not arrogant?' To his surprise she looked at him and then smiled at his comment. And then to his utter astonishment she threw back her head and laughed. A throaty chortle that had his own mouth curve in appreciation.

Her whole face had softened. 'Actually, I've been told I am.'

When she laughed she changed from being a very attractive but moody woman into a delightful seductress he could not take his eyes off, and when she shuffled her chair back and studied him for a change, he felt the shift in their rapport like a fresh breeze. A dangerous, whimsical, warning breeze that he should flee from.

He shifted closer. 'So tell me, Tammy, is this your full name?'

'Tamara Delilah Moore, but nobody calls me that.'

'Delilah I believe. Tamara?' He rolled the name off his tongue as if sampling it, found the taste delightful and he nodded. That suited her better. 'There was a famous noblewoman called Tamara in Roman mythology. She, too, was tall and apparently rather arrogant. How ironic.'

'Really?' She raised those stern eyebrows of hers and Leon realised he liked the way she responded fearlessly to his bait. 'What if I say you're making that up?'

The music lilted around them playfully and helped the mood stay light. 'I would have to defend myself.'

She glanced down at her hands and spread them to look at her fingertips as if absorbed in her French manicure. He almost missed her comment. 'You nearly had to defend yourself in a more physical way earlier.'

So. More fire. He straightened and met her eyes with a challenge. 'I had the utmost faith in your control. You'd exhibited control all day. It's a wonder your teeth aren't aching.'

She blinked, glanced at him with an arrested expression and then laughed again. He felt the smile on his face. A deeper more genuine smile than he'd had for a long time. It felt surprisingly good to make her laugh.

Not something he'd been known for much in the past but her amusement warmed him in a place that had been cold for too long. 'Of course I also have a slight weight advantage.'

'And I have a black belt in karate.' She picked up one of the biscotti favours from a plate on the table and unconsciously broke a piece off, weighing it in her hand before putting it to her mouth. That curved and perfect mouth he'd been trying not to look at for the past ten minutes.

Karate. He searched for an image of sweating women in tracksuits he could call to mind, or the name of the white pyjamalike uniform people wore for martial arts, anything to take his mind off the sight of her lips parting as she absently turned him on.

'How long are you staying before you head back to Italy?' she said carelessly as she raised the biscuit shard. His gaze followed her fingers, drawn by invisible fields of magnetism and, unconsciously, he held his breath. Gi. The uniform was called gi.

Her lips opened and she slid the fragment in and licked the tips of her fingers, oblivious to his fascinated attention as she glanced at the dancers. His breath eased out and his body stirred and stretched in a way it hadn't in a long time.

Then she glanced back at him and he had to gather

his scattered wits. When was he leaving? Perhaps sooner than he intended if this was how tempted he'd already become. 'Gianni and Emma are away for the first few days of their honeymoon, and then Paulo and I will join them at the airport before we all return to Italy.' He was rambling.

He focused on the plans he'd finalised before he left for Italy. 'We were held up.' He paused. His grip tightened unconsciously on the glass in his hand and he looked away from her—that brought him back to earth. There was no time for this when the real world required constant and alert attention.

He shook his head and went on. 'We were held up on the way over and arrived later than expected. It will give Paulo a few days to get over the "excitement" before we have to return.' She nodded.

Jack appeared at her side and tugged on her dress. 'Excuse me, Mum. Can we go and play spotlight?'

Tammy looked away from this suddenly much more attractive man to her son and the world started again. What was she thinking? She blinked again to clear her head and swallowed the last of the biscuit. 'Who with?' she asked Jack, and looked beyond him to the milling group of young boys and girls.

'Dawn and Grace, and Peta and Nicky. And some of the older kids as well.' He glanced at Leon. 'And Paulo if he wants to?'

Leon frowned and looked across to where his son

was talking to Grace and another girl. 'What is this "spotlight"?'

Tammy shrugged. 'Hide-and-seek in the dark and the seeker has a handheld torch or spotlight. The children play it all the time here when parties like this stretch into evening.'

Leon's frown didn't lighten. 'Even young girls? Without parents supervising?'

'They won't go far.' She looked at Paulo, who pretended he didn't expect his father to say no. 'Let him go. He'll be fine.'

Leon hesitated, and she wondered if he'd been this protective since the boy's mother had died. Overprotecting children made her impatient but she held her tongue, if not her expression, and then finally he nodded.

'Perhaps for a short while.' He tilted his head at his son and Paulo approached them. He spoke in Italian and Tammy looked away but she couldn't help overhearing.

She had no trouble interpreting Leon's discussion with his son. She'd been able to speak Italian since her teenage years in a dingy Italian coffee shop in Sydney, dark with dangerous men and a tall Italian youth she hadn't seen since but wasn't allowed to forget. Those memories reminded her why she wasn't attracted to Leonardo Bonmarito.

'Do you wish to play this game?' Leon said to his son.

'*Sì*,' said Paulo, and he looked away to the other children.

'Be aware of your safety,' Leon continued in his native language, and Tammy frowned at the tablecloth in front of her. It seemed a strange thing to say at his brother's wedding in a country town.

'*Sì, Padre*, of course,' Paulo said again, and when his father nodded he ran off to join the children. Tammy hoped she wiped the expression from her face before she glanced back at Leon. Listening to Leon talk to his son brought back many memories and it had surprised her how easily she slipped back into recognising the words.

'Your son has beautiful manners. Is he allowed to play with other children much?'

It was her turn to be frowned on. 'Of course.' No doubt she'd offended him. Oops, she thought without remorse.

Leon went on in a low, steely voice that made her eyebrows rise. 'He attends school. And your Jack? He appears very confident.' His eyes travelled over her. 'Like his mother.'

She shrugged. Tough if he had a problem with that. 'There's only been Jack and me together, although my father and my stepmother have always been very much a part of his life since he was born. They live next door.'

She saw his gaze drift to his brother and the planes of his angular face softened as he nodded. 'Family is important. Especially when one's family is smaller than God intended.'

There seemed a story there. She wasn't quite sure what he was getting at. Did he have plans to enlarge his family? Was he here to convince his brother to take his wife back to Italy for good? Perhaps it would be better to know one's enemy, as good as an excuse as any for plain old nosiness, but she had to admit to herself he intrigued her. 'So, both your parents are gone?'

'*Sì.*' Reluctance in the answer. 'They died when we were young.'

She should stop the questions, but maybe now a silence would be even more awkward, or that's what she told herself as she asked the next. 'To lose a parent is hard, to lose both would be devastating. Especially as I believe you are the eldest of the two of you?'

He shrugged and his voice had cooled. 'By four years. It was my responsibility to be the head of the family.'

At how old? she wondered. 'No other relatives to look after you?'

He answered almost absently as his attention was distracted by the calls and laughter of the children. 'An elderly widowed aunt who has since passed away.' He frowned again as Paulo ducked with a grin behind a dark bush.

He really did have issues with Paulo playing with

the other children, Tammy decided. 'And Emma says you lost your wife last year?'

His gaze snapped back to her and this time he raised haughty brows at her. *'Molto curioso,'* he said.

Yes, she couldn't deny she was curious. She looked at him blandly as if she had no idea what he said, until he inclined his head and continued on a different topic. 'It is good to see Paulo with a smile on his face. They have been too rare in the past year.'

The pang of sympathy for both of them reminded her of the past as well. 'And now your own son has lost his mother. It's hard to lose your mother.'

Now that brought back memories she'd rather forget but felt obliged to share as she'd been so nosy. 'Even difficult mothers. I was fifteen when I lost mine. Went to live with my mother's mother.' She laughed with little amusement. 'Who said my living there made her feel too old. Such a silly woman.'

'Perhaps it is my turn to be curious?' It seemed Leon waited for her to enlarge on the topic. Not a hope in Hades.

She said the first thing she could think of to avoid a discussion of her ridiculous past. 'Would you like to dance again?' She discovered as she waited for his answer the idea held definite appeal.

His mouth tilted and she knew he was aware of her sudden change of subject. 'I would like that very much.'

The palpitations came out of nowhere. Just started to thump in her chest as he stood—and from where she sat he filled her vision; he truly was magnificent—then drew her up, with that strong hand of his closing on hers. She felt weightless, like a feather, and a little airy like a feather too, which wasn't like her as she drifted across to the floor where the piano accordion was valiantly attempting to play a waltz.

It was okay to enjoy a dance. With a skilled partner. Nothing wrong with that. His arms came around her and she closed her eyes, giving in to the moment for once, not fighting the magic that had surprised her earlier in the evening. This was what dancing was for. She just hadn't realised she'd been searching for the right partner.

CHAPTER TWO

TAMMY missed the moment when the music stopped until Leon's arm drifted down her back to her hip and he angled her towards the bridal table. The tiny, secret smile on her face fell away with her trance. How embarrassing.

His fingers were warm on her skin through the thin material of her bridesmaid dress as he led her back to her chair.

Both of them were silent. And that serves me right for letting my guard down, Tammy thought, as she tried to think of something to say that would dispel the myth she'd been lost in his arms.

In the end she was saved by the bride. 'You two seem to be getting along *very* well.' A glowing Emma grinned at them as she and Gianni approached the table. When her husband held her chair for her Emma sank thankfully down and fanned her face. She looked from one to the other but neither spoke.

Leon murmured his thanks as he lifted his hand in a 'spare me a moment' gesture to his brother. Then he slanted a glance at Tammy, his face serious as he caught her eye, before he and his brother walked off just a few paces.

Tammy saw Leon's glance flick to the boys as they disappeared around the corner of the building but her attention was brought back to the table by Emma's excitement. 'The dancing is such fun.' Emma waved her hand some more as she tried to stir the warm air. 'Did you have a good chat with Leon before the dance? I wondered if you'd find much to talk about.'

'We talked about the boys,' Tammy said, and then she heard Leon ask Gianni, in Italian, if he thought the spotlight game was safe enough. He was back to that.

Tammy strained her ears for Gianni's answer, his affirmative clear, but then something Leon said very quietly made Gianni stop suddenly and stare and the two men moved further out of earshot, both bristling, and she had the sudden ridiculous thought that they were like a pair of wolves hunting in the night.

The darkness of a black shadow ran icy fingers over her neck and she shook the feeling off mostly because she didn't do premonitions, and secondly because it wasn't a happy wedding-day vibration at all and a far cry from the heady bubble of the dance floor.

She turned to Emma and worked to dispel the unease that lingered despite her efforts to banish it. 'So what were you so anxious to tell me that I had to sit beside your brother-in-law and wait with bated breath?'

'Poor you. Was he such a hardship?' Emma teased.

Tammy glanced towards the spot where the men had disappeared. 'It's been a long day,' she said cryptically, 'but perhaps he might not be as bad as I thought.'

Emma's brows crinkled. 'Good.' Though now there was a trace of doubt in her voice. 'Because I want everyone to get on well.' Emma looked for the men too, and back at Tammy. Then all the excitement caught up with her again and Tammy vowed to be more careful not to blemish her friend's day.

'My news?' She smiled happily. 'Well, first Leon's talking to your father about some project in Rome so he and Paulo are not flying back immediately.'

Tammy knew that, and didn't see much there to be excited about. She didn't like the uncomfortable feeling the man left her with.

Emma bubbled on. 'So Leon and Paulo are staying here until after we come back from our mini honeymoon and then we're going to Italy for a month's holiday. Gianni asked if in a couple of weeks you and Jack might like to come over and be with me while he has to sort out work commitments with his brother.'

Tammy raised her eyebrows and her friend went on. 'So Grace and I won't get bored?' Emma looked at her expectantly. 'What do you think?'

What did she think? That this was the last thing she'd expected. Did she want to go to Italy? While she could admit Emma's new husband had turned out to be a delightful and doting husband, initially she hadn't been overly impressed with his brother.

And now it was more the effect he had on her that had her squirming to find a matching excitement her friend would like. 'I guess I'd have to think about it. See if Montana has enough staff to cover at the birth centre, work out which of my birthing women are due.'

She shook her head. 'Take Jack overseas? I don't know.' To Italy of all places.

Emma nodded her understanding. 'Think about it. Oh, and I gave Leon your mobile number. Hope you don't mind. In case we're out of range and he needs something.' Emma seemed to think it was no great moment. She was still focused on the Italian trip. 'It's just an idea but I love the sound of both of us in Italy.'

Tammy could see she did. And normally she'd like the idea too. Overseas travel was something she'd done a lot of in her early teens with her parents and she'd been to Italy once. Maybe that had been the start of her attraction to Italians. She tried not to think of him having her number and then decided he didn't look like a stalker. He only had a few days to stalk anyway.

The men came back, both faces too angled and

sombre for a wedding feast, though Gianni smiled at his wife when he reached her side. He held out his hand. 'Do you still wish to circulate through the guests, *cara*? I believe a few of the older guests are starting to leave.'

Emma allowed herself to be drawn up and against her husband's chest for a brief hug, as if the two of them had spent a day apart and not a few minutes, and Tammy couldn't help but wonder if she'd ever have such a love as that. She damped down the almost irresistible urge to sneak a glance at Leon's face to see what he was thinking. When she did he was looking at her and for some bizarre reason her face flamed.

Thankfully, her friend seemed oblivious to Tammy's own embarrassment as she stepped, pink-cheeked, back out of her husband's arms. 'I haven't spent much time with Louisa. Shall we see her before she goes?'

'Indeed.' Gianni smiled warmly. 'I will inquire if she thinks my brother can be as excellent a guest as when I stayed with her.'

They walked away and Leon sat down. She saw him again seek the boys out in the shadows. 'Everything okay?' Tammy searched his face but the mask he'd arrived with earlier in the day was firmly back in place. She could read nothing and it irritated her for no good reason.

He inclined his head. 'Of course.'

'So you and Paulo have settled into the old doctor's residence with Louisa for a few days?'

'She has made us very welcome.' This time he did smile and the sudden warmth in his eyes did strange, unsettling things to her stomach. Things she hadn't had a problem with for nearly ten years. Maybe she was hungry. Though that seemed unlikely as the wedding feast had more choices than a country fete.

The thought came out of nowhere. What would he be like to kiss? Her belly twisted. Great, she'd bet. He had amazing lips, like sculptured marble on a work of art. Good grief. She checked out her nails again, to hide her eyes.

He went on. 'Paulo has never had so many affectionate embraces and we have only been there since last night.'

'Louisa loves a cuddle.' It was amazing she could carry on a conversation and be so focused on his mouth. She risked a glance. 'She's a recent widow.' Yep, they still looked good.

Leon concentrated on Louisa, whom he could see behind the dancers, the little woman who'd made his son so welcome, and thankfully the tension eased. He wasn't sure where it came from but he'd felt the sudden rise between them. 'My brother told me of her loss. And that is why he asked we stay there. It is no hardship.'

He kept his eyes on his brother and his wife across the floor. In fact, even this wedding had become no hardship. It was surprising how resigned he'd become to his brother's fate. And in a few short hours, partly because no one could doubt the true bond between the newlyweds, and partly because all of the people he'd met here tonight had exuded such warmth and generosity towards him and his son.

Except this woman.

The thought made him smile for some reason, as if the challenge for supremacy between them had taken on a new urgency. He fought the errant concept away. No. Perhaps it had been too long since he had set aside time to share intimacy with a woman. The chance of a brief liaison with this Tamara was tantalising but remote. Too much was happening.

And she would be the last to welcome him. The thought made him smile again. He'd somehow offended her, and he searched his memory for that ridiculous saying he'd heard today—he'd got up her nose. And such a delightful nose it was. He smiled again. She was not showing a warm or generous side to him at all but he perceived she had one, which in fact was lucky, because he became more intrigued every minute he spent with her.

Tammy saw him smile at the thought of Louisa. So he did have a soft spot for elderly widows. The idea dangerously thawed a little more of her reserve and she reached for another unwanted biscuit to distract her concentration from this handsome, brooding man beside her.

She felt his attention and when she glanced at him there was a sudden darkening of his eyes that arrowed that sharp sensation of hunger right back through her midsection. She felt the wave of heat between them like a furnace door opening.

'Not again,' he murmured. And then more strongly, 'If you delicately consume another biscotti I will not be responsible for my actions.' His voice was very quiet, and she realised they were alone at the table—in fact, alone at their side of the dance floor. The children shrieked with laughter in the distance just in view, Emma and Gianni were across talking to Louisa, and suddenly she couldn't look away from him. Her stomach kicked again. She got the message.

She wasn't sure what to do now with the biscuit she didn't want, but blowed if she'd let him know he'd rocked her.

Did she look away and nonchalantly put it down or did she pull the tiger's tail? There was no choice really.

Unhurriedly, with great deliberation, Emma raised the shard of almond to her mouth. With her eyes on his she parted her lips with seductive exaggeration and slid it slowly in, and chewed. It was hard to swallow with a dry mouth but she did. Choking would have ruined the impact. To drive home her point she calmly licked the sugar from her finger. One raised eyebrow left him in no doubt of her message. *Don't dare me.*

Leon stood, took the arm that reached towards him—surely she hadn't asked her fingers to do that—and Tammy found herself whisked back into the shadows with her hand in his. In an instant she was in his arms and his body felt warm and inflexible against hers. It had all happened so fast she doubted anyone had noticed she'd been abducted.

His eyes glittered in the low light. 'You do not follow orders well, I think.' She barely heard him over the thumping in her chest as he stared down at her, and there was something primal about the tree branch casting shadows across his face. 'This night has been filled with intriguing moments. I cannot allow it to conclude without this.' He bent his dark head towards her with such intent she froze as he brushed her neck with his lips. She shivered and all the hair on her arms whooshed into an upright position on little mountains of goose flesh.

'Your scent has been driving me wild all night.' His words hummed against her ear and thrummed down her throat as his lips travelled the sensitive skin around her jaw. She'd never felt exposed and vulnerable and yet starving for more.

His mouth took flight across her cheek like a hot moth that dusted both eyes before homing in on her mouth. Every nerve in her skin seemed to lean his way for attention, drawn to the light like a kamikaze insect, and she shuddered at the delicious sensations his whispered caress invoked.

Somehow her arms had wound themselves round his neck and she could feel the sinew and muscle in his shoulders, rock hard beneath her fingers. He had the power to snap her in two and they both knew it.

Then his mouth found hers, her stomach jolted and she swayed against him suddenly weak at the knees like an old-fashioned heroine. She'd never believed this would happen to her. A swoon from a man kissing her. It was ridiculous, and crazy, and…

'It was a funny wedding,' Jack said as he drove home with his mother.

'Funny in what way?' Tammy said extremely absently as she turned along the sweeping driveway out of the lakeside complex. When Leon had kissed her Tammy realised what she'd been missing for too many years. She'd kissed a few men, more to reassure herself she could get a man to the point, but never been enamoured enough to want to repeat the experience.

With Leonardo Bonmarito she'd wanted to do more than repeat it. She wanted next verse. Next chapter. The whole darn book and she knew where that could leave her. She prayed he hadn't realised because she'd managed to step back before she'd dragged the buttons from his shirt. But only just. So she'd stepped away further, called her son and left fairly quickly after that.

'Just different.' The childish voice beside her reminded her why she'd stepped away. 'And that kid's different too.'

'Paulo? I imagine they'd be saying the same thing about you if you turned up at a wedding in Italy.'

She glanced at Jack. Her miniature man in the house, whom she adored but had no blinkers about. 'Which reminds me, you were impolite to push into that dance with Grace and Paulo.'

He looked away from her and squirmed a little. 'She didn't want to dance with him.'

'That's not what I saw.'

Jack sniffed and avoided his mother's glance. 'She danced with him later anyway,' he muttered.

Tammy dimmed her lights for a passing car. 'I wouldn't like to think you were rude or acting the bully to a visitor, Jack.'

'I don't like him.' More muttering.

Tammy frowned. Jealous brat. 'Even more reason to be nice to him.'

Jack sniffed again. 'Like you were nice to his father?'

Now where had that come from? Thank goodness it was dark and he couldn't see the pink flooding her neck. Little ankle biter. She certainly wasn't going there. Of course the children hadn't seen. 'Yes.' She took the easy way out. 'Did you all have fun playing spotlight?'

She caught the movement of his shoulder beside her as he shrugged. 'He was scared half the time.'

The dark cloud of uneasiness slid new tendrils through her mind. Tammy glanced at her son and then back at the road. 'Why do you think he was scared?'

Jack swivelled and she could tell without turning her head that he was looking at her. 'What would you do if a man tried to kidnap me?'

Tammy blinked at the unexpected question and her hands tightened until they were almost white on the wheel. Someone take her son? Harm Jack? Threaten to kill him? 'Tear him limb from limb.' She shook the power of the unexpected passion off. Good grief, there'd been some emotional roller-coasters tonight. 'What made you ask that?'

Such a little voice from the darkness. 'He said it sometimes happens in Italy for ransom money.'

'Who? Paulo?' She'd read of it but didn't want to think about such a crime actually happening. Europe was a long way from Lyrebird Lake. 'Well, let's hope someone doesn't want to ransom you.'

Then he said it. Explained it. Let loose the cloud that turned from dark to black. 'Just before they left to come to Australia somebody tried to take Paulo. That's why they didn't get here till yesterday.'

That couldn't be true. 'What do you mean? Who

did?' She slowed the car, then slowed it some more, which didn't really matter because there wasn't that much traffic around Lyrebird Lake. It would be better if she didn't run into anyone.

'They don't know. His father caught them before they could get away but they put a bag over Paulo's head and knocked him out.'

Tammy's heart thumped under her ribs and she shivered at the thought of someone attempting to steal a child. Any child. Her child.

Then she remembered how she'd been less than diplomatic about Leon's reluctance with the children's game and she winced. Every instinct urged her to turn the car around and apologise to Leon for her ill judgement. Poor Paulo, poor Leon. And the kidnappers had struck a child. 'Paulo told you this?'

Jack was losing interest. 'No, Grace did. Paulo told her.'

Good grief. No wonder Leon hadn't wanted him to play spotlight. It was amazing he'd let his son out of his sight at all. She glanced at Jack. 'If that's true, even you should understand why he was scared in spotlight.'

'I guess.' He looked at his mother. 'You'd find me, wouldn't you, Mum?'

She stretched her arm across and ruffled his hair with her fingers. The strands were fine and fragile beneath the skin of her fingertips and the sheer fragment of the concept of losing him tightened a ball of fear in her chest. 'I wouldn't rest until I did.'

Jack snuggled down in his seat. 'I thought so,' he said, and yawned loudly.

Tammy was glad to get to work the next morning. The night had been a sheet-crunching wrestle for peace that she'd only snatched moments of and this morning a rush to get a tired and cross Jack through the fence to Misty's house.

Leon Bonmarito had a lot to answer for. She'd walked straight into a birth and thankfully hadn't given the man a thought for the past three hours.

Tammy wrapped the squirming newborn infant in a fluffy white towel and tucked him under her arm like a football. Little dark eyes blinked up at her out of the swathe and one starfish hand escaped to wave at her. She tucked the tiny fingers in again and ran the water over his head as she brushed the matted curls clean. She grinned at his mother. 'I haven't seen such thick hair for a long time.'

Jennifer Ross watched with adoration as the little face squinted and frowned at the sensation in his scalp. 'He's gorgeous.' She sighed and rubbed her stomach and her son turned his head in her direction.

'Thanks for rinsing his hair for me, Tammy. I'm just not up to it.' Even in the dimly lit corner of the room where the sink nestled Tammy could see him try to focus on the familiar sound of his mother's voice.

'We'll just use water today. We'll bath Felix properly tomorrow so we don't overload his poor nose with baby bath perfume.' Tammy combed a little curl onto his forehead and smiled. 'He needs to feel secure, with your skin and his smelling the same as he remembers from inside you. It all helps with establishing breastfeeding. Like the way you waited for him to find the breast and didn't push him on for that first feed.'

'I can't believe he moved there himself.' Jen's face was soft with wonder.

'He'll do it again too. That's why it's better not to wash your own hair with shampoo the first twenty-four hours. A strong scent like shampoo has can confuse and even upset his nose during that time.'

'I'll let Ken's mum know when I ring her. She likes a heavy perfume but she's a sweetie. She'll give it a miss if I ask.' Jen reached out and touched his little hand that had escaped again. 'I remember when you told my sister only Mum and Dad should snuggle babies for the first twenty-four hours. She swears her second baby is much more settled.'

'Best practice. But sometimes it's hard to manage when everyone wants a hold.'

Jen rubbed her stomach again. 'Better to do it right. If the after pains get much worse I might not have a third one,' Jen said with a rueful smile.

'Have a lie-down. You've had a big day and there's a warm wheat pack on your bed. I'll bring Felix in when I've dressed him and check your tummy.' She cast her eye over the mum and decided she looked okay. 'Let me know if you start to bleed more heavily.'

'Thanks, I'll do that.' Jen smiled and turned gingerly with her hand holding her stomach. 'I'm looking forward to that wheat pack. Ken's so disappointed he wasn't home for the birth. And I have to ring his mother and sister as well.'

'Since when do babies wait for truck-driving daddies? Ken will just be glad you're both well. Off you go. I'll be in soon.' She narrowed her gaze as the other woman hobbled out. Tammy wished Ken could have made it too. She wanted every mother's birth to be perfect for them but sometimes babies just didn't wait.

When Ben brought Leon in to see the unit Tammy had just towelled Felix's hair dry. She was laughing down at him as she tried to capture the wriggling limbs and they'd moved to the sunny side of the room as she began to dress him. The early-afternoon sunlight dusted her dark hair with shafts of dancing light and her skin glowed.

For Leon, suddenly the day was brighter and even more interesting, although his tour of the facilities had captured his attention until now. Strangely all thoughts of bed numbers, ward structure and layout seemed lower in his priorities than watching the expressions cross this woman's face. And brought back the delightful memory of a kiss that had haunted him long into the night in his lonely bed.

'Hi, there, Tam,' Ben said as he crossed the room. Tammy looked up at her father and smiled. Then she looked at Leon and the smile fell away. He watched it fall and inexplicably the room dimmed.

'Hi, Dad. Leon.' She looked at her father. Or perhaps she was avoiding looking at him, Leon surmised, and began another mind waltz of piqued interest that this woman seemed to kick off in him. 'What are you men up to?'

'I'm showing Leon the facilities. His board's been thinking of adding maternity wards to their children's hospitals and I thought you might like to hint him towards a more woman-friendly concept.'

Leon watched the ignition of sharper concentration and the flare of captured interest. She couldn't hide the blue intensity in her eyes and silently he thanked Ben for knowing his daughter so well. So, Leon mulled to himself, he'd suddenly become a much more interesting person?

'Really?' She tossed it over her shoulder, as if only a little involved, but she couldn't fool him—he was learning to read her like a conspiracy plot in a movie, one fragmented clue at a time.

She dressed the baby with an absentminded deftness that reassured the infant so much he lay compliant under her hands. Mentally Leon nodded with approval. To handle infants a rapport was essential and he was pleased she had the knack, though it was ridiculous that such a thing should matter to him.

When the newborn was fully clothed she nestled him across her breasts and Leon had a sudden unbidden picture of her with her own child, a Madonnalike expression on her face, and a soft smile that quickened his heart. More foolishness and he shook his head at the distraction the fleeting vision had caused.

Tammy tilted her determined chin his way and Madonna faded away with a pop. 'I'll just take this little bundle into his mother and come back.'

He watched her leave the room, the boyish yet confident walk of an athletic woman, not a hint of the shrinking violet or diffident underling, and he was still watching the door when she returned. That confidence he'd first seen was there in spades. She owned the room. It seemed he activated her assertiveness mechanism. He couldn't help the smile when she returned.

She saw it and blushed. Just a little but enough to give him the satisfaction of discomfiting her and he felt a tinge of his awareness that he'd felt the need to do so.

She looked away to her father and then back at him. 'What sort of unit were you looking at?'

Enough games. 'Small. One floor of the building.

Midwife run and similar to what your father has explained happens here, though with an obstetrician and paediatrician on call because we have that luxury in the city.'

He went on when her interest continued. 'It would be situated in a wing of the private children's hospital we run now. The medical personnel cover is available already, as are consulting rooms and theatres.'

She nodded as if satisfied with his motives and he felt ridiculously pleased. 'We promote natural birth here and caseload midwifery. Do the women in your demographic want that sort of service? What's your caesarean rate, because ours is the lowest in Australia.' She was defiant this morning. Raising barriers that hardened the delicate planes of her face and kept her eyes from his. He began to wonder why she, too, felt the need. *Molto curioso*.

'I'm not sure of the caesarean rate—obstetrics is not my area—but in my country most of our maternity units are more in the medical model and busy. Often so understaffed and underfinanced that the families provide most of the care for the women after birth.'

Tammy nodded and spoke to her father. 'I'd heard that. One of my friends had a baby in Rome. She said the nurses were lovely but very busy.'

He wanted her to look back at him. 'That is true of a lot of hospitals. This model would be more midwifery led for low-risk women.' He paused, deliberately, before he went on, and she did bring her gaze back his way. Satisfied, he continued. 'Of course, my new sister-in-law, Emma, is also interested and I believe there is a small chance you and your son could come to Italy in a few weeks?' He lifted the end of the sentence in a question. 'Perhaps the two of you could discuss what is needed and what would work in my country that is similar to what you have here.'

Tammy intercepted the sudden interest from her father and she shook her head at Ben. 'I haven't even thought much about the chance of travelling in Italy.' Liar. The idea had circled in her head for most of the night. 'I won't say your idea of setting up midwife-led units isn't exciting.' *But that's all that's exciting and you're the main drawback.* She repeated the last part of the sentence to herself. 'But thanks for thinking of me.'

He shrugged those amazing shoulders of his, the memory of which she'd felt under her hands more than once through the night despite her attempts to banish the weakness, and she frowned at him more heavily.

'It is for my own benefit after all,' he said.

She remembered Jack's disclosure, and the idea she'd had to apologise if she saw him, but it wasn't that easy. All the time they talked, at the back of her mind, she wanted to ask about Paulo, about the truth in Jack's revelation, and to admit she hadn't understood his reserve and his protectiveness. But it didn't seem right with her father there just in case Leon didn't wish to discuss it. Or she could just let it go.

She owed him an apology. 'Maybe we could meet for lunch and talk more about your idea,' she offered, though so reluctantly it seemed as if the words were teased out of her like chewing gum stuck on a shoe. He must have thought so because there was amusement in his voice as he declined.

'Lunch, no. I'm away with your father for the rest of the day but perhaps tonight, for dinner?' His amusement was clearer. 'If I pick you up? My brother and I share a taste in fast cars and we could go for a drive somewhere to eat out.'

She did not want to drive somewhere with this guy. A car. Close confines. Him in control. 'No, thank you.' Besides. It was her invitation and her place to say where they met. 'You could come to my house, it's easier. Bring Paulo if he'd like to come and he can play with Jack.'

She had a sudden vision of her empty pantry and mentally shrugged. 'At six-thirty? I'm afraid Jack and I eat early or I can't get him to bed before nine.'

He shook his head. 'That does not suit.'

Tammy opened her eyes slow and wide at his arrogance and his inability to accept she wanted to set the pace and choose a place that would be safe.

But he went on either oblivious or determined to

have his own way. 'I will come after nine. When Paulo, too, is in bed. I am away all day tomorrow and we will be able to discuss things without small ears around us.'

Tammy caught the raised eyebrows and stifled smile on her father's face and frowned. She'd never been good at taking orders. She bit back the temptation to say nine didn't suit her, but apart from being different to what she usually did, she never slept till midnight anyway.

It would be churlish to stick to her guns. This once she'd let him get away with organising but he wouldn't be making a habit of it.

She conceded, grudgingly. 'I don't normally stay up late but a leisurely after-dinner coffee could be pleasant.'

'I'll see you tonight, then.' He inclined his head and Tammy did the same while Ben looked on with a twinkle in his eye. Tammy glared at her father for good measure which only made his eyes twinkle more as they left.

Tammy could hear the suddenly vociferous new arrival in with his mother and, glad of the diversion, she hastened to the ward to help Jen snuggle Felix up to her breast. She couldn't help the glance out the ward window as the two men crossed the path to the old doctor's residence.

She'd always thought her father a big man but against Leon he seemed suddenly less invincible. It was a strange feeling and she didn't like it. Or maybe she didn't like being so aware of the leashed power of Leonardo Bonmarito.

CHAPTER THREE

LEON arrived at nine.

'So, tell me about your private hospitals. What made you choose paediatrics as a main focus?'

Be cool, be calm, say something. Leon made her roomy den look tiny and cramped. Not something she'd thought possible before. Tammy had run around madly when Jack had gone to bed and hidden all the school fundraising newsletters and flyers in a big basket and tossed all evidence of her weekly ironing into the cupboard behind the door.

She'd even put the dog basket out on the back verandah. Stinky didn't like men. Then she'd put the Jack Russell out in the backyard and spent ten minutes changing her clothes and tidying her hair. Something else she hadn't thought of before at this time of night.

But now she sat relaxed and serene, externally anyway, and watched Leon's passion for his work flare in his eyes. She could understand passion for a vocation; she had it herself, for midwifery and her clients in Lyrebird Lake.

'It's the same in a lot of hospitals in the public system. The lack of staff, age of buildings and equipment and overcrowding means the convalescing patient is often cared for with less attention than necessary. With children that is doubly tragic.'

She couldn't help but admire his mastery of English. Her understanding of Italian was more than adequate but her conversational ability was nowhere near as fluent and his occasional roll of the *r*'s made his underlying accent compellingly attractive. It did something to her insides. She obviously had a dangerous fetish for Italians.

'This has concerned me,' he went on, 'and especially in paediatrics because children are vulnerable, more so when they are sick.'

That brought her back to earth. Children were vulnerable. He had great reason to believe that after Paulo's incident but she'd get around to that. Get around to the fact she'd thought him overprotective. 'I can see what you're getting at. It's hard because of priorities with those more ill. But I agree a lonely and convalescing child needs special care.'

He sat forward in his chair and his shirt tightened impressively across his chest. She didn't want to notice that. '*Sì.*' He was obviously pleased with her. 'There is a shortage of empathetic time for those children on the mend but not yet well enough to go home. I had hoped to prevent their stay from becoming a more traumatic experience than necessary.' He glanced up to see if she agreed and she nodded.

He was determined to ensure his goals were realised. 'This is especially important if these children are dealing with other issues, such as grief from loss of loved ones, or difficult family circumstances.'

There was an added nuance in his voice that spoke of history and vast experience. An aversion to children suffering, perhaps more personal than children he'd seen in wards. The reason teased at her mind. 'Was there something in particular that made you so aware?'

His answer seemed to come from another direction. 'In our family all sons have entered the medical profession, though disciplines were left to our personal preferences. My grandfather was intrigued by surgery, my father ophthalmology. My passion lies with paediatrics and Gianni's with emergency medicine. Paolo's area is yet to be discerned.'

That made her smile. 'Paulo's a bit young to be worrying about disciplines, don't you think? I doubt Jack would have a thought in his head about what he'll do when he grows up.'

Leon shook his head. 'In Italy a man learns at an early age that he will be responsible for others.'

'Like dancing,' she suggested. 'A man must be able to lead?'

He returned her smile. *'Sì.'*

She couldn't resist teasing him again. 'So you turned your father's eye hospitals into paediatric wards?'

He raised one stern eyebrow but something made her wonder if he was secretly smiling. 'You do not really think that I would?'

There was a lot going on below the surface here. From both of them. She shook her head. 'No.' He wouldn't do that. She knew little of him but already she could tell he would hold his father's wish to provide service to the blind sacrosanct. 'So the eye hospitals are thriving.'

There it was. A warm and wicked grin that wrapped around her like a cloak dropping over her shoulders. A cloak that enveloped her in all the unusually erotic thoughts that had chased around her head for far too long last night in bed. She was in trouble.

'*Sì*. I built more hospitals. Designed especially for children and staffed with nurses who have much to offer an ailing or grieving child.'

He leaned back in the chair and the fine fabric of his handmade shirt again stretched tight across his chest. He picked up the tiny espresso coffee she'd made for him, black and freshly ground from the machine she couldn't live without, and sniffed it appreciatively. He took a sip, and those large hands looked incongruous around the tiny cup. '*Perfetto*.'

She'd learned to make good coffee years ago and

it was her one indulgence. She dragged her eyes away from his hands because down that road lay danger.

She remembered he and Gianni were orphans and the pieces fell into place. 'How did your parents die, Leon?'

She had connected with his previous statement and why she could sense and understand meanings so easily from a man she barely knew was a puzzle she didn't want to fathom. She wondered if it worried him as much as it worried her.

To her relief he didn't try to avoid her question. 'My parents drowned off the Amalfi Coast from our yacht in a storm.'

Drowned. Poor little boys. 'Storms at sea.' She sighed. 'Mother Nature's temper can be wild and indiscriminate,' she said softly. His eyes gazed off into the distance and she was with him. She could almost feel the spray in her face and hear the scream of the wind and she nodded. 'I've lived by the sea. The weather can be unexpected and fierce. My father still has a house on a fabulous beach, but even he nearly drowned one day when he was washed off the rocks.'

He was watching her, listening to her voice, but she could tell half of him was in another place. 'What happened with you and Gianni?'

He looked through her and his voice dropped. 'Gianni almost died, and I, too, had pneumonia.' She glanced at his face and couldn't help but be touched by his effort to remain expressionless.

'And you were both in hospital afterwards?' Spoken gently, because she didn't want to break the spell.

He nodded and now she understood where his empathy for those in similar circumstances had grown from because she could see the suppressed emotion, even in the careful blankness. That concept hit her hard, in mutual empathy from her early teens and the scars she still bore. 'How old were you when they died?'

Leon shrugged the pain away. 'Fourteen.' Grieving, convalescing, in a hospital that was rushed and old and unintentionally uncaring. With a ten-year-old brother he'd nearly lost as well.

She could see he knew she'd connected the dots. And wasn't happy. 'It is better in my hospitals now.' He changed the subject. 'To see what you do here, in your maternity section, is good too.'

She allowed the change of subject, aware instinctively how privileged she'd been to glimpse into the private man and sensitive to his need to close the subject. 'The maternity hospital concept is an exciting idea. I'll certainly talk to Emma about it.'

No doubt he would also be happy because it would mean his brother's new wife would be interested in staying more often in Italy. She didn't fully trust his superior motives without a thought for his ulterior ones.

He was watching her again and she wondered what he'd seen of her thoughts. Not much, she hoped.

'So you, too, have suffered the loss of a parent?' His turn to pry. 'You said you lost your mother young, also?'

Not going there. Fifteen hadn't been a good age to be allowed to run free. 'Yes.' The less said there, the better.

'And that you lived with your grandmother?' So he remembered. Deep creases marred his forehead. 'Why did you not go with your father when your mother died?'

'It's a long story and maybe another day.' She and her father would have preferred that and maybe her life would have been different. She shrugged her shoulders for something she'd no control over. Fifteen had also been a bad age to be told Ben wasn't her real father.

Rebellion saw Tammy spend many hours loitering at that Italian coffee shop. Months had passed without her father's knowledge of how little supervision her grandmother had exercised.

Rides in fast cars she later found out were stolen. Dark and dangerous men that even her boyfriend was wary of. Secret meetings she'd had to stay silent in.

The day Ben, her father in all that counted if not legally, had arrived to rescue her.

He'd picked her up from the coffee shop when she'd rung him to say she was pregnant and whisked her to Lyrebird Lake. He'd told her then they were petty criminals. Not long later she'd read that her baby's father had been sent to jail for a long time.

No wonder she'd found it all so dreadfully, horribly exciting. That risk-taking and foolish time in her life was something she'd buried when she'd become a responsible mother.

Until Gianni had arrived in Lyrebird Lake and wooed her best friend, she'd covered the Italian episode in her life. Hadn't even tried her language skills out on Gianni so she doubted there was anyone except her father, and maybe his wife, Misty, in Lyrebird Lake who knew her secret.

Emma's betrothal had been such a whirlwind affair she hadn't even mentioned it when her friend had fallen for Gianni.

But she had Jack. The light in her life. And she'd change nothing now. Except maybe the subject again.

She had other motives for asking him here and he'd stayed a while already. 'There's something I want to ask you, though you may not want to discuss it. Something that means I should apologise for my presumption without knowing the facts.'

He frowned and inclined his head.

She hesitated, because she didn't really know him or how he'd react, and then typically, she dived in anyway. 'Was Paulo almost abducted before you came here?'

His brows snapped together. 'Who told you this?'

She straightened in her seat, refusing to be cowed. 'Paulo mentioned it to Emma's daughter, Grace.' She didn't say Grace had told Jack and Jack had told her.

His hand tightened on the cup he held and for a fleeting moment she had the ridiculous thought he might crush it without realising. Surely a man's hand couldn't really do that? In the silence she imagined she could hear the porcelain creak in protest.

'This is true.' He glanced at his white fingers and carefully put the cup down, then ran his other hand through thick black curls. She glimpsed the flicker of white-hot fury in his eyes and it was a warning of what he would be capable of. Strangely she had no problem with that. She'd almost pity the men who tried to harm his son if he caught them.

'I was stupidly distracted by my wish to arrive well before the wedding and took too little care. We are not the first family to be targeted by those who wish to benefit financially from people they see as too wealthy.'

So it was true. The thought made her want to clutch at her throat but she kept her hands together in her lap as if to hold onto the pictures that wanted to rise up and fill her mind. 'Good grief. What about the police?'

He inclined his head but the movement was non-committal. 'The police do their best to capture these criminals but by then it is often too late for the one abducted. This will not happen to my son or anyone in my family. I have a private investigator and bodyguards working with me full-time now. Experienced operatives whose records are impeccable and that I trust with my and my family's lives.'

There was almost an aura around him and she recognised the implacable determination that would see him succeed in whatever he set his mind to. 'So you believe Paulo is safe, now that these people work for you?'

He inclined his head. 'Already they have paid tenfold for the money I retain them with. Those responsible have been passed over to the police. Paulo is safe now. No more at risk than any other boy, but it is hard not to look into the dark for danger.'

Who were these Bonmaritos her friend had bound herself to? These superficially cultured men who hid wolves beneath their Italian suits and hired bodyguards. More gangsters she'd fallen in with? Or truly philanthropic doctors merely protecting their own from a culture she didn't understand.

'This all sounds very James Bondish. Not something Lyrebird Lake would ever have to worry about.' She said it firmly, and perhaps a little too quickly, but she really didn't want to think of this scenario in her own home. In the lives of people she knew. In the man opposite her she was strangely drawn to. Dark forces she never wanted to be involved with again. It was too unsettling.

'So my brother says. He does not believe I need the bodyguards here but, for the moment, it is for me. These and other reasons are perhaps why my brother and I should return to our homeland.'

Surely nothing would happen here? In Australia? She didn't like any of this conversation and regretted what she'd discovered. She wondered if Emma was aware of the more menacing undercurrents of the Bonmarito family. 'This seems a long way from discussing children's hospitals and maternity wings.'

Visibly Leon forced his shoulders to relax. 'I'm sorry, Tamara. I apologise if I've upset you. I still struggle with allowing Paulo out of my sight.' But his face remained changed. Harshly angled and fierce. The face of the stranger he really was.

Her chin was up as if she needed to rise and meet the challenge of this warrior of a man. He didn't frighten her but she gave him the respect he deserved. 'And I apologise for judging your need to know where Paulo was the other night.'

He inclined his head. 'You could not know.' While the dangerous side to this handsome Italian made her uneasy, it was less upsetting when she thought of her own response when Jack had asked what she would do—limb from limb seemed pretty similar to Leon's response. 'The lives of children should be protected.'

'*Sì*. And I should go to check Paulo. It is late.' He stood and she rose also, and couldn't squash the tiny irresponsible hope he would kiss her before he left. She walked him to the door and paused as she opened it. When she turned to him some of the hardness had faded from his face but there was enough of the wolf in him to still keep her head up as she met his eyes.

He had no difficulty seeing into her mind. His brows lifted. 'Do you want to play dare again, little one?'

So he thought she was little? Danger shuddered deliciously along her veins and made her remember a time in her dim past when she'd put her ear to a train track, the early rumbles of an approaching train, the danger, the paralysing fear that screamed to move. 'Should I in this mood you're in?'

He stepped in. 'That is enough answer for me.'

This kiss was different. Harder, decidedly more dominant with her crushed against his chest, and she pulled him against herself more to keep her feet on the ground and show she wasn't subdued by him. But she was. They leaned into each other, searching out secrets, showing each other hidden facets of their souls rarely exposed like little shafts of moonlight illuminating the areas used to darkness. All the more penetrating because there was no future in it.

When he left her, she leaned her forehead against the closed door with her eyes shut and listened to his car purr away in the darkness.

'Hit by the train,' she murmured into the darkness.

The next day as Tammy worked her early shift in the birthing centre she found herself glancing out the windows whenever she heard male voices, and once she saw her father in the distance with Leon, two dark heads together. One that made her smile and one that burned her with the heat of that last hard kiss.

It was strange how Leon and Ben seemed to find a common ground and mutual respect when there was a good fifteen years difference in age. And she trusted Ben's instincts implicitly so Leon must be 'good people'.

Her stepmother, Misty, the second of the midwives to move to Lyrebird Lake Birthing Centre, arrived to take over the shift. She joined Tammy on the steps to wave goodbye to this morning's new family.

'So Gloria did well.' They walked inside together and Misty grinned down at the birth register open on the desk. 'And they finally have a daughter?'

'In the bath at 10:00 a.m. She came out in three pushes and Gloria's over the moon with how much better this birth was.'

Misty ran her finger along the page and raised her

eyebrows at the baby's weight. 'Lovely. And you're dropping there after work?'

Tammy bulldog-clipped the folder she'd completed. 'I said around four. Give them all time to have a sleep. I said I'd pick up their Jimmy after school and give him a chance to meet his new sister.'

'Sounds great.' Misty glanced at her with an unusual thoroughness and Tammy felt as if her stepmother chose her words carefully. 'Your father seems very impressed with Gianni's brother.'

'I was thinking that this morning.' Tammy looked back at Misty with a smile. 'What're your instincts?' There was more to the question than seemed on the surface. By 'instincts' Tammy meant those intangible nuances Misty was known for. Or even more to the point, had Misty had any of those eerie premonitions she occasionally experienced with startling accuracy?

Tammy didn't try to understand Misty's special gift, just accepted it for the reality it was and the fact that Misty had shown on occasion how useful her premonitions could be.

'There's something happening but I'll let you know if I get worried. But I like Leon too. I think despite an illusion of aloofness he's a man to be sure of in tough times. A man's man perhaps, but I've always thought you hadn't yet found a man you couldn't walk over. He could be one of those and I'm looking forward to the tussle with great anticipation.'

Tammy slanted a look at her. 'Not very motherly of you.'

Misty just smiled. 'You never wanted me to be your mother, Tam. I'm grateful to be your friend.'

Tammy felt the prickle of tears. Not something she did often and she impulsively hugged Misty. 'I'm the lucky one.' She stepped back and straightened. 'And I'm out of here. Jen's staying another night until Ken comes home—the truck broke down at Longreach.'

She picked up her bag. 'Trina's at home in early labour, and she missed her last two appointments while away in Brisbane, so I'm not sure of her baby's size. He was a little bigger than expected last time I saw her. She knows I'm concerned. She's ringing after five so let me know if you need a hand. I'm on call tonight. Have a good shift.'

'I understand Leon Bonmarito is visiting?' Misty's face was bland.

Tammy tilted her head. 'That was last night.'

'So it was.' Misty nodded with a smile. 'Enjoy your evening.'

CHAPTER FOUR

SO TAMMY wasn't surprised when the doorbell rang at nine-thirty that night. Nor was she surprised at the identity of the caller. 'Come in. I'm guessing Paulo's asleep.'

'And Louisa is watching over him. I am learning to trust he is safe again.' Leon's strong white teeth flashed in the low light. 'I would like to take Louisa home to Italy. Perhaps a change of scenery would be good for her. Do you think she'd come?'

'No.' Louisa had been housekeeper at the old doctor's residence, a short-term accommodation house for visiting doctors and nurses for a lot of years. Her husband had established Lyrebird Lake hospital and recently passed away.

'I'm sure my brother has suggested I stay at the residence and not at the resort because he wants me to fall in love with Louisa's cooking. And her stories. Has she told you about the myth of the lyrebird?'

Tammy had never been a fan of fairytales. 'I've heard of it. In all my years at the lake I've never seen one. Emma has, twice, once with your brother.' She smiled at how that ended. 'You'd better watch out.'

He, too, smiled. 'I think to see a bird will not change my life.'

'Louisa's husband used to say the lyrebird heals those in pain.' She had the feeling Leon could do with a spot of healing but it was none of her business.

She returned to the notion of Leon worrying about Louisa. 'Louisa spends time with her stepson's family.' She couldn't help but think it strangely endearing that this big, quiet man was concerned for an elderly widow he barely knew. She'd made a mental note to visit Louisa herself in case she needed more company. 'We won't let you steal her. We'd all miss her too much.'

She glanced at the clock. 'If you want a coffee, I'll offer you one now. I'm on call and I know one of the girls has come in to birth with Misty and there's another woman due out there.'

'Please, to the coffee.' He followed her when she stood and moved into the kitchen and she put her hand up to halt him at the door. He kept coming until his chest touched her fingers, a wicked glint in his eye that warned he didn't take orders easily either, but then he stopped.

She shifted her fingers quick-smart and tried not to recognise how good the warmth of his solid chest had felt beneath her palm. She needed at least three feet between them for her to breathe. 'If you can make my den feel small you'll crowd my kitchen. Just stay there and let me work.'

He lifted one brow but obediently leaned against the doorframe, relaxed but alert, and they were both aware he was capable of swift movement, if he wished.

She breathed out forcefully as she turned away. Thank goodness he'd stopped. The guy was too much of a man to ignore when he was this close and a powerful incentive to get her chore done quickly and move out of here.

Then he said quietly, as if the thought had just occurred to him, 'If you are called in to work, who is here for your Jack?' Was that censure in his voice? Disapproval?

It had better not be. Nobody disapproved of her mothering. She flicked him a glance and his face was serious. 'We have an intercom between the houses and I switch it on for my father to listen in. Jack knows he can call for his grandfather if I'm not around and Dad takes him next door.' She glared at him and pressed the button on the machine for espresso and the beans began to grind—like her teeth.

'And what if Ben is called out?' Still the frown when it was none of his business but then, suddenly, she remembered he'd had a recent fright himself. One she'd put her foot in at the wedding. She eased the tension that had crept into her neck.

Of course he'd be security conscious. She didn't

need to be so quick to take offence. 'We don't do the same nights on call,' she explained. 'That's the beauty of a small town and friends who organise rosters between families.'

The aroma of fresh beans made her nose twitch with calmer thoughts and she forced herself to stay relaxed. The guy could make her nerves stretch taut like a rubber band ready to snap back and sting her.

He nodded and looked at her almost apologetically, as if aware he may have overstepped a boundary. 'I begin to see the sense of this place.'

To her further astonishment he smiled and added, 'Perhaps I am less surprised at my brother's decision to spend half his time here.'

She had the feeling that could've been a huge admission for him but she didn't pursue it. She didn't want him to think it mattered to her. It didn't. Really. Time for a subject change. The coffee spurted from the twin spouts and filled their cups and she turned with them in her hands to face him.

He didn't move initially and she realised her hands were full. He could touch her if he wished. She was defenceless. Something told her he realised it too. She lifted her brows at him and waited.

He grinned and heaved himself off the doorframe and stepped back to allow her past him into the den.

'See how I understand your look?'

She bit back her smile as she sat his coffee on the low table almost on top of another of those fund-raising pamphlets. She shifted it and her eye was caught by the title.

"Wanted! Man Willing To Wax Chest For Fund-raising."

She had a sudden image of Leon and the gurgle of laughter floated up like the brown bean froth in the cup.

'You find that funny?'

She shook her head and bit her lip. She handed him the flyer. 'Lucky you're not here for long.'

He looked down at the paper and grimaced. 'And a man would do this?'

She couldn't help her glance at his broad chest, a few dark hairs gathered at the neck. 'They haven't found a volunteer yet. Want to offer?'

'No.' He shook his head with a smile. 'Though—' he paused and eyed her '—it would depend on who is doing the waxing.' The look he sent her left no doubt there'd be a price paid for the privilege.

Tammy felt the heat start low down, potent and ready to flame, like a hot coal resting on tissue paper. Yikes. She snatched the flyer from him and stuffed it behind a cushion on the sofa. 'Do you have much to do with young babies in your hospital?'

He settled back with a hint of smile and left the topic, clearly amused by her pink cheeks. 'No. Neonatal surgery is too specialised and we don't have a neonatal intensive care. But perhaps we would need a special care nursery if the maternity wing went ahead.'

He leaned forward and she could tell he was weighing possibilities and scenarios. She could see the big businessman she'd mentally accused him of being before she'd known him better, before she'd been kissed by him perhaps. But she had no doubt that if such a venture could be successful, then Leon would be the man to do it.

'These are all things to be taken into consideration if we opened a midwifery service. I'm sure a lot has changed since my obstetric rotation a decade ago. At the moment of birth, I mean.'

She could talk about that all day—and night. 'You're right. Things have changed a lot.' She tried to imagine Leon as a young medical student, diffident and overawed like those she'd seen in her training, but he was too strong a personality for her to imagine him ever being daunted by setting. 'I think the biggest change here is to keep the baby with the mother at all times from the moment of birth. Not separate in a cot. With emphasis on skin-to-skin contact for the first hour at least. At birth, we try not to clamp the umbilical cord for a few minutes either, unless we really have to.'

He nodded with a little scepticism. 'If the baby requires resuscitation?'

'Sure.' She brushed the hair out of her eyes.

'Though not always. It's a little trickier but the latest studies have shown that not cutting the umbilical cord for at least three minutes after birth is beneficial, though perhaps not that long in resuscitation.'

His face said he couldn't see how that would work so she explained more. 'We can give oxygen and even cardiac massage on the bed with the mother and that allows us to keep the blood flow from the cord as well. We've had great success with it. But then all our babies that come through the centre are low risk so any problems they have at birth are usually transient and should be resolved fairly quickly.'

He looked unconvinced and she couldn't help teasing him. 'Or is this a little too radical for your maternity hospital idea?'

'I'm always willing to see and hear of new ideas.' He raised his eyebrows at her comment, so quick to respond to any negative feedback she gave him, but she had no time to go on before the phone rang.

She dug her mobile out of her pocket. It was Misty and she had to leave.

'Sorry. I'm needed in birthing. You'll have to go.' Leon's eyebrows rose haughtily and Tammy almost smiled. She could tell he wasn't used to that. A woman had to go and he would be left cooling his heels.

He stood, though to say he did it obediently didn't suit the way he complied. 'You are not in awe of me at all, are you, Tamara?'

She didn't have time for this, unfortunately. 'Should I be?' She switched on the intercom between the two houses. 'I hope I haven't jinxed us talking about resuscitation and healthy babies.'

She saw his mind switch to the medical urgency. 'What was said?'

She gave him half an ear as she scooped up her keys. 'On the phone? Misty's concerned at the delay in second stage, and there's some unease with the baby's heart rate,' she murmured as she closed the front door behind them both. 'If it was bad she'd ship them out to the base hospital, but backup is always good when the back of your neck prickles. Do you want to come?'

He shrugged. 'I'm not registered in this country but happy to advise you if needed. Please.'

'Fine. People know Gianni so they'll have no problem accepting your presence.'

He hesitated at the two cars. 'I'll meet you there. No sense leaving your car or mine here because we don't know how long you'll be.'

They met outside the hospital and she let them in through the side entrance. Trying to remain unobtrusive they drifted into the birthing room and over to Misty. The lighting was still dim but Tammy saw the heater on for the infant resuscitation trolley and the preparations Misty had made. And the birthing mother, Trina, was beside the bed and not in the bath.

There was even a flicker of relief in her stepmother's eyes when she saw Leon. Tammy's stomach tightened. With uncomplicated births the midwife called a staff member from another part of the hospital as an extra pair of hands. If the midwife was uneasy she called the on-call midwife or doctor as a more experienced backup.

Misty spoke quietly so as not to disturb the couple who were leaning over the bed together. 'Trina's been pushing for an hour and a half now and everyone's getting tired. There's good descent of the head but there's still a heck of a lot of baby to come.'

Tammy nodded. 'Do you want to transfer?'

Misty shook her head. 'Maybe earlier would have been better but Trina didn't want to go. We're just getting a head-on view now and we don't want a difficult birth lying down in an ambulance. Trina's done an amazing job.' She eased her neck stiffness. 'Thanks for coming. I wanted some backup for the end. We'll move to all fours when the head's almost here.'

'Sure. Good call.' Tammy was peripherally aware that Leon had moved to the resuscitation trolley and was checking the drawers. Excellent. It would be much easier if he knew what they had and where it was. He shut the bottom drawer, glanced up and nodded.

She hoped they wouldn't need him.

The next pain came and the expulsive efforts from

Trina were huge. Tammy could see why Misty was impressed with Trina's progress. Slowly a thatch of baby's hair could be seen and Misty helped Trina down onto her hands and knees, the position least likely to result in a baby's shoulder becoming lodged behind the pubic bone of the mother.

During the next contraction the baby's head was born. Tammy raised her eyebrows at Misty. Not a small head and the fact didn't auger well for small shoulders. Tammy glanced at the clock.

'If your baby's shoulders feel tight remember you can help by bringing your chest in close. Nipples to knees. That flattens the curve of your coccyx and allows baby an extra centimetre or two.' All calm and quiet instructions that Tammy knew Misty would have given before this stage as well.

As the seconds passed and they waited for the next contraction, the skin of the baby's scalp faded from pink to pale blue, and Tammy could feel her own heart rate begin to gallop as the handheld Doppler amplified the way Trina's baby's heart rate slowed. The contraction finally began again and baby's head seemed to try to extend but didn't move and Tammy crouched down beside Trina's ear. 'Bring your knees together as close as you can and flatten your breasts down towards your knees. You're doing awesome.'

Trina squashed down as much as she could and Misty supported the baby's head. The contraction built. 'Okay, Trina, push now.'

Trina pushed and suddenly her baby eased under the arch of her mother's pelvis and tumbled limply into Misty's hands. 'Flip around, Trina, so we can lay baby on your warm stomach and have a look at this little bruiser.'

Misty wiped the baby briskly with a warm towel and passed her baby, all cord and limbs and damp skin, back to Trina between her legs, and the new mother shifted around until she was lying on her back with her stunned baby flaccid on her stomach.

Misty used the little handheld Doppler directly against the baby's chest and the comparatively slow thump-thump-thump of the baby's heart rate made them all look at the clock.

'Over a hundred,' Leon said, 'and some respiratory effort.' He leaned down and held the green oxygen tubing near baby's face until the little body became gradually more pink.

'Thirty seconds since birth,' Tammy said, and as if on cue Trina's baby screwed her face up and began to cry in a gradually increasing volume. Except for the slight blueness in her face from the tight fit, Trina's baby was vigorous and pink all over now as she roared her disapproval of the cool air Leon was holding near her nose.

He took it away and watched Tammy and Misty exchange smiles, and Misty's shoulders dropped with relief. She slid the baby up Trina's body to her breasts and put a warm blanket over both of them.

'What do you think she weighs?' Trina's husband seemed to have missed the tenseness the attendants had felt and Misty wiped her forehead with the back of her wrist.

'I'd say at least eleven pounds.' She looked at Trina. 'What do you think, Trina?'

Trina looked away from her baby and grinned widely up at Misty. 'She's as big as a watermelon. And I'm stiff and sore but glad it's over. She's definitely my biggest—' she glanced at her husband '—and my last.'

'I'm glad you mentioned you don't cut the cord immediately,' Leon said quietly into Tammy's ear. 'Or I would have been expecting a different sequence of events.'

They'd moved back away from the birthing couple to the sink to strip off their gloves and wash their hands. Tammy nodded. 'Do you think it would have made much difference if we'd clamped and cut and moved the baby to the resuscitation trolley?'

'Not with an adequate heart rate like that.' He paused and she wondered if he was comparing this with other occasions he'd known. 'Actually, no, and I can see advantages. It is always good to see differences in the way things are managed in other hospitals, let alone other countries.'

They waved to Misty and let themselves out. The parents were absorbed in their new daughter and waved absently.

Tammy smiled at the man walking beside her. 'It was good to know you were there. If those shoulders had been more stubborn we would have had a baby in much poorer condition, and in resuscitation the more hands the better.'

'The maternal positioning worked very well. My memories of shoulder dystocia were always fraught with a dread that was missing tonight.' He smiled. 'You were both remarkably calm.'

'There's some anxiety when you see a very large baby like Trina's. But we do drills for that scenario at least once a week so if there's a delay we can move straight into the positions. Because we knew Trina's baby was larger, Misty would have spoken to her about what to do if needed and good positions to try. But it can happen with small babies too.'

He dropped his arm around her shoulders, and it was companionable, not sexual. Not something she would have believed possible earlier. 'You must be very proud of your team here.'

'We are.' His arm felt warm and heavy but not a heaviness she wanted to shrug off. A heaviness of wanting to snuggle in and encourage more snuggling. She shifted away from that concept quick-smart and he picked up the tiny movement and slid his arm away. She pretended she didn't miss it. 'And the women and their families love the centre and the choice it gives them. We've quite a clientele from the larger centres coming here to birth and then going home from here.'

They were crossing the car park to Tammy's car and Tammy suddenly realised how at ease she felt with this big, quiet Italian. How she'd just expected that if Trina's baby had been compromised by a long delay before the rest of her body was able to be birthed, that Leon would be there to help. Despite his denial that he'd had much to do with new babies, she had unshakable conviction that his skills would be magnificent.

You can't tell that, a voice inside her insisted. But just like she knew that Misty could see things without proof or concrete evidence, she knew that Leon Bonmarito would be a great asset in Lyrebird Lake. Not that there was much chance of him hanging round.

She paused beside her car to speak and he took the opportunity to open her car door for her. She frowned. No one had done that for her for years and she wasn't sure she liked the warm and pampered feeling it left her with. As if abdicating her independence. But that uneasiness didn't stop her invitation. 'Perhaps I'll see you tomorrow night. If you find yourself at a loose end after Paulo's in bed.'

He inclined his head. 'Three in a row? What will people say?' At her arrested expression he laughed softly and looked around at the sleeping town. 'Your townspeople bed early, I doubt anyone is awake to notice.'

What would they notice? There was nothing to see. She'd done nothing wrong. Nobody could construe otherwise but it was as well he reminded her. She'd vowed to remain squeaky clean and the soul of discretion once she'd had Jack. Lyrebird Lake had given her tarnished youth a brand-new, shiny start, and there'd never been any hint of wayward behaviour to jeopardise that from Dr Ben's daughter.

She looked up at him, confident she'd done nothing wrong, nothing remotely possible to compromise her good name, and her chin lifted as she peered up at him in the dimness. Unexpectedly she perceived the unmistakable glint in those bedroom eyes of his. The breath caught in her throat and she moistened her lips to make the words, at the very least, sound relaxed. 'Notice what?'

'Perhaps this?' His hands came up and cupped both cheeks to prevent her escape, not with force but with warmth and gentleness and definite intent. His head bent and his chiselled lips met hers with an unmistakable purpose that spun her away from streetlights and neighbours and petty concerns of her good name, until she kissed him back because that was more natural than breathing, more satisfying than a heartfelt sigh, and kindled the smoulder of heat in her belly he'd started with a dance two days before.

When Leon stepped back she swayed until he cupped his hand on the point of her shoulder and held her steady.

Her hand lifted to her mouth of its own accord—suddenly sensitive lips tingled and sang—and she could feel the sleepiness in her eyes until she blinked it away. She glanced at the silent streets. The only lights shining were the street lamps. And no doubt her eyes.

Where had all these feelings come from? How could she feel so attuned and connected to this man she barely knew? How could she be tempted in a way she hadn't been since Jack was conceived? The depth of her response scared the pants off her. And she knew what had happened last time she'd felt like that.

He's right, she thought with convoluted logic, this was dangerous, and she'd need to think what she was doing before she ended up as the latest discussion point at the local shop.

She moved back another step. 'I could see how people could form the wrong idea,' she said wryly, and then she swallowed a nervous laugh as she slipped past him into the car. She stared straight ahead as she turned the key. 'Thanks for the reminder and for being there for all of us tonight.' And for the kiss, but she wasn't saying that out loud.

As an exit line it wasn't bad. Showed she had presence of mind—something she wouldn't have bet on one minute ago. 'If you visit, maybe you could walk to my house tomorrow night, instead of driving. More discreet.'

As she drove away she decided the invitation had been very foolish. And not a little exciting. She was a sad case if that was how she got her thrills.

CHAPTER FIVE

LEON glanced in the oval hallway mirror beside the door and grimaced at the five-o'clock shadow that darkened his jaw. His watch said it was too late to shave again this evening. And no time to walk.

Paulo had been unsettled tonight and Leon doubted Tamara would appreciate a ten-o'clock visit. If he didn't know better he would say he was wary of upsetting her.

Little firebrand. He could feel the tilt of his mouth as he remembered the wedding and her not so veiled threats of violence to his person. And the kiss last night under the street lamp. That had been bad of him. The man in the mirror smiled. Not that he wouldn't do it again if he had the chance. The result had far exceeded his wildest expectations and the ramifications had disturbed his slumber again for much of the night. It was fortunate he'd never required much sleep.

She amused him, intrigued him, but most of all she burned his skin with Vesuvian fire whenever he touched her and that should be enough to warn him off. He couldn't deny the danger but then she was so different than the women he was used to.

There was no fawning or attempts to use guile. He laughed out loud as his hired car ate up the short distance to her house—she did not know the meaning of the word *subtlety*.

Though no doubt she'd prefer he walked and with less fanfare of his arrival, and he needed to remind himself this town was different to Rome. Even Gianni had told him that. Perhaps he would walk tomorrow if he was invited again.

Another smile twitched at his lips. That would be two days before they left and each day he was becoming more interested in the concept of his new sister-in-law bringing her friend to visit his homeland.

When he knocked quietly on the door, it wasn't Tamara who opened the door, but her father, Ben, with his grandson standing behind his back. The degree of Leon's disappointment was a stern warning of how quickly he was becoming accustomed to Tamara's company.

'Evening, Leon. Tammy said you might call. She's over in the birthing unit with Misty.'

Another crisis? 'Do they need a hand?'

Ben shrugged but there was tension in his smile. 'Haven't asked for one but you could hang around outside on standby. Misty said it was good having you there last night. Or you could wait with us?'

'Perhaps I will return to the hospital and check. It will be too late for visitors when she's finished anyway.'

'I'll give her a quick ring and let her know you're available, then.'

'Thank you.' He nodded at Ben and turned away. He could hear Tammy's son asking why he had come. Perhaps a question he should be asking himself. But at the moment he was more interested in his instinct that he be there in case Tamara needed him.

Leon had intended to poke his head into the birthing room and then wait at the nurses' station until he heard the sound of a well baby. What he did hear when he arrived was the sound of the suction and oxygen and the murmur of concerned voices. When he opened the door his eyes caught Tammy's and the urgent beckon of her head had him beside her before he realised he'd moved.

'Will you tube this little guy, please, so we can have a look? He's not responding as well as I'd like.' She had the equipment ready to hand him, the laryngoscope, the endotracheal tube and introducer, even the tape. 'I thought I was going to have to do it myself but I'd rather you did.'

Easily, but that would not help her next time. 'Then go with that thought. You do it and I'll help. Better for when I am not here.' She swallowed and nodded and he tapped the dispenser of hand cleaner on the side of the trolley and quickly cleaned his hands before handing the laryngoscope to her.

'No rush,' he said conversationally, and steadied her hand with his as she fumbled a little. 'His colour is adequate so your resuscitation has maintained his oxygen saturation but a direct vision and an airway into his lungs is a good idea if he's not responding.'

He handed Tammy the equipment in order as she gently tilted the baby's head into the sniffing position as she'd been taught, and viewed the cords with the laryngoscope.

Misty murmured background information to fill Leon in. 'A true knot in his very short umbilical cord and it must have pulled tight as he came down.' They all glanced at the manual timer on the resuscitation trolley as the second hand came around to the twelve. 'So quite stunned at birth. Heart rate's been sixty between cardiac massage, and he's two minutes old. We've been doing intermittent positive pressure since birth and cardiac massage since thirty seconds. He's slow to respond.'

Tammy passed the suction tube once when the laryngoscope light bulb illuminated a tenacious globule of blood that must have occluded half of the baby's lungs from air entry.

'That will help,' she murmured. This time when they connected the oxygen to the ET tube she slid down his throat, his little chest rose and fell and his skin quickly became pink all over.

'Heart rate one hundred,' Misty said when she ceased the chest compressions to count, and they all stood back as the baby began to flex, wince and finally attempted to cry around the tube in his throat.

'I love the way all babies wish to live,' Leon murmured. 'It is their strength.' He nodded at Tammy and gestured with his hand. 'Slide the tube out. He doesn't need it now.' He felt the pride of her accomplishment expand in his chest and smiled at her as the little boy began to wail his displeasure. 'Well done.' He nodded his approval of her skill. 'How did that feel?'

Tammy's voice had the slightest tremor that matched the one in her fingers now it was all over. 'Better now I've done it again. Thanks.'

Misty lifted the crying babe and carried him back to his mother, who sat rigidly up in the bed with her empty arms outstretched to take him.

Tears ran down her face and even her husband wiped his eyes as their baby cried and the mountain of fear gradually faded from their eyes like dye from new denim.

'Don't do that to Mummy, Pip,' the dad said as his wife's arms closed over her baby and she hugged him to her chest. Her husband's arms came around them both and their heads meshed together in solidarity. The baby blinked and finally settled to squint at his parents through swollen eyelids.

The dad looked across at Misty. 'He'll be all right, won't he, Misty?'

'He's good, Trent.' She glanced at Tammy and Leon to include them. 'A clot of blood was stuck in his throat. We'll watch him for the next twenty-four hours but Pip responded well once the airway was clear. No reason to think otherwise.'

'That was terrifying,' the mother said with a catch in her voice.

Leon smiled. 'Yes. Always. Of course this is the beginning of many frights this child will give you.' He smiled again. 'I know. I have a son.' He bent and listened with the stethoscope to the baby's little chest. 'Your son sounds strong and healthy, and obviously he was born under a lucky star.'

His mother shivered. 'How's that lucky?'

'A true knot in the umbilical cord is dicing with danger. The knot could have pulled tight much earlier when there was nothing we could do but he waited until it was safe to do so. And in such a good place as this.'

Misty and Tammy smiled and the parents looked at each other as if to say, Thank goodness we have a clever child.

'If you excuse me, I'll leave you to enjoy your family.' He leaned across and shook the father's hand, nodded at the mother and smiled at Misty.

'I'm ready to come with you,' Tammy said as she glanced at Misty for confirmation.

'Go. I'm fine. Thanks again. Both of you.'

They left, shutting the door behind them, and

when they reached the outside, Tammy inhaled the night air deep into her lungs and let it out as if her very breath had been hung with lead weights. 'I hate that floppiness in a compromised infant.' She shuddered with relief.

He could see that. Clearly. 'Of course. Everyone does. You did well,' Leon said quietly at her shoulder, and to his surprise he realised she was wiping at tears. Instinctively he pulled her gently into his chest and held her safe against him with her nose buried in his shirt. This time only for comfort and he was surprised how good it felt to be able to offer this.

But Tamara in his arms was becoming a habit. She felt warm and soft and incredibly precious within his embrace and the fragrance of her filled his head. His hand lifted and stroked her hair, hair like the softest silk, and the bones of her skull under his fingers already seemed familiar. He accepted he would find her scent on his skin when she was gone. Like last night. And the night before. And the night before that. The thought was bittersweet. 'You did beautifully.'

Her head denied his approval and her voice was muffled by his shirt. 'I should have done it earlier.'

'You could not know there was an obstruction there. To decide to intubate is no easy decision. And the time frame was perfect because he was well perfused while the decision was made.'

She unburrowed her head from his chest. Obviously she'd just realised she was in his arms again and wondering how that happened. He couldn't help the twitch of his lips.

'This is becoming a bit of a habit.' She said it before he could.

'Hmm. So it is.' He could hear the smile in his voice as she stepped back.

'I'll be more confident next time.' There was no amusement to spare in hers. His arms felt empty, like the mother must have felt before she was given her baby, but he felt anything but maternal towards Tamara. Probably better that she stepped away because his thoughts had turned from mutual comfort to mutual excitement in a less public place.

He forced himself to concentrate on her concerns. 'Do not disparage yourself. I'm impressed. Intubation is a skill that not all midwives have and very useful for unexpected moments. It was very brave of you to conquer your fears.'

She straightened and met his eyes. 'I felt better once I knew you were there as backup.'

He was glad he could help. The streetlight illuminated the delicate planes of her face, the shadows lengthened her already ridiculously long neck and his fingers tensed inside his pocket where he'd sent them to hide because he itched to cup her jaw. Already his mouth could imagine the taste of her, the glide of his mouth along that curve that beckoned like a siren, but a siren unaware of her power. He drew a low breath and looked away. 'I'm glad I was there.'

'So am I.' He felt she avoided his eyes this time and maybe it was better. 'I should get home to Dad and Jack. They'll be worried.'

He wasn't sure either of them would be worried but he could tell she was uncomfortable and maybe a little aware of the danger she was in. Her night had been stressful enough without him adding pressure. 'And I will see you tomorrow. Sleep well, Tamara.' He wouldn't.

'Tammy,' she corrected automatically. And then she smiled. 'Goodnight, Leonardo.' He liked the sound of his name on her lips.

The next afternoon Tammy and Misty stood beside Pip's wheeled cot and stared down at him as he slept. 'Lucky little guy.'

Misty shook her head. 'It's always when you least expect it. The labour was perfect, Pip's heart rate all the way was great, and then I just started to feel bad, edgy for no reason, and I had to call you.'

Tammy gave a quick squeeze of her stepmother's arm for comfort. 'Your instinct has always been terrific.'

Misty rolled her eyes. 'I did wonder if Trina's birth from the night before had given me the willies and I was losing my nerve. You know, doubting myself by wanting to call you.' She looked at Tammy. 'You were great. I'm really pleased you came.'

'Your turn to intubate next time. I'm pleased that

Leon came as well. I know that if we do what we did, just keeping the oxygen and circulation going until they recover, we're going to be fine. I *know* babies want to live.'

They stared down at Pip and Tammy went on. Voicing what they both knew. 'The horrible thing is that every now and then, for their own reasons, babies don't do what we expect. On that day I want to know we did everything we could. Maybe we could ask Leon about the latest resuscitation techniques before he leaves?'

Misty nodded. 'I think everyone would be interested in a discussion and the practise too. I know your father would. We need to include it more, like we practise the emergency drills.'

That was the beauty of working at Lyrebird Lake. Everyone wanted to keep their skills top notch. Wanted to support growth and competency and faith in one another. 'We need to include new trends in Resus more.'

'Next time I see him I'll ask him.' Probably tonight, she thought with a bubbling anticipation she tried to ignore. 'It'll have to be soon because he'll be gone.' She hoped she didn't sound plaintive.

Misty missed nothing. 'Sunday, isn't it? I think you'll miss him. You okay with that?'

Tammy reached for a pile of nappies to restock Pip's cot. At least she could avoid Misty's eyes that way. 'Fine. No problem.' She didn't want to think about it. Something she hadn't been able to achieve in reality. She shrugged. 'I've enjoyed his company, but really, we barely know each other.'

And yet on another level they knew each other far too well.

Misty might have been able to read her mind but there was no pressure in her comment. 'Sometimes it doesn't take long to feel that connection.'

Tammy smiled at the pile of nappies. 'Like you did with Dad?'

She could hear the returning smile in Misty's voice. 'I can remember driving away as I tried to deny it.'

She'd heard the story many times and never tired of it. 'And he followed you to Lyrebird Lake.' Tammy stood and glanced over at her stepmother. 'I'm glad he did, and glad he brought me with him. But I can't see Leon hanging around here for me and I'm certainly not moving to Italy.'

She thought about the differences in their cultures and she thought about distance and all she'd achieved here. Then she thought about her bad run with Italians and finally the kidnap attempt on Leon's son, even though the criminals had been caught and Paulo was safe now. She couldn't imagine living a life like that.

Misty handed her some clean singlets to put under the cot. 'I'm sure your father told me once you can speak Italian?'

She didn't know why she wanted to hug that to herself. 'Only a little.'

'Does Leon know?' Tammy shook her head.

Misty smiled. 'Isn't that interesting.' She moved away from Pip's bed to change the subject. 'I'm actually glad it's my last evening tonight. Peta and Nicky want to go to the beach house on the weekend and your father says he's not going without me. It'll be good to relax.'

Tammy thought of her father and the run-around her stepsisters would give him if Misty wasn't there to gently control their exuberance. 'I don't blame him. The girls are full-on.'

Misty laughed. 'And Jack isn't?'

'Must be in the genes.' They smiled at the family joke. Though Ben wasn't Tammy's biological father they'd decided Tammy had inherited all her bad traits from him.

'Actually—' Misty paused as if weighing her words '—I was wondering if Jack would like to come with us? Give you a weekend off.'

Tammy frowned at the sudden unease the thought left her with. All this talk of kidnapping and violence and her son away. Then she thought of her response when she'd thought Leon was coddling his own son. 'Maybe not this weekend. But another time, sure. As long as I can take the three of them some weekend and you and Dad could have a weekend off?'

'We could do that.' Misty glanced at the clock and

saw it was almost time for Tammy to go. 'Has Jack been keeping Paulo company?'

She'd tried to encourage her son to visit but he'd resisted. 'Not yet. I'm not sure they get on. I have a feeling they both like being only children. Rivalry. I'm taking him around to Louisa's this afternoon to play.'

Tammy glanced at her watch. 'Did you want to send the girls around after school? Louisa would love it. The more children, the happier she is. Just until Dad gets home with Leon? I'll be there too.' Not to mention she'd be there when Leon came home. She wouldn't have to wait until late that night to see him and the thought sat warmly just under her throat.

Misty glanced at her own watch and weighed up the time she had to change plans. 'Instead of after-school care? They'd like that.'

'It was Louisa's idea for the children to visit.' And Tammy had been quick to agree. 'I've been meaning to catch up with her for a few days.'

Misty nodded as they both paused and thought about Louisa's loss and Tammy went on. 'Leon says she's lonely. That the residence is too big and empty for her.'

Misty bit her lip. 'Poor Louisa. Maybe she needs a change of scenery to help her think of something else for a while?'

'Leon says he's trying to get her to move to Italy with him.' She was starting all her sentences with

'Leon says.' Good grief. She needed to watch that and she'd bet her stepmama wouldn't miss it either. She changed the subject. 'I wonder where Gianni took Emma for the Australian leg of their honeymoon?'

Tammy saw Misty bite back her smile as she accepted the change. 'She'll send us a postcard, I'm guessing. It's not long till they fly out.'

Tammy glanced at her watch. It was time for her to go before she said something else she'd regret. 'Yep. Imagine—Italy on Sunday.' She didn't look at Misty as she left. Just waved and stared straight ahead.

'I don't want to play with him. I'm not a little kid, Mum, you can't make me.' Tammy glanced across and checked that Jack had done up his seatbelt before she started the car. Stinky pulled against his dog restraint and panted longingly at the window.

'Sure I can.' She ruffled Jack's black hair. 'So stop acting like a baby and be nice. The girls are coming too. The poor kid's probably bored out of his skull not being able to go to school.'

Jack screwed up his nose. 'Poor Paulo. Imagine not having to go to school? How terrible.'

'Don't be sarcastic. It doesn't suit you.' Tammy tried to keep a straight face. There was a lot of muttering going on under Jack's breath and she thought she heard, 'I'd kill to not have to go to school.' She could remember thinking the same thing a lot of years ago.

She parked outside and walked the path of the old doctor's residence and up the stairs onto the verandah. Tammy knocked and opened the door. The residence was always open and Louisa would be out the back in the kitchen.

The tantalising aroma of fresh baking wafted down the hallway and she sighed philosophically about her new jeans that were a little tight already. Louisa's scones were legendary.

'Hello, Jack.' Tiny Louisa held out her snuggly-grandma arms and smiled hugely as she enveloped him in a big hug. Louisa was the only person he'd suffer a hug from and the sight made Tammy smile too.

Jack emerged pink cheeked, grinned shyly, and he leaned up and kissed Louisa's cheek. 'Hello, Aunty Lou.'

'You need fattening up, my boy. You and Paulo are like two skinny peas in a pod.' She glanced fondly over at Paulo, who sat beside the window with an open book in front of him. 'Paulo's been forcing down my scones. Haven't you, Paulo?'

Paulo smiled shyly at Louisa and kissed his fingers. *'Delizioso.'*

Tammy stepped in for her own hug, and she squeezed Louisa's waist which suddenly seemed smaller than she remembered. She frowned. 'You losing weight, Louisa?'

Louisa patted her round tummy. 'Oh, I'm not

cooking as much, though I've put on a pound or three since two more gorgeous Italians moved in.'

Tammy felt slightly reassured but decided she'd mention Louisa's health to her dad next time she saw him.

She noticed Jack had wolfed down his scones by the time Peta and Nicola arrived. Misty and Ben's girls were both fair-headed like their mother and Nicola stood half a head taller than her sister.

More hugs and more homemade strawberry jam and freshly whipped cream to be piled onto disappearing scones and then the children all trooped off to play outside. Tammy felt Paulo dragged his feet a little and she frowned after him.

She glanced at Louisa. 'Maybe I should ring Montana? Paulo seemed happiest talking to Grace at the wedding.' Grace was staying with Montana and Andy's daughter while Gianni and Emma were on their first few nights of the honeymoon.

Louisa laughed. 'She'll be here soon. She and Dawn have been over every afternoon after school. The three get on very well.'

Tammy nodded, and helped Louisa carry their tea to the verandah. The women sat looking out over the green lawns, talked together easily while the children played and drank tea.

The sun shone on the red roof of the hospital across the road and fluffy white clouds made magical shapes in the blue of the sky. The breeze from the lake helped keep the temperature down and Tammy decided the two boys seemed to be getting on well enough.

The children's games started simply, though even to a casual observer the boys competed for most stakes. They always seemed to be the last two to be found in hide-and-seek and were the fastest at finding people. Both were better than the girls at shooting hoops and it quickly became apparent how important it was to be the boy with the best score. Tammy shook her head as Jack whooped when he won the latest game.

The afternoon sun sank lower and Louisa went back inside to start dinner while Tammy flicked through a magazine as she watched them play.

Leon would be home soon, and her thoughts returned to the man who had erupted into her life with a compelling force she wasn't prepared for.

She'd already seen his concern for Louisa but what was he like while he stayed here? Was he tidy and thoughtful? Did he wait to be served his meals or jump up to help? Was he a good father, attending to all Paulo's needs? At the last thought she pulled herself up. It didn't matter what the answer was to any of these questions, he was leaving on Sunday. And she was not going to waste her time wondering about things that didn't concern her.

She called out to the children to suggest they finish off their games and come in. Stinky barked as he tried to join in and the sound echoed over the quiet, tree-lined street.

Tammy glanced at her watch again. He'd be here soon. The questions she'd asked herself itched like a raised rash at the back of her mind and she gave in to the urge to search out Louisa for some of the answers before it was too late.

Her mind wandered to whether or not Leon would visit her house tonight as well.

Wandered to the night after he left for his home country and how empty her den would feel.

Wandered to whether the tension she could feel heating between them could be contained to prevent an inferno, a conflagration that could damage them both as they went their separate ways in the very near future.

Her hip buzzed and she reached for her phone. It was Misty and she opened it with a smile.

Her smile fell at the unease plain in her stepmother's voice. 'I've got a bad feeling.' Misty sounded shaky and Tammy felt her stomach drop. Misty went on. 'Where's your car?'

Tammy frowned into the phone. 'Outside. Why?'

'I'm coming over.' Misty hung up.

Outside, the girls were happy to quit but the boys had one more point they wanted to settle and the ultimate test was Jack's idea.

'Just one last race. A longer one. I'll race you past

the last tree and around that car down the end of the road and back. No stopping.'

Paulo looked at the distance, pondering the slight incline in the hill over the rough stones and the fact that they both had bare feet. He'd always run well in bare feet. And he was fast.

'*Sì*. Then we must go in, for my father will be here soon.'

'You're on.' Jack looked at the girls. 'Grace? You be starter.'

Paulo looked confused and Grace whispered, 'I say, "Ready, set, go." On "go" you run like the clappers.'

Paulo nodded. He understood 'go'.

The other girls were silent as Grace counted. 'Ready. Set. Go.' The two boys took off like deer in the bush, along the path, down the hill, and Stinky ran with them, barking the whole way. The girls cheered as the two distant figures ran neck and neck and then split each side of the car as they came to it and turned for the return journey. Then a strange thing happened.

The car doors opened wide and two men got out and suddenly the boys disappeared. Almost as if they were sucked into the vehicle. Both of them. The doors shut and the car pulled away on the road out of town in a skid of gravel and the roar of an engine even the girls could hear.

All that was left was the dust and the tiny four-legged figure of Stinky chasing the black sedan down the road.

Grace blinked and looked at Nicky and Peta and then she spun on her heel and raced into the house. 'Tammyyyyy. Someone's taken them!'

Grace ran full pelt into Tammy, who'd just shut her phone and was staring at it as if trying to understand. She steadied the girl against her chest. When she realised Grace was crying, dread curled like a huge claw in her chest and she looked at the empty lawn. Where were the boys?

She thrust Grace aside into Louisa's arms and rushed out into the street. A white car backed out of a driveway down the road and drove away; otherwise, the road was deserted in every direction. No Jack. No Paulo. Just Nicky and Peta with their arms around each other in fright outside the door.

Tammy spun on her heel. 'Who took them, Grace?' Her brain searched for a reason. More kidnappers? 'What did they look like? It wasn't a white car, was it? What were they driving?'

Grace sniffed valiantly and her mouth opened and closed helplessly. Louisa hugged the little girl into her side as the older woman, too, tried to make sense of what had happened.

Grace swallowed a sob that blocked her throat. 'It was a black car.' She sniffed hugely and then the words tumbled out. 'It was parked down the road.

The boys had a race and, when they ran past, men came out of the car and pushed them inside and drove off. Stinky's run after them.'

Tammy grabbed the keys to her own car off the table. 'Mind the kids, Louisa. I'm going after them.'

'Is that wise?' Louisa's vice trembled. 'It could be dangerous.'

'Dangerous for them,' Tammy snarled. 'Ring Dad to find Leon. Let Leon ring the police if he wants to.' Tammy was having trouble seeing through the thick fear in her head. How dare they take her son? And Leon's.

'They had black shirts and black trousers on,' Nicky said suddenly.

'And it was a car like Grandpa's,' Peta added.

Tammy's brain was chanting Jack's words over and over. *You'd find me, wouldn't you, Mum?*

Peta's words sank in as she threw her bag over her shoulder. 'A Range Rover?'

Peta nodded. 'Sort of. A big black four-wheel drive.'

'Right, then.' And Tammy was gone, running for her car and roaring away from the kerb as she fumbled with her seatbelt. They probably only had about three minutes head start on her and she knew the road. Misty's phone call came back to her. 'Where's your car?' And here she was in her car. She hoped to hell that Misty's premonition had seen a good end to the scenario.

The winding road into Lyrebird Lake could be treacherous for those who didn't know it. But then if they were Italians as she expected they were, they'd be used to driving on treacherous winding roads. Damn them. She pushed the pedal down harder and she flew past a gliding Maserati she barely recognised coming into town. A minute later her mobile phone rang and she snatched it up and didn't even consider it unusual she knew who it was. 'I can't drive and talk.'

'Put it on speaker.' Leon's order was calm, yet brooked no refusal. She flicked the speaker on impatiently and his voice echoed in the cabin. 'Stop your car, Tamara. Do not chase these people.'

Her foot lifted off the accelerator and then pushed down again. 'No. I won't stop.' She hung up and pushed the pedal down harder. And nearly ran over Stinky, who appeared as she rounded a bend.

She skidded to a halt, reversed, leaned over to the passenger's side and opened the door. She breathed deeply in and out several times. She wasn't surprised when she looked in the rearview mirror and Leon's car was behind her.

Stinky's tongue was hanging twice its length as he gulped air. 'Get in, Stinky.' Stinky leaned his paws on the frame and sighed. Such was his dedication to chasing the boys he didn't have the energy left to jump in.

Tammy pulled on the handbrake, opened her door, dashed around the car and picked up the little dog, but before she could bundle him in, Leon pulled up behind her. He was out of his car in a flash.

'Do not follow them. That's an order. You do not understand and will cause more harm than help.'

His words dashed over her like a bucket of cold water and she didn't reply as he went on implacably. 'Your son will be safer if you do not confront them.' His voice lowered. 'And so will mine.'

Her footsteps stopped beside her car, as did the frozen focus that had consumed her, and she slumped, horrified again at what had happened and chillingly aware of how the fear in her chest was almost choking her. She turned and leaned her face on her arm against the roof of her vehicle and then she felt Leon's hands as he pulled her back into his body.

She almost sank into him until she remembered he'd brought this on her. They'd taken Paulo and now he'd brought this agony to her when they'd taken Jack too. He wrapped his arms around her stiff body, but there was no yielding, no relief he could give her. Nothing would help the cold that seeped into her as if she were being slowly submerged in an icy blanket of dread. Her son had been abducted.

Her chest ached with the spiralling fear started by Misty's call and the empty yard.

And they sped away further as she stood here. She yanked herself free of his embrace. He was letting them get away. 'I could have caught them.' She threw her head back and glared into his face. 'Seen where they went.'

His voice was flat. Cold. Implacable. A stranger. 'I will know where they went. Those who follow them are better prepared to apprehend than you or me. I told you I had people protecting my family.'

Great. That was just great. 'And what about mine? Whose protection does my son have?'

'My protection too, of course,' he ground out. Her eyes flashed a deep fear at him that tore at his faith in his men and his belief he'd done the right thing to stop her. He'd done this to her. Why had he left Paulo again today? He'd created a pattern. The first rule of prevention. So much for his belief the threat had passed. So much for his efforts to not be too protective of his son. Now his nightmare had spilled over onto Tamara.

But he hadn't believed they'd follow him here. It didn't make sense. Why would they do such a thing? Was it not easier to wait until he returned to Italy? Even Gianni had thought danger in Australia highly unlikely. But thinking these thoughts brought no solace at this point.

She was waiting for a crumb of reassurance and he was too slow with it. 'Of course he will be safe. You have to trust me.'

She stepped back, further out of his arms, and spun away. 'You're asking a lot,' she threw over her shoulder as she paced. 'To trust you with the most important person to me in the world.'

He knew it was such a huge thing she entrusted to him. Her shoulders were rigid with it. 'I know,' he said.

She narrowed her eyes as she turned to face him. With her arms crossed tight across her breasts as if to hold in the fear, she searched for a hint of unsureness or ambivalence on the rightness of his actions. He hoped there was none.

Did she trust him? It was achingly important she could. Her chest rose and fell in a painful rasping breath full of unshed tears that tore at his own pain like the claws of a bird.

He saw the moment she accepted there was nothing physical she could do. He'd taken that away from her but he'd had to, for her own safety, and for the boys. She sagged back against her car. 'What happens now, then?'

'We go back home and wait.'

She shook her head angrily at the passiveness of the action, then threw herself off the car and back into action. 'I'm going to see Misty.'

CHAPTER SIX

'My mum's going to rip your arms off!'

'And my father will see you in hell.'

Both boys looked at each other and nodded. The captors, three dark-clothed Italian men, laughed as they drove.

Jack screwed up his face at the men and patted Paulo's leg. 'Don't worry, Paulo. She'll come.'

Paulo hunched his shoulders. 'It is my father who will come. And these dogs will pay.' The bravado was wearing a little thin but it still helped the fear that crept up their arms and settled around their tight little bellies as they sat wedged between two burly men. Two small boys in a situation they shouldn't have had to deal with.

'How have we two of them?' The Italian accent was coarser than Paulo's dad's and his partner shrugged.

'Didn't know which to take. We can get rid of the other one.'

In the back the boys huddled closer together.

* * *

Tammy parked her car outside Louisa's house and left the door gaping as she ran straight into Misty's arms. Ben came out of the house to meet them.

Leon heard Misty say, 'I feel they're fine. Honestly,' and he grimaced at the strange comment. He passed Tammy's open car door and shut it with tightly leashed control before he followed her in.

He felt suspended above himself, detached and icy cold as though he were peering down a long tunnel when all he wanted to do was find the people who had taken their sons and crush their throats. But he needed to stay calm for Tamara—and for the boys. He'd been speaking to his bodyguards and they had caught up with the car but were keeping distance between them. They had to find a way to stop the vehicle and keep the boys safe.

When he entered the residence it seemed the room was full of people. Louisa, her lined face white and shaking, stared at him as if she didn't understand. Kidnappings and violence were not in her life and Leon moved swiftly across and folded her in his arms. He stroked her hair. Nothing like this would have ever happened before in Lyrebird Lake.

Leon remembered his hope he wouldn't need to call on his brother's help for just such a situation. Gianni wasn't here but it seemed he'd get as many people as he needed. But for the moment he had to trust his own men and, now that he'd just contacted them, the Australian police. They would ring him if he could do anything.

And past his fear for his son was Tammy, and her son's kidnapping, leaving Leon devastated he'd brought this on her by association, and regretful of her pain. His own agony was like a gaping wound in his chest and no doubt it would be as bad if not worse for a mother. Louisa shuddered in his arms and he rested his chin on the top of her grey head. Poor Louisa. Poor Tammy. And what of the boys?

The afternoon stretched into evening and then to night. Six hours after his return to the lake Leon stood tall and isolated in Tammy's den. He searched her face for ways to help but he knew she wasn't able to let herself relax enough to take the comfort he wanted to offer.

He carried the coffee he'd made her from the machine in the kitchen and the strong aroma of the familiar beans made him think of home. At home he would have more access to resources.

His arms ached to pull her against him and transfuse the strength she needed in the closing of this tumultuous day. Her distress left him powerless in a way he wasn't used to and he placed the cup on the mantel, then sighed as he reluctantly lowered himself to the sofa to watch her. 'I stay until we have them back.'

Tammy heard him. The coffee aroma drifted past her nose. She was glad he'd finally sat down. It gave her more room to pace and her eyes closed as she processed his words. *Until we have them back.* 'I want my son.' She wanted to wring her hands. 'I want Jack now. I don't want you.'

That wasn't strictly true. She'd driven everyone else away—her father, her stepmother—but she'd been unable to evict Leon from her presence. He'd flatly refused to leave her. And she needed him near her so she could know she was kept in the loop. Despite her wall of pain she seemed to be able to draw some strength from Leon which seemed absurd when he was the reason she was going through this.

She reached for the cup and took a sip. It was strong, and black, as she liked it. She'd drunk her coffee that way since she'd been that impressionable teen who'd fallen for a man similar to this one. Or was that unfair to Leon?

What was it with her and men that attracted trouble and danger?

At sixteen Vincente Salvatore had taught her to love his language, his country, all things Italian, with a heady persistence that endeared her to him. An Italian with trouble riding his shoulders, hot-headed and hot-blooded. Then he blew it all away with a reckless abandon for right and wrong that left her with the realisation of just how dangerous his lifestyle was. She swallowed a half-sob in a gulp of coffee. Maybe Vincente's friends could find Jack.

How on earth had she embroiled herself and her son in trouble without realising it? But she would have to deal with that. It was her fault. She couldn't believe she'd been so irresponsible as to let the children out of her sight. Couldn't forgive herself for daydreaming her way to negligence. Such stupidity could have cost Jack his life. And Paulo his.

It wasn't as if she hadn't known of the possibility of danger. Even though Leon had said it was past. And what had she been doing? Daydreaming about a man. Following Louisa for titbits of gossip about his presence at the old residence. Anything to feed her growing fascination for Leon.

Well, it would all stop. Now. She would promise anyone who would listen that the risk of danger to her family far outweighed any fleeting attraction this dark Italian held over her.

A bargain.

Jack and Paulo back safe and she'd never think of the man again. Honest.

She should have learned that she was destined to be brought down by her heart, and the menace of these Mediterranean men, her nemeses. Now their sons had paid the price.

Unfortunately, at this moment, it was hard to keep those thoughts clear in her mind because her shattered emotions were torn—torn between guilt for her negligence, spiralling fear for the outcome and the gnawing need for comfort from the very man who caused it all.

Louisa had been gathered up from the residence by

her stepson and whisked away. And Leon was here, the only barrier to the emptiness of this house.

It was eerie how she could imagine the outside of her empty house, dark and forlorn in the moonlight, and she glanced out the window to the shifting shadows in the street outside. Strained her ears for imagined sounds and then turned abruptly from the window and put the cup down.

She even ran her fingertips along the mantelpiece as if to catch dust and at least do something useful. Her mind was fractured into so many fear-filled compartments and what-ifs she couldn't settle.

She wanted both boys asleep in Jack's room, with Stinky's head on his paws as he watched his master—glancing at her every time she went in as if to ask if he could stay.

But the blue room at the end of the hall stayed empty like an unused shrine.

And Leon watched her.

It had taken until midnight for Tammy to decide she couldn't stay at her father's house. She'd said she wanted to be near Jack's things. Leon had refused to allow her to go alone and he was still glad he'd come. But as he watched her, she glittered like glass in moonlight with nervous energy. Every sound made her jump, every creak of the polished floorboards made her shiver, and Leon ached for the damage he'd caused to this sleepy town and to this woman.

He patted the sofa beside him and held out his

hand. 'Come. Sit by me. Let me help you rest for a few moments at least.'

She turned jerkily towards him. 'I can't believe he's not here.' Staccato words stabbed the air in the room like little knives, tiny steel-tipped blades of guilt that found their mark on him.

'They will have them by morning. My men have promised me.' Leon rose to slide his arm around her stiff shoulders and pull her down to sit beside him so their hips touched. She was so cold and stiff and he nudged more firmly against her hip, offering comfort to both of them, and a safe place to rest if only for a moment, and if only she could.

'Your men?' She sniffed. 'If they were so good the boys would never have been taken at all.'

'Nobody expected this here. We were lucky they were still with us.' Leon had his own demons. Paulo gone and he didn't know if he was alive. Or Jack. Surely they would get them back.

There had been no demand yet. Would they discard the boy they didn't need? Would they leave him alive? It had been his choice to delay the police while his men followed the trail initially.

The trail Tamara had wanted to chase. His first sight of her face as she drove past him like a woman possessed still affected him. Her little car pushed to its limits to the point where his more powerful motor could barely catch her. His throat tightened. 'I can't believe you pursued them in your car.'

She brushed the hair out of her eyes impatiently. 'Why would I not?' Her eyes searched his. 'I could still be chasing them if you hadn't stopped me. What if they've disappeared and we never find where they went? What, then?'

He shook his head at the thought. No! It would not be like that. He had to trust what his operatives told him. Tomorrow in the early morning, it would be okay. 'I was terrified for you as well. What were you going to do if you caught them?'

Her eyes burned. 'Whatever I had to. They have my son.'

And mine. She had no idea. And he did and should never have brought this on these people. He knew what loss and guilt did to people. 'What you did was too dangerous.'

Another swift scornful search of his face. 'For them?'

'For you and for the boys.'

She shook her head. 'For the first time in a lot of years I don't know what to do. You tell me to wait. But how long must I wait? I want him now.' Her shoulders slumped and slowly, like the deflation of an overstretched balloon, all the fight leaked out of her and she sagged against him as she buried her face in his shoulder.

He smoothed her hair. Had to touch her and try to soothe her agitation as she went on. 'There's never been such hard waiting. I've never had such fear.

Make me forget the horror I can't shake. Talk to me. Tell me something that helps.'

He pulled her onto his lap and hugged her, still smoothing her hair and whispering endearments she wouldn't understand. Assuring her the boys would be returned. That he knew she was scared. That he was scared.

His hand travelled over her hair and his mind seemed to narrow its focus, the room faded until only the sheen of silk beneath his fingers existed. Rhythmically he stroked as he murmured until suddenly he began to speak more easily.

In his own language, not hers. All the things he'd bottled up for years but never said.

He said he knew how scared she was. How scared one could be in that moment of loss. He could taste his first moment of absolute fear and horror, all those years ago on the ocean, at fourteen, not yet a man but about to become one.

The storm upon them before his father realised, the sudden wave that washed he and his brother overboard, and his father throwing them the lifebuoy just as the boom smashed him and his mother into the water after them.

He'd grabbed Gianni's collar and heaved him against his chest so his head was out of the water. He could remember that frozen instant in time. Them all overboard, Gianni unconscious and only he with something to cling to. He couldn't let go of his brother and, screaming out against God, he'd watched his parents sink below the surface.

So alone in the Mediterranean under a black sky. It had grown darker as the night came; Gianni awoke, and he'd had to tell him of their parents' fate.

Such fear and swamping grief as they'd bobbed in the dark, imagining sharks and trying not to move too much, chilled to the core, fingers locked to the rope of the buoy. Knowing they would die.

Their rescue had been an anticlimax. A fishing boat pulled them in. Then the week in hospital alone and grieving, with visits from lawyers and one old aunt and her change-of-life son who'd hated them both.

He'd vowed that day he would be strong. And he had been.

He'd married Maria as his parents had betrothed them, and finally they'd had Paulo. His heritage safe again.

Then Maria had died and Paulo had been almost taken. He'd realised his life could fall apart again any moment and he'd needed to see his brother, his only family.

He, who'd never spoke of anything that exposed his soul, poured it all out to Tammy. It eased the burden of guilt he carried to tell her how he felt, without the complication of her knowing. From somewhere within it was as if the walls he'd erected around his emotions began to crumble, walls he'd erected not just since Maria's death, but since that lost summer all those years ago when he'd felt he failed his parents. Walls that prevented him being touched by feelings that could flay him alive.

He continued to murmur into her hair as her softness lay against his chest. His native tongue disguising the compromise and giving freedom to express the beginning of something he hadn't admitted to himself as he held her warmth against his heart. Her healing warmth. The way she touched his soul. He told the truth.

How sorry he was to have brought this on her. How the lure of her physical attraction for him had begun to change to a more complete absorption. How she made him feel alive as he hadn't felt for years, even if sometimes it was with impatience or frustration when she thwarted him.

How beautiful she was, how she'd captured his attention after their first dance at his brother's wedding, how he'd never felt that connection before with another woman, even his wife, and that made him feel even worse.

How these past few days he couldn't stay away, spent his mornings and afternoons dragging his thoughts away from her so he could concentrate on business—something he had never had trouble with before—when in fact he was waiting for the evening when he could call on her.

The lonely nights dreaming of her in her house a

street away, staring out through the window all night so he could start the whole process again.

How he'd glimpsed the promise of what could have grown between them, but now that had changed. Had to change. Once the boys were returned he would sit on a plane and watch the ground fall away beneath him, knowing she was still in Australia. So she and Jack would be safe, apart from the danger that followed him.

Knowing the distance of miles would not be the only distance that grew between them every second. But he would. Because she would be safe. Her son would be safe. His life was too complicated for this, the ultimate complication, but he could never regret these past few days. And he would never forget her.

Tammy listened. Her head on his chest, the regular beat of his heart under her cheek as his liquid words flowed over her. Some words and phrases she didn't catch but most she did, like the honesty in his voice and the gist of his avowal. The sad acceptance of his promise brought tears to her eyes.

When she lifted her face to his, he saw the tears and softness in her eyes and he could no more stop himself from kissing the dampness away than he could stop himself drawing breath. Her arms came up around his neck and her face tilted until she lay suspended below him, mute appeal his undoing.

He stood with her in his arms, cradled against him,

and strode to her room, a dim and disconnected haven from the reality which they both sought to escape.

To hide in each other, buffer the pain of their fears with the physical, the warmth and heat of each other's bodies. At the very least the release might let them sleep.

Tammy knew she would regret this. But there were so many huge regrets—this tiny one was nothing if it gave her some flight from the pain, and comfort to them both.

He lowered her feet to the floor until she stood next to him, beside the bed, eyes locked as slowly they peeled away each other's clothes, layer by layer, like the emotions Leon had peeled away for her, until she was as bare as him.

She stepped forward until her breasts brushed his chest and with a muffled groan he crushed her to him. And she knew it was her turn to comfort him. She needed to comfort someone because she couldn't comfort Jack. Her hands curved around his neck and she pulled him closer so she could wrap herself around him, and draw his pain into her. In some unexplained way it eased her own suffering as they stood locked together in a ball of consolation that slowly unravelled into something else.

It started with a kiss, a slow gathering of speed. Kissing Leon was like running beside the wolf she thought him, down an unexpectedly steep hill, barely able to keep her feet. The momentum grew and her heart shuddered and skipped as she was swept alongside the rush of Leon, the heat of his chest, his powerful hands, his eyes above her, burning fiercely down as he searched her face for consent.

She reached up and pulled his mouth to hers again and she could feel the need in her chest and belly and in the heart of her as he gathered her closer, stroked her, murmured soft endearments of wonder in Italian which deepened the mist of escape and made her want to melt into him even more.

His hands slid down her back, marvelling at the smoothness of her skin, curling around her bottom and lifting her until her weight was in his hands. When he lifted her higher she rose against his chest. She'd never felt so small and helpless, dominated yet so safe and protected. She ran her cheek against the bulge of his arms, savouring the tension of steel beneath her skin from this mountain of a man who made her feel like a feather, as effortlessly he carried her until she felt the wall behind her. Then the nudge of him against her belly.

In a moment of clarity that came from the coolness of the wall on her back, she told herself she shouldn't do this, didn't deserve to experience this man at this moment in this way, would not die if she didn't. But she didn't really believe it.

She did believe she'd always regret not taking the gift of solace they offered each other in their darkest hour. And soon he would be gone.

He stilled, as if sensing her thoughts, and when she looked again into the midnight of his eyes, she knew she could stop this. Her heart felt the tear of denial, the breath of resolution and the tiniest lift of her skin away from his but something inside her snapped. No. She needed this for her sanity because with that one millimetre of distance between them, the outside world pummelled her and the pain made her wrap her legs around his corded thighs, hook her ankles and implore him to save her.

Afterwards, they lay together on the bed, entwined, her head on his chest as he stroked her hair and, against her will, against any conviction she'd be able to, she fell into a dreamless sleep and rested.

Leon listened to the slowing of her breathing and his arm tightened protectively around her. How would he forget this woman? What had happened between them was something he hadn't expected and he certainly hadn't foreseen the severity of the impact of their collision.

More barricades had tumbled under her hands, barriers he'd closely guarded and never planned to breach. He would regret this night and yet could not wish it undone. His eyes widened in the dark when he realised what else he'd done. Or not done.

His sins compounded. Not only had he not protected her son, he'd not protected her.

The flash of light on his silenced phone was muted by his shirt pocket on the floor but he saw it. He buried the enormity of that other problem for another time as he slipped his arm out from under her head. She snuggled back into him and he paused until her breathing resumed before he slid from the bed.

His brow creased as he read the message, then he gathered his clothes swiftly and left the room.

CHAPTER SEVEN

SHE was woken by ringing as he came back into the room. He leaned over and switched on the bed lamp before he reached for the phone beside the bed and gave it to her. 'Yes,' she listened, mouthed, 'the police' at him and then said, 'I understand.' She listened again and then nodded, her eyes closing with relief. He could read it in her face. She put the phone down. 'They're safe.'

He didn't tell her he'd known already. Just turned her into his body and hugged her. It was her he needed to hug and not just because of the boys. Crushed her into his chest and closed his eyes as if blotting out all the terrifying pictures his mind had been filled with before his bodyguards had rung him.

Tammy pulled back and her tear-streaked face looked up into his. Searched his eyes, searched his face. 'They wouldn't have made a mistake. Would they?'

He shook his head. 'They're on their way home now.' He didn't tell her there had been a gunfight.

Between two groups. Coming on them his men had scooped the boys from the confusion, had been fortunate one unidentified man had thrown himself in front of the boys to save them and been badly wounded. They'd left the dead and dying where they were for the police. He didn't say his bodyguards wanted to know what enemies he had that they knew nothing of.

Perhaps it wasn't over yet. It was an unexpected nightmare he'd dragged her into and he would never forgive himself. How many people were after him in his life? But there was much he didn't understand.

She searched his face and pulled away a little. 'There's more, isn't there?'

How could she tell? 'The boys aren't hurt.'

Still she watched him. Closely. 'Your people?'

He shook his head. 'No.'

Her head lifted as if she could scent danger. 'Then something went wrong with the kidnappers. So it's not finished.'

He squeezed her shoulders tight beneath his hands. 'It will be finished.'

She moved out of his embrace and her narrowed eyes flicked over him and away. 'You can't promise that.'

'I promised the boys would be returned.'

She looked at him and slowly she nodded. 'You did.' He could feel the distance grow between them. Despite what had passed only an hour ago. Or perhaps because of it. He thought briefly of a subject they hadn't broached but she went on.

'And I trusted you. But I don't know if I could do that again with my son's life.' And there was more there than was spoken and they both knew.

He inclined his head. 'I understand.'

She moved to slide out of the bed and he laid his hand on her shoulder to stay her. 'There is another thing we must discuss.'

She wrinkled her forehead. 'Yes?'

'I did not protect you when we made love. What of those chances?'

She shook her head. 'I'm meticulous.'

'Then there is nothing else you need to worry about.'

'Or you,' she confirmed.

The Saturday night before they left was so much harder to have Leon in the house, Tammy reflected with a sigh, thanks to a moment of weakness.

When she'd finally held her son safe in her arms that morning, Jack had asked if Paulo and his dad could stay their last night with them. Of course she'd said yes. She understood Jack's need and would have given her son anything he desired in that moment, that precious, arm-filling, flesh-and-blood hug of her unharmed child.

Both boys hadn't wanted to be separated after their ordeal and the day had been spent quietly watching over them as they slept and feeding them when they were awake. Leon had spent hours with the police.

How could she say no? What could she say, that she needed as much space as she could get from Leon now that she knew the man? Knew him with a depth and intensity and physical knowledge that scared the living daylights out of her.

Had heard his deepest fears exposed, had wept for the young orphan, had seen a little of his growing feelings for her. During her darkest hour those things had immeasurably comforted. Now they would both pay the price and tonight was incredibly awkward. And on top of it all was the guilt that Leon didn't know she'd understood his words.

Then there were the secrets he held. Where had he been when she'd been woken by the phone? Certainly not beside her in a state of undress. Plus the fact that two quiet men were outside, somewhere watching over her house and the people inside. She felt as if her world was spinning out of her control. She, who prided herself on control.

Leon had been reluctant to confirm their presence, but she'd seen them leaning on the tree across the road, and another out the back against her father's fence. His bodyguards.

Again she thought of Vincente and his cronies and the secrets and murky dealings she'd learned more of each day, and it hardened her resolve to stay aloof from this other dark man. But she needed all that resolve to not seek the same comfort she knew she could lose herself in.

The boys were finally asleep for the night. She'd been in and checked on them so many times she was almost dizzy with it.

Leon circled her, wary of intruding on her space, wary of her, as he should be. She was afraid of herself, her thoughts, her dilemmas that loomed large in the emotionally fogged compartments in her brain.

He came closer until he stopped in front of her. Lifted his hand and brushed the hair out of her eyes.

She shrugged and shifted out of his reach because she knew how easily she could have thrown herself back into his arms and that was the last thing she wanted communicated to him.

For Leon it was confirmation that she didn't need him. She had her son back. He was just prolonging her embarrassment. He watched her turn away again and search the room for the peace she obviously hadn't found next to him. 'The boys are safe now,' he said.

'Are they?' She sighed. 'Really? I have to bow to your superior knowledge, there, don't I?'

It was his fault. Letting her guess it was all not finished. He laughed without humour. Still she didn't trust him. 'Why don't I believe you could bow before anyone?'

Her eyes pinned him. 'Well, what if these criminals do come back to hurt the boys?'

He ran his hand down her arm. His aim had been to gentle her but all he seemed to achieve was to reinforce her agitation and his own aching feeling of loss. In the past twenty-four hours he'd changed.

Making love with Tamara had changed him. Had cost him something he hadn't wanted to give, ever again. But now was not the time to rail at himself for something he'd had no control of. Later he would sift what could be salvaged from the wreckage. He said again, 'The boys are safe.'

'You don't know that.' She looked at him. 'You can't lie that you aren't frightened they'll come back for Paulo.'

He sighed and he fought the dark pictures away. The way he'd only just caught them last time, Paulo pale and almost lifeless in his arms, the panic at the airport. The sickness of dread. And now again, unexpectedly, in this far-off land, and the fact that no ransom had been demanded. 'But there was no reason to take Jack.'

'There wasn't yesterday.' Tammy shook her head. 'But now he knows what the men look like.'

He raked restless fingers through his hair. Nearly all the men had been caught. With one close to the end when last he'd heard. 'What if it was not Paulo they were after?'

She shook her head. 'I don't understand.'

Neither did he. 'Is there any reason somebody would want Jack?'

Her hand flew up as if to brush aside the idea. Vehemently. 'Of course not. They were after Paulo.'

He watched her, narrowed his eyes as he tried to understand the nuance he was missing. Something that didn't ring true, though she'd never given him cause to disbelieve her before. It was hard to pinpoint his unease. 'My bodyguard was told they were delivering Jack.'

She shook her head. 'They made a mistake.'

He heard her words but this was what he couldn't understand. There had to be a connection. 'What about his father?'

She avoided his eyes. 'He's never seen his father.' He'd been in jail for all of Jack's life, but she didn't want to share that delightful pearl of information. She shook her head again. 'Jack knows I haven't seen or heard from his family since Ben moved me out of Sydney eight years ago. Before Jack was born. Jack's father was not someone I'm proud of falling in love with.' *And I'm not making the same mistake twice.*

Leon sat and pulled her down next to him. 'How old were you, Tammy?'

She stood again and walked away. She didn't want to talk about this now. When she had her back to him she answered, 'Does it matter?'

Leon persisted and she didn't understand why.

'Does anyone in this man's family know about Jack?'

She shook her head but she didn't even know that. She'd been pregnant, fifteen, with belly quietly bulging under the bulky clothes she'd worn. Her grandmother had panicked and her father had arrived. Thank goodness for the love of Misty and her dad. She was fairly sure Vincente was working himself up from a petty gangster and she would have been in the thick of it.

'I guess his mother knew I was pregnant because she worked for my grandmother, but whether or not she knew who the father was, I'm not sure. The whole world knew when I left.'

'So perhaps they could know?'

What was he getting at, digging through this old history? That horrible black trepidation was creeping over her again and she hated the feeling. Mistrusted it more than ever after yesterday.

She felt cold and she rubbed the goose flesh on her arms. It wasn't a cool night. 'This has nothing to do with the fact your son was kidnapped and mine was taken as well. Don't try and blame this on me. Our life was normal before you came.'

'I'm sorry.' He thrust his fingers deep through his hair. 'You're right. Unless he was Italian there can be no connection.'

Tammy's breath jammed in her throat and she hoped Leon didn't hear it stick. Another shiver ran through her as her heart slowed and then sped up twice as fast. She could feel her blood trickling coldly in her chest as she tossed that idea around like a hard lump of ice. No way.

Leon crossed to her. Her face gave away the turmoil he'd caused. He was a fool and a thoughtless one. 'Forget I asked. Please, Tamara, forgive me.' And he could do little else but gently draw her into his arms and kiss her.

She was so soft beneath him. Her cheek like satin against his face, her hair fluid under his fingers in that way he would never forget. How could he cause her more distress? He stroked her arm. 'Come lie down with me. Just to hold you. Nothing else. Let me keep you warm.'

She wanted to. So badly. It was a great theory to just hug and wrap themselves around each other and drift off to sleep but she doubted it would end that way.

She shivered again. 'I am cold.'

Was it wrong to want to lie with this man? To experience the immersion in another human being, to feel the power of her inner woman that she'd only just discovered because he'd shown her? She wanted to lose herself in him, or perhaps truly find herself, and in doing so maybe gain some peace. Why did this man, a man leaving tomorrow, have to be the one who had shown her that? The only man she'd ever sought peace from. Why was that? Why did everything go so wrong?

She wrapped her arms across her chest and attempted humour. 'If you took me to bed I don't know if I could keep my hands off you.'

The worried crease across his brow jumped and the tiniest twinkle lit his eyes. 'Perhaps I could sacrifice myself to your needs. If that should happen I would forgive you. Medicinal purposes, of course.'

No. They couldn't. There was the chance of the boys wandering in. 'I don't think so.'

'I could stay on top of the bedclothes.'

'And how would you warm me, then?' Perhaps that would work. She was so tired and cold and miserable and the thought of leaving her troubles for him to mind while she rested was beyond tempting.

'I'll be out in a minute.' She dived into the bedroom and shut the door. She imagined his face when he saw her in her too-big, dark blue striped, flannelette pyjamas.

But when she returned he didn't comment. Just took her hand and led her to the bed. She doubted he wanted to risk her changing her mind and making him sleep in the den. When she stood before him he took both her hands and kissed them.

'Tonight will look after itself.'

Sometime in the night she awoke, her pyjamas strangling her. Her arm had little movement where she lay on the ungiving fabric and she felt trapped.

Trapped and claustrophobic by the material and ripped off by the thought that tomorrow Leon would be gone. The bare skin of her feet had wormed between his legs and soaked in his heat and his hand had slipped between the buttons of her shirt and rested like a brand to cup her breast.

She lifted her free hand up to move his fingers but instead she stroked the back of his hand. He kissed her neck.

So he was awake also. *'Stai bene?'* Then, 'Are you okay?'

She almost said *sì*. 'I'm a little uncomfortable.'

'Your pyjamas?' She could hear the laughter in his voice and the sound was more precious than she expected.

'Yep.'

'I have a solution.'

'I'm sure you do.' The solution was delightful.

The next morning dawned clear and bright. Unlike her head. Tammy still felt fogged with the twists and turns of the past few days, let alone the disaster of sleeping with Leon again. Her face flamed in the privacy of the bathroom. Goodness knows how she was going to face the boys. At least Leon had been up and dressed before either boy had appeared.

Today they left for Italy. She was still telling herself his leaving was a good thing.

Emma and Gianni returned to Brisbane today

from their honeymoon and Montana was also driving up with Dawn, taking Grace to meet up with her mother and new step-father, before they all flew out.

Leon had taken the boys to the shop while she showered, to buy bread rolls and cold meats for brunch, a last-minute attempt to create some normalcy from Paulo's trip to Australia. A family picnic by the lake before they left.

She'd told Jack they weren't seeing them off at the airport. It was the last thing Tammy wanted—a long, drawn-out goodbye in front of strangers or even to sit opposite Leon at a small café table and make small talk in front of their sons. The picnic would be hard enough but at least it was private.

Tammy was meeting them back in the kitchen in half an hour to make the hamper. When they'd gone she slipped next door in search of her father.

Ben was painting the bottom of his old rowboat down the long yard that backed onto the lake. No trip to the beach this weekend. The ghost gum towered into the sky and shaded the grassy knoll above the water where he worked. The boatshed was where her father came when he was stressed.

She'd spent months of lazy summer afternoons with Ben and Misty here, watching swans and ducks when Jack was a baby. She realised time, peaceful and trouble-free time, so different to now, had drifted by like the floating leaves from the overhanging trees.

'Hello, there, Tam.' Her father looked up with a smile and his piercing blue eyes narrowed at the strain in her face.

He wiped the excess paint off the paintbrush and balanced it carefully across the top of the open paint tin before he stood. 'How are you? How's Jack? What's happened was huge. Bigger than anything we've had to cope with before.' He came closer. 'You okay, honey?'

She watched one large drip of red paint slide down the end of the brush and fall onto the grass like a drop of blood. A spectre of foreboding. But she didn't have premonitions—that was Misty's way. She shivered. She was here for a reason. 'I'll be fine when Leon's gone and Jack's safe.' As if to convince herself?

Her father's dark brows, so like her own, raised in question. He slid an arm around her shoulders and drew her to sit beside him on the circular iron stool that ringed the trunk of the biggest gum.

'You think the two go together, do you? Leon and trouble?'

'Of course.' So quickly she could say that but still there was that tiny seed of doubt planted last night, an illogical but still possible seed that maybe the trouble had come from her.

She wasn't sure how to broach a subject everyone in her family had left alone for more than eight years.

'Do you remember when you came for me that last time at Grandma's?'

Ben's black brows rose in surprise. 'Of course.'

'Did you ever learn much about Jack's father?'

Ben's arm slid away and he straightened and gazed across the lake. 'Yes. A little.'

She wouldn't have been surprised if he'd said, 'No—nothing,' so the other answer made her curious. She couldn't read his face. 'What could you know? I didn't tell you much.'

Still he didn't look at her. 'I found out what I needed to. To be sure you were safe when I took you away. To be sure Jack was safe.'

She really didn't want to hear those words. *To be sure Jack was safe*. Her stomach plummeted as she watched his profile. 'I think Vincente was involved with the mob on a small scale.'

Ben winced. 'I believe he was. I spoke to his mother and he was betrothed to a woman in Italy so he was never going to marry you.'

'Do you think there is any reason they'd want Jack now?' She'd said it. Out loud because she needed her father to deny, say it was nonsense, because she couldn't say it to Leon, whom she needed to tell.

Ben looked away again and didn't meet her eyes. Her stomach sank and she didn't want to think about the ramifications of that. He hesitated but then he said, 'Can't think of one.'

Tammy sighed with relief. 'Of course not.'

CHAPTER EIGHT

THE picnic had been Jack's idea. The boys kicked a soccer ball between them as they walked down to the water along the shaded path and every now and then Jack cupped his hands around his mouth and called, 'Coo-ee,' across the lake. Paulo would imitate him. The echoes bounced off the hills across the lake and rolled back over the water and Tammy could hear the boys giggle up ahead as they trickled the ball between them.

Somewhere to the right a kookaburra laughed at nothing in particular and she drew the moment in with the breath of freshly mown grass that drifted across the street. It was good to remember what normal felt like.

Not that it was normal to have a gorgeous Italian man by her side. 'The hamper not too heavy, Leon?' Tammy glanced across as they strode down the leaf-strewn path.

Leon swung the hamper as if it was filled with

fluff and nonsense but Tammy knew it must have weighed a ton. 'It's fine.'

Like heck it was. She'd put cans of soft drink, a thermos of freshly brewed coffee, mountains of savoury mini quiches, cold sausage rolls and a full bottle of tomato sauce in with the meat and rolls. Small boys could eat man-size portions. Then there were the sweets on plates Misty had forced on her.

As she walked she kept glancing at his bulging biceps and, becoming more noticeable, the veins in Leon's right arm. She clamped her lips on the smile that wanted to spread across her face. She could tell there was a little strain adding up. He swapped to the other arm.

By the time they'd reached one of the picnic tables under the trees she could've put a drip in his veins with a garden hose. She waited for the sigh as he lifted the bag onto the table and wasn't disappointed. She had to laugh.

He slanted a glance at her. 'And what amuses you?'

'How useful a man's arm is when you need it.' She grinned down at the hamper. 'I'm afraid I loaded the food up. On my own I'd have put it in the car and driven it down.'

He smiled and said cryptically, 'It kept my hands busy.'

Just one little comment like that and a dragon unfurled inside her stomach. He could seduce her in an instant in an open park with children a few feet away. How did he do that?

When the soccer ball came out of nowhere and almost hit her in the head, it put paid to the dragon and she stumbled back. Leon's hand speared out to knock the ball away, then caught her arm to help her balance. He turned and raised his brows at the boys.

'Oops. Sorry, Mum.' There was a pause and then Jack added, 'Sorry, Mr Bonmarito.'

'Perhaps you could aim for those trees behind you,' Leon suggested mildly, but the boys immediately spun to face the other way.

'You're proving handy this morning.'

'*Sì.*' Very quietly, under his breath, she heard him add, 'And sometimes at night.'

Tammy fought the tide of colour away from her cheeks and just managed to keep it in check as she began to unpack the hamper. Change subject. 'What time do you meet Gianni and Emma at the airport?'

'Five. Our plane leaves at eight.' Leon reached across and took the heavy thermos and weighed it in his hand. He raised his brows at her. 'Could you not find a house brick to place in the bag as well?'

She grinned. He made her smile and she sneaked a look at his handsome profile as he gazed across the lake. She'd miss him. More than a little. She couldn't remember ever being so at ease with a man on one hand and so supersensitised on the other.

Leon reached in and stole a juicy prawn wrapped in lettuce and she offered the tiny plastic container with seafood sauce.

He smiled and dipped, then took his time raising it to his mouth, a teasing light in his dark eyes and she couldn't help but follow it. He was laughing at her but it was nice. She watched him indulgently as he closed his eyes in pleasure. But when he licked those glorious lips, capable of such heat and hunger, last night flooded back and she wished she'd just given him the sauce and run away.

'Your seafood is amazing.'

'Ah.' Brain dead. Wake up. 'Yes. I love it.' She replaced the lid on the sauce in such a hurry it splashed over her hand, but before she could wipe it clean he'd taken her wrist and brought it to his mouth. A long slow sip of sauce and she was undone. Her dragon breathed a spurt of fire as her belly unfurled and there was no hope of keeping the pink out of her face this time. She glanced hurriedly at the boys but they were running and whooping between the trees with the ball.

She rushed into speech. 'Misty's excelled herself in sweets. It's almost embarrassing.' She opened the folded cloth to offer the plates with plastic film displaying their contents. 'Let's see,' she garbled. 'Oh, Lamingtons.' Bite-size Lamingtons, chocolate eclairs oozing creamy custard, tiny swirls of meringue with tart lemon sauce in the middle. And another squat steel thermos jammed with homemade ice cream and some waffle cones to hold the ice cream which helped restore her sense of humour. With the crockery and the thermos she'd bet that weighed a ton too.

Leon wasn't seeing the food. He would miss her. His hands stretched in his pockets where he'd thrust them away from her. He wanted to pull her into his arms and lose himself and could feel the tension between them stretching. Perhaps he should kick the ball with the boys as a more useful outlet for unexpected action. 'Do you need help setting out the food?'

She shook her head. 'A bit of space would be great.'

He grinned to himself. 'Always so complimentary. It is fortunate my feelings cannot be hurt.'

'Or mine,' she retaliated, and he turned away with a shake of his head. She could be stubborn and blunt to the point of offence, but despite her efforts he could see through the independent facade she insisted on showing him. He had the impression it was he that brought out this harsher side of her and he acknowledged she had reason to distance him.

'Kick me the ball, Paulo,' he called, and the boys whooped as he joined their game. Fearlessly Jack attempted to tackle and when Leon sidestepped him Jack fell laughing to the ground.

Paulo swooped on his father while he was distracted and stole the ball and the three of them were bumping and pushing one another as they fought for possession. It was no surprise that soon they were all laughing and wrestling on the ground.

The immaculate Leon Bonmarito rolling in the grass with two grubby boys. It hurt too much to watch. This was what she couldn't give her son, though Ben had the same man-versus-man mentality that boys seemed to love. She didn't understand it but could see that Jack was delighted with the rough and tumble.

Leon looked and acted so big and tough and yet he was so good with the boys. She wished she'd been spared this memory. Jack was sent rolling away and Paulo dived on his father. She was sure someone would be hurt soon. Then it would all end in tears. The table was ready, almost groaning under the tablecloth full of ham and silverside rolls and the mountains of cold savouries she suddenly didn't have the stomach for.

She called to the boys. 'Come and eat.'

It took a minute for her voice to soak into the huddle on the ground but then they brushed themselves off and walked back towards her, all smiling and filthy. She pointed to the wipes she opened at the edge of the food.

'You can all wash your hands.'

'Yes, Mama,' Leon said as he shook his head at the

spread. 'I think we need to put out a sign and invite people to share.'

She began to pour drinks. 'That happens. If you see anyone, wave them over.'

Leon believed her. This past week had shown him a town full of generosity and warmth and the concept of sharing was in every connection he made. He bit back the tinge of jealousy that wasn't worthy of him. His own life was different, and he wasn't able to function like this self-sufficient small town could. He had responsibilities, people depending on him and his family business to continue to grow to provide a service for those in need.

He was glad they had the chance today to do something normal. Though the taste of this magical interlude would no doubt come back to haunt in his and Paulo's emptily spacious apartment in Rome.

By the time they'd finished what they could, the boys were groaning and tottering back to their ball and Leon had subsided with a sigh onto the picnic rug.

'Had enough?' Tammy teased, and she looked over at him with satisfaction. When you don't know what to do with a man, you could always overfeed him.

Before she'd been foolish enough to sleep with him he'd taken up a huge portion of her day even when he wasn't there in person. Now, with so many memories in all dimensions, he would be everywhere.

Tonight he would be gone and the long nights ahead promised little rest at all. She was such a fool. But the opportunity for further foolishness was drawing to a close and when he invited her with a questioning look, she eased down beside him on the rug until their shoulders touched. She had no problem imagining more. Her ears heated with the need to tell him her secret.

Last night, in the dark, after he'd warmed her in a way she would never forget, he'd whispered again to her in his native tongue and the burden of her deceit had grown impossible.

He'd whispered softly how being able to hold her in his arms had been the only thing that had kept him sane while the boys were missing.

That his guilt for drawing her into this mess had been very hard and her forgiveness so precious.

How hard it would be to fit back into his life as he remembered the feel of her weight against his chest and how much he savoured the little time they'd had together and the gift she'd given him.

All soul-exposing statements he didn't know she understood.

Maybe it could have been different if he didn't live on the other side of the world. She could never leave the lake, take Jack from his grandparents, leave her friends and her work and, if she was honest, her independence, and just move in with Leon. Not that he'd asked her.

But she knew she'd be unable to go to Rome and not be in his arms again.

'Do you think you will come to Italy next month? For the maternity wing.' It was as if he'd read her mind without looking. He shifted his attention back to her and it was her turn to look out across the water.

The smile fell off her face. 'Perhaps.' No, she didn't think so.

He slid his finger beneath her chin and turned her face towards him. 'You do not seem too sure.'

She met his eyes. 'I'm not. I need to think about the idea when my head isn't full of kidnappings and work crises and other—' she grimaced '—emotionally charged events I'm not sure what to think of.'

He nodded and let her chin go. 'I won't pressure you. Though I'd like to. Perhaps you will think about it. I know my new sister-in-law would be pleased.'

Bring in the big guns, why don't you, Tammy thought with a sigh. Emma would understand though.

She looked back across the lake so he couldn't read her eyes. 'We'll see.'

The boys returned and fell down beside them. She saw the glances they exchanged at the closeness between Leon and herself and she ached for their naiveté. She'd wondered if Jack would be wary of Leon but he seemed to accept that the big man had a place in his mother's attention. Maybe because he knew that place had come to an end?

In the few minutes they all lay there before packing up, the simple pleasures of the morning rolled over them. Even the boys were silent and peace stole over their blanket.

The blue sky through the leaves overhead hurt her eyes it was so bright—or that's what Tammy told herself, why her eyes stung—and small puffy clouds skittered and were reflected in the lake that stretched away through the trees.

It was a perfect day for their overseas visitors to see before they left. The thought bounced around like an echo in her head. That's what they were. Visitors. Tammy felt the emotion and the hopelessness of the dream overwhelm her.

She heard the sharply indrawn breath of Leon beside her, and turned to see a small brown bird poke an inquisitive head out of the bush across from them.

A lyrebird, his beady brown eyes unblinking, tilted his beak at Leon and then stepped fearlessly out into the open less than ten feet from where they lay. The boys froze and covered their mouths with their hands, their little chests almost bursting with suppressed excitement.

The lyrebird lifted his brown, curved tail until it stood behind him like a fan, then shivered and shifted his feathers, until the upright display was to his satisfaction.

Only then did he strut and pivot in a stately dance to show them his glory.

When he opened his mouth the unexpected sound poured out. 'Coo-ee.' The notes from the lyrebird soared across the lake and bounced back at them. Strong and sure and perfectly mimicked on the boys earlier. 'Coo-ee,' the lyrebird trilled again, and he stared at them all as if he'd just given them a very important message. Then his tail fell and with regal disregard for politeness he disappeared back into the bush.

Tammy felt the air ease from her lungs, and the collective sigh almost lifted the paper napkins into the air. Jack whispered, 'A lyrebird. Grandpa told me about them.'

'It copied our call.' Paulo, too, was whispering.

'That's what they do. They imitate noises,' Tammy said quietly. 'They can copy anything. Even a baby crying.' She felt like crying herself it had been so magical. She sighed and somehow the load seemed a little lighter. 'We'd better pack up.'

Leon stared at the bush, his mind strangely less cluttered by the past. But no doubt that was because the present had been so chaotic. The bird had looked at him, and of all the memories of this place he would take with him today, that bird, and these people spellbound by his dance and song, would remain with him.

* * *

It was time for the Bonmaritos to leave. They'd said goodbye to Ben and Misty and Louisa already.

The fierceness of Paulo's hug surprised Tammy, as did her own in return. The lump in her throat grew as she hugged him back.

Paulo's beautiful dark eyes, so like his father's, so serious and young, seemed dreadfully in need of a mother. Her heart ached for him, and for Jack, and the loss of what could have been.

She tried to imagine how this quiet young boy felt, all he'd gone through, even worse than Jack because he'd been taken twice. She hugged him again. Paulo had to feel nervous.

She stroked his shoulder. 'Your dad will mind you.'

'*Sì.*' He nodded, but the concern stayed in his eyes. 'And who will keep you and Jack safe?'

'We'll be fine, honey.' She hugged him for the last time. 'Have a good flight and look after Grace and Aunt Emma for me.'

'Until you come?' He searched her face. 'Jack wants to come.'

'We'll see.' She glanced across to Leon, who seemed just as embroiled as she, with Jack. 'I'll think about it.' Not on your life was she going anywhere near Leon Bonmarito. Hopefully by the time he came back to visit his brother she'd be over this infatuation that had rocked her nice tidy little world.

Jack returned to her side, looked at Paulo and

shook hands and then threw shyness to the winds and hugged the other boy, who hugged him fiercely back.

'You guys got over your mutual dislike, I see,' she teased, and they broke apart, both pink-tinged in the neck.

'He's okay,' Jack said gruffly.

'Too rrright, mate,' Paulo said with a stiff upper lip and a fine attempt at Aussie slang. His accent rolled the *r*'s and made them all laugh.

Then Leon stood beside her. So big and darkly handsome...and so ready to leave.

'*Arrivederci*, Tamara.' His arms came around her for a brief hug and he kissed her in the Italian fashion on both cheeks. Nowhere near her mouth.

It was as if they both knew it would hurt too much. With his head against her hair she heard him say, '*Addio, amore mio.*'

Ciao, Leonardo, she whispered soundlessly into his shirt and then she stepped back. 'Safe trip.'

'Come,' Leon said to Paulo. 'You have forgotten nothing?' Paulo shook his head and Leon closed the boot on their luggage. They would leave the rental at the airport.

It was time. He lifted his hand in salute, no last chance for a kiss goodbye, Tammy thought with an ache she'd have to get used to, but surely it was better this way.

With Jack by her side she watched them drive

away and as they walked back into the suddenly empty house, Tammy felt a gaping emptiness in her chest that made tears burn her eyes.

'I'm going to my room,' Jack said gruffly, and she nodded. She wanted to go to her room too, and crawl under the covers for the rest of the day, maybe the rest of the year.

Five minutes later Jack was back. 'We'll have to see them off now.' When her triumphant son reappeared, brandishing Paulo's backpack like a glorious trophy, she had a ridiculous urge to laugh out loud.

Then common sense stepped in. 'No, we don't. We can post it to him.'

Jack shook his head decisively. 'It's got everything in it. His MP3 player, his phone, diary—' he paused for effect '—his mother's photos.' Jack knew he had the winning hand. 'What if all that gets lost in the post?'

Tammy rubbed her forehead and ignored the stupid leap of excitement in her belly. She'd have to take it. They'd have to take it. Jack wins.

'Maybe we'll catch them. It's three hours to Brisbane and a real pain.' Not that she'd planned anything useful today except feeling sorry for herself.

Tammy grabbed her keys with a heart that was lighter than it should have been. This was not good. She'd have to go through the whole painful farewell routine again and this time she was bound to cry. But if she had to do that, she was darn sure she was at least getting that kiss. A real one. To hell with the consequences.

Her eyes narrowed for a moment on Jack. 'You and Paulo had better not have cooked this up between you. I won't be impressed if we catch them and Paulo's not surprised to see us.'

They didn't catch them and half an hour into the drive Tammy accepted it was a dumb idea to try. Once she thought a police car was following her and she slowed down even more. She wished she'd remembered to bring her phone so she could have called Emma.

The plane didn't leave for another five and a half hours so she wasn't worried about missing them. Leon was meeting Emma and Gianni at the International Departure gates at 5:00 p.m. As was Montana with Grace. She had plenty of time. It was only one-thirty now.

By the time she took her parking ticket from the machine at Brisbane airport Tammy had reached a definite point of regret for her decision to come.

And they'd all, especially Leon, think her mad to chase across the country to give back a bag she could have posted. She could have sent it registered mail, for crying out loud. It was Jack's fault.

Her mood wasn't improved when she realised that she and Jack were in such a hurry they'd forgotten Paulo's bag in the car and they'd had to race back and get it.

Dragging her son through the terminal, she wished herself home until finally she spied the signs directing her to the departure lounge entry. And there, towering above the crowds, big and dark and brooding with his broad shoulders lovingly encased in his grey Italian suit, stood Leon. Her steps slowed and her hand tightened on Jack's as she came closer.

Leon turned, as if sensing her, and his eyes widened with surprise and a warmth that almost had her fan her face.

Jack eased his hand out of hers and ran across to Paulo brandishing the bag. The two boys hugged and Tammy and Leon looked back at each other with raised brows.

Her feet slowed but Leon stepped past the boys without a word and walked straight up to her. *'Ciao, bella.'* His head bent and he stared into her face as if still not sure that she was real.

Her cheeks warmed under his scrutiny. *'Ciao,* Leonardo,' she said. It was safe enough to echo, and of its own accord her hand lifted to brush his cheek. 'You didn't kiss me goodbye.'

His eyes darkened and roamed over her. *'Sì.* For good reason.'

'And what reason would that be?' Her belly kicked with the heat in his scrutiny and suddenly they weren't in a crowded airport. They were alone, in a mist of vision that narrowed to just Leon's face.

'I believe that's a dare.'

Wasn't that how they started? 'It's been done before.'

His head lowered further and just before his lips touched hers she heard him whisper, 'But not like this.'

She should have realised how dangerous it was to challenge this man. Or maybe she was very aware of the consequences. That was the glory of it. When he finally stepped back, the hard floor of the terminal seemed to sway beneath her feet and he kept one hand cupped beneath her elbow until she balanced again. Some kiss.

He lifted her chin with his finger. 'Why are you here?'

Still vague and dreamy she answered absently, 'Paulo forgot his bag.'

They both turned to the boys, forgotten in the heat of the moment, a few feet away only minutes ago, but the place they'd occupied stood vacant. Two older men moved with a leisurely intent to stand and chat there instead.

Leon craned his neck around the men, and frowned heavily. 'Now where have they gone?'

The boys were running. A vague and nebulous plan had formed in the few moments their parents had ignored them. What if they ran away? Together. Somewhere safe, of course, just long enough to miss the flight, and ensure their parents had more time together. More chance to stay longer in Lyrebird Lake for the Bonmaritos.

A family in front of them were heading for an arriving bus, pushing luggage and laughing, and the boys followed them and two older ladies onto the bus.

'What is Long-Stay Parking?' Paulo whispered as they sat unobtrusively behind the noisy family.

'Don't know, but sounds like a good place to sit while we wait for the plane to go,' Jack said.

The bus filled quickly with those returning from holidays and trips to their cars parked in the furthest part of the terminal. 'My father will be very angry,' Paulo whispered, regretting their daring already.

'So will Mum, but they'll get over it.' Jack's voice wobbled only a little. 'It's for their own good.'

'What if we get lost?'

'You've got your mobile in the bag. We'll ring your dad. Which reminds me, you'd better turn it off now.' He looked at Paulo. 'In case he rings?'

Paulo paled and hastily dug in his bag. '*Sì.*' He flipped open the phone and held down the key until the screen changed. They sat there and stared as the light dimmed and disappeared. Both gulped.

The bus revved and moved off. The trip seemed to take a long, long time. When it pulled up, the jerk thrust them forward in their seats while all around them people stood and lifted bags and shifted in a line towards the exit and a huge area with rows of parked cars. In every big square of cars, a brick waiting room sat on edge of the bus line, to provide shelter in case of rain.

'We could sit in that shed,' Jack said, less sure of the brilliance of his plan now that they were there.

Paulo didn't say anything but he followed the other boy with his head down, his backpack bumping on his shoulder like the weight of the world.

Both boys' eyes lit up when they saw the snack vending machine in the corner of the waiting room. 'You got money?' Jack said.

'*Sì.*' Finally Paulo smiled.

'I can't believe this.' Tammy felt sick and frightened and most of all incredibly angry and disgusted with herself. And the man beside her.

Leon was reaching for his phone. A muscle jerked in his cheek and his mouth had thinned to a grim line. 'This, I think, is a trick thought up by your son.'

The possibility had crossed her mind. A bit like the suddenly found backpack of Paulo's. But she couldn't admit that. Surely Paulo had some say. 'Why does it have to be my son?'

Leon's hand tightened on the phone. 'Because mine is aware of consequences.'

Not true but she wasn't going to fight about it now. She was too scared to have lost Jack again. 'Where are your clever bodyguards? What if someone's taken them again?'

'One has left to organise our safe arrival and the other I gave leave for a few minutes. He approaches now.'

Leon launched into a flood of Italian and Tammy battled to keep up. It seemed the bodyguard had gone to buy a drink and also not seen the boys disappear. So Leon wasn't discounting the chance of abduction. Tammy turned to the elderly men beside them. 'Excuse me. Have you seen two little boys, dark hair, about eight years old?'

One of the men shook his head and the other stroked his chin. 'I might have, actually. Did one have a backpack?'

'*Sì*,' Leon broke in. 'Did you see where they went?'

The gentleman lifted his hand and waved. 'Running towards the exit. I thought it strange but they caught up with a family and I assumed they were with them. I'm sorry.'

'Thank you. You've been very helpful.' Leon gestured to the bodyguard and the man jogged quickly towards the exit. He slanted a grim I-told-you-so glance at Tammy.

Tammy's head ached with the beginning of a tension headache. How could the boys have done this to them? They knew how frightened she'd been. She couldn't believe this was happening and all because they'd brought a stupid bag to the airport. When would she learn that this man was trouble? Where were Jack and Paulo?

Leon flipped open his phone again. Then he swore in Italian. Graphically.

'Don't swear,' she said—anger was the last thing she needed—and rubbed her face.

Leon blinked. '*Scusi*. Paulo has switched off his phone.' He narrowed his eyes at her. 'And how did you know I was swearing?'

Good grief. She didn't have time for this. She shrugged and avoided his eyes. 'I didn't really. It just sounded like swearing.'

His eyebrows raised but he said nothing more. 'I will try the washrooms. Perhaps you could check the shops.'

She nodded but the fear was forming a monster in her throat. 'And what if we can't find them?'

'Then we'll check with the police.'

The next hour was fraught with false leads, and small boys that for a moment made her heart leap, and then ache with growing fear. The police had faxed through the photos of the boys to airport security and the inspector in charge of the previous kidnapping was on his way.

Tammy slumped against a pole outside the terminal and searched out groups for small boys. 'I can't believe we've lost them again.'

Leon ran his hand through his hair and glanced at

his watch. 'Nor I. There will be retribution for those responsible.' The underlying menace in his voice made Tammy shiver and for a second she almost hoped for Jack's sake that they'd been kidnapped.

Leon glanced at his watch again. 'I must meet the inspector and Gianni should also soon be at the departure gate. And Montana with Grace. Do you wish to come with me or remain searching?'

What? And stay here by herself, imagining the worst? 'I'll come.'

When they returned to the terminal again only Emma and Gianni were there. Leon broke into a flood of Italian and when he said to his brother that no doubt it was a hoax dreamed up by Tammy's son, Tammy shot him a look of such pure dislike, he paused midsentence.

Leon held his hand up to his brother and turned to Tammy. Her heart thumped at his comprehension. He searched her face, took her arm above the elbow and steered her away from the others.

His grip was more than firm. 'You understood everything I said?' The question came in Italian.

'*Sì,*' she spat back.

He dropped her arm as if it was suddenly dirty. 'This we will discuss later.'

'Or not,' Tammy replied, and closed her eyes as he walked away. She felt like burying her head in her hands but it wouldn't help. He'd never forgive her. But it didn't matter. Nothing mattered. The boys were the important thing.

The inspector arrived accompanied by his constable. 'I do not think they have been taken by the same people.'

'Why are you so sure?' Tammy had to ask.

The inspector shrugged. 'We have all except one of the men responsible for the kidnapping in custody or in the morgue. It seems the shootout was between two warring Mafia gangs. They planned to hostage the one man's son for the location of stolen property.'

Leon's brow furrowed and his impatience with this diversion was plain. 'What has this to do with my son?'

'Nothing, I'm afraid.' The inspector scratched his ear. 'It's the other boy. Our informant believes Miss Moore's son was the illegitimate child of one Vincente Salvatore. Mr Salvatore was killed in the battle. It is believed he protected the boys with his life.'

Tammy felt the look of incredulity Leon shot at her and she shook her head. Vincente was dead. He'd saved the boys. She looked at Leon but he didn't hide his contempt for more lies. She hadn't known Vincente knew. How could she have known that Paulo's abduction had been mistaken identity? All this fear and danger her fault—for a hidden heist. And all the time she'd blamed Leon for the boy's danger. 'I'm sorry.'

'I wonder what else I do not know,' he said quietly in Italian, and she could tell he didn't care if she understood.

The inspector went on. 'There's still one man at large so we will be keeping an eye out. Might be prudent to be careful, Miss Moore.'

The airport security chief arrived at that moment to join the inspector and Tammy turned still-stunned eyes on him. 'We've isolated the video coverage in the time frame the boys went missing. It seems there's a chance they boarded the long-stay car-park bus. We're waiting for a patrol car now so we can check that out.'

Leon's phone rang. He glanced at it with an arrested expression and closed his eyes with relief. 'Paulo?'

He paused as the boy spoke. *'Sì.'*

He looked at first Tammy and then the police inspector. 'We will come,' he said in English. 'Long-stay car park. It seems they have run out of money for the vending machine.'

'I'll go,' Tammy said quickly. 'My car's just outside.'

There was an awkward pause as they all looked at Leon. The security chief pulled a pad and pen from his pocket. 'Give me the registration and they'll let you through.' Tammy wrote down the number.

'I, too, will come.' Leon's tone brooked no argument and Tammy was too emotionally exhausted to care. It was her fault the boys had been kidnapped. Vincente's fault. The fact rotated in her mind like a clothes line in the wind. Around and around. Leon's words sank in. It was a wonder he'd travel with her but she guessed he'd handed his own car in. 'Feel free. What the hell.'

'Don't swear,' he mocked as they walked away together. She gave him the keys in the hope he wouldn't get out of the car when they first saw the boys. At least driving back to the terminal would give them some cooling-off period.

Leon glared down at her as they walked. 'So, all this time it is you who has placed my son in danger—not, as I thought, my imposition on you. You should have told me his father was a criminal. And Italian.'

She ignored the part she had no defence for. 'It was more than an imposition to almost lose the lives of two children,' she said wearily, 'and I had no idea that Vincente knew about Jack.' That wasn't strictly true. She'd *hoped* Vincente hadn't known about Jack.

'Is that the truth or more lies?' He didn't believe her. Couldn't say she blamed him.

She rubbed her aching temples. 'Nothing warned me the Salvatores, or their enemies, knew of my son's connection to their family. As far as I was aware, there was no connection.'

Leon strode forward more quickly when he spotted her car. She had to almost run to keep up. 'It is well there is still time to leave today because I find myself wanting to shake you for destroying my trust in you. That you speak my language.'

She wasn't happy being in the wrong either. 'I know. If it's any consolation I'm embarrassed I didn't let you know earlier. But the longer I left it, the harder it was to tell you.'

He speared a glance at her across the roof of her car. 'So I have told you what is in my heart, my most inner secrets, and you are the one to feel embarrassed? My sympathies.'

He came back to her side and opened her door, and his courtesy while he waited for her to get in was an insult.

His sarcasm flayed her and she could feel the tears she refused to let fall. Would this horrible day never end?

She'd witnessed his utter emotional devastation, and for a proud man who barely showed emotion normally, of course it must be mortifying. He'd never forgive her. 'I can only say I'm sorry. And that I wish I could have told you myself before you found out.'

It seemed she could look forward to years of distrust and dislike whenever he visited his brother in

Lyrebird Lake. At least there was no decision now about visiting Rome.

It wouldn't matter how hard she tried to re-establish their mutual trust after this.

CHAPTER NINE

Leon drove with icy precision.

They followed the signs to the long-stay car park and the operator at the booth magically waved them on when their car appeared.

Two small and forlorn boys stood sheepishly outside the brick shelter, little white faces pointed to their shoes as Leon and Tammy pulled up beside them.

There was silence until Leon spoke very quietly. *'Arrivare,'* he said to his son. 'Get in,' he said to Jack. Then he glanced at Tammy. 'Or does your son understand Italian too?'

'No.' Tammy didn't offer anything else. The silence stretched and remained in the car until Leon reparked in the terminal car park.

They all heard his deep breath. 'I do not want to know whose idea this was—' his cold glance brushed them both '—but I wish you to appreciate how frightened and upset both Tamara and I were when we found you gone. This has been a difficult week for everyone and I would prefer if no further problems arise.' His voice remained low but every word made Tammy wince. 'Or there will be retribution.'

Paulo held back his tears. '*Sì, Padre. Mi dispiace.*' He looked at Tammy. 'I'm sorry.'

Jack sniffed and nodded, then he, too, took a deep breath. 'It was my idea, Mr Bonmarito. Not Paulo's. I'm sorry.'

'It is to your mother you owe an apology, Jack.'

She watched her baby struggle to hold back the tears. 'I'm sorry, Mum.' Tammy just wanted to hug him but she couldn't risk him thinking he could run away ever again. And if she was honest, she was a little nervous of Leon, in the mood he was in.

'Thank you, Jack. And Paulo.' She fought back her own tears. 'Let's just get you Bonmaritos on that plane.'

They all climbed out of the car and walked silently back towards the departure gate. Incredibly there was still time for boarding. Tammy was so emotionally punch-drunk she couldn't wait to make her own exit.

She saw Gianni and Emma up ahead and it was like a seeing a drink machine in the desert. They had Grace so Montana must have been gone. Emma, her best friend—a welcoming face, thank goodness, from a world she understood and felt comfortable in, a face from home. Her steps quickened and she threw herself into Emma's arms and hugged her fiercely.

Emma hugged her back. The loudspeaker called another flight and reminded them all that time was running out and they hadn't been through customs yet. Emma searched Tammy's face and then looked to Leon and gave her friend one last hug. She blinked back the tears and glanced at her husband before she took her daughter's hand and they moved through the departure gate into customs. One wave and then they were gone from sight.

Which left Tammy with the thundercloud, two subdued boys and a goodbye that never seemed to end.

'Say goodbye to Tammy,' Leon said quietly to his son, and perversely Tammy wished Leon had called her Tamara.

'Goodbye.' Paulo moved in against her as she held open her arms. She cradled his dark head against her chest and her heat ached for him. *'Ciao, Paulo. Hanno un buon volo.'* Have a good flight. She may as well tell everyone she could speak it if she wanted to. Now.

Paulo's eyes widened at her faultless Italian and then he smiled. A beautiful smile. *'Sì.'*

Leon took the insult on the chin. She was mocking him. It seemed she had always mocked him. He'd made a fool of himself with her deceit. Did she have no shame? How had he allowed himself to be fooled by her smile? And yet he was tempted to throw everything to the winds and demand to know if she cared for him a little. He bit the impulse stubbornly back. Did he have no pride? Did he want to lower himself again? He was a Bonmarito! 'Goodbye, Jack. Look after your mother.' He inclined his head and it should not have been so hard to brush past her and walk away. But it was.

Tammy watched Paulo follow his father, his eyes shadowed as he waved one last time to Jack and her. Then it was too hard to see because her eyes were full of tears. But still she couldn't look away from the broad back that finally disappeared through the gate.

He'd gone. Leon's gone. She'd tried to apologise in the car, but maybe she should have tried again before he left. Of course she should have. Should have thrown herself on his chest. Should have made him see she hadn't meant to continue the lie, but opportunities had slipped away. And in those last few seconds, she'd only alienated him more. With her pride. Lot of good that would do her now.

The fact slapped her in the face. She loved him. Loved Leon. And she should have told him she loved him. At least then they would have both been exposed. The fact stared her mockingly in the face as she watched strangers disappear into the void that had taken the only man she should have fought for.

And she'd been too stubborn and too cowardly to beg him to forgive her. Too proud to share the same thoughts and emotions he'd shared with her more than once. She felt the tearing in her chest as she realised her loss. The tears welled thicker and her throat closed.

Jack tugged on her hand, then jerked hard, and she brushed her hand across her eyes and turned back to look. What was the boy doing now?

She looked again. A man with a barely hidden wicked-looking knife had taken Jack's other hand and was pulling him away from her. Again. They were trying to take her son again.

A red haze crossed her vision; all thought of self-defence she'd learned for years flew out the window in this recognition of danger and she raised her handbag like a club and rushed at him, threshing at his face and head until he let Jack go. She kept hitting him until something hot and yet chilling struck her chest.

People stopped and stared as Tammy blinked at the sudden heat in her chest and the last thing she heard was Jack's scream. She fell as the air seemed squeezed out of her lungs and a steel band tightened slowly and relentlessly across her chest. The world went dark.

Leon made it to the first checkpoint, clicked his pen to complete the departure form and suddenly a word leapt out. *Departure.* His hand stopped. His fingers refused to write a letter and he'd grabbed Paulo's hand and spun back towards the entry.

Making their way backwards through the crowd had taken agonising seconds and he prayed she hadn't gone far through the terminal. He didn't know what he was going to say but leaving without a kind word because of stupid, stubborn Italian pride would not happen. He'd made the gate just as Jack had been accosted. His heart exploded in his torso as he'd pushed past people to where he could see Tammy flailing at the man. He saw it happen with a horror he would never forget, the awfulness of the knife, and seeing her eyes close as she fell.

He hit the man once, with a force that snapped the man's head back, and the knife flew into the air and then clattered to the ground. The assailant slid to the floor where he lay unmoving and for a few seconds Leon hoped he was dead. Then he fell to his knees beside Tammy and slid his hand to her neck to feel her pulse. 'Can you hear me? Stay with me, Tamara. You'll be okay.'

He found her pulse. It was there, beneath his fingers, rapid and thready, as the bright red blood poured from the wound in her chest. He pulled his handkerchief from his pocket and tried to staunch the flow, glancing around for help.

'She's alive,' he said to Jack, beside him, and then Paulo was there too. 'Look after Jack,' he said to his son, and white-faced Paulo nodded and put his arm around his friend as both boys looked on in horror.

A security guard arrived and Leon snapped orders

at him. 'He's stabbed her. I'm a doctor. Call for an ambulance.' All the time his brain was screaming, *No, not Tamara. Not here. Not now. Not ever.* Wrenching his mind away from the unthinkable he clinically assessed her. With one hand he lifted her eyelids and no flicker of recognition eased his fear. 'Stay with me, Tamara,' he said again. He rechecked her pulse, still fast but it was her pallor and the unevenness of her breathing that terrified him.

Then he saw it in her throat. The sign of imminent death. The tracheal shift from internal pressure within her chest. The veins in her neck began to bulge as the pressure of one lung expanding from within its layers squeezed the air out of the underlying lung and crushed her heart.

Gianni and Emma arrived, pushing though people who crowded around them. 'Thank God.' Leon gestured from where he was crouched. 'He's stabbed her lung.'

Without a word, Gianni took over holding the wound as Leon rolled her gently to check there was no exit wound.

'Where are the paramedics? There is very little time to decompress her lung.'

Emma fell to her knees and put her arms around both boys. 'What happened?'

Leon spoke across Tammy's body. 'He stabbed her. An ambulance is on its way.'

Jack sobbed and Leon grasped his shoulder to give him strength. 'Move the boys away, please.'

The paramedics arrived and they all moved back. Except Leon. 'I'm a doctor. Tension pneumothorax. It needs releasing. Now.'

The paramedics, young and a little unsure, gulped, looked at each other and nodded. With barely controlled haste they opened their kit and removed their largest cannula normally used for rapid infusion of intravenous fluids.

The paramedic wiped the area with a swab but his hand shook so that he dropped the swab. The bleeding sped up. He hesitated. The gauge looked huge and Leon could feel the sweat bead on his brow as her veins stood rigid from her neck. Come on, he thought.

Still they hesitated, perhaps unsure, and Gianni leaned across his brother. 'Here.' He pointed to the precise spot. 'Between the second and third intercostal space.' Of course his brother had dealt with this many times in rescue from flying debris and it was enough to galvanise Leon.

He ripped Tammy's shirt where the knife had gone in and her skin looked alabaster in the artificial light of the terminal, with a slash of sluggish blood. Her low-cut lacy bra was stained a garish red and he pulled it down further with one hand. Her collarbone lay round and fragile and he slid his finger along halfway, then down, one, two spaces between the ribs.

He glanced at her face, her beloved face, and she had the blue of death around her mouth. Leon snatched the cannula from the man and slid it with precision between her ribs and through Tammy's chest wall. The hiss of air escaping made him want to cry. He who never shed a tear could barely see.

Leon sat back and the paramedic, spurred on by Leon's decision, apologised for his slowness and hastened to remove the stylet so that only the thin plastic tube remained in her chest. 'Sorry. Never done it before, sir.'

His partner handed the tubing that would connect the indwelling catheter to the Heimlich valve that stopped the air from leaking back in and immediately the blueness began to recede from around her mouth.

Leon felt the weight ease in his chest. Slowly her chest began to rise and fall with inflation as the air between the layers in her lung escaped and allowed the tissue beneath to expand.

Her breathing became more rapid and the blueness faded more. 'We'll cannulate before we move her, sir.' The paramedic was all efficiency now and Leon winced for his love when they inserted the intravenous line in her arm. Seconds later the cardiac monitor assured them all her heart was beating fast but in a normal rhythm. A few more seconds and she was on the trolley and they were all moving swiftly towards the ambulance.

Still she didn't regain consciousness. Leon's fear escalated. 'How far to the hospital?'

'Brisbane Central. Five minutes, tops.'

'We'll follow and take the children with us in Tammy's car,' Emma said, and she clutched Tammy's bag so fiercely it was as if she was holding her friend's life in her hands. They peeled away with Grace and the boys.

By the time they had her settled in the ambulance, Tammy's pulse was still rapid but appeared stable.

Leon took her hand and leaned down near her ear so she could hear him over the sound of the siren. 'I'm here, Tamara. It's Leon. I need you to listen to me. Jack is fine. We're all fine. We need you to hang on.'

He didn't know what he was saying. He just knew he needed to make sure she could hear his voice. Unconsciously he switched to Italian and he didn't care that if she woke she would understand every word. He ached for her to do so.

'I love you, Tamara Moore. The thought of you dying right there, in front of me, will live with me for ever. Why did I think I could go and leave you when it is plain to see you need me around you all the time?' He smoothed the hair from her still-pale features. 'I adore you with all my heart, my love. I need you. You must get well and we will plan our life together. If you will have me.' He rested his face against her cheek and to hear her breath was all he needed to keep going.

They kept him from her in Emergency, but after beginning one tedious form he brushed them off and at his most imperious he cornered a doctor and gained entry to her side.

He oversaw them insert the underwater sealed drain that would keep her lung from collapsing again, and watched the colour return to her face with bags of blood they replaced.

He followed her to the intensive care unit and supervised her transfer into the bed. The only person he couldn't bully was the specialist nurse who stared him down and told him to step back.

'She's my patient. When she's stable you can have her back.' And to the surprise of the other medical staff he did back down. Because, he thought with a wry smile, how like his beloved Tamara she was.

When Tammy woke up, she saw him asleep in the chair pulled up to her bed. His dark hair was tousled, his five-o'clock shadow heavily marked around his strong jaw. He was a disgustingly handsome wreck of a man as his cheek rested on her bed. She'd done this to him.

'I've been meaning to tell you,' she whispered, and the air stirred between them. He shifted in his chair and opened his eyes. The warmth that poured over her brought the heat to her cheeks. No one had ever looked at her like that. As if her presence had brightened his whole world. As if the sun had just risen with six words.

His hand tightened where it still held hers and he raised it slowly to his mouth and kissed her palm.

'Meaning to tell me what, *amore mio*?'

'That I speak Italian. Have done since I was a teenager.'

'So we discussed,' he said, but he was smiling. 'But now you have told me yourself and I am glad you can.'

She searched his face. 'What you said in the ambulance. Was it true?'

'You heard me, then?' Such love shone from his eyes she couldn't doubt him.

'I was trying to stay away from the light,' she only half teased.

He squeezed her hand and kissed it again. 'Nothing I have told you is not true.'

She closed her eyes and relaxed back into the pillow. 'In that case, yes, I will you marry you.'

'Sleep, my love. And when you wake I will ask you properly.'

CHAPTER TEN

LEON BONMARITO allowed the blessing to flow over him as the priest joined him and Tamara Delilah Moore in holy matrimony. His heart filled with the joy he'd once avoided on his brother's face and he thanked God again for allowing him to find and keep his love.

He had no doubt that somewhere ethereal above them all his parents were smiling down at them.

The tiny family chapel on the hillside at Portofino, filled with the scent and delicacy of flowers, held smiling people most important to them both.

Their two sons, dressed again in their tuxedos, tried hard to contain their mischief in the front row with the flower girls but he had no doubt Tamara's parents would quieten them if they exploded.

His brother and his wife, her pregnancy just showing, stood at the altar as their attendants but could not keep their emotion-filled eyes off each other.

His housekeeper and her husband, who had served the Bonmarito family all of their lives cuddled up to

Louisa, who had come for a holiday and to share their happiness.

There would be a party at Lyrebird Lake when they returned but this day, far away from the magic of the lake, was for them. To savour the solemnity of their vows and celebrate their love in front of a special few in a special place.

Afterwards, Leon took Tammy to honeymoon at the Hotel Macigno in Ravello. Their suite of rooms perched high above the cliffs where at night, when the boys were asleep, he showed her how much he truly adored her.

In the blue-skied days the boys flew kites under the watchful gaze of the nanny Leon had insisted on so they could relax, and the nanny was watched by Louisa.

As Leon and Tammy walked the cliff paths hand in hand, the spectacular Amalfi Coast shimmered below them and he pointed out traditional fishing villages and the reflected blue of the Mediterranean.

Nearby Amalfi, Positano, Capri and Pompeii beckoned for day trips and the boys flourished in the warmth of love that radiated from both parents as they played in the sea and explored the ruins of ancient cities.

Gradually Jack began to call Leon Dad, and though Tammy had told Paulo he could always call her Tammy, the boy asked, diffidently, if he could call her Mum. 'That is different to *Madre*, if that is okay?' And slowly their family melded, became one with a solidarity Leon thanked God for every day.

EPILOGUE

One year later

'We don't have to go to hospital. You could call Misty and Emma and they could look after me here.'

'*Cara*, I would give you anything. But what is the use of following your every wish for the centre and then you choose to birth at our villa in Rome?'

Tammy shook her head stubbornly. 'I don't want to get out of this bath.'

Leon perched on the edge of the tub and regretted he'd made it so large. Large enough for two but not for two and the birth of his child. 'They will have the pool ready for you at the centre. I promise. They're dying to have someone use it. You could be the first.'

'Misty and Emma have to be there.' She sounded plaintive and he wanted to smooth the worry lines from her face.

'Of course.' He'd agree to anything. He was

confused and anxious and totally bewildered by the sudden change in his calm and level-headed Tamara.

The boys were with Gianni and what had begun as a slow romantic day before the birth of their child had suddenly turned into a mutiny he hadn't expected.

He smoothed the hair from her forehead. 'Come, *cara*, I will lift you out.'

She sighed and he watched her gorgeous shoulders sink below the surface of the water as if savouring the last pleasure to be had from the day. 'I'm sorry, Leon.' She gazed up at him and he saw the flicker of uncertainty in her beautiful eyes. 'I think I had a panic attack when I realised today was the day.'

She reached for the handles at the edge of the bath and quickly he lent down to take her hand. She smiled with relief as she slipped her hand into his and prepared to climb out. 'Which is silly. Because I've done it before, and I know I'm designed to do this.' He didn't know if she was talking to herself or to him so he nodded encouragingly, trying not to pull her up so fast she'd realise how scared he was she'd change her mind.

She went on musingly now. 'But for a minute there I didn't want to admit that the time is here.'

She stood, her magnificent roundness running with water and bubbles and acres of shiny taut skin that made him bless the magic day he was allowed into her heart.

'You are such a beautiful Madonna with child, my wife.' His words came out gruffly, filled with bursting pride and a smattering of fear for the unknown. He needed to have her and their baby safe and then all would be fine.

The drive to the hospital was accomplished with typical Italian chaos but, for once, traffic parted before the assertiveness of an extremely worried father.

Their journey from the front door to the birth room was faster than the speed of light so that Tammy felt quite giddy in the chair Leon had cajoled her into. 'Slow down, for goodness sake, before all my endorphins run for the hills.'

He slowed, just, and she chuckled to herself at this man, her husband, this anxious, gruff, darling man who was so unsure of the next few hours that his usual calm had been totally misplaced.

Her own moment of doubt was long gone. She knew all would be well. She knew her baby was waiting to meet them with the same anticipation she felt.

The ripples of conversation followed them. The Bonmarito baby was coming. No doubt there would be a hundred people in the waiting room when the boys arrived. It wasn't her problem. Her husband would sort that out.

They were through into the birth suite now. The eggshell blue of the rounded walls greeted her like a long-lost friend. She'd spent hours pouring over designs and new innovations to create the perfect birth space. No angles or corners, just soft and rounded curves and a welcome like a mother's arms.

The pool water lapped gently, waiting for her arrival, and against the large window overlooking the shifting branches of a huge tree outside, Misty and Emma also waited. Both women smiled in understanding at the harried look on Leon's face when he came to a halt in front of them. He looked down at his precious cargo and began to smile sheepishly. 'I may have panicked for a moment there.'

'For only a moment,' his wife murmured with a smile as she lifted herself out of the chair and was embraced first by Misty and then by Emma. She glanced at Leon. 'Perhaps you could ask someone to take the chair away, darling, while I get organised.'

Leon nodded and hurried away. The three women laughed softly until Tammy began to sway as the contraction built and they stood holding her as she leaned against them. She breathed in deeply, her belly pushed low with the breath in her lungs, and then a downward out breath full of power and rightness.

Misty held the Doppler and they listened to the steady clopping of Tammy's baby's heartbeat as the contraction faded away and was gone. Then a quick rest back on the couch while Misty ran her gentle hands over the smooth mountain of Tammy's stomach, finding the baby's head well fixed deep in the pelvis, baby's back to the right and all as it should be for the final descent.

'The bath, I think,' said Misty.

Tammy nodded and her loose sarong fell to the floor with her underwear. Before they could move, the next pain was upon her and her two attendants smiled at each other and glanced at the door.

'I want Leon.' Barely had the words left her mouth and he was there. Kicking off his shoes and snatching at socks, shedding his trousers and plucking off his shirt until his powerful shoulders rippled freely as he leaned down and lifted her back against him for a moment before he stepped easily into the bath with Tammy safe in his arms. 'I am here, my love. Lean back against me.' And they sank into the water.

Tammy lay back against her man, safe and secure, surrounded by the warm cradle of buoyancy and her husband's arms. The bath gave the ease of movement she hadn't wanted to leave at home and the ability to move her cumbersome body to each new position with a gentle shift of her arm. As the next pain rolled over her she closed her eyes and breathed. The water rose and fell and her belly heaved with the life of her baby within.

She knew Leon's arms held safe around them both. Her fellow midwives would watch over them all until the journey was complete, and her heart was calm.

When Tammy's baby entered the world she was born into the silence of warm water, the welcoming hands of her mother about her, and lifted gently to the surface to breathe her first breath under the awestruck eyes of her family.

Perfetto. Except her father was crying.

Paulo and Jack Bonmarito scowled at the visitors. The new Lyrebird Wing of the Bonmarito Cura Nella Maternitá postnatal wing in Rome was crowded with well-wishers and they couldn't get near the door to their new baby.

'It'll be a boy. For sure,' Jack muttered, and Paulo nodded glumly. With three boys the new one would have to be favourite but neither said that out loud.

The boys looked at each other and shrugged and searched for Leon in the crowd.

'Who are all these people?' Jack asked.

Paulo chewed his lip. 'Acquaintances of my father. Business partners, patients, relatives of people from our village.' He shrugged. 'They will go soon.'

'Jack?' Paulo tapped his shoulder to attract his stepbrother's attention. 'I do not understand how the baby is born.'

Jack looked at him. He had a hazy idea but didn't really think about it. Or want to. 'Ever been to a farm? Seen animals give birth?'

Paulo nodded and then paled. 'You are serious? Who told you this?'

'Mum. That's what she did at Lyrebird Lake. What all the midwives do. Usually in the bath. People go there to have their babies. Mum catches 'em and cleans 'em up when they come out.'

Paulo had trouble getting his head around that. 'Does it hurt, do you think? For the woman?'

Jack shrugged and packed away the deep fear he'd been fighting with all morning. What if his mother died like Paulo's mother had? 'I've never heard a cat or dog complain. What about you?'

Paulo shook his head weakly. 'I feel sick.'

Jack grinned, suddenly glad his new brother shared his fear. It was amazing how much better he felt when he realised he wasn't the only one afraid. 'And you're going to be a doctor? Let's find Dad.' In the end it wasn't hard to find him because the door opened and their father towered over everyone else in the room.

Leon gestured to the boys and they pushed their way through. 'Come, boys. Come and meet your new sister.' Jack and Paulo looked at each other and a slow, incredulous smile mirrored on both faces. Jack fisted the air. 'Yes!'

Leon swept them in and they saw Tammy. Serene and smiling, sitting calmly in a recliner chair, not looking like she'd done much at all.

Jack sighed with relief. She was okay. Mum was okay. That hard lump in his throat was going away. Well, he guessed all she'd done was catch a baby of her own in the water.

Nestled in Tammy's arms, curled like a kitten, was

a tiny, pink-faced baby, with dark, soft curls piled on her head. She had the softest, rounded arms and tiny starfish hands that fisted up to her chin and mouth. She blinked at them.

'Look at her eyes,' Jack whispered, and he peered over Tammy's arm at the baby and Isabella blinked as if desperate to focus on her new big brother.

Paulo nodded. 'And her fingers,' he whispered back. 'She's got tiny fingernails.'

And across their heads, Leon and Tammy exchanged loving smiles full of promise and pride and wonder at the blessings that surrounded them.

THE PLAYBOY OF ROME

JENNIFER FAYE

For Ami.
To a wonderful friend who has kept me company
as we've walked a similar path.
Thank you for your friendship
and unwavering encouragement.

CHAPTER ONE

"SCUSA."

Dante DeFiore stepped into the path of a young woman trying to skirt around the line at Ristorante Massimo. Her long blond hair swished over her shoulder as she turned to him. Her icy blue gaze met his. The impact of her piercing stare rocked him. He couldn't turn away. Thick black eyeliner and sky-blue eye shadow that shimmered succeeded in making her stunning eyes even more extraordinary.

Dante cleared his throat. "Signorina, are you meeting someone?"

"No, I'm not."

"Really?" He truly was surprised. "Someone as beautiful as you shouldn't be alone."

Her fine brows rose and a smile tugged at her tempting lips.

He smiled back. Any other time, he'd have been happy to ask her to be his personal guest but not tonight. Inwardly he groaned. Why did he have to have his hands full juggling both positions of maître d' and head chef when the most delicious creature was standing in front of him?

He choked down his regret. It just wasn't meant to be. Tonight there was no time for flirting—not even with this stunning woman who could easily turn heads on the runways of Milan.

He glanced away from her in order to clear his thoughts. Expectant looks from the people waiting to be seated reminded him of his duties. He turned back to those amazing blue eyes. "I hate to say this, but you'll have to take your place at the end of the line."

"It's okay." Her pink glossy lips lifted into a knowing smile. "You don't have to worry. I work here."

"Here?" Impossible. He'd certainly remember her. By the sounds of her speech, she was American.

"This is Mr. Bianco's restaurant, isn't it?"

"Yes, it is."

"Then I'm in the right place."

Suddenly the pieces fell into place. His staff had been cut in half because of a nasty virus running rampant throughout Rome. He'd called around to see if any business associates could loan him an employee or two. Apparently when Luigi said he might be able to track down a friend of one of his daughters, he'd gotten lucky.

Relief flooded through Dante. Help was here at last and by the looks of her, she'd certainly be able to draw in the crowds. Not so long ago, they hadn't needed anyone to draw in customers; his grandfather's cooking was renowned throughout Rome. But in recent months all of that had changed.

"And I'd be the luckiest man in the world to have such a beauty working here. You'll have the men lined up down the street. Just give me a moment." Dante turned and signaled to the waiter.

When Michael approached Dante, the man's forehead was creased in confusion. "What do you need?"

In that moment, Dante's mind drew a blank. All he could envision were those mesmerizing blue eyes. This was ridiculous. He had a business to run.

When he glanced over at the line of customers at the door, the anxious stares struck a chord in his mind. "Michael, could you seat that couple over there?" He pointed to an older couple. "Give them the corner table. It's their fortieth anniversary, so make sure their meal is on us."

"No *problema*."

Lines of exhaustion bracketed Michael's mouth. Dante couldn't blame the guy. Being shorthanded and having to see to the dining room himself was a lot of work.

Dante turned his attention back to his unexpected employee. She had her arms crossed and her slender hip hitched to the side. A slight smile pulled at the corners of her lush lips as though she knew she'd caught him off guard—something that rarely happened to him.

He started to smile back when a patron entered the door and called out a greeting, reminding Dante that work came first. Since his grandfather was no longer around to help shoulder the burden of running this place, Dante's social life had been reduced to interaction with the guests of Ristorante Massimo.

After a brief *ciao* to a regular patron, Dante turned back to his temporary employee. "Thanks for coming. If you give me your coat, I can hang it up for you."

"I've got it." She clutched the lapels but made no attempt to take it off.

"You can hang it over there." He pointed to the small cloakroom. "We can work out everything later."

"You want me to start right now?"

That was the plan, but perhaps Luigi had failed to make that part clear. "Didn't he tell you that you'd be starting right away?"

"Yes, but I thought I'd have a chance to look around. And I didn't think I'd be a hostess."

"Consider this an emergency. I promise you it's not hard. I'm certain you'll be fantastic...uh..." Did she give him her name? If she had, he couldn't recall it. "What did you say your name is?"

"Lizzie. Lizzie Addler."

"Well, Lizzie, it's a pleasure to meet you. I'm Dante. And I really appreciate you pitching in during this stressful time."

"Are you sure you want me out here? I'd be a lot more help in the kitchen."

The kitchen? With her looks, who would hide such a gem behind closed doors? Perhaps she was just shy. Not that anything about her stunning appearance said that she was an introvert.

"I'd really appreciate it if you could help these people find a table."

She nodded.

An assistant rushed out of the kitchen. "We need you."

By the harried look on the young man's face, Dante knew it couldn't be good. He turned to his new employee. There would be time for introductions and formalities later. Right now, he just needed to keep the kitchen from falling behind and giving the patrons an excuse to look for food elsewhere.

"Sorry for this rush but I am very shorthanded." When the girl sent him a puzzled look, he realized that Luigi might not have filled her in on the details of her duties. "If you could just get everyone seated and get their drinks, Michael can take their orders. Can you do that?"

She nodded before slipping off her long black coat to reveal a frilly white blouse that hinted at her willowy figure, a short black skirt that showed off her long legs and a pair of knee-high sleek black boots. He stifled a whistle. Definitely not the reaction a boss should give an employee, even if she was gorgeous enough to create a whirlwind of excitement on the cover of a fashion magazine.

He strode to the kitchen, hoping that nothing had caught fire and that no one had been injured. When was this evening going to end? And had his grandfather's friend Luigi been trying to help by sending Lizzie? Or trying to drive him to distraction?

Once the kitchen was again humming along, he retraced his steps just far enough to catch a glimpse of the blonde bombshell. She moved about on those high-heeled boots as if they were a natural extension of her long legs. He swallowed hard as his eyes followed her around the dining room. He assured himself that he was just doing his duty by checking up on her.

When she smiled and chatted with a couple of older gentlemen, Dante's gut tightened. She sure seemed far more at ease with those men than when he'd been talking with her. How strange. Usually he didn't have a problem making conversation with the female gender. Lizzie was certainly different. Too bad she wouldn't be around long enough to learn more about her. She intrigued him.

Obviously there was a misunderstanding.

Lizzie Addler frowned as she locked the front door of Ristorante Massimo. She hadn't flown from New York to Italy to be a hostess. She was here to work in the kitchen—to learn from the legendary chef, Massimo Bianco. And to film a television segment to air on the culinary channel's number-one-rated show. It was a dream come true.

The strange thing was she'd flown in two days early, hoping to get her bearings in this new country. How in the world did this Dante know she was going to show up this evening?

It was impossible. But then again, this smooth-talking man seemed to know who she was. So why put her on hostess duty when he knew that her true talents lay in the kitchen?

Her cheeks ached from smiling so much, but all it took was recalling Dante's flattering words and the corners of her lips lifted once again. She'd heard rumors that Italian men were known to be charmers and now that she knew that it was true—at least in Dante's case—she'd have to be careful around him. She couldn't lose focus on her mission here.

She leaned her back against the door and sighed. She couldn't remember the last time her feet ached this much.

Why in the world had she decided to wear her new boots today of all days?

Oh, yes, to make a good impression. And technically the boots weren't new—just new to her. They were secondhand, like all of Lizzie's things. But in her defense, some of her things still had the tags on them when she'd found them at the gently used upscale boutique. And boy, was she thankful she'd splurged on the stylish clothes.

Her gaze strayed to the wall full of framed pictures of celebrities. There were black and whites as well as color photos through the years. Massimo was in a lot of them alongside movie stars, singers and politicians from around the world. As Lizzie scanned the many snapshots, she found Dante's handsome face. In each photo of him, he was smiling broadly with his arm around a beautiful woman.

"Pretty impressive?"

She knew without looking that it'd be Dante. "Very impressive." She forced her gaze to linger on the army of photos instead of rushing to ogle the tall, dark and undeniably handsome man at her side. "Have all of these people eaten here?"

"Yes. And there are more photos back in the office. We ran out of space out here." His voice was distinguishable with its heavy Italian accent. The rich tones flowed through her as seductively as crème brûlée. "We should add your photo."

"Me." She pressed a hand to her chest. "But I'm a nobody."

"You, my dear, are definitely not a nobody." His gaze met hers and heat rushed to her cheeks. "Is everything wrapped up out here?"

Her mouth went dry and she struggled to swallow. "Yes...yes, the last customer just left."

Lines of exhaustion etched the tanned skin around his dark eyes. His lips were lifted in a friendly smile, but something told her that it was all for her benefit and that he didn't feel like doing anything but calling it a night.

"I can't thank you enough for your help this evening." His gaze connected with hers, making her pulse spike. "I suppose you'll be wanting your pay so that you can be on your way. If you would just wait a moment."

Before she could formulate words, he turned and headed to the back of the restaurant. Pay her? For what? Playing hostess for the evening? She supposed that was above and beyond her contract negotiations with the television network.

Dante quickly returned and placed some euros in her hand. His fingers were warm as the backs of his fingers brushed over her palm, causing her stomach to quiver. She quickly pulled her hand away.

"Thank you so much. You truly were a lifesaver." He moved to the door to let her out.

She didn't follow him. She wasn't done here. Not by a long shot. "I'm not leaving. Not yet."

Dante shot her a puzzled look. "If this is about the money, this is the amount I told Luigi I was willing to pay—"

Lizzie shook her head. "It's not that. I came here to meet with Chef Massimo."

"You did? You mean Luigi didn't send you?"

"I don't know any Luigi."

Dante reached in his pocket and pulled out his smartphone. A few keystrokes later, he glanced up. "My mistake. Luigi wasn't able to find anyone to help out. Thank goodness you showed up."

"And I was happy to help. Now if you could introduce me to Chef Massimo."

Dante's forehead creased. "That's not going to happen." His tone was firm and unbendable. "He's not here. You'll have to deal with me."

"I don't think so. I'll wait for him."

Dante rubbed the back of his neck and sighed. "You'll be waiting a long time. Chef Massimo is out of town."

"Listen, I know I'm here a couple of days ahead of time, but we do have an agreement to meet."

"That's impossible." Dante's shoulders straightened and his expression grew serious. "I would have known. I know about everything that has to do with this place."

"Obviously not in this case." Lizzie pressed her lips together, immediately regretting her outburst. She was tired after her long flight and then having to work all evening as a hostess.

"You're obviously mixed up. You should be going." He pulled open the front door, letting a cool evening breeze sweep inside and wrap around her.

She couldn't leave. Her whole future was riding on this internship, and the money from participating in the upcoming cooking show would pay for her sister's grad school. She couldn't let her down. She'd promised Jules that if she got accepted to graduate school she'd make sure there was money for the tuition. Jules had already had so many setbacks in her life that Lizzie refused to fail her.

She stepped up to Dante, and even though she was wearing heeled boots, she still had to tilt her chin upward to look him in the eyes. "I did you a big favor tonight. The least you can do is hear me out."

Dante let the door swing shut and led her back to the dining room, where he pulled out a chair for her before he took a seat across the table. "I'm listening."

Lizzie wished it wasn't so late in the evening. Dante looked wiped out, not exactly the optimal position to gain his understanding. Still, she didn't have any other place to go.

Her elbows pressed down on the white linen tablecloth as she folded her hands together. "Chef Massimo has agreed to mentor me."

Dante's gaze narrowed in on her. "Why is this the first I'm hearing of it?"

"Why should you know about it? My agreement isn't with you."

"Massimo Bianco is my maternal grandfather. And with him away, I'm running this place."

This man wasn't about to give an inch, at least not easily. "When will he return so we can straighten things out?"

Dante leaned back in his chair and folded his arms. His dark eyes studied her. She'd love to know what he was thinking. Then again, maybe not. The past couple of days had been nothing but a blur. She'd rushed to wrap up her affairs in New York City before catching a transatlantic flight. The last thing she'd wanted to do was play hostess, but she figured she'd be a good sport. After all, Dante seemed to be in a really tight spot. But now she didn't understand why he was being so closemouthed about Massimo.

"All you need to know is that my grandfather won't be returning. So any business you have with him, you'll have to deal with me. Tell me about this agreement."

Uneasiness crept down her spine. This man had disbelief written all over his handsome features. But what choice did she have but to deal with him since she had absolutely no idea how to contact Chef Massimo? The only phone number she had was for this restaurant. And the email had also been for the restaurant.

"The agreement is for him to mentor me for the next two months."

Dante shook his head. "It isn't going to happen. I'm sorry you traveled all of this way for nothing. But you'll have to leave now."

Lizzie hadn't flown halfway around the globe just to be turned away—she'd been rejected too many times in her life. Her reasons for being here ran deeper than appearing on the television show. She truly wanted to learn from the best and Massimo Bianco was a renowned chef, whose name on her résumé would carry a lot of weight in the culinary world.

"Surely you could use the extra help." After what she'd witnessed this evening, she had no doubt about it.

"If not for this virus going around, Massimo's would be fully staffed. We don't have room for someone else in the kitchen."

"Obviously Chef Bianco doesn't agree with your assessment. He assured me there would be a spot for me."

Dante's eyes darkened. "He was mistaken. And now that I've heard you out, I must insist that you leave."

These days she proceeded cautiously and was always prepared. She reached in her oversize purse and pulled out the signed document. "You can't turn me away."

When she held out a copy of the contract, Dante's dark brows rose. Suddenly he didn't look as in charge as he had just a few seconds ago. Funny how a binding legal document could change things so quickly.

When he reached for the papers, their fingers brushed. His skin was warm and surprisingly smooth. Their gazes met and held. His eyes were dark and mysterious. Instead of being intimidated by him, she was drawn to him.

Not that she was in Italy to have a summer romance. She had a job to do and this man was standing between her and her future. He may be stubborn, but he'd just met his match.

CHAPTER TWO

WHAT WAS IT about this woman that had him feeling off-kilter?

Could it be the way her touch sent currents of awareness up his arm? Realizing they were still touching, Dante jerked his hand away. He clenched his fingers, creasing the hefty document.

Or maybe it was those cool blue eyes of hers that seemed to study his every move. It was as though she could see more of him than he cared for anyone to observe. Not that he had any secrets to hide—well, other than his plans to sell the *ristorante*.

His gaze scrolled over the first lines of the document, pausing when he saw his grandfather's name followed by Ristorante Massimo. He continued skimming over the legalese until his gaze screeched to a halt at the mention of a television show. His gut twisted into a knot. This was much more involved than he'd ever imagined.

"You said this was for an internship. You didn't mention anything about a television show."

Her lips moved but nothing came out. It was as though she wasn't sure exactly how to proceed. If she thought he was going to make this easy for her, she'd have to think again. She'd tried to get him to agree to let her work here under false pretenses when in fact she had much bigger plans.

When she didn't respond fast enough, he added, "How

long were you planning to keep that little bit of information a secret?"

Her forehead wrinkled. "Obviously I wasn't keeping it a secret or I wouldn't have handed you the contract."

She had a valid point, but it didn't ease his agitation. He once again rubbed at his stiff neck. It'd been an extremely long day. Not only was he short-staffed but also the meeting with the potential buyers for the *ristorante* hadn't gone well. They didn't just want the building. They also wanted the name and the secret recipes that put his grandfather's name up there with the finest chefs.

Dante didn't have the right to sell those recipes—recipes that went back to his grandmother's time. They were special to his grandfather. Still, selling them would keep them alive for others to enjoy instead of them being forgotten in a drawer. But could he actually approach his grandfather and ask for the right to sell them? Those recipes were his grandfather's pride and joy. In fact, employees signed a nondisclosure agreement to maintain the secrecy of Massimo's signature dishes. The thought of selling out left a sour taste in Dante's mouth.

"As you can see in the contract, the television crew will be here on Tuesday." Her words brought Dante back to his latest problem.

"I also see that you've arrived a couple of days early." He wasn't sure what he meant by that statement. He was stalling. Thinking.

"I like to be prepared. I don't like surprises. So I thought I'd get settled in and maybe see some of the sights in Rome. I've heard it's a lovely city."

"Well, since my grandfather isn't going to be able to mentor you, perhaps you can have an extended holiday before heading back to—"

"New York. And I didn't come here for a vacation. I came here to work and to learn." She got to her feet. "Maybe I should just speak with one of the people in the kitchen. Perhaps they can point me in the direction of your grandfather."

"That won't be necessary."

His grandfather didn't need to be bothered with this—he had more important issues to deal with at the moment. Dante could and would handle this woman. After all, there had to be a way out of this. Without reading the rest of the lengthy details, he flipped to the last page.

"It's all signed and legal, if that's what you're worried about." Her voice held a note of confidence, and she sat back down.

She was right. Right there in black and white was his grandfather's distinguished signature. There was no denying the slope of the *M* or the scroll of *Bianco*. Dante resisted the urge to ball up the document and toss it into the stone fireplace across the room from them. Not that it would help since the fire had been long ago extinguished.

He refused to let the sale of the *ristorante*—the deal he'd been negotiating for weeks—go up in smoke because of some promotional deal his grandfather had signed. There had to be a way around it. Dante wondered how much it'd take to convince Lizzie to quietly return to New York.

"I'm sure we can reach some sort of agreement." He was, after all, a DeFiore. He had access to a sizable fortune. "What will it take for you to forget about your arrangement with my grandfather?"

She sat up straighter. "Nothing."

"What do you mean nothing?"

"I mean that I'm not leaving." She leaned forward, pressing her elbows down on the tabletop. "I don't think you understand how serious I am. I've cut out months of my life for this internship. I've said goodbye to my family and friends in order to be here. I had to quit my job. Are you getting the picture? Everything is riding on this agreement—my entire future. I have a signed agreement and I intend to film a television segment in that kitchen." She pointed over her shoulder.

She'd quit her job!

Who did something like that? Obviously someone very trusting or very desperate. Which type was she? Her beautiful face showed lines of stress and the darkness below her eyes hinted at her exhaustion. He was leaning toward the desperate scenario.

Perhaps he'd been too rough on her. He really hadn't meant to upset her. He knew how frustrating it could be to be so close to getting what you wanted and yet having a barricade thrown in the way.

"Listen, I know this isn't what you want to hear, but I'm sure you'll be able to land another job somewhere else—"

"And what are you planning to do about the film crew when they arrive?"

Dante's lips pressed together. Yes, what was he going to do? This situation was getting ever so complicated. He eyed up the woman. Was she on the level? Was she truly after the work experience? The opportunity to learn? Or was she an opportunist playing on his sympathies?

He certainly didn't want to spend his time inflating her ego in front of the camera crew for the next two months—two very long months. But he was getting the very unsettling feeling that there was no way over, around or under the arrangement without a lengthy, messy lawsuit, which would hold up the sale of the *ristorante*.

This was not how things were supposed to go.

Lizzie resisted the urge to get up and start pacing. It was what she usually did when she was stuck in a tough spot. While growing up in the foster care system, she'd found herself in plenty of tough spots. But the one thing she'd learned through it all was not to give up—if it was important enough, there had to be a solution. It'd worked to keep

Jules, her foster sister, with her through the years. She just had to take a deep breath and not panic.

Dante appeared to be a businessman. Surely he'd listen to logic. It was her last alternative. She sucked in a steadying breath, willing her mind to calm. "If you'll read over the contract, you'll see that your grandfather has agreed not only to mentor me but also to host a television crew. We're doing a reality spot for one of the cooking shows. It's been in the works for months now. Your grandfather was very excited about the project and how it'd give this place—" she waved her hand around at the restaurant that had a very distinct air about it "—international recognition. Just think of all the people that would know the name Ristorante Massimo."

Dante's eyes lit up with interest. "Do you have some numbers to back up your claims?"

She would have brought them, if she'd known she'd need them. "Your grandfather is confident in the value of these television segments. He has made numerous appearances on the culinary channel and has made quite a name for himself."

"I know. I was here for every one of those appearances."

She studied Dante's face for some recollection of him. His tanned skin. His dark eyes. His strong jaw. And those lips... Oh, they looked good enough to kiss into submission... She jerked her attention back to the conversation. "Why don't I recall seeing you in any of them?"

"Because I took a very small role in them. I didn't understand why my grandfather would sign up for those television appearances."

Her gaze narrowed in on him. "Do you have something against people on television?"

"No." He crossed his arms and leaned back, rocking his chair on the rear two legs. "I just think in a lot of cases they misrepresent life. They give people false hope that they'll be overnight successes. Most of the time life doesn't work that way. Life is a lot harder."

There was a glimmer of something in his eyes. Was it regret? Or pain? In a blink, his feelings were once again hidden. She was locked out. And for some reason that bothered her. Not that it should—it wasn't as though they were friends. She didn't even know him.

Not about to waste her time debating the positive and negative points of television, she decided to turn the conversation back around to her reason for being here. "Surely your grandfather will be back soon. After all, he has a restaurant to run."

"I'm afraid that he won't be returning."

"He won't?" This was news to her. Surely he couldn't be right. "But we have an agreement. And he was so eager for us to begin."

Dante rubbed his jaw as though trying to decide if he should say more. His dark gaze studied her intently. It made her want to squirm in her seat but she resisted.

"Whatever you're thinking, just say it. I need to know what's going on."

Dante sighed. "My grandfather recently experienced a stroke. He has since moved to the country."

"Oh, no." She pressed a hand to her chest. This was so much worse than she'd imagined. "Is he going to be all right?"

Dante's brows lifted as though he was surprised by her concern. "Yes, it wasn't as bad as it could have been. He's getting therapy."

"Thank goodness. Your grandfather seemed so lively and active. I just can't imagine that happening to him."

She thought back to their lively emails and chatty phone conversations. Massimo's voice had been rich and robust like a dark roast espresso. He was what she thought of when she imagined having a grandfather of her own. "He was so full of life."

"How exactly did you get to know him?"

Perhaps she'd said too much. It wasn't as if she and Massimo were *that* close. "At first, the production group put us in touch. We emailed back and forth. Then we started talking on the phone, discussing how we wanted to handle the time slots. After all, they are short, so we couldn't get too elaborate. But then again, we didn't want to skimp and do just the basics."

"Sounds like you two talked quite a bit."

She shrugged. "It wasn't like we talked every day. More like when one of us had a good idea. But that was hampered by the time difference. And then recently the calls stopped. When I phoned here I was merely told that he wasn't available and that they'd give him a message."

Dante's eyes opened wide as though a thought had come to him. "I remember seeing those messages. I had no idea who you were or what you wanted. I was beginning to wonder if my grandfather had a girlfriend on the side."

"Nope, it was me. And now that you know the whole story, what's yours?"

"My what?"

"Story. I take it you run this place for your grandfather."

His brows furrowed together as though he knew where this conversation was leading. "Yes, I do."

"Have you worked here long?" She wanted as much information as possible so she could plot out a backup plan.

He hesitantly nodded.

"That must be wonderful to learn from such a talented chef." There had to be a way to salvage this deal. But she needed to know more. "When did you start working with your grandfather?"

"When I was a kid, I would come and visit. But it wasn't until later that I worked here full-time."

She noticed that his answers were vague at best, giving her no clue as to his family life or why he came here to work. Perhaps he needed the money. Still, as she stared across the table at him, his whole demeanor spoke of money and culture. She also couldn't dismiss the fact that most women would find him alarmingly handsome. In fact, he'd make some real eye candy for the television spot. And if that was what it took to draw in an audience, who was she to argue.

She'd been earning money cooking since she was fourteen. Of course, being so young, she'd been paid under the table. Over the years, she'd gained more and more experience, but never thinking she'd ever have a shot at owning a restaurant of her own, she'd taken the safe route and gone to college. She'd needed a way to make decent money to keep herself and Jules afloat.

But then Jules entered her application for a reality TV cooking show. Jules had insisted that she needed to take a risk and follow her dream of being a chef in her own five-star restaurant.

Winning that reality show had been a huge stepping-stone. It gave her a television contract and a plane ticket to Rome, where she'd learn from the best in the business. Jules was right. Maybe her dream would come true.

All she needed was to make sure this deal was a success. One way or the other. And if Chef Massimo couldn't participate then perhaps his grandson would do.

She eyed him up. "Your grandfather must have taught you all of his secrets in the kitchen."

His body noticeably stiffened. "Yes, he did. How else would I keep the place running in his absence?"

She knew it was akin to poking a sleeping bear with a stick, but she had to confirm her suspicions before she altered her plans ever so slightly. "But do your dishes taste like your grandfather's?"

"The customers don't know the difference." The indignity in his voice rumbled through the room. "Who do you think took the time to learn every tiny detail of my grandfather's recipes? My grandfather insisted that if you were going to do something, you should learn to do it right. And there were no shortcuts in his kitchen."

From the little she'd known of Massimo, she could easily believe this was true. During their phone conversations, he'd made it clear that he didn't take shortcuts with his recipes or with training people. She'd have to start from the beginning. Normally, she'd have taken it as an insult, but coming from Massimo, she had the feeling that he only wanted the best for both of them and the television spotlight.

"Will you continue to run the restaurant alone?"

Dante ran a hand over his jaw. "Are you always this curious about strangers?"

She wasn't about to back off. This information was important and she had learned almost everything she needed. "I'm just trying to make a little conversation. Is that so wrong?"

There was a look in his eyes that said he didn't believe her. Still, he didn't press the subject. Instead he surprised her by answering. "For the foreseeable future I will continue to run Massimo's. I can't predict the future."

"I still wonder if you're as good as your grandfather in the kitchen."

"Wait here." He jumped to his feet and strode out of the room.

Where in the world had he gone? She was tempted to follow, but she thought better of it. She'd already pushed her luck as far as she dared. But her new plan was definitely taking shape.

The only problem she envisioned was trying to keep her mind on the art of cooking and not on the hottie mentoring her. She knew jet lag was to blame for her distorted worries. A little uninterrupted sleep would have her thinking clearly.

This arrangement was far too important to ruin due to some sort of crush. She pursed her lips together. No matter how good he looked, she knew better than to let her heart rule her mind. She knew too well the agonizing pain of rejection and abandonment. She wouldn't subject herself to that again. Not for anyone.

She pulled her shoulders back and clasped her hands in her lap. Time to put her plan in motion.

One way or the other.

CHAPTER THREE

How dare she question his prowess in the kitchen?

Dante stared down at a plate of *pasta alla gricia*, one of his favorite dishes. The fine balance of cured pork and *pecorino romano* gave the pasta a unique, tangy flavor. It was a dish he never grew tired of eating.

He proceeded to divvy the food between two plates. After all, he didn't need that much to eat at this late hour. As he arranged the plates, he wondered why he was going to such bother. What was so special about this golden-haired beauty? And why did he feel a compulsion to prove himself where she was concerned?

It wasn't as if he was ever going to see Lizzie again. Without his grandfather around to hold up his end of the agreement, she'd be catching the next plane back to New York. Still, before she left, he needed to prove his point. He'd taken some of his grandfather's recipes and put his own twist on them. And the patrons loved them. This meal was sure not to disappoint the most discerning palate.

He strode back into the dining room and placed a plate in front of Lizzie. She gazed up at him with a wide-eyed blue gaze. Her mouth gaped as though she were about to say something, but no words came out.

He stared at her lush lips, painted with a shimmery pink frost. They looked perfectly ripe for a kiss. The urge grew stronger with each passing second. The breath hitched in his throat.

"This looks delicious." She was staring at him, not the food. And she was smiling.

"It's an old family recipe." He nearly tripped over his own feet as he moved to the other side of the table. "The secret to the dish is to keep it simple and not be tempted to add extras. You don't want to detract from the flavor of the meat and cheese."

He couldn't believe he was letting her good looks and charms get to him. It wasn't as if she was the first beautiful woman he'd entertained. But she was the first that he truly wanted to impress. Safely in his seat, he noticed the smallness of the table. If he wasn't careful, his legs would brush against hers. If this were a casual date, he'd take advantage of the coziness, but Lizzie was different from the usual women he dated. She was more serious. More intent. And she seemed to have only one thing on her mind—business.

"Aren't you going to try it?" Dante motioned to the food. Just because he wasn't interested in helping her with her dreams of stardom didn't mean he couldn't prove his point—he could create magic in the kitchen.

He watched as she spun the pasta on her fork and slipped it in her mouth. He sat there captivated, waiting for her reaction. When she moaned her approval, his blood pressure spiked and his grip tightened on the fork.

"This is very good. Did you make it?"

Her question didn't fool him. He knew what she was digging at—she wanted him to step up and fill in for his grandfather. Him on television—never. That was his grandfather's dream—not his.

"It's delicious." She flashed him a big smile, seemingly unfazed by his tight-lipped expression.

Her smile gave him a strange feeling in his chest that shoved him off center. And that wasn't good. He didn't want to be vulnerable to a woman. He knew for a fact that romance would ultimately lead to disaster—one way or the other.

He forced himself to eat because he hadn't had time to since that morning and his body must be starved. But he didn't really have an appetite. In fact, the food tasted like cardboard. Thankfully Lizzie seemed impressed with it.

When she'd cleaned her plate, she pushed it aside. "Thank you. I can't wait for you to teach me how to make it."

Dante still had a couple of bites left on his plate when he set his fork down and moved the plate aside. "That isn't going to happen."

"Maybe you should at least consider it."

Her gaze strayed to the contract that was still sitting in the middle of the table and then back to him. What was she implying? That she'd drag him through the courts?

That was the last thing he needed. He already had enough important issues on his mind, including fixing his relationship with his family. And the closer it got to putting his signature on the sale papers, the more unsettled he'd become about his decision.

"You can't expect me to fulfill my grandfather's agreement."

"Why not?" She smiled as though it would melt his resistance. Maybe under different circumstances it would have worked, but not now.

"Because I don't want to be on television. I didn't like it when those camera people were here before. All they did was get in the way and create a circus of onlookers wanting to get their faces on television."

He didn't bother to mention that he was just days away from closing a deal to sell Ristorante Massimo. But it all hinged on those family recipes. And somehow parting with those felt treasonous. His grandfather had signed the entire business over to him to do as he pleased, but still he couldn't make this caliber of decision on his own.

But how did he approach his grandfather? How did he tell him that he felt restless again and without Massimo in the kitchen, it just wasn't the same? It was time he moved on to find something that pacified the uneasiness in him.

He'd been toying with the thought of returning to the vineyard and working alongside his father and brother. After all of this time, perhaps he and his father could call a truce—perhaps Dante could in some small way try to make up for the loss and unhappiness his father had endured in the years since Dante's mother had died. But was that even possible considering their strained relationship?

"It isn't me you have to worry about." Lizzie's voice drew him back to the here and now. She toyed with the cloth napkin. "The television people will want to enforce the contract. They're already advertising the segment on their station. I saw it before I left New York. Granted, we won't have a show of our own. But we will have a daily spot on the most popular show on their station."

He'd forgotten that there was a third party to this agreement. A television conglomerate would not be easily deterred from enforcing their rights. "But what makes you think that they would want me instead of my grandfather?"

"I take it your grandfather truly didn't mention any of this to you?"

Dante shook his head. A sick feeling churned in the pit of his stomach.

"That's strange. When he brought your name up to the television people, I thought for sure he'd discussed it with you." She shrugged. "Anyway, they are eager to have you included in the segments. They think you'll appeal to the younger viewers."

Dante leaned his head back and expelled a weary sigh. Why hadn't his grandfather mentioned any of this to him? Maybe Massimo just never got the chance. Regardless, this situation was going from bad to worse. What was next?

When Dante didn't say anything, Lizzie continued, "I'm sure when I explain to them about your grandfather no longer being able to fulfill his role, they will welcome a young, handsome replacement."

She thought he was handsome? He sat up a little straighter. "And if I don't agree—"

"From what I read, there are monetary penalties for not fulfilling the contract. I'm not an attorney but you might want to have someone take a look at it."

A court battle would only extend the time it would take to sell the *ristorante*. Not to mention scare off his potential buyer—the one with deep pockets and an interest in keeping Ristorante Massimo as is.

Dante's gaze moved to the document. "Do you mind if I keep these papers for a little while?"

"That's fine. It's a copy."

"I'll get back to you on this." He got to his feet. He had a lot to think over. It was time to call it a night.

"You'll have to decide soon, as the film crew will be here in a couple of days."

His back teeth ground together. Talk about finding everything out at the last minute. No matter his decision, resolving this issue would take some time. Agreeing to the filming would be much quicker than a court suit. And in the end, would he win the lawsuit?

But then again, could he work with Lizzie for two months and ignore the way her smile made his pulse race? Or the way her eyes drew him in? What could he say? He was a red-hot Italian man who appreciated women. But nothing about Lizzie hinted at her being open to a casual, gratifying experience. And he was not about to get tangled up in something that involved his heart. Nothing could convince him to risk it—not after the carnage he'd witnessed. No way.

He was attracted to her.

Lizzie secretly reveled in the knowledge. Not that either of them would act on it. She'd noticed how he kept his distance, but his eyes betrayed him. She wondered if his demeanor had cooled because of the television show. Or was there something more? Her gaze slipped to his hands, not spying any rings. Still, that didn't mean there wasn't a significant other.

Realizing the implication of what she was doing, she jerked her gaze upward. But that wasn't any better as she ended up staring into his bottomless eyes. Her heart thudded against her ribs. This was not good. Not good at all.

She glanced down at the gleaming black-and-white floor tiles. She could still feel him staring at her. With great effort, she ignored him. Her trip to Rome was meant to be a learning experience, not to partake in a holiday romance.

Putting herself out there and getting involved with Dante was foolish. She had the scars on her heart to prove that romance could come with a high price tag. Besides, she was certain she wouldn't live up to his expectations—she never did.

It was much easier to wear a smile and keep people at arm's length. It was safer. And that was exactly how she planned to handle this situation.

Dante cleared his throat. "Well, since you're a couple of days early, I'm sure you'll want to tour the city. There's lots to see and experience." He led her to the front door. "Make sure you visit the Colosseum and the catacombs."

"I'm looking forward to sightseeing. This is my first trip to Italy. Actually, it's my first trip anywhere." She pressed her lips together to keep from spilling details of her pitiful life. She didn't want his sympathy. She was just so excited about this once-in-a-lifetime experience. Years ago in those foster homes, she never would have imagined that a trip like this would be a possibility—let alone a reality.

"I'd start with the Vatican Museums."

"Thanks. I will."

He smiled as he pulled open the door. The tired lines on his face smoothed and his eyes warmed. She was struck by how truly handsome he was when he let his guard down. She'd have to be careful and not fall for this mysterious Italian.

She glanced out into the dark night. "Is this the way to the apartment?"

His brow puckered. "Excuse me."

"The apartment. Massimo told me that he had a place for me to stay?"

"He did?" Dante uttered the words as though they were part of his thought process and not a question for her.

She nodded and reached into her purse. She fumbled around until her fingers stumbled across some folded papers. Her fingers clasped them and pulled them out.

"I have the email correspondence." She held out the evidence. "It's all right here."

Dante waved away the pages. "Are you this prepared for everything?"

She nodded. She'd learned a long time ago that people rarely keep their word. Just like her mother, who'd promised she'd do whatever it took to get Lizzie back from social services. In the beginning, Lizzie had gone to bed each night crying for the only parent she'd ever known—the mother who was big on neglect and sparing on kindness. At the time, Lizzie hadn't known any other way. In the end, that mother-daughter reunion was not to be. Her mother had been all talk and no follow-through, unable to move past the drugs and alcohol. Lizzie languished in the system.

She'd grown up knowing one simple truth: people rarely lived up to their word. There was only one person to count on—herself.

However, in Massimo's case, breaking his word was totally understandable. It was beyond his control. Her heart squeezed when she thought of that outgoing man being forced into retirement. She truly hoped while she was here that she'd get the opportunity to meet him and thank him for having such faith in her. It was as though he could see through her brave front to her quivering insides. During moments of doubt, he'd calmed her and assured her that all would be fine with the television segments.

She glanced at Dante. He definitely wasn't a calming force like his grandfather. If anything, Dante's presence filled her with nervous energy.

He leaned against the door. "There's no apartment available."

Her eyes narrowed on him. "Does everything with you have to be a struggle?"

"I'm not trying to be difficult. I simply don't have any place for you to stay."

"Why is it your grandfather seemed confident that I would be comfortable here?"

"Probably because there was a remodeled apartment available, but since I wasn't privy to your arrangement with my grandfather, I just leased it. But I'm sure you won't have a problem finding a hotel room nearby."

Oh, yes, there would be a big problem. She didn't have money to rent a hotel room. She could only imagine how expensive that would be and she needed every penny to pay down her debts and to pay tuition for Jules's grad school. Every penny from the contract was already accounted for. There was nothing to spare.

"It was agreed that I would have free room and board." Pride dictated that she keep it to herself that she didn't have the money to get a hotel room.

He crossed his arms and stared at her as though debating his options. "What do you want me to do? Give you my bed?"

The words sparked a rush of tempting images to dance through her mind. Dante leaning in and pressing his very tempting lips to hers. His long, lean fingers grazing her cheek before resting against the beating pulse in her throat. Her leaning into him as he swept her up in his arms.

"Lizzie, are you okay?" Dante's eyes filled with concern.

She swallowed hard, realizing that she'd let her imagination get the best of her. "Umm, yes. I'm just a little jet-lagged. And things were busy tonight, keeping me on my toes."

His eyes probed her. "Are you sure that's all it is?"

She nodded.

Where in the world had those distracting images of Dante come from? It wasn't as though she was looking for a boyfriend. The last man in her life had believed they should each have their own space until one day he dropped by to let her know that he was moving to California to chase his dream of acting. No *I'll miss you*. Or *Will you come with me?*

He'd tossed her aside like the old worn-out couch and the back issues of his rocker magazines. He hadn't wanted her except for a little fun here and there. She'd foolishly let herself believe that they were building something special. In the end, she hadn't been enough for him—she always came up lacking.

"I'd really like to get some rest." And some distance from Dante so she could think clearly. "It's been a long evening and my feet are killing me."

Was that a hint of color rising in his cheeks? Did he feel bad about putting her to work? Maybe he should, but she honestly didn't mind. She liked meeting some of the people she'd hopefully be cooking for in the near future. That was if she ever convinced Dante that this arrangement could work.

"Putting you to work was a total mix-up. My apologies." He glanced down at the floor. "I owe you."

"Apology accepted." She loved that he had manners. "Now, does this mean you'll find me a bed?"

CHAPTER FOUR

THE QUESTION CONJURED up all sorts of scintillating scenarios.

Dante squelched his overactive, overeager imagination. Something told him that there was a whole lot more to this beautiful woman than her desire to be on television and to brush up on her skills in the kitchen. He saw in her eyes a guardedness. He recognized the look because it was something he'd witnessed with his older brother after his young wife had tragically died. It was a look one got when life had double-crossed them.

Lizzie had traveled to the other side of the globe from her home without knowing a single soul, and from the determined set of her mouth, she wasn't about to turn tail and run. She was willing to stand her ground. And he couldn't help but admire her strength.

He just hoped his gut feeling about this woman wasn't off target. What he had in mind was a bold move. But his grandfather, who'd always been a good judge of character, liked her. He surely wouldn't have gone out of his way for her if he hadn't. But that didn't mean Dante should trust her completely, especially when it came to his grandfather.

Nonno had enough on his plate. Since he'd been struck down by a stroke, he'd been lost in a sea of self-pity. Dante was getting desperate to snap his grandfather back into the world of the living. And plying the man with problems when Nonno was already down wouldn't help anyone.

"Have you told me everything now? About your agreement with my grandfather."

She nodded.

"You promise? No more surprises?"

"Cross my heart." Her finger slowly crossed her chest.

Dante cleared his throat as he forced his gaze upward to meet her eyes. "I suppose I do have a place for you to stay."

"Lead the way."

With the main doors locked, he moved next to her on the sidewalk. "It's right over here."

He led the way to a plain red door alongside the restaurant. With a key card, the door buzzed and he pulled it open for her. Inside was a small but lush lobby with an elevator and a door leading to steps. He'd made sure to give the building a face-lift when his grandfather handed over the reins to him. That was all it took to draw in eager candidates to rent the one available unit that he'd been occupying until he'd moved into his grandfather's much larger apartment.

"Where are we going?" She glanced around at the new furnishings adorning the lobby.

"There are apartments over the *ristorante*."

A look of dawning glinted in her eyes. "Your grandfather mentioned those. It's where he intended for me to stay while I am here. Are they nice?"

"Quite nice." In fact the renovations on his apartment had just been completed.

As the elevator doors slid open, she paused and turned to him. "But I thought you said that you leased the last one."

"Do you want to see what I have in mind or not?"

She nodded before stepping inside the elevator.

Good. Because he certainly wasn't going to bend over backward to make her happy. In fact, if she walked away now of her own accord, so much the better. As it was, this arrangement would be only temporary. He'd pacify her until he spoke to his solicitor.

In the cozy confines of the elevator, the faint scent of her floral perfume wrapped around him and teased his senses. If she were anyone else, he'd comment on its intoxicating scent. It was so tempting to lean closer and draw the perfume deeper into his lungs. But he resisted. Something about her led him to believe that she'd want more than one night—more than he was capable of offering her.

The thought of letting go and falling in love made his gut tighten and his palms grow damp. He'd witnessed firsthand the power of love and it wasn't all sappy ballads and roses. Love had the strength to crush a person, leaving them broken and angry at the world.

He placed a key in the pad, turned it and pressed the penthouse button. The hum of the elevator was the only sound. In no time at all the door swished open, revealing a red-carpeted hallway. He led her to his door, adorned with gold emblems that read PH-1.

Dante unlocked the door and waved for her to go ahead of him. He couldn't help but watch her face. She definitely wouldn't make much of a poker player as her emotions filtered across her face. Her blue eyes opened wide as she took in the pillar posts that supported the open floor plan for the living room and kitchen area.

He'd had walls torn down in order to create this spacious area. He may enjoy city life but the country boy in him didn't like to feel completely hemmed in. He'd paid the men bonuses to turn the renovations around quickly. Though it didn't come close in size to his family's home at the vineyard, the apartment was still large—large enough for two people to coexist without stepping on each other's toes. At least for one night.

She walked farther into the room. She paused next to the black leather couch and turned to him. "Do you live here alone?"

"I do. My grandfather used to live here. When he got

sick, he turned it over to me. I made some changes and had everything updated."

"It certainly is spacious. I think I'd get lost in a place this size." Her stiff posture said that she was as uncomfortable as he felt.

He wasn't used to having company. He'd been so busy since his grandfather's sudden exit from the *ristorante*—from his life—that he didn't have time for a social life. In fact, now that he thought about it, Lizzie was the first woman he'd had in here. He wasn't sure how he felt about that fact.

"Can I get you anything?" he asked, trying to ease the mounting discomfort.

"Yes—you can tell me what I'm doing here."

Oh, yes. He thought it was obvious but apparently it wasn't to her. "You can stay here tonight until we can get this whole situation cleared up."

"You mean when you consent to the contents of this contract."

His jaw tightened, holding back a string of heated words. "Don't look like it's the end of the world." Lizzie stepped up to him. "With your good looks, the camera is going to love you. And that's not to mention the thousands of women watching the segment. Who knows, maybe you'll become a star."

Dante laughed. Him a star. Never. Her lush lips lifted. The simple expression made her eyes sparkle like blue topaz. Her pale face filled with color. And her lips, they were plump and just right to lean in and snag a sweet taste. His head started to lower when she pulled back as though reading his errant thoughts.

He cleared his throat and moved to the kitchenette to retrieve a glass. "Are you sure you don't want anything to drink?"

"I'm fine. Have you lived here long?"

He ran the water until it was cold—real cold. What he

really needed to do was dump it over his head and shock some sense back into himself.

"I've lived in this building since I moved to Rome. I had a smaller apartment on another floor before moving to this one. You're my first guest here." He turned, waiting to hear more about what she thought of the place. "What do you think of it?"

He was genuinely curious about her take on the place. It was modeled in black-and-white decor. With the two colors, it made decorating easier for him. He sensed that it still needed something, but he couldn't put his finger on what exactly was missing.

"It's...it's nice." Her tone was hesitant.

Nice? The muscles in his neck tightened. Who said "nice"? Someone who was trying to be polite when they really didn't like something but they didn't want to hurt the other person's feelings.

She leaned back on the couch and straightened her legs. She lifted her arms over her head and stretched. He tried to ignore how her blouse rode up and exposed a hint of her creamy skin. But it was too late. His thoughts strayed in the wrong direction again. At this rate, he'd need a very cold shower.

He turned his attention back to the apartment and glanced around, trying to see it from her perspective. Everything was new. There wasn't a speck of dust—his cleaning lady had just been there. And he made sure to always pick up after himself. There wasn't a stray sock to be had anywhere.

"Is it the black-and-white decor you don't like?" He really wanted to know. Maybe her answer would shed some light on why he felt something was off about the place.

"I told you, I like it."

"But describing it as *nice* is what people say to be polite. I want to know what's missing." There, he'd said it.

There was something missing and it was going to drive him crazy until he figured it out.

He looked around at the white walls. The modern artwork. The two pieces of sculpture. One of a stallion rearing up. The other of a gentle mare. They reminded him of home. When he turned around, he noticed Lizzie unzipping her boots and easing them off. Her pink-painted toes stretched and then pointed as though she were a ballerina as she worked out all of the muscles. When she murmured her pleasure at being free of the boots, he thought he was going to lose it. It took every bit of willpower to remain in his spot and not go to her.

He turned his back. He tried to think of something to do. Something to keep him from going to her. But there was nothing that needed straightening up. No dirty dishes in the sink. In fact, he spent very little time here. For the most part, he slept here and that was it. The rest of his time was spent either downstairs in the *ristorante* or at the vineyard, checking on his grandfather.

"You know what's missing?" Her voice drew his attention.

He turned around and tried to ignore the way her short black skirt had ridden even higher on her thighs. "What would that be?"

"There are no pictures. I thought there'd be one of you with your grandfather."

Dante glanced around, realizing she was right. He didn't have a single picture of anyone. "I'm sorry. I don't have any pictures here. They are all at my family's home."

"Do they live far from here?"

He shrugged. "It's a bit of a drive. But not that far. I like to go home on the weekends."

"But isn't the restaurant open?"

"It's open Saturday. But then we're closed Sunday and Monday. So my weekend is not the traditional weekend."

"I see. And your grandfather, is he with your family?"

Dante nodded. "He lives with my father and older brother."

Her brows drew together but she didn't say anything. He couldn't help but be curious about her thoughts. Everything about this woman poked at his curiosity.

"What are you wondering?"

She shook her head. "Nothing."

"Go ahead. Say what's on your mind."

"You mentioned a lot of men. Are there no women?"

"Afraid not. Unless you count my aunts, but they don't live there even though they are around so much that it feels like they do." He didn't want to offer a detailed explanation of why there were no women living at the vineyard. He tried to avoid that subject at all costs. He took it for granted that the DeFiore men were to grow old alone. But that was a subject best left for another day.

"Sounds like you have a big family."

"That's the understatement of the century." Anxious to end this line of conversation, he said, "We should get some sleep. Tomorrow will be here before we know it."

"You're sure you want me to stay here?" She stared directly at him.

Their gazes connected and held. Beyond the beauty of her eyes, there was something more that drew him to her—a vulnerability. In that moment, he longed to ride to her rescue and sweep her into his arms. He'd hold her close and kiss away her worries.

Lizzie glanced away, breaking the special moment.

Was she thinking the same thing as him? Did she feel the pull of attraction, too? Not that he was going to act on his thoughts. It wasn't as though he couldn't keep himself in check. He could and would be a gentleman.

"I'll deal with it. After all, you said this is what my grandfather agreed to. There are a couple of guest rooms down the hallway." He pointed to the right. And then for good measure he added, "And the master suite is in that direction." His hand gestured to the left. "Plenty of room for both of us."

"My luggage hasn't arrived yet. I have nothing to sleep in."

"I can loan you something."

Just as he said that, there was a buzz from the intercom. He went to answer it. In seconds, he returned to her. "Well, you don't have to worry. Your luggage has arrived."

She smiled. "That's great."

A moment of disappointment coursed through him. What in the world was the matter with him? Why should he care one way or the other if she slept in one of his shirts or not? Obviously he was more tired than he'd thought.

CHAPTER FIVE

Lizzie grinned and stretched, like a cat that had spent the afternoon napping in the sunshine. She glanced around the unfamiliar surroundings, noticing the sun's rays creeping past the white sheers over the window. She rubbed her eyes and then fumbled for her cell phone. She was shocked to find that she'd slept away half of the morning. It was going to take her a bit to get her internal alarm clock reset.

Last night, she'd been so tired that she'd barely gotten off a text message to Jules to assure her that she'd arrived safely before sleep claimed her. This was the first time in their lives that they'd been separated for an extended period and Lizzie already missed her foster sister, who was also her best friend. She had promised to call today to fill her in on her trip. But after converting the time, Lizzie realized it was too early in New York to call.

She glanced around, not surprised to find the room done up in black and white. The man may be drop-dead gorgeous but when it came to decorating, he definitely lacked imaginative skills. What this place needed was some warmth—a woman's touch.

She thought back to his comment about her being his first guest here. She found that surprising. For some reason, she imagined someone as sexy and charming as him having a woman on each arm. Perhaps there was more to this man than his smooth talk and devastating smile. What was the real Dante like? Laid-back and flirtatious? Serious and a workaholic?

She paused and listened for any sounds from him. But then again, with an apartment this big, she doubted she'd hear him in the kitchen. She'd be willing to bet that her entire New York apartment could fit in this bedroom. She'd never been in such a spacious home before. Not that she'd have time to get used to it. She was pretty certain that Dante was only mollifying her. Today he would have a plan to get her out of his life and his restaurant.

With that thought in mind, Lizzie sprang out of bed and rushed into the glass block shower enclosure with more water jets than she'd ever imagined were possible. But instead of enjoying the shower, she wondered what Dante's next move would be concerning the agreement.

Almost thirty minutes later, her straight blond hair was smoothed back into the normal ponytail that she wore due to its ease at pinning it up in the kitchen. She slipped on a dark pair of designer jeans. Lizzie didn't recognize the name, but the lady at the secondhand store had assured her that they were the in thing right now.

Lizzie pulled on a white tiny tee with sparkly silver bling on the front in the shape of a smiley face. It was fun, and today she figured she just might need something uplifting. There were decisions to be made.

After she stepped into a pair of black cotton shoes, she soundlessly made her way to the living room, finding it deserted. Where could Dante be? She recalled their conversation last night and she was certain that he'd said the restaurant was closed today.

"Dante?" Nothing. "Dante?" she called out, louder this time.

Suddenly he was standing in the hallway that led to the master suite. "Sorry, I didn't hear you. Have you been up long?"

She shook her head. "I'm afraid that my body is still on New York time."

"I've spoken to my grandfather."

Lizzie's chest tightened. "What did he say?"

Dante paused, making her anxiety even worse. She wanted to yell at him to spit it out. Did Massimo say something that was going to change how this whole scenario played out?

"He didn't say much. I'm getting ready to go see him."

She waited, hoping Dante would extend an invitation. When he didn't, she added, "How far did you say the vineyard is from here?"

He shrugged. "An hour or so out of the city."

She glanced toward the elongated window. "It's a beautiful day for a drive."

He said nothing.

Why wasn't he taking the hint? If she laid it on any thicker, she'd have to invite herself along. She resisted the urge to stamp her feet in frustration. Why wouldn't he give in and offer her a ride? She'd already mentioned how much she enjoyed talking to his grandfather on the phone.

Maybe Dante just wasn't good with hints, no matter how bold they were. Perhaps she should try another approach—a direct one.

"I'd like to meet your grandfather."

Dante shook his head. "That isn't going to happen."

Oh, no. She wasn't giving up that easily. "Why not? When we talked on the phone, he was very excited about my arrival."

"Things have changed since then." Dante walked over and grabbed his keys from the edge of the kitchen counter. "It just wouldn't be a good idea."

"Did you even tell him that I was here?"

Dante's gaze lowered. "In passing."

He was leaving something out but what? "And did you discuss the contract?"

"No. He had a bad night and he was agitated this morning. I didn't think him hearing about what has transpired since your arrival would help things." He cursed under his breath and strode over to the door and grabbed his overnight bag.

He was leaving without her.

Disappointment washed over her. She just couldn't shake her desire to meet the man who reminded her of what she imagined her grandfathers would have been like, if she'd ever met either of her own. But she couldn't tell Dante that. He'd think she was a sentimental dreamer—and she couldn't blame him.

How could she ever explain to someone who grew up in a big, caring family with parents and grandparents about the gaping hole in her heart? She'd forever been on the outside looking in. She knew all too well that families weren't perfect. Her friends in school had dealt with a whole host of family dynamics, but they had a common element—love to bind them together, no matter what. And to have her very own family was what Lizzie had prayed for each night. And at Christmastime it had been the only thing she had ever asked for from Santa.

Instead of a mom and dad and grandparents, she was given Jules—her foster sister. And she loved her with all of her heart. She would do anything for her, including keeping her promise to help Jules reach for her dreams—no matter the price. Because of their dismal finances, Jules had to put off college for a couple of years until Lizzie got her degree. Jules always talked of helping other kids like them. This was Jules's chance to become a social worker and make a difference, but in order to do that she had to get through grad school first.

Massimo had been insistent that her plan would work. He'd been so certain. And she couldn't shake her desire to meet him and thank him for his encouragement. "Take me with you. I promise I won't say or do anything to upset your grandfather."

Dante eyed her up as though attempting to gauge her sincerity. She sent him a pleading look. Under the intensity of his stare, her insides quivered. But she refused to turn away.

"Even though he insists on meeting you, I will leave you behind if I feel I can't trust you."

"So he does want to meet me." This time she did smile.

"Don't go getting all excited. I still haven't made up my mind about taking you with me. You know it's a bit of a ride."

Meaning Dante didn't like the thought of spending yet more time alone with her. To be honest, she couldn't blame him. She'd basically dropped into his life out of nowhere with absolutely no warning. How could she possibly expect him to react any different?

But then again, she had noticed the way he'd looked at her last night. As if she were an ice cream cone on a sweltering hot day and he couldn't wait to lick her up. To be fair, she'd had similar thoughts about him. No one had ever turned her on with just a look.

She halted her thoughts. It wasn't worth it to go down this path. It'd only lead to heartbreak—her heartbreak. In her experience, men only wanted an uncomplicated good time. And she couldn't separate her heart and her mind. It was so much easier to remain detached. If she was smart, she'd turn and leave now. But she couldn't. Not yet.

"You can trust me," she pleaded. "I won't upset Massimo."

"I don't know—"

"If you won't take me to him, then give me his address. I'll find my own way there."

Not that she had any clue how she'd get from point A to point B without a vehicle, but she was certain that Italy had public transportation. That was one of the things she'd discovered when she'd researched coming here. So now Dante wouldn't stand between her and meeting Massimo.

Dante hated being put in this position.

All he wanted to do was protect his grandfather—well, that wasn't quite the whole truth. He didn't relish the car ride with Lizzie. He was certain she'd keep at him, trying to convince him to change his mind about the television spot. His jaw tightened. He had other priorities with the sale of the *ristorante* to negotiate.

Then this morning when he'd phoned his grandfather to verify that he'd agreed to this television segment, his grandfather had come to life at the mention of Lizzie's name. After weeks of Nonno being in a black mood, this was the first time he'd sounded even remotely like himself. Dante made every excuse to get out of taking Lizzie to meet him. His grandfather would have none of it.

Unwilling to disappoint his grandfather, he said, "You can come with me on one stipulation."

Hope glinted in her eyes. "Name it."

"There will be no talking about the contract or the cooking show this weekend."

"But the camera crew will be here Tuesday morning expecting to begin filming before the restaurant opens. What will we do? We haven't even decided how to proceed."

"Let me deal with them." He'd already called his solicitor that morning. Even though it was the weekend, this couldn't wait. He'd pay the exorbitant fees. Whatever it took to find a way out of this mess.

She narrowed her gaze. "You're going to break the contract, aren't you?"

"Why wouldn't I? I never agreed to give up two months of my life."

"But I...I can't repay the money."

"What money?"

She glanced away and moved to the window that looked

out over the street. "They paid me a portion of the fee up front. And it's already been spent. I can't repay them."

That wasn't his problem. But his conscience niggled at him. All in all, Lizzie wasn't bad. In fact, she was smokin' hot. And when she smiled it was as though a thousand-watt lightbulb had been switched on. But when she opened her mouth—well, that was a different story. She knew instinctively which buttons of his to push.

He wanted to think that she was lying to him just to gain his sympathy, but his gut was telling him that she was being truthful. Those unshed tears in her eyes—those were genuine. There had to be a compromise but he didn't know what that would be at this point.

Until he figured out what that was, he had to say something to ease her worry. "I can't promise you this will work out for you. But if you quit worrying while we're away, I give you my word that I'll share what my solicitor uncovers before I make any moves."

She hitched a slender hip and tilted her head to the side. He couldn't help but smile at the way she was eyeing him, trying to decide if she should trust him. He supposed he deserved it. He had just done the same thing to her.

The strained silence stretched on, making him uncomfortable. "Okay, you've made your point. I'll trust you not to pull the *poor pitiful me* card around my grandfather, if you'll trust me not to take any action without consulting you."

Why did he feel as if he'd just struck up a losing deal? For a man used to getting his way, this was a very unsettling feeling.

CHAPTER SIX

THIS WOULD IMPRESS HER.

Dante maneuvered his low-slung, freshly waxed, candy-apple-red sports car around the street corner and slowed to a crawl as he approached the front of the *ristorante*. Lizzie stood on the sidewalk with an overnight bag slung over her shoulder and her face lifted toward the sun. She didn't appear to notice him. The sun's rays gave her golden mane a shimmery glow. He wondered if she had any clue how her beauty commanded attention. Something told him she didn't. There was an unassuming air about her.

Without taking time to consider his actions, he tramped the brakes and reached for his smartphone to snap her picture. It wasn't until he returned it to the dash that he realized how foolish he was acting. Like some schoolkid with a crush on the most popular girl in school.

Back then he'd been so unsure of himself—not knowing how to act smooth around the girls. That all changed after he moved to Rome. Away from his father and brother, he'd grown more confident—more at ease with the ladies.

His older brother, though, always had a way with the women...but Stefano had eyes for only one girl, even back in school. They'd been childhood sweethearts until it came to a devastating end. The jarring memory brought Dante up short.

He eased the car forward and parked next to Lizzie.

He jumped out and offered to take her bag, but she didn't release her hold. In fact, her grip tightened on the straps. What in the world?

"I just want to put it in the boot. There's no room inside the car. As you can see, it's rather compact."

She cast him a hesitant look before handing over the bag. He opened the door for her. Once she was seated, he stowed her bag with his. He was surprised how light she packed. He'd never met a woman who didn't need everything including the kitchen sink just to go away for the night. Lizzie was different in so many ways.

And now it was his chance to impress her with his pride and joy. Anytime he wanted to make a surefire impression on a woman, he pulled out Red. He'd bestowed the name upon the luxury sports car, not just because of its color but because the name implied an attitude, a fieriness, and that was how he felt when he was in the driver's seat.

"Ready?" He glanced at her as she perched a pair of dark sunglasses on her face, hiding her expressive eyes.

"Yes. I'm surprised you'd choose to drive."

"Why wouldn't I drive?" He revved the engine just because he could, and he loved how the motor roared with power.

Who complained about riding in a fine machine like this one? He'd dreamed about a powerful car like this all of his life, but his father made him wait—made him earn it on his own without dipping into his trust fund. At the time Dante had resented his father for standing in his way. Now Dante found himself grateful for the challenge. He'd learned an important lesson—he could accomplish whatever he set his mind to. Even his father had been impressed with the car, not that he'd said much, but Dante had seen it in his eyes the first time he'd driven up to the villa.

Lizzie adjusted her seat belt. "I thought I read somewhere that people utilize public transportation here."

He glanced at her as he slowed for a stop sign. Was she

serious? She'd prefer the train to his car? Impossible. "I thought the car would be more convenient. We can come and go as we need."

"Oh. Right. And do you always run stop signs?"

"What?"

"There was a stop sign back there. Didn't you see it?"

"Of course I did. Didn't you notice how I slowed down and checked that there was no cross traffic?"

"But you didn't stop."

His jaw tightened as he adjusted his grip on the steering wheel. "Are you always such a stickler for rules?"

"Yes. Is that a problem?"

"It depends."

Silence settled over them as Dante navigated them out of the city. Every now and then he sneaked a glance at Lizzie. She kept her face turned to the side. The tires clicked over the brick roadway as Rome passed by the window. The cars, the buildings and the people. He'd never been to New York City and he couldn't help but wonder if it was as beautiful as Rome. The lush green trees planted along stretches of roadway softened the view of block-and-mortar buildings. Thankfully it was Sunday, so the roadway wasn't congested with standstill traffic.

They quickly exited the city. Now was his chance to find out a little bit more about her before she met his grandfather. His gut told him there was a lot she was holding back. It was his duty to make sure there weren't any unpleasant surprises that might upset his grandfather. Dante assured himself that his interest was legitimate. It had absolutely nothing to do with unraveling the story behind the sad look in her eyes when she thought no one was watching her.

"Where in New York do you come from?"

Out of the corner of his eye he noticed how her head swung around quickly. "The Bronx. Why?"

"Just curious. I figured if we're going to be spending

some time together, we might as well get to know a little about each other."

There was a poignant moment of silence as though she were deciding if this was a good idea or not. "And were you raised at this vineyard we're going to visit?"

Fair was fair. "Yes, I was. It's been in my family for generations. But it has grown over the years. And now our vino is a household name."

"That's an impressive legacy. So how did you end up in Rome helping your grandfather run a restaurant?"

How in the world did this conversation get totally turned around? They were supposed to be talking about her—not him. "It's a long story. But I really enjoyed the time I spent working with my grandfather. I'll never forget my time at Ristorante Massimo."

"You make it sound like you're leaving."

Dante's fingers tightened on the steering wheel. He had to be more careful with what he said. He could feel her puzzled gaze as she waited for him to affirm or deny her suspicions. That he couldn't do. He hadn't even told his family yet that he was planning to sell the place. There was always one excuse or another to put off the announcement.

But now that the negotiations were winding down, he was out of time. He needed to get his grandfather's blessing to include the family's recipes as part of the sale. Dante's gut tightened.

And the other reason he hesitated to bring it up was that he knew his father would use it as one more thing against him. His father always blamed him for Dante's mother's death during childbirth. Though logically Dante knew he wasn't responsible, he still felt the guilt of playing a part in his father's unhappiness. The man he'd known as a child wore a permanent scowl and he couldn't recall ever seeing his father smile. Not once.

When they communicated it was only because Dante

hadn't done a chore or hadn't done it "correctly." Who could blame him for moving away to the city?

But over the years, his father seemed to have changed—mellowed. He wasn't so critical of Dante. But was it enough to rebuild their relationship?

"Dante, are you planning to leave the restaurant? Is that why you're hesitant to help me?"

What was it about this woman that she could read him so well? Too well. "Why would you say that?"

Before she could respond, the strums of music filled the car. He hadn't turned on the stereo and that certainly wasn't his phone's ringtone.

"Oh, no!" Lizzie went diving for her oversize black purse that was on the floor beneath the dash.

"Something wrong?"

"I told my sister to only call me if there was an emergency." She scrambled through her purse. With the phone pressed to her ear, she sounded breathless when she spoke. "Jules, what's the matter?"

Dante glanced at Lizzie, noticing how the color had drained from her face. He wasn't the sort to eavesdrop, but it wasn't as if he could go anywhere. Besides, if she was anything like his younger cousins, it was most likely nothing more than a romantic crisis or a hair emergency—at least he hoped so for Lizzie's sake.

Most of the time when he was out in public, he grew frustrated with people who had their phones turned up so loud that you could hear both sides of the conversation. Lizzie obviously felt the same way as him, as hers was turned down so low that he couldn't hear the caller's voice. Lizzie wasn't much help as she only uttered things like: "Okay."

"Yes."

"Mmm...hmm..."

When her hand started waving around as she talked, Dante didn't know if he should pull over or keep driving.

"He can't do that!"

Who couldn't do what? Was it a boyfriend? Had he done something to her sister? The fact that Lizzie might have a man waiting for her in New York gave him an uneasy sensation.

At last, Lizzie disconnected the call and sank back against the leather upholstery. He wasn't sure what to say because he didn't have a clue what the problem might be. That, and he wasn't very good with upset women. He didn't have much experience in that department as he preferred to keep things light and casual.

Unable to stand the suspense, he asked, "Problems with your boyfriend?"

"Not a chance. I don't have one."

He breathed a little easier. "But I take it there's an emergency?"

"That depends on if you call getting tossed out of your apartment a problem."

"That serious, huh?"

"That man is so greedy, he'd sell his own mother if it'd make him an easy dollar."

"Who's greedy?"

"The landlord. He says he's converting the building into condos."

Dante was truly sorry for Lizzie's plight. He couldn't imagine what it'd be like to get kicked out of your home. Even though he and his father had a tenuous relationship, leaving the vineyard had been completely Dante's idea.

He pulled the car off the road. "Do I need to turn the car around?"

She glanced at him, her brows scrunched up in puzzlement. "Why would you do that?"

"So that you can catch a flight back to New York."

"That's not necessary."

Not necessary. If he was getting evicted, he'd be hightailing it home to find a new place to live. He must be missing something. But what?

"Don't you want to go back and figure out where you're going to live? I can't imagine in such a populated city that it'll be easy to find another place to your liking."

She clucked her tongue. "Are you trying to get rid of me?"

"What?" His tone filled with indignation, but a sliver of guilt sliced through him. "I'm just concerned."

"Well, you don't have to be concerned because the landlord gave us plenty of notice."

"He did?" Lizzie's gaze narrowed on him as he stammered to correct himself. "I...I mean, that's great. Are you sure you'll have time to find another place?"

"My, aren't you worried about my welfare. What could have brought on this bit of concern? Wait, could it be that you thought this might be your out with the contract?"

"No." The word came out far too fast. He wished he were anywhere but in this much-too-small car. There was nowhere to go. No way to avoid her expectant look. "Okay, it might have crossed my mind. But I still wouldn't wish someone to get kicked out of their home just to save me grief."

She laughed.

The sound grated on his nerves. "What's so funny?"

"The guilty look on your face. You're cute. Like a little boy caught with his hand in the proverbial cookie jar."

Great. Now he'd just been reduced to the level of a cute little kid. Talk about taking direct aim at a guy's ego. He eased the car back onto the road. If he'd ever entertained striking up a more personal relationship with Lizzie, it just came to a screeching halt right there. How did one make a comeback from being "cute"?

"So you aren't mad at me now?" He chanced a quick glance her way as she shook her head.

"I can't blame you for wanting an easy solution to our

problem. And after watching how much you worry about your grandfather, I realized that you aren't the sort to revel in others' misfortune."

Wow, she'd read all of that into him not wanting her to drag his grandfather into the middle of their situation? He was truly impressed. But that still didn't erase the *cute little boy* comment. His pride still stung.

After a few moments of silence passed, he turned to the right onto a private lane. "We're here. Are you up for this?"

CHAPTER SEVEN

She was most definitely ready for this adventure.

Lizzie gazed out the car window at the rolling green hills and lines of grapevines. This place was a beauty to behold. Did a more picturesque place exist? She didn't think so.

Of course, it didn't hurt that she was in the most amazing sports car, being escorted by the sexiest man on the planet. But she refused to let Dante know how truly captivated she was by him. She couldn't let him have any more leverage. They still had a contract to iron out.

And whereas he appeared to have plenty of money to hire his own legal dream team, she didn't have two pennies to rub together. She had to play her cards carefully, and by letting him know that she was vulnerable to his gorgeous smile and drawn in by his mesmerizing gaze, she would have lost before she even started.

They pulled to a stop in front of a spacious villa situated atop a hill overlooking the sprawling vineyard and olive grove. The home's lemon-yellow exterior was offset by a red tile roof and pale blue shutters lining the windows and doors. The three-story structure gave off a cheerful appeal that called to Lizzie.

Her gaze came to rest on a sweeping veranda with blue-and-white lawn furniture, which added an inviting quality. What a perfect place to kick back while enjoying a gentle breeze over her sun-warmed skin and sipping an icy lemonade.

"This is where you live?"

Dante cut the engine. "This is where my family lives."

"It's so big."

"It has to be to accommodate so many generations. It seems like every generation expands or adds something."

She especially liked the private balconies. She could easily imagine having her morning coffee there while Dante read the newspaper. "I couldn't even imagine what it would be like to call this my home."

"A little smothering."

"Smothering? You can't be serious." She turned, taking in the endless fields.

He shrugged. "When you have so many people keeping an eye on you constantly, it can be."

"But there's just your grandfather, father and brother, isn't it?"

"You're forgetting about all of my aunts, uncles and cousins. They stop over daily. There's never a lack of relatives. In fact, the dinner table seats twelve and never has an empty chair. They disapproved of my father not remarrying. So they made a point of ensuring my brother and I had a woman's influence."

"And did it work?"

"What? Oh, you mean the woman's-influence thing. I guess it helped. I just know that it was annoying always tripping over family members."

She frowned at him. "You should be grateful that they cared enough!"

His eyes grew round at her agitated tone. "I...I am."

She didn't believe him.

She couldn't even imagine how wonderful it would be to have so much family. He took it all for granted, not having sense enough to count his blessings. She'd have done anything to have a big, loving family.

"Not everyone is as lucky as you." With that, she got

out of the car, no longer wanting to hear how hard Dante had it putting up with his relatives.

He was the luckiest person she knew. He wasn't much older than herself and he already owned his very own restaurant—a successful one at that. Not to mention his jaw-dropping apartment. And she couldn't forget his flashy sports car. And on top of all that, he had a family that cared about him. Stacked up against her life, she was left lacking. She was up to her eyeballs in debt. And without the money from this television spot, she didn't know how she'd survive.

But how did she explain any of that to him? How would he ever understand when he couldn't even appreciate what he had? She'd met people like him before—specifically a guy in college. He was an only child—and spoiled. He thought he understood what hardship was when he had to buy a used car to replace the brand-new one his parents had bought him—a car he'd wrecked while out partying with the guys. She stifled the groan of frustration that rose in her throat. Hardship was choosing between paying the rent or buying groceries.

A gentle breeze brushed over her cheeks and whipped her hair into her face. She tucked the loose strands behind her ear. The air felt good. It eased her tense muscles, sweeping up her frustration and carrying it away.

In this particular case, she'd overreacted. Big-time. She had better keep a firmer grip on her emotions or soon Dante would learn about her past. She didn't want him to look down on her like she was less than everyone else since her mother hadn't loved her enough to straighten out her life and her father was someone without a name—a face. The breath caught in her throat.

She hated that being around Dante was bringing all of these old feelings of inadequacy to the surface. She'd buried them long ago. Coming here was a mistake. Nursing her dream of finding out what it would be like to have a grandfather—a family—was opening Pandora's box and her past was spilling out.

What had set her off?

Dante darted out of the car, but then froze. Lizzie's back was to him. Her shoulders were rigid. Her head was held high. He didn't want to do battle with her. Especially not here, where his family could happen upon them at any moment.

But more than that, he didn't have a clue what he'd done wrong. Did she have that strong an opinion about families? And if so, why?

His questions about her only multiplied. And as much as he'd set out to learn more about his flatmate on the ride here, he truly believed he had gained more questions than answers. Sure, he'd learned that she appeared to be very close with her sister and that she was about to get evicted. Oh, and she was a stickler for following the rules—especially the rules of the road. But there was so much more she was holding back. Things he wanted to know. But that would have to wait.

He could only hope that he could smooth things over with her before his father descended upon them. He didn't need her giving his family the impression that he didn't know how to treat a lady. His father already held enough things against him without adding to the list.

He rounded the car and stopped in front of her. "Hey, I don't know what I said back there, but I'm sorry. You must miss your family."

Her head lowered and her shoulders drooped. "It's me that should apologize. I guess it was just hearing Jules's voice made me realize it's going to be a long time before I will see her again. We've never been apart for an extended period like this."

So that was it. She was homesick. That was totally understandable. Maybe his family could help fill that gap. They certainly were a chatty, friendly bunch—even if they could be a bit overbearing at times.

"Why don't we go inside? I'm sure my father and brother are out in the fields. They keep a close eye on the vines and soil. But my grandfather will be around. Not to mention an aunt or two."

She smiled. "Thanks for including me. I'm really excited to meet your family."

"They're looking forward to meeting you, too."

"They know I'm coming?" When he nodded, she said, "But you made it sound like you'd planned to come without me."

"I had, but my grandfather had other ideas. He insisted I bring you to meet him. He told the family while I was on the phone."

"Would you have really left me behind if I hadn't promised to keep quiet about the contract?"

Dante shrugged. "I guess we'll never know. Just remember our agreement. Don't say or do anything to upset my grandfather."

Her eyes flared with indignation. But before she could say a word, there were footsteps on the gravel.

"Dante, who's your guest?"

He didn't even have to turn around to recognize his older brother's voice. Stefano was the eldest. The son who did no wrong. He'd stayed on at the villa and helped their father run the vineyard as was expected of the DeFiore men. But what no one took into consideration was that Stefano always got along with their father. He wasn't the one their father held responsible for their mother's death.

Dante turned on his heels. "Stefano, this is Lizzie."

Stefano stepped up, and when she extended her hand, he accepted it and kissed the back of it. Dante's blood pressure spiked. What was his brother doing? Wasn't he the forlorn widower?

Not that Dante wished for his brother to be miserable the rest of his life. In fact, he wished that Stefano would be able to move past the nightmare and get on with his life, but Stefano seemed certain that he would remain a bachelor...which seemed to be the destiny of the DeFiore men.

Dante had learned much from his family, especially to keep his guard up around women. He had zero intention of getting caught up in the tangled web of love. It only led to pain. Something he could live without.

While Stefano made idle chitchat with Lizzie, Dante noticed how her face lit up. He swallowed down his agitation. "Is Nonno in the house?"

Stefano turned to him. His whole demeanor changed into something more stoic—more like the brother he knew. "Of course. Where else would you expect him to be?"

Dante rolled his eyes and started for the house. When he realized that Lizzie had remained behind with his brother, he turned and signaled for her to follow him. She smiled at Stefano—a great big, ear-to-ear, genuine smile that lit up the world like a starburst. Dante's jaw tightened.

Why couldn't she be that happy around him? Why did she have to act so reserved—so on guard? After all, he was a nice guy, too. Or so he'd been told by some lady friends. Surely he hadn't lost his touch with the women. Maybe he'd have to try a little harder.

When Lizzie joined him, he said, "My grandfather is probably getting impatient. We should go see him."

Lizzie kept her smile in place and he couldn't help but wonder if it was part of their agreement to keep the mood light and happy. Or perhaps it was lingering happiness from meeting his older brother—Mr. Tall, Dark and Persuasive.

Not that it mattered if Lizzie had a thing for Stefano. It wasn't as if Dante was interested in the woman who was threatening the deal he'd been working for weeks to finalize. And it rankled him that he now felt some sort of responsibility toward Lizzie. Not only did he have to take into consideration what was best for the business, but also he felt compelled to take into account how it impacted her.

Dante stepped into the sunroom. "Nonno."

His grandfather's silver head lifted from reading a newspaper. He removed his reading glasses, focused on Dante and then his gaze moved to Lizzie. A lopsided smile pulled at his lips. Dante inwardly sighed at the effect Lizzie had over the men in his family. They stared at her as if she were a movie star. Well...she was pretty enough. Still, they didn't have to act as though they'd never seen a beautiful female before. Then again, it had been a very long time since a woman that wasn't a relative had visited the DeFiore villa. Okay, so maybe they had a reason to sit up and take notice. He just wished they didn't make it so noticeable.

"Come here." Nonno's deep voice was a bit slurred from the stroke.

His grandfather's gaze clung to Lizzie. She moved forward without hesitation and came to a stop in front of his chair. Then something happened that totally surprised Dante. She bent over and hugged his grandfather. It was as though they'd known each other forever. How did that happen?

The two of them chatted while Dante sat on the couch. He really wasn't needed as neither of them even noticed that he was in the room. And he could plainly see that Lizzie's presence had an uplifting effect on his grandfather. In fact, this was the happiest he'd seen his grandfather since he'd been forced into retirement.

"So that's why you changed your mind about visiting this weekend?" Dante's father entered the room and came to a stop by the couch before nodding in Lizzie's direction.

Dante instinctively followed his father's gaze back to the woman who'd thrown his life into turmoil. "She knows Nonno. He asked me to bring her here."

His father nodded. "If I had that sort of distraction, I might stay in the city, too. After all, it's a lot easier to have a good time with a beautiful woman than it is to do the hard work needed to keep the family vineyard running."

Dante's jaw ratcheted tight. It didn't matter what he said; it never seemed to be the right thing where his father was concerned. Some things never changed.

"At least you have good taste." That was the closest his father had ever come to giving him a compliment.

"Lizzie and I are working together, nothing more."

His father sent him a *you are crazy* look. Dante wasn't going to argue with the man—it wouldn't change things. He never lived up to his father's expectations—not like his brother, Stefano, always did. Just once, he'd like his father to clap him on the back and tell him he'd done something right—something good.

Dante sat rigidly on the couch. Not even his father's jabs were enough to make him leave the room. He assured himself that it was just to keep an eye on what Lizzie said to his grandfather. Because there couldn't be any other reason. Unlike the rest of his family, he was immune to her charms.

Sure, he knew how to enjoy a woman's company. Her smiles. Her laugh. Her touch. But that was as far as it went. He refused to let himself become vulnerable. He'd seen too much pain in his life. It wouldn't happen to him. The *L* word wasn't worth the staggering risks.

CHAPTER EIGHT

"This place is amazing."

Lizzie didn't bother to hide her enthusiasm as she glanced around the spacious living room with a high ceiling and two sets of double doors that let the afternoon sun stream in. She'd trade her Bronx apartment in a heartbeat for this peaceful retreat.

"I love it here." She spoke the words to no one in particular. "Very different from city life."

"It is different." Massimo's words took her full attention between the accent and the slight slur from his stroke. "I'm glad you're here. Is my grandson treating you well?"

Her thoughts flashed back to their first meeting. But she wasn't so sure that Massimo would find it amusing that Dante mistook her presence at the restaurant and put her to work as a hostess. She opted to save that story for a later date.

She glanced across to where Dante was pretending to read a cooking magazine. "Yes. He...he's been a gentleman."

Massimo gave her a quizzical look. "My grandson is a good man. He knows a lot. Make him teach you."

His choice of words struck her as a bit odd. Either the man was eager to shorten his sentences or he sensed that things between her and Dante weren't going smoothly.

"I will. I just wish you could be there. I was really looking forward to working next to such a legend."

Massimo attempted to smile but the one side of his

mouth would not cooperate. Her heart pinched. She had no idea how frustrating it must be for your body not to cooperate. But beyond that, the man's face spoke of exhaustion. Dante had warned her not to overtax him. And she wouldn't do anything to harm Massimo. The place in her heart for him had only grown exponentially since meeting him in person.

"I'll let you get some rest." Lizzie went to stand when Massimo reached for her hand.

His grip was strong but not painful. But it was the look in his eyes that dug at her heart. "Promise me you won't give up. Promise me you'll see through our deal."

"But—" She'd almost uttered the fact that Dante was opposed to the whole idea. "I'll do my best." It was all she could offer the man.

"My grandson needs someone like you."

The following morning Lizzie hit the ground running.

She wasn't about to waste a minute of her time at the villa. The big, brilliant ball of orange was still low in the distant horizon. She stood just outside the kitchen door with a cup of steamy black coffee in hand.

She wandered across to an old wooden fence and gazed out at the endless acres of grapes. The golden rays gave the rows and rows of vines a beauty all of their own. She'd never been someplace so wide open. She reveled in the peacefulness that surrounded her. And that was something she truly found amazing. Normally her nights were full of restless dreams and her days full of running here and there, doing this and that. But here she could take a moment to breathe—just to be.

Her thoughts trailed back to her unusual conversation with Massimo. Was the man some sort of matchmaker? But why? He hardly knew her. How would he know if she would be good for Dante? And why would Dante need her?

The questions followed one after the other. The most

frustrating part was that she didn't have an answer for any of them. Dante was even more of a mystery to her now than he was before.

She'd noticed from the moment they'd arrived here that everything wasn't so perfect in Dante's life. Though she hadn't been able to hear the conversation between father and son, she'd clearly seen the dark look that had come over Dante's handsome face while talking with his father. There was a definite distance between him and his family. Was that what Massimo thought she could help Dante with? But how? She was here for only a matter of weeks, certainly not long enough to change someone's life. And what did she know about the inner workings of families?

Still, she couldn't get her mind to stop replaying the events from the prior evening. When his family grew boisterous talking of the vineyard, she noticed how Dante had become withdrawn as if he didn't feel as though he fit in—or was it that he didn't want to fit in? Either way, she couldn't imagine Dante willingly walking away from such an amazing place.

There had to be something more to his story—something he wasn't willing to share. But what could drive him from the peacefulness of the countryside and the bosom of his family to the city? Unless... Was it possible? Her mind raced. Could he have a passion for cooking that rivaled hers? Was it possible that they at last had something in common?

The thunk of the kitchen door swinging shut startled her. She spun around and there stood the man who'd filled her every thought since arriving here. The heat crept up her neck and settled in her cheeks. She realized that she was being silly. It wasn't as if he could read her mind.

Their gazes met and held. His stare was deep and probing. Unease inched up her spine. There was no way that he could know that just moments ago, she'd been daydreaming about his grandfather's suggestion that she and Dante might be a perfect fit.

"I didn't know if you'd be up yet." His voice was deep and gravelly.

"I set my phone alarm. I didn't want to miss the sunrise."

"And was it worth the effort?"

She nodded vigorously. "Definitely. I'm in love." When his eyes widened in surprise, she added, "With the villa and the vineyard. With all of it."

"I'm glad you like it here."

"I was considering going for a walk."

"Would you care for some company?"

Her gaze jerked back around to his to see if he was serious. "You really want to escort me around? I mean, it isn't like I'll be running into any of your family. You don't have to babysit me."

"I didn't offer so I could play babysitter. I thought maybe you'd want some company, but obviously I was wrong." He turned back to the house.

"Wait." He paused, but he didn't turn around. She swallowed down a chunk of pride. "I would like your company."

He turned to her but his lips were pressed together in a firm line. He crossed his arms and looked at her expectantly. He had a right to expect more. She'd been snippy and he hadn't deserved it. But it wasn't easy for her. For some reason, she had the hardest time dealing with him. His mere presence put her on edge. And he always scattered her thoughts with his good looks and charming smile.

"Okay, I'm sorry. Is that what you want to hear?"

"Yes, it is." He stepped up to her. "Shall we go?"

She glanced down at the almost empty cup. "I need to put this in the house."

He took it from her, jogged back to the kitchen and returned in no time. He extended his arm like a total gentleman, which sent her heart tumbling in her chest. Without hesitation, she slipped her hand into the crook of his arm.

When her fingers tightened around his biceps, she noticed his rock-hard strength.

This wasn't right. She had no business letting her guard down around him. Nothing good would come of it. She considered pulling away, but part of her refused to let go. With a quick glance at his relaxed features, she realized she was making too much of the situation.

He led her away from the house and down a dirt path. "You made quite an impression on my family."

"Is that a good thing?"

"Most definitely. They're all quite taken with you. It was the most excitement they've had around here in quite a while."

Normally she kept up her walls and held everyone at bay, but being here, being around Massimo, she'd let down her defenses a bit. "I noticed you were quiet last night. Was there something wrong?"

"No, not at all. And you were amazing, especially with Nonno. He's been really down in the dumps, but you cheered him up. So I owe you a big thank-you."

She noticed how he didn't explain his quietness. She wondered if he was always so reserved around his family. Granted, she didn't understand how traditional families worked as her life had consisted of foster homes where kids came and went and there wasn't that deep, abiding love that came naturally. But she had Jules and they were as close as any blood relatives.

"Your brother, he's older than you, isn't he?" She wanted to get Dante to open up about his family. She couldn't help it. She was curious.

"Yes. He's a couple of years older."

Well, that certainly didn't strike up the hoped-for conversation. "Are you two very close?"

Dante slanted a gaze her way but she pretended not to notice. "I don't know. We're brothers."

She knew none of this was any of her business but everything about Dante intrigued her. He was like an artichoke and she'd barely begun to pull at the tough outer layer. There was so much to learn before she got to the tender center that he protected from everyone.

"They care a lot about you."

He stopped and pulled her around to look at him. "Why all of this curiosity about my family? What's going on in that beautiful mind of yours?"

Did he just say she was beautiful? Her gaze met his and her breath became shallow. No, he'd said her mind was beautiful. But was that the same thing as saying she was beautiful?

"I was just making small talk." She tried to act innocent. "Why do I have to have ulterior motives?"

"I didn't say you did. But sometimes you make me wonder." He peered into her eyes and for a moment she wondered if he could read her thoughts.

Heat filled her cheeks and she glanced away. "Wonder about what?"

"You. There's more to you than meets the eye. Something tells me that you have an interesting past."

She couldn't hold back a laugh. "You make me sound very mysterious. Like Mata Hari or something." She leaned closer to him and whispered in his ear. "I'm here to find out your secrets."

He grabbed her upper arms and moved her back, allowing her the opportunity to see the worry lines ingrained on his face. "What secrets?"

His hard, sharp tone startled her. "Your secrets in the kitchen, of course. What else did you think I meant?"

His frown eased. "You're having far too much fun at my expense."

So the man was keeping secrets. From her? Or from the whole world? She didn't think it was possible but she was even more intrigued by him.

She gazed into his bottomless brown eyes. "You need

to let your hair down and have some fun. It won't hurt. I promise."

"Is that what all of the smiling and laughing was about last night? Or are you trying to sway my family over to your side so they'll pressure me into agreeing to follow through with the contract?"

She pulled back her shoulders. She knew she shouldn't but she just couldn't help herself. His gaze dipped as her fingers once again made an X over her chest. "I promised not to do that."

The vein in his neck pulsated and when his eyes met hers again, there was a need, a passion in his gaze. Her line of vision dipped to his lips.

"You do know that you're driving me crazy, don't you?"

"Who, me?" This was the most fun she'd ever had. She'd never flirted with a guy before. Sure, they'd flirted with her but she never felt the desire to return the flirtations.

Until now.

His hands encircled her waist. "Yes, you. Do you have any idea what I'd like to do to you right now?"

A few scintillating thoughts danced and teased her mind. She placed her hands on his chest and felt the pounding of his heart. She was certain that hers could easily keep time with his. It was pumping so fast that it felt as if she'd just finished a long run on a hot, muggy day. In that moment she was overcome by the urge to find out if his kiss was as moving in real life as it had been in her dreams last night.

"You know, we really shouldn't do this." His voice was carried like a whisper in the breeze.

"When have you ever done what was expected of you?"

"Not very often." His gaze bored deep into her, making her stomach quiver with need.

"Then why start now? I won't tell, if you won't."

That was all it took. His head dipped and then his lips were there. He stopped just a breath away from hers. She could practically feel the turbulent vibes coming off him.

It was as though he was fighting an inner battle between what was right and what he wanted. She needed to put him out of his misery—out of her misery.

Acting on total instinct and desire, she leaned up on her tiptoes and pressed her mouth to his. His lips were smooth and warm. He didn't move. He wanted it. She knew that as well as she knew that the sun would set that evening. Perhaps he needed just a touch more enticement.

She let her body lean into his as her hands slipped up over his broad shoulders. Her fingertips raked through his dark hair as her lips gently moved over his. And then she heard a hungry moan swell in his throat as he pulled her snug against him.

Perhaps it was the knowledge that this kiss should be forbidden that made it the most enticing kiss she'd ever experienced. Then again, it could be that she was lonely and missing her sister, and being in Dante's arms made her feel connected to someone. Or maybe it was simply the fact that he was the dreamiest hunk she'd ever laid her eyes on, and she just wanted to see what she'd be missing by holding herself back.

He stroked and prodded, sending her heart pounding against her ribs with pure desire. His hard planes fit perfectly against her soft curves. And for the moment, she felt like the most beautiful—most desired—woman in the world.

Dante moved, placing his hands on each side of her face. When he pulled his lips from hers, she felt bereft. She wanted more. Needed more.

He rested his forehead against hers. His breathing was deep and uneven. He'd been just as caught up in the moment as she'd been, so why had he stopped? What had happened?

His thumb gently stroked her cheek. "Lizzie, we can't do this. You know that it's wrong."

"But it felt so right."

She couldn't help it. She wasn't ready for the harsh light of reality. She lived every single day with the sharp edges of reality slicing into her dreams. Just once, she wanted to know what it was like not to have to worry about meeting the monthly bills. She just wanted this one blissful memory.

"Lizzie, this can't happen. You and I…it's impossible."

His words pricked her bubble of happiness. Once again she was being rejected. And the worst part was he was right. And that thought made the backs of her eyes sting.

When was it going to be her turn for just a little bit of happiness without the rug being pulled out from under her? This trip to Rome should be the trip of a lifetime, but now the entire arrangement was in jeopardy and she had no job to return to.

She blinked repeatedly, keeping the moisture in her eyes in check. If she was good at one thing in life, it was being a trooper. When life dropped lemons on her, she whipped up a lemon meringue pie with the fluffiest, tallest peaks. She could do it again.

She pulled back until her spine was straight and his hands fell away. "You're right. I don't know what I was thinking." Her voice wobbled. She swallowed down the lump of emotion. "It won't happen again."

Without meeting his gaze, she moved past him and started for the villa. The tip of her tongue ran over her lower lip, where she found the slightest minty taste of toothpaste he'd left behind. She stifled a frustrated moan, knowing that he was only a few steps behind her.

CHAPTER NINE

HE'D TOTALLY BLOWN IT.

Dante stowed their bags in the car's boot and then glanced back at the villa. Lizzie smiled at his grandfather before hugging him goodbye. A stab of jealousy tore into Dante. She'd barely spoken to him after they'd kissed, and even then, it'd only been one-word answers. Why in the world had he let his hormones do the thinking for him?

He had absolutely no desire to toy with her feelings. Hurting Lizzie was the last thing in the world he wanted to do. And though she appeared to have it all together, he knew that she had a vulnerable side, too. He'd witnessed the hurt that had flashed in her eyes when she realized that he didn't trust her with his grandfather. She wanted him to think she was tough, but he knew lurking beneath the beautiful surface lay a vulnerable woman—a woman that he was coming to like a bit more than he should.

When she at last joined him in the car, she stared straight ahead. The unease between them was palpable. Dante didn't like it one bit, but he had no one to blame but himself. There was no way he could go back in time and undo the kiss. And if he could, he wasn't so sure he would. Their kiss had been something special—something he'd never experienced before.

He cut his thoughts off short. He realized that it was thoughts like this that had gotten him into trouble in the first place. But he couldn't ignore the fact that this silent treatment was doing him in.

"Are you ever going to speak to me again?" He struggled to keep the frustration out of his voice.

"Yes."

More of the one-syllable answers. "Did you enjoy your visit to the vineyard?"

"Yes."

"Enough with the yeses and nos." His hands tightened on the steering wheel, trying to get a grip on his rising frustration. Worst of all was the fact he had no clue how to fix things between them. And whether it was wise or not, he wanted Lizzie to like him. "My grandfather seemed quite taken with you. In fact, the whole family did."

Nothing.

She crossed her arms and huffed. What did that mean? Was she about to let him have it? His muscles tensed as he waited for a tongue-lashing. Not that he could blame her. He deserved it, but it wouldn't make it any less uncomfortable.

Her voice was soft and he strained to hear her. "How do you do it?"

Well, it was more than one syllable, but he didn't have a clue what she meant. And he was hesitant to ask, but what choice did he have?

"How do I do what?" The breath caught in his throat as he waited for what came next.

"How do you drive away from that little piece of heaven at the end of each weekend and return to the city?"

This wasn't the direction he'd expected the conversation to take. His family wasn't a subject he talked about beyond the generalities. *How's your father? Is your brother still working at the vineyard? Did they have a good harvest?* But no one ever probed into his choice to move away—to distance himself from his family.

"I prefer Rome." It wasn't necessarily a lie.

"Don't get me wrong. I love the city life. But I was born and bred in a city that never sleeps. I think it's in my bones to appreciate the chatter of voices and the hum of vehicles. But you, you were raised in the peace and tranquillity."

"It isn't the perfect slice of heaven like you're thinking." He tried not to think about his childhood. He didn't want to remember.

"What wasn't perfect about it?"

He glanced her way, giving her a warning stare to leave the subject alone.

"Hey, you're the one who wanted me to talk. I'm talking. Now it's your turn."

He could see that she wasn't going to leave this subject alone. Not unless he let her know that she was stepping on a very tender subject.

"Life at the DeFiore Vineyard wasn't idyllic when I was a kid. Far from it."

"Why?"

She really was going to push this. And for some unknown reason, he wanted to make her understand his side. "I'm the reason my mother died."

"What?" She swung around in her seat, fighting with the seat belt so that she was able to look directly at him. "But I don't understand. How?"

"She died after she gave birth to me."

"Oh. How horrible." There was an awkward pause. "But it wasn't your fault."

"No, not directly. But my father blamed me. He told me that I took away the best part of his life."

"He didn't mean it. That...those words, they were part of his grief."

Dante shoved his fingers through his hair. "He meant it. I can't help but feel that I bring sadness and misery to those closest to me—"

"Nonsense. Listen, I'm so sorry for your loss. I know

how tough that can be, but you're not to blame for her death or how your father handled his grief. We all handle the death of family members differently."

That caught his attention. A chance to turn the tables away from himself and back to her. "Have you lost a parent?"

Silence enveloped the car. Only the hum of the engine and the tires rolling over the blacktop could be heard. Lizzie turned away to stare out the side window as Dante drove on, waiting and wondering.

"Lizzie, you can talk to me. Whatever you say won't go any further."

He took his focus off the road for just a moment to glance her way. She cast him a hesitant look. He had a feeling she had something important to say—something she didn't normally share. He really hoped she'd let down her guard and let him in. He wanted so badly to understand more about her.

"My mother died." Her voice was so soft.

"I'm sorry. I guess we've both had some hard knocks in life."

"Yes, but at least you have a loving family. And you can always go home when you want to..." It seemed as though she wanted to say more but stopped.

This conversation was much deeper—much more serious than he'd ever expected. He wanted to press for more information, but he sensed now wasn't the time. Spotting a small village up ahead with a trattoria, he slowed down.

"You know, we left without eating. Would you care for a bite of food? And they have the best *caffè* around. I noticed that you have quite a fondness for cappuccino."

"I do. And I'd love to get some."

He eased off the road and maneuvered the car into the lot. Before he got out, he knew there was something more he had to say. "I'm sorry about what happened back at the vineyard. The kiss was a mistake. I didn't mean to cross the line. The last thing I want to do is hurt you."

She turned to him and smiled, but the gesture never quite reached her eyes. "Don't worry. You'd have to do a lot more than that kiss to hurt me. Now let's get that coffee."

Without giving him a chance to say anything else, she alighted from the car. Her words might have been what he wanted to hear, but he didn't believe her. His gut told him that he'd hurt her more deeply than her stubborn pride would let on.

He didn't know what it was about Ms. Lizzie Addler from New York, but she was getting to him. He longed to be a good guy in her eyes, but he was torn between his desire to help her and his need to sell the *ristorante* in order to return to the vineyard and help his family. How was he supposed to make everyone happy? Was it even possible?

How had that happened?

Lizzie had entered the quaint restaurant with no appetite at all. And now as they exited the small family establishment, her stomach was full up with the most delicious sampling of pastas, meats and cheeses.

It had all started when they'd been greeted by the sweetest older woman. She'd insisted that they have a seat while she called to her husband, who was in the kitchen. Apparently they'd known Dante all of his life and were thrilled to see that he'd brought his lady friend to meet them. When Lizzie tried to correct the very chatty woman, her words got lost in the conversation.

"Are they always so outgoing?" Lizzie asked Dante as they approached the car.

"Guido and Luiso Caruso have known my family for years, and yes, they are always that friendly. Did you get enough to eat?"

Lizzie gently patted her rounded stomach. "I'm stuffed."

Dante snapped his fingers. "I forgot to give them a message from my grandfather. I'll be right back."

While Dante rushed back inside, Lizzie leaned against the car's fender and lifted her face to the sun. Perhaps she was hungrier than she thought because now that she'd eaten, her mood was much lighter. And it'd helped that Dante had opened up to her about his family. No matter how little he cracked open the door to his past, every bit he shared meant a lot to her.

But nothing could dislodge the memory of that earth-shattering kiss. It was always there, lurking around the edges of her mind. But the part that stung was how Dante had rejected her. And his reasoning did nothing to soothe her.

Somehow she'd get past this crazy infatuation. Because in the end, he was right. They did have to work together over the next eight weeks. Not to mention that they shared an apartment—anything else, no matter how casual, would just complicate matters.

"Ready to go?" Dante frowned as he noticed her leaning against the flawless paint job.

"Yes, I am."

As he got closer, she noticed how he inspected where she'd been leaning, as if she'd dented the car or something. His hand smoothed across the paint.

"Are you serious?" she asked incredulously.

He turned to her, his face perfectly serious. "What?"

He really didn't get it. She smiled and shook her head. Men and their cars. "Nothing."

"If we get going we should be home in no time. There's not much traffic. And the weather is perfect." He repeatedly tossed the keys in the air.

Lizzie moved in to catch them. "Let me drive."

"What? You're joking, right?" He reached out to take the keys from her.

She pulled her hand behind her back, which drew her

blouse tight across her chest. His gaze dipped and lingered just a moment. When his gaze met hers again, she smiled.

"Come on. You said yourself there is hardly any traffic."

And she'd love to drive an honest-to-goodness exclusive sports car, the kind that turned heads—both men and women, young and old. She may not be a car junkie, but that didn't mean she couldn't appreciate a fine vehicle. And this car was quite fine. Jules would never believe she'd gotten to drive such an amazing sports car.

"I don't think so." The smile slipped from his face. "Can I have the keys so we can get going?"

Enjoying having him at a disadvantage, she felt her smile broaden. She backed up a few steps. She was in the mood to have a little fun, hoping it'd get them back on track. "If you want them, you'll have to come and get them."

He didn't move. "This isn't funny." His tone grew quite insistent. "Hand over the keys."

Her good mood screeched to a halt. He wouldn't even consider letting her behind the steering wheel. Did he really think so little of her that she couldn't drive a car in a straight line?

Hurt balled up in her gut. She dropped the keys in his outstretched hand and strode around the car. "I assume I'm still allowed to sit in the passenger seat."

"Hey, you don't have to be like that. After all, I don't let anyone drive Red."

Her head snapped around to face him. "You named your car?"

"Of course. Why wouldn't I?"

She shook her head, having no words to describe her amazement.

"Besides, I'm sure that you'll enjoy riding in the passenger seat more. You can take a nap or check out the passing scenery."

It hurt her how easily he brushed off her request as though she couldn't possibly be serious about wanting to drive such a fine machine. All of her life people had never seen past her foster-kid status and used clothes. Even now as she sat on the butter-soft upholstery of a car that she would never be able to afford in her entire life, she was wearing hand-me-downs. But at least these clothes fit her and they didn't look as though they'd seen a better day.

She was tired of people underestimating her. She refused to sit by and take it. She would show Dante that she was just as capable as him.

CHAPTER TEN

"I KEPT MY WORD."

The sound of Lizzie's voice startled Dante.

She'd resumed her quiet mode after he'd asked for the keys. He had no idea she was so intent on driving his car—his gem. She obviously didn't know how precious it was to him and he didn't know how to describe it to her. The fact that his father liked this car almost as much as Dante did meant the world to him. And the fact that he'd bought it all on his own had earned him some of his father's respect. He couldn't afford to lose that one small step.

Dante unlocked the penthouse door. "You kept your word about what?"

"The contract. I didn't say a word while we were at the villa. But now that we're back and the film crew will be here tomorrow at 6:00 a.m., I need to know if you're on board with the whole thing." Lizzie strode into the living room. She fished around in her purse, eventually producing her cell phone. Her gaze met his as her finger hovered over the touch screen.

His curiosity was piqued. "Who are you planning to call?"

"My contact at the studio."

"Did you already tell them about my grandfather not being able to fulfill his obligation?"

She nodded. "I told them right away."

He kind of figured she would. "And what did they say?"

He wasn't so sure he wanted to hear the answer because Lizzie looked far too confident. What did she know that he didn't?

Lizzie perched on the arm of the couch. "They were sorry to hear about your grandfather."

"And?"

"And when I mentioned that you'd taken over the restaurant, they were intrigued. They pulled up some old footage of you with your grandfather and they're convinced transitioning the spotlight from your grandfather to you will work."

He should have known that eventually being on television even for a few seconds would come back to bite him. He just never expected this. Who would want him on television? He knew nothing of acting. And he wasn't inclined to learn.

"Lizzie, I haven't agreed to this. Any of it." And he didn't want to either.

"But what choice do you have at this point? If your attorney was going to uncover an easy out, he'd have told you by now."

Dante's hands pressed down on the granite countertop. He wanted to argue with her. He wanted to point out that this idea didn't have a chance to be a success. But even his solicitor wasn't rushing in, promising that all would be fine. In fact, his solicitor had said quite the opposite. That trying to break the contract would cost him money and time.

The television exposure would definitely give the *ristorante* added publicity and the asking price could easily be inflated. As it was, he'd been forced to lower the price to unload it quickly, but now there wouldn't be a rush. He could ask for a more realistic price and perhaps someone else would step forward that would want the *ristorante* without buying the family recipes.

Lizzie tossed her oversize purse on the couch. "Besides, if you help me out, I'll help you out."

"What do you have in mind?"

"If you agree to do the filming each morning before the restaurant opens, I can help you around Ristorante Massimo."

His brows rose. "You're offering to work for me?"

"Sure. What else do I have to do with my time?"

There had to be a catch. There always was. Everybody wanted something. "And what are you expecting me to pay you?"

She shrugged. "Nothing."

"Nothing?"

"I'd just like a chance to do what I would have done with your grandfather."

"And that was?"

"To learn from him. He was planning to teach me as much as he could while I was in town. I came to Italy with the sole intent to work my butt off."

Dante eyed her up. "You really don't want anything else but to learn?"

"Why do you sound so skeptical?"

He shrugged. "I'm not used to people offering me free help."

"I wouldn't get used to it. Not everyone can afford to do it. But the studio is paying me to be here, and with you providing free room and board, it should all work out."

At last he found the rub. "You intend to continue to live here? With me?"

"Is this your way of saying that you plan to kick me out?"

"You have to admit that after what happened in the vineyard the idea of us living and working together isn't a good one."

"Why? Are you saying that you want to repeat that kiss?" She moved forward, only stopping when she stood on the other side of the counter. "Are you wishing that you hadn't stopped it?"

His gaze dipped to her pink frosted lips. Oh, yes, he

definitely wanted to continue that kiss. He wanted it to go on and on. "No. That's not what I'm saying. Quit putting words in my mouth."

Her eyes flashed her disbelief. "I only call 'em like I see 'em."

"It has nothing to do with the kiss. I'd already forgotten about it." No, he hadn't. Not in the least. "It's just..."

"Just what?" Lines bracketed her icy blue eyes as she waited for his answer.

"I just don't know if you understand what will be expected from you."

"You mean you think I'm just another pretty face without anything between my ears."

"Hey, I didn't say that. There you go again, making assumptions."

"Then what did you mean?"

"I have my way of doing things. And I expect you to pay attention to the details—no matter how small or meaningless you might find them." He needed time alone to get his head on straight. There was a lot here to consider. "I'm going to my office. We'll talk more later."

"Do you mind if I go downstairs and have a look around. I want to know what I'm getting myself into."

"Be my guest. Here's the key." He tossed her a key card and rattled off the security pass code.

Her lips pressed into a firm line as she clutched the key card and turned for the door. He stood there in the kitchenette. He couldn't turn away as his gaze was latched on the gentle sway of her hips as she strode away. His pulse raced and memories of holding her and tasting her sweet kisses clouded his mind. How had he ever found the willpower to let her go?

The snick of the door closing snapped Dante back to the here and now. What was so different about her? He'd dated his share of women and none of them had gotten to him like her. But if there was any possibility of them working together and sharing this apartment, he needed to see her as just another coworker. Someone who couldn't get under his skin and give him that overwhelming urge to scratch his itch. Because that would only lead them both into trouble as had already happened back at the vineyard.

He should just show Lizzie the door and forget trying to fulfill his grandfather's wishes. If he was logical, that was what he'd do. But when it came to family, nothing was logical.

Combine that with the desperation he'd witnessed in Lizzie's gaze, and he felt an overwhelming urge to find a way to make this work for both of them. But could he keep his hormones in check around her? Suddenly his apartment wasn't looking so big after all.

She'd prove him wrong.

Lizzie strode into the impressive kitchen of Ristorante Massimo. It was more spacious than it had appeared on television. And she immediately felt at home surrounded by the stainless-steel appliances. She just wished that Massimo would be there instead of his stubborn grandson.

But she had a plan. She was going to prove to Dante that she was talented—that she could hold up her end of the agreement. She looked over the ingredients in the fridge and the freezer. Slowly a dinner menu took shape in her mind. She didn't want it to be pasta as she didn't want to compete in his arena. No, she would whip up something else.

She set to work, anxious to prove to Dante that she belonged here in Massimo's kitchen. She had the ability; she just needed to broaden her horizons with new culinary skills.

She didn't know how much time had passed when she heard a sound behind her. She turned and jumped when she saw Dante propping himself up in the doorway.

"What are you doing there?" She set aside the masher she'd used to whip up the cauliflower.

"I think I'm the one who should be asking you that question."

She glanced around at the mess she'd created. Okay, so she wasn't the neatest person in the kitchen. But to be honest, she had seen worse. And she was in a hurry. She'd wanted it all to be completed before he arrived. So much for her plan.

"I thought I'd put together dinner."

He walked closer. "And what's on the menu?"

She ran over and pressed a hand to his chest to stop him. The warmth from his body and the rhythm of his heart sent tingles shooting up her arm. Big mistake. But her heart wasn't listening to her head. A bolt of awareness struck her and all she could think about was stepping a little closer. The breath caught in her throat as she looked up at his tempting lips.

Memories of his caresses dominated her thoughts. She'd never been kissed like that before. It had meaning. It had depth. And it had left her longing for more. But this wasn't the time or the place. She had to make a point with him. And caving in to her desires would not help her cause.

She pulled her hand back. "I have a table all set in the dining room. Why don't you go make yourself comfortable? The food will be in shortly."

He strained his neck, looking around. "Are you sure I shouldn't stay and help?"

She pressed her hands to her hips. "I'm positive. Go."

He hesitated and she started to wonder if he was going to trust her. But then he relented. And turned. When he exited the kitchen, she rushed to finish up with the things on the stove. She placed them in the oven to keep them warm.

At last, it was time to start serving up the most important meal of her life. Since when had impressing Dante become more about what he thought of her and less about gaining the job? She consoled herself with the thought that it was just nerves. It wasn't as if he was the first man to kiss her. Nor would he be the last.

She pushed aside the jumbled thoughts as she moved to the refrigerator and removed the crab-and-avocado salad. She placed the dish on the tray, took off her apron and smoothed a hand over her hair, worrying that she must look a mess. Oh, well, it was too late to worry about it now.

Then, realizing that she'd forgotten something for him to drink, she grabbed both a glass of chilled water and a bottle of DeFiore white wine she'd picked out to complement the meal.

She carried the tray into the dining room and came to a stop when she noticed the lights had been dimmed and candles had been added to the table as well as some fresh greens and dahlias with hearty yellow centers and deep pink tips. The breath caught in her throat.

The table was perfect. It looked as though it was ready for a romantic interlude. And then her gaze came to rest on Dante. He'd changed clothes. What? But why?

She glanced down at the same clothes she'd worn all day that were now smudged with flour and sauce. She resisted the urge to race out of the room to grab a shower and to change into something that would make her feel sexy and alluring.

She turned her attention to Dante, taking in his creased black slacks, a matching jacket and a gray button-up shirt. Wow. With his tanned features and his dark hair, he looked like a Hollywood star. She swallowed hard. She wondered if he'd remembered to put on a touch of cologne, too. The thought of moving close enough to check was oh, so tempting.

She gave herself a mental jerk. She wasn't here for a date. This was business. She couldn't blow her chance to show him that she was quite competent in the kitchen. She would impress him this evening, but it would be through her culinary prowess and not through flirting or any of the other tempting thoughts that came readily to mind.

"If you'll have a seat, I'll serve you." She tried to act as though her heart wasn't thumping against her ribs.

He frowned. "But I want to get your chair for you."

"You don't need to do that."

"Aren't you joining me?"

She shook her head.

"But you've got to be hungry, too."

She was but it wasn't the food she'd slaved over for the past couple of hours that had her salivating. "I'm fine."

"Oh, come on. You surely don't think that I'll enjoy this meal with you rushing around waiting on me. Now sit."

What was up with him? She eyed him up as she sat in the chair he'd pulled out for her. Was he having a change of heart about teaching her what he knew—in the kitchen, that was?

"I only brought out enough food for one."

"Not a problem." Before she could utter a word, he moved to the kitchen.

This wasn't right. This was not how she'd planned to prove to Dante that she was up to the task of working in Ristorante Massimo. Frustration collided with the girlie part of her that was thrilled to be pampered. It was a totally new experience for her. But it also left her feeling off-kilter. Was she supposed to read something into his actions? The clothes? The flowers and candles? Did any of it have anything to do with their kiss?

When he returned, she gazed at him in the glow of the candle. The words caught in her throat as she realized this was her first candlelit dinner. Romance had never been part of her other relationships. She could definitely get used to this and to Dante—

No. No. She couldn't get distracted again. This was not a date. It was business. So why was Dante acting so strange? So kind and thoughtful?

"Is there something I should know?" she asked, bracing herself for bad news.

A dark brow arched. "Know about what?"

She didn't want to put words in his mouth, especially if they were not what she wanted to hear. "I don't know. I just wondered about your effort to be so nice."

He frowned. "So now you think that I'm not nice."

She groaned. "That isn't what I meant. You're taking my words out of context."

"I am?" He placed a plate and glass in front of her. "Perhaps we should talk about something else, then."

"No. I want to know why you're in such a good mood. Have you made up your mind about the television show?"

Please let him say that he had a change of heart.

His gaze lowered to the table as he took his seat. "Are you sure you know what you're asking?"

"Of course I do. All you have to do is fill in for your grandfather. And teach me everything you know." Did this mean he was truly considering the idea? Were her dreams about to come true?

"You really want to learn from me?"

She nodded.

The silence dragged on. Her stomach knotted and her palms grew damp. Why wasn't he saying anything?

"Well?" She couldn't bear the unknown any longer. "Where does that leave us?"

"It leaves us with a meal that's going to get cold if we don't get through this first course soon."

"But I need to know."

"And you will. Soon."

Was that a promise? It sounded like one. But what was soon in his book? She glanced down at her salad. How in the world was she supposed to eat now?

CHAPTER ELEVEN

HE MUST HAVE lost his mind.

That had to be it. Otherwise why would he even consider going along with this arrangement?

Dante stared across the candlelit table at Lizzie. He noticed how she'd moved the food around on her plate, but she'd barely eaten a bite. She had to be hungry because it'd been hours since they'd stopped at the trattoria on their way back to Rome.

And this food was really good. In fact, he had to admit that he was impressed. Maybe taking her under his wing wouldn't be such a hardship after all. His solicitor definitely thought it was the least painless course of action. Easy for him to say.

But the deciding factor was when the potential buyer of the *ristorante* had been willing to wait the two months. His solicitor said that they'd actually been quite enthusiastic about the *ristorante* getting international coverage.

But what no one took into consideration was the fact that Dante was totally drawn to Lizzie. And that was a serious complication. How in the world were they to work together when all he could think about was kissing her again? He longed to wrap his arms around her and pull her close. He remembered vividly how the morning sun had glowed behind her, giving her whole appearance a golden glow. It had been an experience unlike any other. And when their lips had met—

"Is something wrong with the food?"

Dante blinked before meeting Lizzie's worried gaze. He had to start thinking of her in professional terms. He supposed that if he were going to take her on as his protégée, he might as well get started. He'd teach her as much as possible within their time limit.

"Now that you'll be working here, there'll be no special treatment. You'll be expected to work just like everyone else."

"Understood."

"As for the food, the chicken is a little overcooked. You'll need to be careful of that going forward."

A whole host of expressions flitted across her face. "Is there anything else?"

It wasn't the reaction he'd been expecting. He thought she'd be ecstatic to learn that she'd be working there. And that she'd get her television spot. Women. He'd never figure them out. In his experience, they never reacted predictably.

"And use less salt. The guest can always add more according to their taste and diet."

Her face filled with color. Without a word, she threw her linen napkin on the table and rushed to the kitchen.

He groaned. He hadn't meant to upset her. Still, how was he supposed to teach her anything if he couldn't provide constructive criticism? His grandfather should be here. He would know what to say and how to say it.

Dante raked his fingers through his hair. He'd agreed to this arrangement far too quickly. He should have gone with his gut that said this was going to be a monumental mistake. Now he had to fix things before the camera crew showed up. The last thing either of them needed was to start their television appearances on a bad note—with all of the world watching.

He strode toward the kitchen and paused by the door. What did he say to her? Did he apologize even though he hadn't said anything derogatory? Did he set a precedent that she would expect him to apologize every time she got upset when he pointed out something that she could improve on? An exasperated sigh passed his lips. He obviously wasn't meant to be a teacher.

He pushed the door open, prepared to find Lizzie in tears. Instead he found her scraping leftovers into the garbage and piling the dishes in the sink.

"What are you doing?"

She didn't face him. "I'm cleaning up. What does it look like?"

"But we weren't done eating. Why don't you come back to the table?"

She grabbed the main dish and dumped it in the garbage. "I don't want anything else."

"Would you stop?"

"There's no point in keeping leftovers." With that, she grabbed the dessert.

He knew where she was headed and stepped in her way. What in the world had gotten into her? Why was she acting this way?

"Lizzie, put down the dessert and tell me what's bothering you."

She tilted her chin to gaze up at him. "Why should something be bothering me? You tore to shreds the dinner I painstakingly prepared for you."

"But isn't that what you want me to do? Teach you?"

Her icy gaze bored into him. The temperature took an immediate dive. "Move."

"No. We need to finish talking."

"So you can continue to insult me. No, thank you." She moved to go around him but he moved to block her.

"Lizzie, I don't know what it is you want from me. I thought you wanted me to teach you, but obviously that isn't the case. So what is it you want? Or do you just want to call this whole thing off?"

"I didn't know we were starting the lessons right away.

Or did you just say those things in hopes of me calling off the arrangement?"

"No, that isn't what I had in mind." How the heck had he ended up on the defensive? He'd only meant to be helpful.

"So you truly think I'm terrible in the kitchen?"

He took the tray from her and set it on the counter. Then he stepped up to her, hating the emotional turmoil he saw in her eyes. He found himself longing to soothe her. But he didn't have a clue how to accomplish such a thing. He seemed to keep making one mistake after the other where she was concerned.

"I think that you're very talented." It was the truth. And he'd have said it even if he didn't find her amazingly attractive.

Her bewildered gaze met his. "But you said—"

"That there were things for you to take into consideration while working here. I didn't mean to hurt your feelings."

Disbelief shimmered in her eyes.

He didn't think. He just acted, reaching out to her. His thumb stroked her cheek, enjoying its velvety softness. She stepped away from his touch and his hand lowered to his side.

"Lizzie, you have to believe me. If you're going to be this sensitive, how do you think we'll be able to work together?"

This was all wrong.

Lizzie crossed her arms to keep from reaching out to him. The whole evening had gone off the rails and she had no idea how to fix things. And the worst part was that she'd overreacted. Big-time.

She'd always prided herself on being able to contain her feelings behind a wall of indifference. And Dante wasn't the first to criticize her skills. But he was the first whose opinion truly mattered to her on a deeply personal level. He was the first person she wanted to thoroughly impress.

The thought brought her up short. Since when had his thoughts and feelings come to mean so much to her? Was it the kiss? Had it changed everything? Or was it opening up to him in the car? Had their heart-to-heart made her vulnerable to him?

Panic clawed at her. She knew what happened when she let people too close and she opened up about her background. She'd been shunned most of her life. She couldn't let Dante do that to her. She couldn't stand the thought of him looking at her with pity while thinking that she was less than everyone else—after all, if her own parents couldn't love her, how was anyone else supposed to?

Not that she wanted Dante to fall in love with her. Did she? No. That was the craziest idea to cross her mind in a long time—probably her craziest idea ever.

The walls started to close in on her. She needed space. Away from Dante. Away from his curious stare. "I need... need to make a phone call. I...I'll clean this all up later."

And with that, she raced for the door. She didn't have to call Jules, but she did need the excuse to get away from him. It was as if he had some sort of magnetic field around him and it drew out her deepest feelings. She needed to stuff them back in the little box in her heart.

Being alone in a strange city in a country practically halfway around the world from her home made her choices quite limited. She thought of escaping back to the vineyard and visiting some more with Massimo. He was so easy to talk to. He was her friend. But he was also Dante's grandfather. And the vineyard was Dante's home.

Her shoulders slumped as she headed for the apartment. What she needed now was to talk to Jules. It would be good to hear a familiar voice. She made a beeline for her room and pulled out her phone. She knew the call would cost her a small fortune but this was an emergency.

She dialed the familiar number. The phone rang and

rang. Just when she thought that it was going to switch to voice mail, she heard a familiar voice.

"Lizzie, is that you? What's wrong?"

The concern in Jules's voice had her rushing to reassure her. "I just wanted to check in."

"But you said that we needed to watch how much we spend on the phone. You said we should only call when something was wrong. So what happened?"

"Nothing. I just wanted to hear your voice and make sure you are doing okay."

There was a slight pause. "Lizzie, this is me. You can't lie to me. Something is bothering you. So spill it."

Calling Jules had been a mistake. She knew her far too well. And now Jules wasn't going to let her off the hook. "It's Dante. I think I just blew my chance to work with him."

"Why? What did you do?"

"I...I overreacted. Instead of taking his feedback on my cooking like a professional, I acted like an oversensitive female." Her thoughts drifted over the evening. "All I wanted to do was impress him and...and I failed."

"Don't worry about him. Just come home."

"I can't do that. Remember, I quit my job. And your tuition is due soon."

"You don't have to worry about that. I don't have to go to grad school."

"You do if you want to be a social worker and help other kids like us." The remembrance of her promise to her foster sister put things in perspective. She couldn't let her bruised ego get the best of her. She couldn't walk away. "Just ignore what I said. I'm tired. Everything will work out."

"But, Lizzie, if he's making things impossible for you, what are you going to do?"

There was a knock at her bedroom door.

"Jules, I have to go. I'll call you later."

With a quick goodbye, she disconnected the call. She

worried her bottom lip and waited. Maybe Dante would go away. She wasn't ready to talk to him. Not yet.

Again the tap at the door. "I'm not going away until we talk."

"I don't have anything to say to you."

"But I have plenty to say to you."

That sparked her curiosity, but her bruised ego wasn't ready to give in. She wanted to tell herself that his words and his opinions meant nothing. But that trip to the vineyard and that kiss in the morning sunshine had cast some sort of spell over her—over her heart.

"Lizzie, open the door."

She ran a hand over her hair, finding it to be a flyaway mess. What was she doing hiding away? She was a foster kid. She knew how to take care of herself. Running and hiding wasn't her style. She straightened her shoulders. And with a resigned sigh, she moved to the door and opened it.

Dante stood there, slouched against the doorjamb. Much too close. Her heart thumped. Her gaze dipped to his lips. She recalled how his mouth did the most exquisite things to her and made her insides melt into a puddle. If she were to lean a little forward, they'd be nose to nose, lip to lip, breath to breath. But that couldn't happen again. It played with her mind and her heart too much.

With effort she drew her gaze to his eyes, which seemed to be filled with amusement.

"See something you like?" A smile pulled at his lips and made him even sexier than the serious expression he normally wore like armor.

"I see a man who insists he has to talk to me. What do you want?"

He shook his head. "Not like this. Join me in the living room."

"I have things to do."

"I think this is more important. Trust me." With that, he walked away.

She stood there fighting off the urge to rush to catch up with him. After all, he was the one who'd ruined a perfectly amazing dinner, nitpicking over her cooking. The reminder had her straightening her spine.

Refusing to continue to let him have the upper hand, she closed the door and rushed over to the walk-in closet to retrieve some fresh clothes that didn't smell as if she'd been working in the kitchen for hours. She wished she had time for a shower, but she didn't want to press her luck.

With a fresh pair of snug black jean capris and a black sheer blouse that she knotted at her belly button, she entered the en suite bathroom that was almost as big as her bedroom. She splashed some water on her heated face. Then she took a moment to run a brush through her hair. Not satisfied with it, she grabbed a ponytail holder and pulled her hair back out of her face. With a touch of powder and a little lip gloss to add a touch of color to her face, she decided that she wasn't going to go out of her way for him.

Satisfied that she'd taken enough time that it didn't seem as though she was rushing after him, she exited her room. She didn't hear anything. Had he given up and disappeared to his office?

Disappointment coursed through her. The fact that she was so eager to hear what he had to say should have been warning enough, but curiosity kept her moving forward. When she entered the wide open living area, she was surprised to find Dante kicked back on the couch with his smartphone in his hand. He glanced up at her with an unidentifiable expression.

"What?" she asked, feeling self-conscious about her appearance.

He shook his head, dismissing her worry. "Nothing. It's just that when I think I've figured you out, you go and surprise me."

"And how did I do that?"

He shook his head. "It doesn't matter."

"Yes, it does. Otherwise you wouldn't have mentioned it."

"It's just that as tough as you act, on the inside you're such a girl." His gaze drifted over her change of clothes down to her strappy black sandals. "And a beautiful one at that."

She crossed her arms and shrugged. "I...I'm sorry for being sensitive. I'm not normally like that. I swear. It won't happen again."

But the one subject she didn't dare delve into was that her appearance was an illusion. Unlike his other women friends, her clothes didn't come from some Rome boutique. Her clothes were hand-me-downs. For a moment, she wondered what he'd say if he knew she was a fraud. Her insides tightened as she thought of him rejecting her.

"Apology accepted." He patted a spot on the black leather couch next to him. "Now come sit down."

It was then that she noticed the candles on the glass coffee table. And there were the dishes of berries and fresh whipped cream and a sprig of mint. Why in the world had he brought it up here?

When she sat down, it was in the overstuffed chair. "I don't understand."

He leaned forward. His elbows rested on his knees. Her instinct was to sit back out of his reach, but steely resistance kept her from moving. She wasn't going to let him think that he had any power over her.

"Dante, what's this all about? Are you trying to soften the blow? Are you calling off the television spot?"

CHAPTER TWELVE

LIZZIE'S HARD GAZE challenged him.

Dante wondered if she truly wanted him to step away from this project. Had she gotten a taste of his mentoring skills and changed her mind? Not that it mattered. It was too late for either of them to back out.

Somehow he had to smooth things out with her. And he wasn't well versed with apologies. This was going to be harder than he'd imagined.

"It's my turn to apologize." There. He'd said it. Now he just hoped that she'd believe him.

"For what?"

This was where things got sticky. He didn't want to talk about feelings and emotions. He swallowed hard as he sorted his thoughts.

"I didn't mean to make you feel bad about dinner." Her gaze narrowed in on him, letting him know that he now had her full attention. "See, that's the thing. I'm not a teacher. I have no experience. My grandfather always prided himself on being the one to show people how to do things. He has a way about him that makes people want to learn. If he hadn't been a chef, he should have been a teacher."

The stiffness in her shoulders eased. "But I didn't make you dinner so that you could teach me. I...I wanted... Oh, never mind."

She clammed up quickly. What had she been about to say? He really wanted to know. Was she going to say that she'd made him dinner because she liked him? Did she want to continue what they'd started earlier that day?

No. She wouldn't want that...would she? He had to resolve the uncertainty. The not knowing would taunt him to utter distraction. And if they were going to work together, he had to know where they stood.

He cleared his throat. "What is it you wanted?"

"I just wanted to prepare you a nice dinner as a thank-you for what you did by introducing me to your family. And...and I wanted to show you that you wouldn't be making a mistake by taking me on to work here. But obviously I was wrong."

"No, you weren't."

"Yes, I was. You made it clear you don't care for my cooking."

He shook his head. "That's not it. I think you're a good cook."

"So then why did you say those things?"

"Because good is fine for most people, but you aren't most people."

Her fine brows drew together. "What does that mean? Do you know about my past? Did your grandfather tell you?"

Whoa! That had him sitting up straight. "Nonno didn't tell me anything." But Dante couldn't let it end there. He wanted to believe that he was being cautious because of the business but it was more than that. He wanted to know everything there was about her. "I'm willing to listen, if you're willing to tell me."

Her blue eyes were a turbulent sea of emotions. "You don't want to hear about me."

"Yes, I do." The conviction in his voice took him by surprise.

She worried her lip as though considering what to tell him. "I don't know. I've already told you enough. I don't need to give you more reason to look at me differently."

Now he had to know. "I promise I won't do that."

"You might try, but it'll definitely color the way you see me." She leaned back in the chair and crossed her arms.

He wanted her to trust him although he knew that he hadn't given her any reason to do so. But this was important. On top of it all, if he understood her better, maybe he'd have an easier time communicating with her when they were working together. He knew he was kidding himself. His interest in her went much deeper than employer and employee.

"Trust me, Lizzie."

He could see the conflicted look in her eyes. She obviously wasn't used to opening up to people—except his grandfather. Nonno had a way with people that put them at ease. Dante was more like his father when it came to personal relationships—he had to work to find the right words. Sure, he could flirt with the women, but when it came down to meaningful talks, the DeFiore men failed.

But this was about Lizzie, not himself. And he didn't want to fail her. More than anything, he wanted her to let him in.

Should she trust him?

Lizzie studied Dante's handsome face. Her brain said that she'd already told him more than enough, but her heart pleaded with her to trust him. But to what end? It wasn't as if she was going to build a life here in Rome. Her life—her home—was thousands of miles away in New York.

But maybe she'd stumbled across something.

Whatever she told him would stay here in Rome. So what did it matter if she told him more about her past? It wasn't as if it was a secret anyway. Plenty of people knew her story—and plenty of those people had used it as a yardstick to judge her. Would Dante be different?

With every fiber of her being she wanted to believe that he would be. But she'd never know unless she said the words—words that made her feel as though she was less than everyone else. Admitting to her past made her feel as though she wasn't worthy of love.

She took a deep breath. "Before my mother died, I was placed in foster care."

Dante sat there looking at her as though he were still waiting for her big revelation.

"Did you hear me?"

"I heard that you grew up in a foster home, but I don't know why you would think that would make me look at you differently."

Seriously? This was so not the reaction she was expecting. Growing up, she'd learned to keep this information to herself. When the parents of her school friends had learned that she came from a foster home, they'd clucked their tongues and shaken their heads. Then suddenly her friends had no time for her. And once she'd overheard a parent say to another, *"You can never be too careful. Who knows about those foster kids. I don't want her having a bad influence on my kid."*

The memory made the backs of Lizzie's eyes sting. She'd already felt unwanted by her mother, who'd tossed her away as though she hadn't mattered. And then to know that people looked down on her, it hurt—a lot. But Lizzie refused to let it destroy her. Instead, she insisted on showing them that they were wrong—that she would make something of herself.

"You don't understand what it's like to grow up as a foster kid. Trust me. You had it so good."

Dante glanced away. "You don't know that."

"Are you serious? You have an amazing family. You know where you come from and who your parents are."

"It may look good from the outside, but you have no idea what it's like to live in that house and never be able to measure up." He got to his feet and strode over to the window.

"Maybe your family expected things from you because

they knew you were capable of great things. In my case, no one expected anything from me but trouble."

"Why would they think that?"

"Don't you get it? My parents tossed me away like yesterday's news. If the two people in the world who were supposed to love me the most didn't want me, it could only mean there's something wrong with me—something unworthy." Her voice cracked with emotion. "You don't know what it was like to be looked at like you are less than a person."

In three long, quick strides Dante was beside her. He sat down next to her and draped his arm around her. Needing to feel his strength and comfort, she lowered her head to his broad shoulder. The lid creaked open on the box of memories that she'd kept locked away for so many years.

Once again she was that little girl with the hand-me-down jeans with patches on the knees and the pant legs that were two inches too short. And the socks that rarely matched—she'd never forget those. She'd been incessantly taunted and teased about them.

But no longer.

Her clothes may not come from high-class shops, but they were of designer quality and gently worn so that no one knew that they were used—no one but Jules. But her foster sister was never one to judge. Probably because Jules never went for the sophisticated styles—Jules marched to a different drummer in fashion and makeup.

"I...I never had any friendships that lasted, except Jules. We had similar backgrounds and we leaned on each other through thick and thin."

"I'm so glad she was there for you. If I had been there I'd have told those people what was up."

Lizzie gave a little smile. "I can imagine you doing that, too."

"I don't understand why people have to be so mean."

She swallowed down the lump in her throat. "You can't

imagine how awful it was. At least when I was little, I didn't know what the looks and snide little comments by the mothers were about, but as I got older, I learned."

Dante's jaw tightened and a muscle in his cheek twitched. "Unbelievable."

"The kids were even meaner. If you didn't have the right clothes, and I never did, you'd be picked on and called names. And the right hairstyle, you had to have the latest trend. And my poker-straight hair would never cooperate. It seemed one way or another I constantly failed to fit in."

"I think they were all just jealous. How could they not be? You're gorgeous."

His compliment was like a balm on her old wounds. Did he really mean it? She gazed deep into his eyes and saw sincerity, which stole her breath away. Dante thought she was gorgeous. A warmth started in her chest and worked its way up her neck and settled in her cheeks.

"It's a shame they missed getting to know what a great person you are. And how caring you are."

She lifted her head and looked at him squarely in the eyes. "You're just saying that to make me feel better."

"No, I'm not." His breath brushed against her cheek, tickling it. "You're special."

She moved just a little so that she was face-to-face with him. She wanted to look into his eyes once more. She wanted to know without a doubt that he believed what he was saying. But what she found in his dark gaze sent her heart racing. Sincerity and desire reflected in his eyes.

He pulled her closer until her curves were pressed up against his hard planes. She knew this place. Logic said she should pull away. But the pounding of her heart drowned out any common sense. The only recognizable thought in her head was that she wanted him—all of him, and it didn't matter at that moment what happened tomorrow.

His gaze dipped to her lips. The breath caught in his throat. Her eyelids fluttered closed and then he was there pressing his mouth to hers. Her hands crept over his sturdy shoulders. Her fingertips raked through his short strands.

She followed his gently probing kisses until her mounting desire drove her to become more assertive. As she deepened their kiss, a moan sounded from him. She reveled in the ability to rouse his interest. Sure, she'd attracted a few men in the past, but none had gotten her heart to pound like it was doing now. She wondered if Dante could hear it. Did he know what amazing things he was doing to her body?

Did he know how much she wanted him?

The knowledge that she was willing to give herself to him just for the asking startled her back to reality. She pulled back. She wanted Dante too much. It was too dangerous. And after being a foster kid, she liked to play things safe—at least where her heart was concerned. She'd been burned far too many times.

"What's wrong?" Dante tried to pull her back to him.

She'd been here before, putting her heart on the line. Only then, she'd been a kid wanting to have a best friend and thinking that all would be fine. Then the parents had stepped in and she was rejected.

She remembered the agonizing pain of losing friend after friend. She'd promised herself that she'd never let herself be that vulnerable again. Not for anyone. Not even for this most remarkable man.

She struggled to slow her breathing and then uttered, "We can't do this. It isn't right."

"It sure felt right to me." He sent her a dreamy smile that made her heart flip-flop.

"Dante, don't. I'm being serious."

"And so am I. What's wrong with having a little fun?"

"It's more than that. It's... Oh, I don't know." Her insides were a ball of conflicting emotions.

"Relax. I won't push you for something you don't want to do."

The problem was that she did want him. She wanted him

more than she'd wanted anyone in her life. But it couldn't happen. She wouldn't let it. It would end in heartbreak—her heartbreak.

Dante placed a thumb beneath her chin and tilted it up until their gazes met. "Don't look so sad."

"I'm not." Then feeling a moment of panic over how easy it'd be to give in to these new feelings, she backed away from him. "You don't even know me. Why are you being so nice?"

"Seriously. Are you really going to play that card?" He smiled and shook his head in disbelief. "You aren't that much of a mystery."

She crossed her arms, not sure how comfortable she was with him thinking that he knew so much about her. "And what do you think you know about me?"

"I know that you like to put on a tough exterior to keep people at arm's length, but deep down you are sweet and thoughtful. I saw you with my family and especially Massimo. You listened to him and you didn't rush him when he had problems pronouncing some words. You made him feel like he had something important to say—like he was still a contributing member of the family."

"I'm glad to hear that my visit helped. I wish I could go back."

"You can…if you stay here."

What? Had she heard him correctly? He wanted her to stay? She didn't understand what was happening here. Not too long ago she'd been the one pushing for this arrangement to work and he was the one resisting the arrangement. Now suddenly he wanted her to stay. What was she missing?

"Why?" She searched his face, trying to gain a glimmer of insight.

"Why not?"

"That's not an answer. Why did you suddenly have this change of heart?"

He shifted his weight from one foot to the other. "I've had a chance to think it over. And I think that we can help each other."

"Are you saying this because I told you about my background? Is this some sort of sympathy?"

"No." The response came quickly—too quickly. "Why would you say that?"

She shrugged. "Why not? It's the only reason I can see for you to want this arrangement to work. Or is there something I don't know?"

There was a look in his eyes. Was it surprise? Had she stumbled across something?

"Tell me, Dante. Otherwise, I'm outta here. If you can't be honest with me, we can't work together." And she meant it. Somehow, someway she'd scrape together the money for Jules to go to grad school, to reach her dreams and to be able to help other unfortunate children.

He exhaled a frustrated sigh. "I talked with my solicitor before dinner."

When he paused, she prompted him. "And."

"He said that we could break the contract but it wouldn't be quick or cheap."

Her gut was telling her that there was more to this than he was telling her. "What else?"

Dante rubbed the back of his neck. "Did anyone ever tell you that you're pushy?"

"I am when I have to be—when I can tell that I'm not being given the whole truth."

"Well, that's it. My solicitor advised me that it would be easier to go through with your project. And he mentioned that in the end it would benefit the *ristorante* and bring in more tourist traffic."

So that was it. He was looking at his bottom line. She couldn't fault him for that because technically she was doing the same thing. She was looking forward to the money she earned to help her foster sister. But she just couldn't shake the memories of the past.

"And you're sure this has nothing to do with what I told you about my past."

"I swear. Now will you stay?"

She didn't know what to say. She wasn't sure how this would work now that they'd kissed twice and were sharing an apartment, regardless of its spaciousness. When she glanced into Dante's eyes, the fluttering feeling churned in her stomach. And when her gaze slipped down to his lips, she was tempted to steal another kiss.

"What's the matter?" Dante asked, arching his brow. "Are you worried about us being roommates?"

"How did you know?"

The corner of his tempting mouth lifted in a knowing smile. "Because you aren't the only one wondering about that question. But before you let that chase you off, remember the reason you came here—to learn. To hone your cooking skills."

"But I can't do that if you and I are...you know..."

"How about I make you a promise that I won't kiss you again...until you ask me. I will be the perfect host and teacher— Well, okay, the teaching might be a bit rough at first but I will try my best."

She looked deep into his eyes, finding sincerity. Her gut said to trust him. But it was these new feelings that she didn't trust. Still, this was her only viable option to hold up her promise to Jules, who'd helped her through school and pushed her to reach for her dreams. How could she do any less in return?

With a bit of hesitancy, she stuck out her hand. "You have a deal."

CHAPTER THIRTEEN

What exactly had he gotten himself into?

The sun was flirting with the horizon as Dante yawned and entered the kitchen of Ristorante Massimo. The film crew was quite timely. Dante stood off to the side, watching the bustle of activity as a large pot of *caffè* brewed. The large kitchen instantly shrank as the camera crew, makeup artist and director took over the area. In no time, spotless countertops were covered with equipment, cases and papers. The place no longer looked like the kitchen his grandfather had taught him to cook in—the large room that held some of his happiest memories.

Dante inwardly groaned and stepped out of the way of a young assistant wheeling in another camera. So much for the peace and tranquillity that he always enjoyed at this time of the day. He slipped into the office to enjoy his coffee.

"Hey, what are you doing in here?" Lizzie's voice called out from behind him.

He turned to find her lingering in the doorway. The smile on her face lit up her eyes. She practically glowed. Was it the television cameras that brought out this side of her? The thought saddened him. He wished that he could evoke such happiness in her. But it was best that they'd settled things and agreed that from now on she was hands off for him.

"I'm just staying out of the way. Is all of that stuff necessary?"

"There's not much. You should see what they have in the studio."

"I don't remember all of those things when they filmed here before."

She shrugged. "Are you ready for this?"

He wasn't. He really didn't want to be a television star, but he'd given his word and he wouldn't go back on that—he wouldn't disappoint Lizzie. She'd been disappointed too many times in her life.

"Yes, I am. We need to get this done before the employees show up to get everything started for the lunch crowd. What do we need to do first?"

"You need makeup."

"What?" He shook his head and waved off the idea. "I don't think so."

His thoughts filled with images of some lady applying black eyeliner and lipstick to him. His nose turned up at the idea. No way. Wasn't happening. Not in his lifetime.

"Is it really that bad?" Lizzie's sweet laugh grated on his taut nerves.

"I agreed to teach you to cook in front of the cameras, but I never agreed to eyeliner."

Lizzie stepped closer. "What? You don't think you need a little cover stick and maybe a little blush."

His gaze narrowed on her as she stopped right in front of him. The amusement danced in her eyes. He truly believed, next to her visit with his grandfather, this was the happiest he'd seen her. He didn't want it to end, but he had to draw a line when it came to makeup.

"I'm not doing it. And you can keep smiling at me, but it isn't going to change my mind."

Her fingertip stroked along his jaw. "Mmm, nice. Someone just shaved."

Yes, he had. Twice. "That doesn't have anything to do with makeup."

Her light touch did the craziest things to his pulse. And was that the sweet scent of her perfume? Or was it the lingering trace of her shampoo? He inhaled deeper. Whatever it was, he could definitely get used to it.

Her fingertip moved to his bottom lip, which triggered nerve endings that shot straight through to his core. Her every touch was agonizing as he struggled not to pull her close and replace her finger with her lips. But he'd once again given his word to be on his best behavior.

He caught her arm and pulled it away from his mouth. "You might want to stop doing that or I won't be responsible for what happens next."

Her baby blues opened wide and her pink frosty lips formed an O.

She withdrew her arm and stepped back. He regretted putting an end to her fun as she seemed to regress back into her shell. He wished she'd let that side of her personality out more often. But obviously he'd have to get a better grip on himself so that next time he didn't chase her away.

She was so beautiful. So amazing. So very tempting. And he'd been the biggest fool in the world to promise to be a gentleman. But he had no one to blame for this agonizing torture except himself.

"You need to loosen up. Act natural."

Lizzie glanced up at the director, thinking he was talking to Dante. After all, she'd done this sort of thing before—acting in front of the cameras. But instead of the young guy giving Dante a pointed look, the man was staring directly at her. Her chest tightened.

"I...I am."

The man shook his head and turned to his cameraman to say something.

Dante moved to her side. "What's the matter, Lizzie? Where's the woman who just a little bit ago was teasing me about makeup?"

She refused to let him get the best of her. "Speaking of which, I see that you're wearing some. Looks good. Except you might want a little more eyeliner."

"What?" He grabbed a stainless-steel pot and held it up so he could see his reflection. His dark brows drew together. "I'm not wearing eyeliner."

She smiled.

"That's what I want." The director's voice drew her attention. "I want that spark and easy interaction on the camera."

Lizzie inwardly groaned. The man didn't know what he was asking of her. She chanced a glance at Dante as he returned the pot to a shelf. She wasn't the only one who'd reverted back behind a wall. He had been keeping his distance around her, too. She wondered if he regretted their kissing? Or was it something deeper? Did it have something to do with the reason Dante lived all alone in that spacious apartment that was far too big for just one person?

"Okay, let's try this shot again."

Lizzie took her position at the counter, trying her best to act relaxed and forget about the camera facing her. But as Dante began his lines and moved around her, showing her how to prepare the *pasta alla gricia*, she could smell his spicy aftershave. It'd be so easy to give in to her desires. But where would that leave her? Brokenhearted and alone. Her muscles stiffened.

"Cut." The director walked up to her. "I don't understand. We've worked together before and you did wonderfully. What's the problem now?"

The problem was Dante looked irresistibly sexy in his pressed white jacket. She swallowed hard. As she took a deep calming breath, she recalled his fresh, soapy scent.

Mmm...he smelled divine. What was she supposed to do? When he got close enough to assist her with the food prep, she panicked—worried she'd end up caring about him. That she'd end up falling for him. And that just couldn't happen. She wouldn't let it.

"Nothing is wrong." She hoped her voice sounded more assured than she felt at the moment. "I'll do better."

The director frowned at her. "Maybe you should take a break. We'll shoot the next segment with just Dante."

Lizzie felt like a kid in school that had just gotten a stern warning from the principal before being dismissed to go contemplate her actions. Keeping her gaze straight ahead and well away from Dante, she headed for the coffeepot, where she filled up a cup. After a couple of dashes of sugar and topping it off with cream, she headed for the office. It was her only refuge from prying eyes.

She resisted the urge to close the door. She didn't need them speculating that she'd dissolved into a puddle of tears. It would take a lot more than messing up a shot to start the waterworks.

More than anything, she was frustrated. She grabbed for her cell phone, wanting to hear Jules's voice. Her foster sister always had a way of talking her off ledges. But just as she was about to press the last digit, she realized that with the time difference, Jules would still be sound asleep.

Lizzie slid the phone back in her pocket. What was she going to do now? Dante was totally showing her up in there. The thought did not sit well with her at all.

Since when did she let a man get to her? She could be a professional. She wasn't some teenager with a crush. She was a grown woman with responsibilities. It was time she started acting that way before this whole spotlight series went up in flames.

"Are you all right?" Dante's voice came from behind her.

"I'm fine. Why does everyone keep asking me that?"

"Because you haven't been acting like yourself." Concern reflected in his eyes. "Tell me what's bothering you. I'll help if I can."

"Don't do that."

His forehead wrinkled. "What?"

"Act like we're something we're not." If he continued to treat her this way, her resolve would crack. And she didn't want to rely on him. She knew what would happen then. He'd pull back just like her ex had done. Men were only into women for an uncomplicated good time.

And she was anything but uncomplicated.

"I don't know what you're talking about." Dante's voice took on a deeper tone. "All I wanted to do was help." He held up his hands innocently. "But I can tell when I'm not wanted."

He stormed back out the door.

Good. Not that she was happy that he was upset. But she could deal with his agitation much easier than she could his niceness. Each kind word he spoke to her was one more chip at the wall she'd carefully built over the years to protect herself. And she wasn't ready to take it down for him or anyone.

At last, feeling as though she had her head screwed on straight, she returned to the kitchen. The director looked at her as though studying her. "You ready?"

She nodded. "Yes, I am."

The director had them take their places as Lizzie sensed Dante's agitation and distance. She was sorry that it had to be this way, but she could at last think straight. And when the director called a halt to the filming, it was Dante who fouled up the shot. They redid it a few times until the director was satisfied.

This arrangement may have been her idea, but at the time she hadn't a clue how hard it was going to be to work so closely with Dante. Still, she had to do this. She didn't have a choice. There were bills to meet and grad school to pay.

She just had to pretend that Dante was no one special. But was that possible in the long run? How was she supposed to ignore these growing feelings when she found Dante fascinating in every way?

She was in trouble. Deep trouble.

CHAPTER FOURTEEN

NOT TOO BAD.

Lizzie stifled a yawn as she poured herself a cup of coffee. Thankfully it was late Friday night and the restaurant was at last closed. She was relieved that there was no filming in the morning. Those early wake-up calls were wearing her down. The next morning the crew was off to shoot some footage of Rome to pad their spotlights. And she couldn't be happier.

Lizzie pressed a cup of stale coffee to her lips.

"You might not want to drink that."

She turned at the sound of Dante's voice. "Why not?"

"That stuff is strong enough to strip paint off Red. You'll never get to sleep if you drink it."

She held back a laugh. "Don't worry. I'll be fine."

Dante raised a questioning brow before he turned back to finish cleaning the grill. He really was a hands-on kinda guy. She didn't know why that should surprise her. He'd never once sloughed off his work onto his staff. Everyone had their assigned duties and they all seemed to work in harmony.

Dante had been remarkable when it came to the filming, too. He may grump and growl like an old bear about things like makeup, but when the cameras started to roll, he really came through for her—for them. Maybe he hadn't nailed every scene but he'd been trying and that was what counted. And if she didn't know better, she'd swear he'd been enjoying himself in front of the cameras.

It was amazing how long it took to shoot a short segment to splice into the station's number-one-rated cooking show. But it was so worth it. What a plum spot they'd been given. It'd definitely make her credentials stand out from the competition when she returned to New York and searched for a chef position at one of the upscale restaurants in Manhattan.

She took the cup of coffee to the office and cleared off a spot at the end of the couch. No sooner had she gotten comfortable than Dante sauntered into the room.

"See, you should have taken me up on my offer to take the afternoon off." He sent her an *I told you so* look.

She shrugged. "I wanted to get a feel for how everything works around here."

"And now you're exhausted."

"Listen to who's talking. You worked just as many hours as I did."

"But I'm used to it."

Now, that did surprise her. What was a young, incredibly sexy man doing spending all of his time at the restaurant? Surely he must have an active social life away from this place. The image of him dressed in a sharp suit filled her mind. And then a beautiful slip of a woman infiltrated her thoughts. The mystery woman sauntered over and draped herself on his arm. Lizzie's body tensed.

"Is something the matter?"

She glanced up at Dante. "What?"

"You were frowning. Is it the *caffè*? I told you not to drink it."

Not about to tell him her true thoughts, she said, "Yes, it's cold. I'll just dump it out and head upstairs. Are you coming?"

He glanced around at the messy office. "I should probably do a little work in here."

She stifled a laugh. This place needed a lot more than a "little" help. "Have you ever thought of hiring someone to sort through all of these old papers?"

"I don't think there's a person alive that would willingly take on this challenge. My grandfather was not much of a businessman. He did the bare minimum. And I'm afraid that I'm not much better. I'd rather be in the kitchen or talking with the patrons."

She could easily believe that of him and his grandfather. They were both very social people, unlike her. She could hold her own in social scenes but her preference was the anonymity of a kitchen or office.

"Well, don't stay up too late." She headed for the door. "We wouldn't want you having bags under your eyes for the camera."

"Is there an in-between with you?"

She turned. "What do you mean?"

"You are either very serious or joking around. Is there ever a middle ground?"

She'd never really thought that much about it. "Of course. See, I'm not making any jokes now."

"And you're also being serious. You're wondering if I'm right."

Her lips pursed together. Did Dante see something that she'd been missing all along? And was he right?

He stepped closer. "If you control the conversation then nothing slips out—those little pieces of your life that let a person really know you. You can then keep everyone at a safe distance."

Her gaze narrowed in on him. "Since when have you become such an expert on me?"

"I'm good at reading people. And you intrigue me."

Any other time she might have enjoyed the fact that she intrigued a man but not now. Not when he could see aspects of her that made her uncomfortable.

"Are you trying to tell me that you're a mind reader—

no, wait, maybe a fortune-teller? I can see you now with a colorful turban, staring into a glass ball." She forced a smile, hoping to lighten the conversation.

"And there you go with the jokes. My point is proven."

He was right. Drat. She'd never thought about how she'd learned to shield herself from other people. When conversations got too close, too personal, she turned them around with a joke. Anything to get the spotlight off herself.

After all this time of putting up defensive postures, she didn't know if she could let down those protective walls and just be—especially around a man who could make her heart race with just a look. But something within her wanted things to be different with Dante. It was lonely always pushing people away.

"I'm just me." She didn't know how to be anyone else. "I'm sorry if that doesn't live up to your idea of the perfect woman."

He stepped closer to her. It'd be so easy to reach out to him—to lean into his arms and forget about the world for just a moment. Every fiber of her body wanted to throw herself into his arms and feel his lips against hers.

"Lizzie, you don't have to be perfect." His voice was soft and comforting. "You just have to be honest with yourself and realize that not everyone is out to hurt you. I won't hurt you."

Hearing those last four words was like having a bucket of ice water dumped over her head. Her ex had said the same thing to her to get her into bed. But when opportunity came knocking on his door, she was relegated to nothing more than an afterthought. He couldn't wait to leave New York—to leave her. The realization of how little he'd cared for her cut deep.

She wasn't going to fall for those words again.

She stepped back out of Dante's reach.

His dark gaze stared straight at her as though searching for answers to his unspoken questions.

When his gaze dipped to her lips, the breath hitched in her throat. What was he going to do? He'd promised not to kiss her until she asked him to. Would he keep that promise?

Factions warred within her. One wanted to remain safe. The other part wanted to sweep caution aside and lean into his arms. Was it possible that being safe wasn't always the best choice? Was a chance at happiness worth the inherent risks?

Dante cleared his throat. "You better go upstairs now." His voice was deeper than normal and rumbled with emotion. "If you don't, I might end up breaking my word. And a DeFiore never goes back on his word."

She turned on legs that felt like rubber and headed for the door. The warm night air did nothing to soothe her heated emotions. She needed a shower to relax her or she'd never get any sleep tonight. And Dante was worried the coffee would be stimulating. It was nothing compared to his presence.

It was on the elevator ride upstairs that she realized if he had reached out to her, she wouldn't have resisted. She wanted him as much as he wanted her. He didn't have to say the words. It was all there in his eyes. The need. The want. The desire.

Sleep was not something that was going to come easily that night.

What was wrong with him?

Dante got up from the desk in his study and strode to the window. The lights from the city obscured the stars, but he knew they were there, just like he knew there was something growing between him and Lizzie. He couldn't touch it. He couldn't see it. But there was definitely something real growing between them.

She'd appeared in his life out of nowhere. At every turn, she challenged everything he believed he wanted in life.

But above and beyond all of that, she brought the "fun factor" back to his life. He enjoyed sharing the kitchen with her. He even went to bed each night anticipating the next morning. What was it about Lizzie that had him feeling things that he'd never experienced before?

Images of her curled up in bed just down the hall from him had him prowling around his study instead of sleeping. The only good news was that there was no filming tomorrow. But it wasn't as if they had the next day off. It was Saturday, the busiest day of the week for the *ristorante*. The responsible side of him told him to go to bed this second or he'd pay for it in the morning. But he didn't relish the idea of lying there in the dark while images of the alluring woman who now shared his apartment teased and danced through his mind.

He clenched his hands as a groan rose in his throat. Pacing around his study was not doing him a bit of good. At least if he went and lay down, his body would get some much-needed rest. If he was lucky, maybe sleep would finally claim him. But first he needed a drink.

In nothing but his boxers, he quietly padded to the darkened kitchen. When he rounded the corner, the door of the fridge swung open and he stopped in his tracks, thoroughly captivated with the sight before him.

Lizzie bent over to rummage through the contents of the fridge. A pair of peach lacy shorts rode up over her shapely thighs and backside. He swallowed hard, unable to pry his eyes away from her.

Then, realizing he was spying on her, he cleared his throat. His mouth suddenly went dry. He hoped when he spoke that his voice would come out clearly. "Something you need?"

Lizzie jumped and turned around. "I didn't mean to wake you."

"You didn't."

She closed the fridge, shrouding them in darkness.

Dante moved to switch on the light over the stove. He couldn't get enough of her beauty.

She turned, casting him a questioning stare. "You couldn't sleep either?"

"Too much on my mind." He wasn't about to admit that she was on his mind. Her image had been taunting him. But those images had been nothing compared to the real thing that was standing in front of him.

The spaghetti straps of her top rested on her ivory shoulders as her straight flaxen hair flowed down her back. He didn't know that she could look even more beautiful, but he'd never be able to erase this enchanting image from his mind. He stifled a frustrated sigh and turned to the fridge. He pulled it open but nothing appealed to him. When he turned back around, her intent gaze met his.

Her fingers toyed with the lace edging of her top. "What are you worried about?"

"Nothing in particular." He really didn't want to discuss what was on his mind. "I just came out to get a snack."

He was hungry but it wasn't food he craved. When his gaze returned to her face, he noticed how she crossed her arms over her breasts. It was far too late for modesty.

"You know, you don't have to be so uncomfortable around me." He stepped forward. "I promise I just want to be your friend."

"I think it's more than that." She arched a brow. "More like friends with benefits?"

"Hey, now, that's not fair. I've kept my word. I haven't touched you." His voice grew deep as his imagination kicked into high gear. "I haven't wrapped my arms around you and pulled you close." He took another step toward her. "I haven't run my fingers up your neck and over your cheeks or trailed my thumb over your pouty lips."

Her gaze bored deep into his. The desire flared in her baby blues. He knew she wanted this moment as much as he did. He also knew that opening this door in their relationship would change things between them dramatically. But that didn't stop him. He'd gotten a glimpse of life with Lizzie in it and he wanted more of her—no matter the cost.

Damn. Why had he given his word to keep his hands to himself? Now all he had to work with were his words. He wasn't a poet, but suddenly he felt inspired.

"I...I thought you said you were going to be a gentleman?" Her gaze never left his.

"I said that I wouldn't touch you—wouldn't kiss you—not until you asked me to. But I never said anything about telling you how I feel."

She took a step toward him until their bodies were almost touching. "And how do you feel?"

His heart slammed into his ribs. He swallowed hard. "I want you so much that it's all I can think about. I can't eat. I can't sleep. All I can think about is you. Do you have any idea how much I want to wrap my arms around you and pull you close? Then I'd press my mouth to yours. I'd leave no doubt in your mind about how good we can be. Together."

She looked deep into his eyes as though she could see clear through to his soul. No one had ever looked at him that way before. The breath caught in his throat as he waited, hoping she'd cave. He wasn't so sure how long his willpower would hold out.

Her head tilted to the left and her hair swished around her shoulder. "Do you really mean it?"

"Yes, I mean it." Second by second he was losing his steadfast control. "You are driving me to distraction. It's a miracle I haven't accidentally burned the *ristorante* down."

Her lips lifted. "You're too much of a professional to do something like that."

"We'll have to wait and see. After tonight, I don't know if I'll ever get the image of you in that barely-there outfit out of my mind." He groaned in frustration. "Talk about a major distraction."

A sexy smile tugged at her lips as desire sparkled in her

eyes. Her hands reached out to him, pressing against his bare chest. He sucked in an even breath as her touch sent tremors of excitement throughout his body. Did she have any idea what she was doing to him?

This was the sweetest torture he'd ever endured. It'd take every bit of willpower to walk away from her. But he had to keep his promise to her—he couldn't be like those other people in her life who'd let her down. But he didn't want it to end—not yet.

She tilted her chin and their gazes locked. All he could think about was pressing his mouth to hers. He desperately wanted to show her exactly how she made him feel.

He was in trouble—up to his neck in it. And as much as he savored having Lizzie this close and looking at him as if he was the only man in the world for her, his resolve was rapidly deteriorating. Was this what it was like to fall in love?

Not that he was going there. Was he?

He gazed deep into her eyes, and in that moment, he saw a flash of his future—a future with Lizzie. He wanted her to look at him with that heated desire for the rest of their lives. The revelation shook him, rattling his very foundation and jarring him back to reality.

He shackled his fingers around her wrists and pushed her away from him, hoping he'd be able to think more clearly.

"You're really as good as your word, aren't you?" There was a note of marvel in her voice.

"I'm trying. But if you keep this up, I'm going to lose the battle."

"Maybe I want you to lose."

What? His gaze studied her face. A smile tugged at her lips and delight danced in her eyes. He honestly didn't know if this was another of her tests. Or was it an invitation. With a frustrated groan, he let go of her wrists and backed up until the stove pressed into his backside. He slouched against it. Defeat and frustration weighed heavy on his shoulders.

"Don't look so miserable." She stepped toward him.

When she went to touch him again, he said, "Don't, Lizzie. You've had your fun but now let me be... Please go."

"I don't want to leave you alone. Maybe I want you to pull me into your arms and do those things you mentioned."

His back straightened. "Is that an invitation?"

She nodded. "Dante, I want you just as much—"

That was all he needed to hear. In a heartbeat, he had her in his arms and his mouth claimed hers. She tasted of mint and chocolate like the after-dinner treats they handed out with the checks. He'd never taste another of those little chocolates without thinking of her.

And though the thought of letting her slip through his fingers was agonizing, he had to be absolutely sure that she wanted this, too. With every last bit of willpower, he moved his mouth from hers. "Are you sure about this? About us?"

Her big round eyes shimmered with desire. "Yes, I'm positive."

In the next instant, he swung her up into his arms and carried her back down the hallway to his master bedroom— a room he'd never shared with another woman.

But Lizzie was different. Everything about her felt so right. It was as though he'd been waiting for her to step into his life. Things would never be the same.

But exactly where they went from here, he wasn't quite certain.

He'd think about it later.

Much later.

CHAPTER FIFTEEN

DROP BY DROP...

The icy walls around her heart had melted.

Lizzie felt exposed. Vulnerable. A position she'd promised herself she'd never put herself in again. She rushed downstairs to the restaurant. When she got there she couldn't fathom how she'd found the willpower to leave Dante's side—where she longed to be right now. But she couldn't stay there. She couldn't afford to get in even deeper.

Her time in Italy was limited. In just a few weeks, she'd be preparing to return to the States—back where her responsibilities were awaiting her. And then what? She'd leave her heart in Italy. No, thank you. She had no intention of being some kind of martyr to love.

What she and Dante had was…was a one-night stand. This acknowledgment startled her. She'd never thought of herself as the type to have a fling. And now that the scratch had been itched, they'd be fine. They could go back to being coworkers.

With a fresh pot of coffee, she filled a mug and headed to the office. She had no idea how Dante could stand such a mess. It was the exact opposite of the immaculate study in his apartment, which probably explained why almost everything in here dated back years. And she couldn't find any current invoices or orders. He probably did his work upstairs and left this place as a reminder of his grandfather. Dante must miss him terribly. Her heart went out to both of them.

She knew what it was like to miss someone terribly. Her thoughts strayed to Jules. She wondered if she was still awake. She glanced at the big clock on the wall. It should be close to midnight now. Jules wasn't a partyer, but she was a night owl who had a thing for watching old movies until she fell asleep.

Needing to hear her foster sister's voice to remind her of why she should be down here instead of snug in bed with Dante, she reached for her phone. It rang once, twice, three times—

"Hey, Lizzie, what's going on?" Jules's voice was a bit groggy. "Is what's-his-face still giving you a hard time?"

"I...I just wanted to touch base and make sure things are okay with you." Her voice wobbled. Usually she told Jules everything, but suddenly she felt herself clamming up.

A groan came through the phone, the sound Jules made when she was stretching after waking up. Lizzie smiled. She could just imagine Jules stretched out on the couch. She really did miss her. They were like two peas in a pod. She couldn't imagine they'd ever move far from each other—no matter what happened in life.

"Lizzie, I can hear it in your voice. Talk to me." Her concern rang through the phone, crystal clear and totally undeniable.

This call had been a mistake. How could she tell Jules—that she'd slept with the dreamiest man on earth? She didn't want Jules adding one plus one and ending up with five.

Because there was no way she was in love with Dante. He liked fast cars and beautiful women draped on his arm. She recalled the photos of him with various stunning women hanging in the dining room. The strange thing was she hadn't found any evidence that he was anything more than a caring, compassionate man who appeared to be as commitment-phobic as herself.

"Stop worrying. I'm fine. Dante and I worked things out." Lizzie ran her thumb over the edge of a tall stack of papers. "What's new with you?"

There was a moment of strained silence.

"I had an interview for grad school. Actually, it was an all-day event. They even took the candidates out for a fancy dinner."

"I hope you didn't scare them off with all of your makeup and your black-and-white ensemble," she said in a teasing tone.

Jules sighed. "You ought to give me more credit. Actually, I borrowed some of your clothes. I even received a couple of compliments."

Excitement swirled in Lizzie's chest and had her smiling. "Does that mean you're ready for a wardrobe makeover?"

"Not a chance. I'm good the way I am."

"Yes, you are."

Jules used the makeup and clothes as camouflage—so people couldn't see the real her. But someday she hoped Jules would feel secure enough to move beyond the walls she hid behind. Whereas Lizzie's scars were all on the inside, Jules wasn't so lucky—she had them both inside and out, and she took great care to hide them.

"Anyway, it went really well and I was told unofficially that I got in. But it'll take a bit of paperwork before I get my official notification." There was a distinct lack of excitement in Jules's voice. "Lizzie? Are you still there?"

"Uh, yes. That's great! I knew you could do it. And don't worry about anything but getting through your final exams. I've got everything else under control."

"I can tell you have something on your mind. If you aren't happy there, come home."

"It's not that." And it wasn't even a lie. "I'm just tired. I didn't sleep much. That's all it is."

"Are you sure that Dante guy doesn't have anything to do with it?"

"I promise he's been great." Lizzie blinked repeatedly, keeping her emotions at bay. "If you must know, I'm a bit homesick. I miss my sidekick."

"I miss you, too. But you'll be home soon."

"I know. I'm looking forward to it."

"And here I thought Rome would be your trip of a lifetime. I was worried that you'd fall in love and I'd never see you again."

Jules was so close to the truth. Perhaps she really could use someone else's thoughts. "The truth is, Dante and I... we...umm..."

"You slept together?" The awe in Jules's voice echoed through the phone.

"Yes. But it was a one-time thing. It didn't mean anything." In her heart she knew it was a lie, but it was the reassurance Jules needed to hear to keep her calm before her finals. "Don't worry. I'll be home soon."

And the truth was it wouldn't happen again. They'd gotten away with making love once, but to have a full-blown affair with him would run the real risk of breaking her heart. Already she felt closer to him than any other man she'd ever known.

It didn't mean anything.

Those words smacked Dante across the face.

When he'd woken up, he'd reached out and found a cold, empty spot next to him. He'd begun to wonder if he'd just dreamed the incredible night. If it hadn't been for the impression of Lizzie's head in the pillow next to his and the lingering floral scent, he might have written it off as a very vivid dream. Maybe that would have been best for both of them.

By the time he'd searched the whole apartment, he'd started to panic. Where could she have gone? Why had she left? Did she regret their moment of lovemaking?

And now as he stood in the doorway with the doorjamb

propping him up, his worst fears were confirmed. Lizzie regretted last night. While he was thinking that this could possibly be the start of something, she was thinking that it would never happen again. His gut twisted into a painful knot.

Gone were the illusions that last night meant something special—for both of them. He'd been so wrong about so many things. He knew that Lizzie wouldn't intentionally hurt him. She had a good heart even though she kept it guarded.

Hearing those painful words was his own fault. He shouldn't be eavesdropping. Still, not even Red could drag him away from the spot on the white tiled floor. It was better to hear the truth than to misread things and get lost in some fantasy that wasn't real.

How could he have been such a fool? He couldn't believe he'd given in to his desires. He never lost control like that. But when he'd thought she'd finally let down her guard and let him in, he'd gotten carried away. In the end, it had all been in his imagination.

She had only one goal. To finish her job here and return to New York. Well, that was fine with him. She didn't have to worry about him clinging to her. That wasn't about to happen. No way.

Finding this out now was for the best. In the end, committed relationships didn't work out for DeFiore men. One way or another, when one of them got too close, they ended up getting burned. Luckily he'd only gotten singed, unlike his father and brother, who'd had their hearts and lives utterly decimated.

Dante stepped into the office. "So this is where you're hiding."

Lizzie jumped and pressed a hand to her chest. "I'm not hiding. And how long have you been standing there?"

"Long enough. A more important question is why did

you disappear without a word?" He should leave the subject alone but he couldn't.

His pride had been pricked and it demanded to be soothed. Because his bruised ego had to be what was causing him such discomfort. It couldn't be anything else. He refused to accept that he'd fallen for a woman who had used him for a one-night stand.

Lizzie's gaze moved to the papers on the desk. "I couldn't sleep."

Because she was horrified by what she'd let happen between them. He stifled a groan of frustration. "Something on your mind?"

Her gaze avoided his. "Uhh...no. I...ah, you must have been right. I had too much caffeine last night."

He cleared his throat, refusing to let his voice carry tones of agitation. "And you thought you'd come down here and what? Clean up the office?"

Her slender shoulders, the ones he'd rained kisses down on just hours ago, rose and fell. "I thought maybe I could organize it for you."

"And you were so excited to sort papers that it had you jumping out of bed before sunrise?"

Her gaze didn't meet his. "I like office work."

"You must."

She nodded. "I have a business degree."

He struggled to keep the surprise from showing on his face. Just one more thing to prove how little he knew about her...and yet he couldn't ignore the nagging thought that he still wanted to learn more about the beautiful blonde with the blue eyes that he could lose himself in.

He crossed his arms as his gaze followed her around the office as she moved stacks of papers to the desk. "You know, office work isn't part of the contract."

"I didn't know that we were being formal about things."

"I think it would be for the best. We don't want to forget the reason you're here."

Her forehead crinkled. "If it's about last night—"

"It's not. That was a fun night, but I'm sure neither of us plans to repeat it." *Liar. Liar.*

"So we're okay?" Hope reflected in her eyes.

"Sure." He was as far from "sure" about this as he could get, but he'd tough it out. After all, he'd given his word. A DeFiore wasn't a quitter. "You still want to complete the filming, don't you?"

There was a determined set of her jaw as she nodded. He didn't want to admit it, but he admired the way she stuck by her commitments, even if she didn't want to be around him. But there was something more. He peered closer at her, noticing the shadows beneath her eyes.

"You don't need to waste your time in here." He didn't want her wearing herself out on his behalf. "You should get some sleep since you…you were up most of the night. I don't need you walking around here in a sleep-filled haze."

"I'll be fine. I…I don't sleep much."

He wasn't going to argue with her. If she found some sort of comfort in sorting through this mound of paperwork that stretched back more years than he wanted to know, why should he stop her?

"Fine. Sort through as many papers as you like."

Her brows lifted as her eyes widened. "You mean it?"

"Sure. But I do have one question. How do you plan to sort everything when it's in Italian?"

She shrugged. "I'll muddle through. I took Italian in school."

And yet another surprise. They just kept coming, and without the aid of caffeine, he had problems keeping the surprise from filtering onto his face. He scrubbed his hand over his head, not caring that he was making a mess of his hair.

He noticed the eager look on her face. "Whatever. It has to be done soon anyway if I plan to…"

"Plan to what?"

He couldn't believe that he'd almost blurted out his plans to sell the *ristorante*. He hadn't even discussed it with Nonno. There was just something about Lizzie that put him at ease and had him feeling as though he could discuss anything. But obviously the feeling didn't go both ways.

"Once there's room, I was planning to move the business files I have upstairs in my study down here."

"Understood." She gave him a pointed look. "Before you go, we really should talk about last night—"

"It was late. Neither of us were thinking clearly. It's best if we forget about it. We still have to work together."

Her mouth gaped but no words came out. The look in her eyes said there were plenty of thoughts racing round in her mind, but that wasn't his problem. By admitting it'd been a mistake, he'd beaten her to the punch. That was fine with him.

He refused to think about how she'd discarded him and his lovemaking so readily. Soon she'd be gone. He'd just have to figure out how they could avoid each other as much as possible between now and then.

CHAPTER SIXTEEN

PRETEND IT HADN'T HAPPENED?

Was he kidding? The thought ricocheted through Lizzie's mind for about the thousandth time since Dante had spoken the words. His solution was paramount to pretending there wasn't a thousand-pound pink polka-dot elephant in the room. Impossible.

How could he just forget their lovemaking?

As the days rolled into weeks, he acted as though that earth-moving night had never happened. And he didn't leave her any room to explain or make amends. He only interacted with her on a minimal basis. The easy friendship they'd developed had crashed upon rocky shores. She missed her newfound friend more than she thought possible.

And worse yet, their chilly rapport was now apparent on the filmed segments. The director appeared to be at a loss as to how to regain their easy camaraderie. Their television segment was in jeopardy. And Lizzie couldn't let things end like this—too much was riding on their success.

While spending yet another sleepless night staring into the darkness, she'd stumbled across an idea. A chance to smooth things out with Dante.

Instead of spending another lonely weekend sightseeing while Dante visited the vineyard, she'd invited herself to accompany him to the country. Armed with an old family recipe she'd found while straightening the office and with

Massimo by her side, she'd commandeered the kitchen. She would cook the family a feast and in the process hopefully she'd mend a fence with Dante.

"Do you really think they'll like it?" She glanced at Massimo as he sat at the large kitchen table near the picture window.

"Don't you mean will Dante like it?"

The more time she spent with Massimo, the less she noticed his slurred speech and the more he could read her mind. "Yes, I want Dante to like it, too."

A knowing gleam glinted in the older man's eyes. "Something is wrong between you two."

It wasn't a question. It was a statement of fact. She glanced away and gave the sauce a stir. She didn't want Massimo to read too much in her eyes. Some things were meant to stay between her and Dante.

"We'll be fine."

Massimo got to his feet and, with the aid of his walker, moved next to her. "Look at me."

She hesitated before doing as he'd asked. She didn't know what he was going to say, but her gut told her that it would be important.

"My grandson has witnessed a lot of loss in his life. He's also been at the wrong end of his father's grief over losing my daughter. I know all about grief. When I lost my dear, sweet Isabelle, it nearly killed me. It can make a good man say things he shouldn't. It can cause a person to grow a tough skin to keep from getting hurt again."

The impact of his words answered so many questions and affirmed her suspicions. "But why are you telling me all of this? It's none of my business."

"I see how my grandson looks at you. It's the same way I looked at his grandmother. But he's afraid—afraid of being hurt like his father and brother. If you care about my grandson like I think you do, you'll fight for him."

"But I can't. Even if there was something between Dante and me, my life—it's in New York."

"Love will always find a way—"

"Mmm... What smells so good?"

Stefano strode into the kitchen, followed closely by Dante and his father. Their hungry gazes roamed over the counter and stove. She shooed them all away to get washed up while she set the dining room table.

Soon all four men were cleaned up in dress shirts and slacks. Thankfully, she'd had a couple of minutes to run to her room and put on a dress. Still, next to these smartly dressed men, she felt underdressed.

"I hope you all like tonight's dinner. Thanks to Massimo, I was able to cook some old family recipes."

"I'm sure it will be fantastic," Dante's father said as he took a seat at the head of the table.

She wished she was as confident as he sounded. It felt like a swarm of butterflies had now inhabited her stomach as she removed the ceramic lids from the serving dishes. This just had to work. She had to impress them—impress Dante.

She sat back, eagerly watching as the men filled their plates. It seemed to take forever. She didn't bother filling hers yet. She already knew what everything tasted like as she'd sampled everything numerous times in the kitchen. In fact, she wasn't even hungry at this point.

But as they started to eat, a silence came over the table. The men started exchanging puzzled looks among themselves. Lizzie's stomach tightened. What was wrong?

She glanced Dante's way but his attention was on the food. She turned to Massimo for some sort of sign that all would be well, but before he could say a word, Dante's father's chair scraped across the tiles. In the silent room, the sound was like a crescendo.

The man threw down his linen napkin and strode out

of the room. Lizzie watched in horror. She pressed a hand to her mouth, holding back a horrified gasp.

Dante called out, "Papa."

The man didn't turn back or even acknowledge him.

"Let him go." Stefano sent Dante a pointed look.

As more forks clattered to their plates, the weight of disappointment weighed heavy on Lizzie. Her chest tightened, holding back a sob. This was absolutely horrific. Instead of the dinner bringing everyone together and mending fences, it'd only upset them.

Unable to sit there and keep her emotions under wraps, Lizzie pushed back her chair. She jumped to her feet, and as fast as her feet would carry her, she headed for the kitchen.

Her eyes stung and she blinked repeatedly. She'd done something wrong. How could she have messed up the recipe? She'd double-checked everything. But her Italian was a bit rusty. Was that it? Had she misread something?

Not finding any solace in the room where she'd created the dinner—the disaster—she kept going out the back door. She had no destination in mind. Her feet just kept moving.

The what-ifs and maybes clanged about in her head. But the one thought that rose above the others was how this dinner was supposed to be her peace offering to Dante. This was what she'd hoped would be a chance for them to smooth over their differences. But that obviously wasn't going to happen when no one even wanted to eat her food.

She kept walking. She didn't even know how much time had passed when she stopped and looked around. The setting sun's rays gave the grape leaves a magical glow. Any other time she'd have been caught up in the romantic setting, but right now romance was the last thing on her mind.

She should turn back, but she wasn't ready to face anyone. Oh, who was she kidding—she wasn't willing to look into Dante's eyes and to find that once again in her life, she didn't quite measure up.

When others looked at her as though she were less than

everyone else, she could choke it down and keep going. After all, those people hadn't meant anything to her. It'd hurt—it'd hurt deeply, but it hadn't destroyed her. And she'd clung to the belief that whatever didn't destroy you made you stronger.

But Dante was a different story. A sob caught in her throat. She couldn't stand the thought of him thinking that she was inept at cooking—the one ability that she'd always excelled in—her one hope to gain his respect.

And now she'd failed. Miserably.

"Are you serious?"

Dante sent Stefano a hard stare. The main dish Lizzie had prepared was his mother's trademark dish. She only prepared it on the most special occasions.

"Of course I'm serious. Did you see how all of the color drained from Papa's face? It was like he'd seen a ghost or something."

Dante raked his fingers through his hair. "I guess I was too busy watching the horrified look on Lizzie's face. She worked all day on that meal. She wouldn't say it but I know that she was so anxious to please everyone—"

"You mean anxious to please you, little brother."

"Me? Why would she do that?" He wasn't about to let on to his older brother that anything had gone on between him and Lizzie. No way! He'd never hear the end of it. "We're working together. That's all."

Stefano elbowed him. "Whatever you say."

Dante leaned forward on the porch rail and stared off into the distance, but there was no sign of Lizzie.

"I just have one question."

Dante stifled a groan. "You always have a question and most of the time it's none of your business."

"Ah, but see, this does have to do with me. Because while you're standing there insisting that you don't care about Lizzie, she's gotten who knows how far away. So is it going to be me or you that goes after her?"

Dante hated when his brother was right. She had been gone a long time. Soon it'd be dark out. He'd attempted to follow her right after the incident, but Massimo had insisted she needed some time alone. But the thing was she didn't understand what had happened to her special dinner and he needed to explain that it had nothing to do with her. Still, he figured that after her walk she'd be more apt to listen to him.

"Dante, did you hear me?"

He turned and glared at Stefano. "How could I help but hear you when you're talking in my ear?"

"You're ignoring the question. Are you going? Or should I?"

"I'm going."

"You might want to take your car. Hard to tell how far she's gotten by now."

"Thanks so much for your expert advice."

Stefano sent him a knowing smile. "You always did need a little guidance."

They'd probably have ended up in a sparring match like they used to do as kids, but Dante had more important matters than showing his big brother that he was all grown up now. Dante jumped in Red and fired up the engine. He headed down the lane to the main road, not sure he was even headed in the right direction. No one had watched Lizzie leave, but he couldn't imagine that she'd go hiking through the fields in a dress and sandals.

He slowly eased the car along the lane, doing his best to search the fields while trying to keep the car from drifting off the road. Thankfully it was a private lane as he was doing a good deal of weaving back and forth.

Where was she?

As he reached the main road, his worries multiplied. Had he missed her? Had she wandered into the fields and somehow gotten lost? He pulled to a stop at the intersection and pounded his palm against the steering wheel. Why had he listened to his grandfather? He should have gone after her immediately.

A car passed by and his gut churned. Was it possible she was so upset that she hitched a ride from a passing motorist? A stranger?

His whole body stiffened. This was his fault. He'd been so upset by her rejection that he'd built up an impenetrable wall between them. Maybe if he hadn't been so worried about letting her hurt him again, she wouldn't have been trying so hard to impress him and his family—his dysfunctional family. If he couldn't please his father—his own flesh and blood—how was she supposed to succeed?

Dante's gaze took in the right side of the main road, but there was no sign of Lizzie. And then he proceeded to the left, the direction they'd come from the city. That had to be the way she'd gone. He could only hope that she was wise enough to keep to herself and not trust any strangers. If anything happened to her—

He cut off the thought. Nothing would happen to her. She would be fine. She had to be.

And then he spotted the back of her red dress. He let out a breath that had been pent up in his chest. He sent up a silent thank-you to the big man upstairs.

He pulled up next to her and put down the window. "Lizzie, get in the car."

She didn't stop walking. She didn't even look at him. He was in a big mess here. He picked up speed and pulled off the road. He cut the engine and jumped out of the car.

By this point, Lizzie was just passing the car. She was still walking and he had no choice but to fall in step next to her. It was either that or toss her over his shoulder. He didn't think she'd appreciate the latter option. And he didn't need any passing motorists calling the *polizia*.

"Lizzie, would you stop so we can talk?"

Still nothing. Her strides were long and quick. His car was fading into the background. He should have locked it up, but he never imagined she'd keep walking.

"What are you going to do? Walk the whole way back to Rome?"

She came to an abrupt halt and turned to him with a pained look. "It's better than going back and facing your family."

"Lizzie, they didn't mean to hurt you. It's just...just that your food surprised them."

"I know. I saw the looks on their faces. Your father couldn't get away from the table fast enough. It was as if he was going to be sick." A pained look swept over her face. "Oh, no. He didn't get sick, did he?"

"Not like you're thinking." Dante really didn't want to discuss his family's problems here on the side of the road. "Come back to the car with me. We can talk there."

She crossed her arms. "We can talk here."

"Fine. The truth is your cooking was fantastic."

She rolled her eyes. "Like I'm going to fall for that line."

She turned to start walking again when he reached out, grabbing her arm. "Wait. The least you can do is hear me out."

Her gaze moved to his hand. He released his hold, hoping she wouldn't walk away.

"I'm listening. But don't feed me a bunch of lies."

"It wasn't a lie," he ground out. "The honest-to-goodness truth is your dinner tasted exactly like my mother's cooking. At least that's what I'm told since I never had the opportunity to taste anything she prepared."

Lizzie pressed a hand to her mouth.

"It seems that particular dish was her favorite. She made it for special occasions—most notably my father's birthday. He hasn't had it since she was alive. So you can see how it would unearth a lot of unexpected memories."

She blinked repeatedly. "I'm so sorry. I never thought—"

"And you shouldn't have to know these things. It's just that my family doesn't move on with life very well. They have a tendency to stick with old stories and relish memories. If you hadn't noticed, my mother's memory is quite alive. And Massimo had no clue that the dish was special to my mother and father."

"I feel so awful for upsetting everyone."

"You have nothing to worry about. In fact, you might be the best thing that has happened to my family in a very long time."

Her beautiful blue eyes widened. "How do you get that?"

"My family has been in a rut for many years. And you're like a breath of fresh air. Instead of them going through the same routine day in and day out, now they have something to look forward to."

"Look forward to what?"

"To you."

"Really?" When he nodded, she added, "But the dinner was supposed to be special—for you."

"For me?" He pressed a hand to his chest. "But why?"

"Because ever since that night when we...uhh...you know..."

"Made love." It had been very special for him—for both of them. There was no way he could cheapen it by calling it sex. No matter what happened afterward.

"Uh, yes...well, after that you grew cold and distant. I was hoping that this dinner would change that."

"But isn't that what you wanted? Distance?"

Her fine brows rose. "Why would you think that?"

Now he had to admit what he'd done and he wasn't any too proud of it. "I heard you."

"Heard me say what?"

He kicked at a stone on the side of the desolate road. It skidded into the field. "When I found you gone that morning, I went searching for you. I knew that the night wasn't anything either one of us planned and I was worried that maybe you'd regretted it."

"But I didn't...not like you're thinking."

He pressed a finger to her lips. "Let me finish before I lose my nerve." He took a deep breath. "I'm not proud of what I have to say."

Her eyes implored him to get to the point.

"After I'd searched the whole apartment including your bedroom and found it empty, I panicked. I'd thought you'd left for good. But then I saw your suitcase. So I went down to the *ristorante* and that's when I heard your voice. When I moved toward the office, I heard you on the phone. And when you said that what we had was a one-time thing—that it didn't mean anything—I knew you regretted our lovemaking."

"Oh, Dante. I'm so sorry you overheard that."

Hope swelled in his chest. "Are you saying that all of this time I misunderstood?"

Her gaze dipped. "I wish I could tell you that, but I can't."

Piercing pain arrowed into his chest. His jaw tightened as he took a step back. He was standing here making a fool of himself for a lady who wanted nothing but to put thousands of miles between them.

"We should get back to the house and get your things." He turned for the car feeling lower than he'd ever felt in his life.

"Wait! Please." The pleading tone in her voice caused him to pause. She rushed to his side. "When I said those words, I was in the midst of a panic attack. That night had been so special. It had me reconsidering my future. I didn't know what I was feeling for you. I just knew that I didn't want to get hurt."

"And then I turned around and hurt you by putting so much distance between us."

She bit down on her lower lip and nodded.

Damn. What he knew about dealing with women and relationships couldn't even fill up the thimble his father kept on his dresser as a reminder of his mother. "I'm sorry. I didn't mean to hurt you. That's the last thing in the world I wanted to do."

"I never wanted to hurt you either. Is there any way we can go back to being friends?"

"I think we can do better than that." His head dipped and caught her lips.

Not sure that he'd made the right move and not wanting to scare her off, he restrained himself, making the kiss brief. It was with great regret that he pulled away. But when she looked up at him and smiled, he knew that he'd made the right move. There was still something there. Something very special.

"See. Your dinner was very successful. It brought us back together. Thank you for not giving up on me and for going to all of the trouble to get through my thick skull."

She lifted up on her tiptoes and pressed her lips to his. No way was he letting her get away twice. His arms quickly wrapped around her waist and pulled her close. It seemed like forever since he'd tasted her and held her. He didn't ever want this moment to end. When she was in his arms, the world felt as if it had righted itself.

The blare of a horn from a passing motorist had Lizzie jumping out of his arms. Color filled her face. "I don't think we should put on a show for everyone."

"Why not?" He didn't feel like being proper at the moment. He had more important things on his mind, like getting her back in his arms. "Who doesn't enjoy a couple—" he'd almost said "in love" but he'd caught himself in time "—a couple enjoying themselves on a summer evening."

"Is that what we were doing?"

Not comfortable exploring the eruption of emotions that plagued him when they'd kissed, he didn't answer her question. Instead he slipped his arm over her shoulders and pulled her close. "How about you and I head back to the villa?"

"I don't know. Couldn't we just go back to the city?"

"But your things are still there."

She didn't move. Then he noticed her gaze searching out his car that was a ways back the road. In that moment he knew how to get her back to the vineyard.

He jangled the car keys in front of her. "I'll let you drive Red."

Her surprised gaze searched his face. "Are you serious?"

"I'd never joke about driving Red."

She snatched the keys from his hand and started for the car.

"That's it?" He started after her. "You just take the keys and don't say a word. You know I never let anyone drive Red, right?"

"I know. But you owe me."

"And how do you get that?"

"I put up with your moodiness lately." She smiled up at him, letting him know that her sense of humor had returned. "And I didn't complain."

He stopped in his tracks and planted his hands on his sides. "I wasn't moody!"

"Oh, yes, you were," she called over her shoulder. "Worse than an old bear awakened during a snowstorm. You better hurry or you'll miss your ride."

"You wouldn't…"

Then again, she just might, depending on her mood. He smiled and shook his head. Then, realizing that she hadn't slowed down for him, he took long, quick strides to catch up with her.

CHAPTER SEVENTEEN

LIZZIE CHECKED HER tattered pride at the door. With her shoulders pulled back, she entered the DeFiore home once again. She didn't know what she expected but it certainly wasn't everyone relaxing. Massimo was reading the newspaper. Stefano was in another room watching a soccer game on a large-screen television. She'd been corrected numerous times that on this side of the pond, it was referred to as football. Not that it mattered one way or the other to her. She'd never been a sports fan.

"See. Nothing to worry about." The whisper of Dante's voice in her ear sent a wave of goose bumps down her arms.

She moved to the kitchen. Everything had been cleaned and put away. "I still haven't seen your father anywhere."

Dante shrugged. "He isn't one for sitting around. He's always complaining that there aren't enough hours in the day."

"I'd really like a chance to talk to him—to apologize."

Dante moved in front of her. "You have nothing to apologize about."

"Yes, I do. I made him unhappy and that's the last thing I meant to do."

"He should be the one apologizing to you. That man always has to have things his way—even if it makes the rest of us miserable."

She studied Dante's furrowed brow and darkened eyes. He wasn't talking about her or the disastrous dinner. There was something else eating at the relationship he had with his father.

Maybe she could do something to help. "Have you tried talking to him? Telling him how you feel?"

"Don't go there." Dante's brusque tone caught her off guard.

She took a second to suck down her emotional response. "Listen, I know there's something wrong between you and your father. When he enters the room, you leave. Your contact is bare minimum."

Dante shrugged. "It's nothing."

"No. It's definitely something. And take it from someone who never knew their father and would have moved heaven and earth to get to know him—you need to fix this thing before it's too late."

"But it's not me. It's him. There's nothing about me that he approves of."

"Aren't you exaggerating just a bit?"

"Not really." Dante raked his fingers through his hair. "But you don't want to hear any of this. Compared to you, I have nothing to complain about."

She worried her bottom lip. In her effort to make him realize how lucky he was to have a family, she'd made him feel worse. "My background has nothing to do with yours. But I would like to hear more about you and your father, if you'll tell me."

Dante stared at her as though trying to decide if she was being on the level or not. The silence grew oppressive. And just when she thought he was going to brush her off, he started to talk.

"We didn't exactly get off to a good start as he got stuck with a newborn baby in exchange for losing his wife. Not exactly a fair trade."

"Still, it's nothing that you can be held responsible for."

"I resemble my mother in more than just my looks. Instead of being drawn into the vineyard like my brother, I got restless. My father didn't understand why I wasn't interested in the family business. We fought about it continually until I moved to Rome."

"And that's where you found your passion for cooking."

He nodded. "I thought I had found my calling until Massimo left. It hasn't been the same since." Dante turned to her and looked her straight in the eyes. "If I tell you something, will you promise it'll go no further?"

She crossed her heart just like she used to do as a kid with Jules. "I promise."

"I'm in negotiations to sell the *ristorante*—"

"What? But why?"

"I figured that it's time I moved home. Make amends. And do my part."

"And you think that'll make you happy?"

He shrugged and looked away from her. "I think it's the best thing I can do for my family. Maybe at last it'll make my father happy."

Lizzie bit back her opinion. She'd have to think long and hard about what to say to him because she didn't have much experience when it came to families. With it just being her and Jules, they'd been able to work things out pretty easily. But this bigger family dynamic had her feeling like a fish out of water.

"Why don't you talk to your father? Tell him your plan."

He shrugged. "Every time I try, we end up arguing. Usually over the choices I've made in my life."

She heard the defeated tone in his voice and it dug at the old scars on her heart. "Don't give up. Promise me. It's too important."

Dante's eyes widened at her plea. "I'll do my best."

That was all she could ask of him. And she believed him. Though she didn't think that selling the restaurant and moving back here was the answer to his problems. But that was for Dante to figure out on his own.

"Now, where did you say I could find your father?"

* * *

Was she right?

Dante rolled around everything they'd talked about in his mind as he led Lizzie to the barrel cellar. When his father wasn't out in the fields checking the grapes or the soil, he was in the cellar—avoiding his family. As a young child, Dante resented anything and everything that had to do with the vineyard. He blamed the grapes for his father's notable absence.

But as Dante grew up, he realized it wasn't the vineyard he should blame—it was his father. It was his choice to avoid his children. And though his father wasn't as remote as he used to be, some habits were hard to change.

Dante glanced over at Lizzie. "Are you sure you want to do this?"

She threaded her fingers with his. With a squeeze, she smiled up at him. "I'm positive. Lead the way."

He wanted to lean over and press his mouth to hers—to feel the rightness of holding her in his arms. But with his father close by, Dante would settle for the comfort of her touch. He tightened his grip on her much smaller hand and led her down the steps.

As they walked, Lizzie asked about the wooden barrels containing the vineyard's bounty. The fact that she was truly interested in his family's heritage impressed him. He and his father may not hit it off, but he still had pride in his family's hard work. It was why he showcased DeFiore vino exclusively at the *ristorante*.

"This is so impressive." Lizzie looked all around at the walls of barrels. "And they're all full of wine?"

He nodded. "This place has grown a lot since I was a kid."

"Dante, is that you?"

They both turned to find his father holding a sample of vino. "Hey, Papa. I thought we'd find you down here."

"I was doing some testing." His father glanced at Lizzie.

"We do a periodic analysis of the contents and top off the barrels to keep down the exposure to oxygen due to evaporation."

"With all of these barrels, I'd say you have a lot of work to stay on top of things."

"It keeps me busy." His father smiled, something he didn't do often. "Is there something you needed?"

Lizzie glanced at Dante, but if she thought he was going anywhere, she was mistaken. He wasn't budging. He crossed his arms and leaned against a post. His father could be gruff and tactless at times. Dante wasn't about to let him hurt Lizzie's feelings any more than had already been done.

Lizzie turned to his father. "Mr. DeFiore, I owe you an apology for tonight. I'm so sorry I ruined your dinner and…and brought up painful memories. I had absolutely no idea that the recipe held such special meaning for you. If I had, I never would have cooked that meal."

There was an awkward pause. Dante's body tensed. Please don't let his father brush her off as though her apology meant nothing. Lizzie didn't say it, but she wanted his father's approval. And Dante wanted it for her. He didn't want her to feel the pain of once again being rejected.

Dante turned his gaze on his father, planning to send him a warning look, but his father was staring down at the vino in his hand.

The breath caught in Dante's chest as tension filled the room. When his father spoke, his voice was softer than normal and Dante strained to hear every word.

"I am the one who owes you an apology. I reacted badly. And I'm sorry. The meal, it…it caught me off guard. It tasted exactly like my wife's."

The pent-up breath released from Dante's lungs like a punctured balloon. He didn't know what was up with his father, but Dante was thankful he'd paid Lizzie such a high compliment. As far as Dante knew, there was no higher compliment than for his father to compare Lizzie's cooking to that of his mother. Was it possible his father truly was changing for the better?

"I'll try not to cook any of your wife's favorites in the future—"

"No. I mean I'd like you to. I know this meal caught me off guard, but it brought back some of the best memories." His father set aside the vino and reached for Lizzie's hand. "I hope I haven't scared you off. I'd really like you to come back and cook for us. That is, if you'd still like to."

"I would...like to cook for you, that is."

"Maybe next weekend?"

Dante at last found his voice. "Papa, we can't be here next weekend. There's been a change in the filming schedule and they're pushing to wrap up the series, so we'll be working all next weekend."

"Oh, I see." His father turned to Lizzie. "So what do you think of my son? Is he good in the kitchen?"

Lizzie's eyes opened wide. "You don't know?"

His father shook his head. "He never cooks for us. Always says it's too much like work."

Lizzie turned an astonished look to Dante. Guilt consumed him. He shrugged his shoulders innocently.

The truth was that cooking was an area where he'd excelled and he didn't want his father's ill-timed, stinging comments to rob him of that special feeling. But witnessing this different side of his father had him rethinking his stance.

"We'll have to change that." Lizzie turned back to his father. "Your son is an excellent cook and he's turning out to be an excellent teacher."

"I have an idea." There was a gleam in his father's eyes. "I'm sure Dante has told you that Massimo hasn't had an easy time moving away from the city and leaving the *ristorante* behind."

Lizzie nodded. "He mentioned it. What can I do to help?"

"That's the spirit." Papa smiled. "I was thinking that we should celebrate his birthday."

"You mean like a party."

He nodded. "Something special to show him that...well, you know."

"To let him know that everybody loves him."

Papa nodded. "I'll hire the musicians."

Lizzie's face lit up and she turned to Dante. "What do you think? Would you be willing to bring me back here?"

He couldn't think of anything he'd like more. "I think it can be arranged."

She smiled at him and a spot in his chest warmed. The warmth spread throughout his body. And he realized that for the first time he was at total ease around his father. Lizzie was a miracle worker.

"Don't worry about a thing." She patted his father's arm. "Dante and I will take care of all the food. Although your son might have to get a bigger vehicle to haul everything."

That was not a problem. Her wish was his command. He had a feeling that this party was going to be a huge deal and not just for his grandfather. He had a feeling his own life would never be the same again.

CHAPTER EIGHTEEN

AND THAT WAS a wrap!

Two weeks ahead of schedule, the filming was over. Lizzie was exhausted. They'd worked every available minute to get enough footage for the studio to splice together for the upcoming season.

And so far Dante hadn't said a word about everything they'd shared at the vineyard. Every time she'd worked up the courage to ask him about it, there was no opportunity for them to talk privately. And it was driving her crazy wondering where they went from here. Technically, she still had another two weeks in Rome to learn as much as she could from him. But her biggest lessons hadn't been taught in the kitchen.

Somewhere along the way, she'd fallen in love with Dante. Oh, she'd been in love with him for longer than she'd been willing to admit. And she accepted that was the reason she'd been so freaked out after they'd made love. She just couldn't bear to have him reject her, so she did the rejecting first. Not her best move.

"Something on your mind?" Dante asked as he strolled into the living room Saturday morning.

"I was thinking about you." She watched as surprise filtered across his handsome features.

"You were?" In a navy suit, white dress shirt and maroon tie, he looked quite dashing. "Only good thoughts, I hope."

"Definitely." Her gaze skimmed down over him again, enjoying the view. "You look a bit overdressed to be heading downstairs to help with the lunch crowd."

"That's because I'm not. I made arrangements so the kitchen is covered today. You, my pretty lady, have the day off." His smile sent her heart tumbling.

To spend with him! She grinned back at him.

She shouldn't have worried. It'd been the rush of the filming and keeping up with the increasing crush of patrons that had kept him from following up on those kisses at the vineyard. She was certain of it now.

"I like the sounds of that. What shall we do with the day?"

"I don't know about you, but I have a meeting."

"A meeting?" The words slipped past her lips.

A questioning brow lifted. "Is that a problem?"

"Umm...no. I just thought we could do something, you know, together." Did she really have to spell it out for him?

The intercom buzzed. Who in the world could that be? From what she'd gathered living here for the past several weeks, Dante didn't entertain much, and when he did, it was down in the restaurant.

"That'll be for me. They sent a car."

"Who did?"

His face creased with stress lines. "The people interested in buying the *ristorante*."

His words knocked her off-kilter. She sat down on the arm of the couch. And here she'd been daydreaming about them one day running the restaurant together. She didn't have a clue how she'd work things out with Jules being so far away, but Massimo's words came back to her: *Love will always find a way.* Now all of her daydreams were about to be dashed.

"You're really going through with it?" Her voice was barely more than a whisper.

"Why do you seem so surprised? I told you I was considering it. And thanks to you, things between me and my father are looking up. It's time I do what's expected of me."

He was trying to be noble and earn his father's respect and love. That she could admire. But at what cost?

"Dante, do you really think that you'll be happy working at the vineyard? After all, you couldn't wait to leave when you were younger. Do you really think it'll have changed?"

His gaze darkened. "Maybe I've changed."

"And you aren't going to miss the restaurant—your grandfather's legacy? Have you even told Massimo?"

Dante's brows gathered. "When I took over the *ristorante*, he gave me his blessing to do what I thought was appropriate with it. And that's what I'm doing."

She knew the decision was ultimately up to him, but if she didn't say something now, she'd regret it—they both might regret it. "Don't do it. Don't sell the restaurant."

Dante grabbed his briefcase and headed for the door. "I've got to go."

"Wait." She rushed over to him. "I'm sorry. I'm butting in where I don't belong, but I don't want you to have any regrets."

"I won't. I know what I want."

And it wasn't working here side by side with her. Her heart sank.

"We'll do something when I get back." The buzzer sounded again. "I really do have to go."

He rushed out the door. She willed him to come back, but he didn't. Deep down she had a bad feeling that Dante was about to make a decision that he would come to regret. But there was nothing else she could do to stop him.

Not quite an hour later, as Lizzie was trying to find a television show to distract her from thinking of Dante, the phone rang. Maybe it was him. Maybe he had come to his senses and couldn't wait to tell her.

"Hello."

"Lizzie, is that you?" Definitely not Dante's voice, but still it was familiar.

"Yes."

"This is Dante's father."

"Oh, hi. Dante isn't here. But I can give him a message."

"Actually, you're the one I wanted to speak to. I wanted to know if you needed any help with the food for the party tomorrow. My sisters have been pestering me to know how they can help."

How in the world had she let Massimo's party slip her mind? Of course, with the crazy filming schedule and the vibes of attraction zinging back and forth between her and Dante, it culminated into a surge, short-circuiting her mind.

"Don't worry about a thing. I have everything under control." No way was she telling him the truth. Not after that disastrous dinner.

"I knew I could count on you." His confidence in her only compounded her guilt. "This party is going to be just what Massimo needs. A houseful of family and friends with great food, music and the best vino."

They talked for a few more minutes before she gave in and said that his sisters could do the appetizers, but the entrées were her and Dante's responsibility.

As she hung up the phone, her mind was racing. That was when she realized they hadn't picked up the collage of photos of the restaurant through the years to hang in Massimo's room at the vineyard. A quick call assured her that the order was complete, but she'd have to get there right away. In twenty minutes, they closed for the weekend. She tried calling Dante's cell phone but it went straight to voice mail.

A glance at the clock told her that she didn't have time to wait. She needed to go right now. She wouldn't let Dante down in front of his family. Not when he was so anxious to fix things with his father. This gift was from the both of them, but it was more Dante's idea than hers.

Spotting the keys to Red on the counter, she wondered

if Dante would mind if she borrowed the car. After all, this was an emergency and he had let her drive it when they were in the country. What could it hurt? The shop wasn't too far away.

Before she could change her mind, she grabbed the keys and headed out the door. Her stomach quivered with nerves as she fired up the engine. As she maneuvered Red down the street, heads turned. She could only ever dream of having a luxury sports car for herself. Without even checking, she knew that the price tag on this gem was not even in her realm of possibilities...ever.

In no time, she placed the large framed collage in the passenger seat. Being cautious, she used the seat belt to hold it in place. She didn't want anything to happen to the gift. It was perfect. And she was certain that Massimo would treasure it.

Mentally she was listing everything she needed to start preparing as soon as she got home. The fact that there would be a hundred-plus people at this "small" gathering totally boggled her mind. When she and Jules had a birthday party, it usually ended up being them and a handful of friends—less than ten people total. The DeFiore clan was more like a small village.

She would need at least four trays of lasagna alone. Thankfully the restaurant was kept well stocked. When they'd talked about the party previously, Dante had told her to take whatever she needed and just to leave him a list of what she used. That was a big relief—

The blur of a speeding car caught her attention. Lizzie slammed on the brakes. Red immediately responded. Her body tensed. The air became trapped in her lungs.

The blue compact car cut in front of her, narrowly missing her.

Lizzie slowed to a stop. She blew out the pent-up breath. Thank goodness nothing had happened to Red. Dante would have freaked out if she'd damaged his precious car. The man truly loved this fine vehicle—

Squeal!

Thunk!

Lizzie's body lurched forward. Her body jerked hard against the seat belt. The air was knocked out of her lungs.

CHAPTER NINETEEN

"THAT'S NOT POSSIBLE. Lizzie wouldn't be out in Red." Dante gripped the phone tighter. "You're sure it was her?" He listened intently as though his very life depended on it. "What do you mean you don't know if she's okay?" His gut twisted into a painful knot. "I'm on my way."

Was it possible his newly hired busboy was mistaken? Lizzie had been in a car accident with Red? The kid didn't know Lizzie very well. He had to have her mixed up with someone else.

Dante strode toward the elevator of the corporate offices after his meeting. He could only hope the hired car would be waiting for him. When the elevator didn't come fast enough, he headed for the stairwell. Lizzie just had to be okay. His feet barely touched the steps as he flew down the two flights of stairs.

After nearly running into a half-dozen people, he made it to the street. The black car was waiting for him. When the driver went to get out to open his door for him, Dante waved him off. There wasn't time for niceties. He had to know if Lizzie was okay.

It seemed to take forever for the car to get across the city. He tried calling her. She didn't answer at the apartment and she didn't pick up her cell phone. Dante's body tensed. Was the kid right? Had she been in an accident? Was she hurt?

Then feeling utterly helpless, Dante did something he

hadn't done since he was a kid. He sent a prayer to the big guy upstairs, pleading for Lizzie's safety.

What had she been doing? Where had she gone? And what was she doing with Red? He couldn't come up with any plausible answers. All he could do was stare helplessly out the window as they slowly inched closer to the accident site.

"This is as close as I can get, sir. Looks like they have the road shut down up ahead." The driver sent him an apologetic look in the rearview mirror.

"Thank you."

Dante sprang out of the car and weaved his way through the throng of people on the sidewalk, sidestepping a cyclist and a few strollers. He inwardly groaned. Just his luck. Everyone seemed to be out and about on such a sunny day.

And then he saw the familiar candy-apple-red paint, but his gaze kept moving, searching for Lizzie's blond hair. She wasn't by the car. And she wasn't standing on the sidewalk.

And then he spotted the ambulance. His heart tightened. *Please. Please. Don't let her be hurt.*

He ran to the ambulance and moved to the back. Lizzie was sitting there with a stunned look on her face. His gaze scanned her from head to foot. No blood. No bandages.

Thank goodness.

"Lizzie."

It was all he got out before she was rushing into his arms and he nearly dropped to the roadway with relief. As his arms wrapped around her, he realized that he'd never been so scared in his entire life. If he had lost her— No, he couldn't go there. Losing her was unimaginable.

As he held her close and felt her shake, he realized that he loved her. Not just a little. But a whole lot. In that moment, he understood the depth of love his father had felt for his mother. He'd never before been able to comprehend why his father never remarried—why his father kept all of the memories of his mother around the house. Now he understood.

Lizzie pulled back. "Dante, I'm so sorry. I...I—"

"Are you okay?" When she didn't answer right away, his gaze moved to the paramedic. "Is she okay? Does she need to go to the hospital?"

"She refused to go to the hospital."

Dante turned to her. "You've got to go. What if something is wrong?"

"It looks like she's going to be bruised from the seat belt and a bit sore in the morning, but she should be okay."

Lizzie patted Dante's arm to get his attention. "He's right. I'm fine. But..."

"But what?" If she so much as had a pain in her little finger, he was going to carry her into that ambulance himself.

"But Red isn't in such good condition. Oh, Dante, I'm sorry..." She burst out in tears.

What did he do now? He didn't know a thing about women and tears. He let his instincts take over as he pulled her against his chest and gently rubbed her back. "It's okay. I'm just glad you're okay."

He truly meant it.

While she let her emotions flow, he realized how close he'd come to losing her in a car accident. He knew this scene. He'd lived through it with his brother. Stefano's wife had died so tragically—so unexpectedly.

The memory sent a new cold knife of fear into Dante's heart. He'd watched the agony his brother had endured when he'd joined the ranks of the DeFiore widowers' club. Dante had sworn then and there that wouldn't be him. He'd never let someone close enough to make him vulnerable. And that was exactly what was happening with Lizzie. Every moment he was with her. Every time he touched her, she got further under his skin and deeper in his heart.

He had to stop it.

He couldn't go through this again. Because next time they both might not be so lucky.

As though sensing the change in him, Lizzie pulled back and swiped quickly at her cheeks. "Dante, I'm so sorry."

"It's not your fault."

"Of course it is. I didn't ask you...I tried. But your phone was off. And I had to hurry."

"I had my phone switched off for the meeting."

"I'd forgotten. Then your dad called. And there wasn't time to wait. Then this car cut me off—"

"Slow down. Take a breath." In her excitement she wasn't making much sense and he was worried she might hyperventilate.

"The car—Red—it's not drivable. They called for a flatbed."

This was the first time he truly looked at Red. Any other time that would have been his priority. Warning bells went off in his head. He loved Lizzie more than anything in the world. When his gaze landed on the crumpled rear corner panel, he didn't feel anything. Maybe he was numb with shock and worry after seeing Lizzie in the back of the ambulance.

She sniffled. "I can't believe it happened. I was on my way home when this little car cut me off. I braked just in time. Before I could get moving again, I was hit from behind by that delivery truck."

Dante's gaze moved to the nearby white truck. The size of it was much, much larger than he'd been anticipating. The damage could have been so much worse. The thought that Lizzie could have been seriously injured...or worse hit him in the gut with a sharp jab.

"I don't know if they can repair the car but...but I'll pay the bill or replace it. Whatever it takes."

She didn't have that kind of money. Not that he'd accept it even if she did. The only important part was that she was safe. He'd be lost without her. The words teetered on his tongue, but he couldn't vocalize them. Telling her that would just be cruel. He refused to get her hopes up and have her think they were going to have a happily-ever-after ending. That simply couldn't happen.

Stifling his emotions, he said, "I still don't understand why you took the car without asking."

She turned and stared directly at him. "I told you. I tried to call you but it went straight to voice mail. And I couldn't be late. Otherwise they would have closed."

"Who would have closed? What was so damn important that you almost got yourself killed?"

Pain flashed in her eyes. "Listen, I know you're worked up about your car, but I was trying to do you a favor."

"A favor? You call totaling my car and scaring me *doing me a favor*?" He rubbed the back of his neck. His words were coming out all wrong. His gut continued to churn with a ball of conflicting emotions.

Lizzie glared at him. "I told you I'm sorry."

"But that won't fix anything." And it wouldn't ease the scare she'd given him.

The groan of the motor hauling his car up onto the back of the tow drew his attention. The bent, broken and cracked car was slowly rolled onto a flatbed. It was a miracle Lizzie had escaped serious injury.

If this worry and agony was what loving someone was about, he didn't want it. He didn't want to have to care so deeply—to depend on someone. The price of loving and losing was too steep. He didn't care if that made him a wimp or worse. He wasn't going to end up a miserable old man like the rest of his family—with only memories to keep him company on those long lonely nights. No way.

"Stay here." He wanted to keep her in sight just in case she started to feel ill. "I need to speak to the *polizia* and the tow driver."

In truth, he needed some distance. A chance to think

clearly. He had to break things off with Lizzie. It was the only logical thing to do. But why did it feel so wrong?

What was his problem?

Lizzie had never seen Dante in such a black mood. Did he really care about his car that much? She glanced over to see broken bits of the car being cleaned up. Okay. So she had totally messed up today. She knew it was her fault, but did he have to be so gruff? This wasn't the man—dare she say it—the man she loved.

After he spoke with the tow driver and the *polizia*, he returned to Lizzie. His face creased into a frown. "I'll call us a taxi."

There was no way she wanted to spend any more time around him. She already felt bad enough and had offered to pay for the damages. There was nothing else she could do to make things better. "I'd rather walk."

"You aren't up for walking." His gaze wouldn't even meet hers. "You were just in an accident."

His body was rigid. A vein pulsated in his neck. He was doing his best to bottle up his anger but she could feel it. And she couldn't stand it. He hated her for wrecking his car. "Just say it."

"I don't know what you're talking about, but I'm calling a taxi." He placed the call, ignoring her protests. "The taxi will be here shortly."

She wished he'd get it off his chest. If they couldn't even talk to each other, how in the world did she think they were going to have an ongoing relationship? Her mind was racing. She had to calm down. Everything was under control... except Massimo's birthday party.

And that was when she realized that the gift—the whole reason for this illuminating calamity—was about to be hauled away inside Red. Her gaze swung around to the damaged car atop the tow. Anxious to get to the truck before it pulled out, she took off at a brisk pace. Her heeled black boots kept her from moving quicker.

"Lizzie!" Dante called out behind her. "What's wrong? Would you talk to me?"

She kept moving until she was next to the truck. She reached up and knocked on the window. When the driver rolled down his window, she explained that she needed a package out of the vehicle.

"Couldn't this have waited?" Dante sighed.

"No. It couldn't." Lizzie stood there ramrod-straight, staring straight ahead. She refused to let Dante get to her. Instead she watched as the driver climbed up to the car and retrieved the large package.

When the man went to hand it down, Dante intercepted it. "Let me guess. This is the reason you couldn't wait for me."

She nodded. "It's the gift for your grandfather."

The tension on his face eased. It was though at last he realized she'd been trying to do something for him and she hadn't taken his car for a joyride.

When the taxi pulled up and they climbed inside, exhaustion coursed through Lizzie's veins. It was so tempting to lean her head against Dante's shoulder. They'd both been worked up. They'd both said things that they regretted. Everything would be all right when they got back to the apartment.

Satisfied that everything would work itself out, she leaned her head against him. She enjoyed the firmness of his muscles against her cheek and the gentle scent of his fresh cologne. She closed her eyes, noticing the beginning of the predicted aches setting in. But if that was all she ended up with, she'd be grateful. It could have been so much worse.

But she noticed how Dante didn't move. He didn't attempt to put his arm around her and draw her closer. He sat there stiffly and stared out the window. Maybe he was embarrassed about his heated reaction. That was understandable. She was horrified that she'd wrecked his car. Once they were home and alone, they could sort this all out.

CHAPTER TWENTY

IF THERE WAS another way to do this, he didn't know what it was.

Guilt ate at Dante. Though the ride back to the apartment was only a few minutes, it felt more like an eternity. And having Lizzie nestled against him only made him feel worse about his decision to end things. But he just couldn't live like this—always wondering when the good times would come to a crashing halt. And now that he'd had a small sample of what the pain and agony would be like—he just couldn't commit himself to a relationship.

The sooner he did this—laid everything on the table with Lizzie—the less pain they'd both experience. It was what he kept telling himself on the elevator ride to the penthouse. But somehow he was having trouble believing his own words.

It was nerves. That was it. He didn't want to hurt Lizzie any more than he had to. But in the end, this was what was best for both of them. After all, her life was in New York.

Once they stepped inside the apartment, Lizzie moved to the kitchen area. "I'll need to make a list of what we need from downstairs."

"For what?"

"The party. Remember, we're in charge of the food. Your father wants to taste your cooking."

The party where she would be introduced to his extended family—the party where people would start hint-ing about a wedding. His aunts were notorious for playing the part of matchmakers. That was why he ducked them as much as possible.

Dante sighed. This was all getting so complicated now. "Lizzie, can you come in here so we can talk?"

She rummaged through a drawer, pulling out a pen and paper. "It's already getting late. We really need to get to work on the food prep. You never did say how we're going to get all of this to the vineyard. You know, it might be easier if we'd take the supplies there and prepare it—"

He'd heard her ramble on a few occasions and each time she'd been nervous. "Lizzie, stop!"

She jumped and turned wide eyes in his direction. He felt even worse now that he'd scared her than he did before. He was making a mess of this.

"I'm sorry. I didn't mean to startle you. I just wanted your attention." He walked toward the black leather couch. "Come here. There's something I need to say."

Lizzie placed the pen and paper on the kitchen counter and hesitantly walked toward him. She knew what was coming, didn't she? It was obvious this wasn't going to work. He just wasn't cut out to be anyone's better half. He'd laugh at the thought if he wasn't so miserable.

She perched on the edge of the couch with her spine straight. "Is this about the restaurant? About your meeting today. Did you go through with the sale?"

That was what she thought he wanted to talk about? He scrubbed his hand over his face. "No, this isn't about that."

"Oh. But did you sell it? Not that it's any of my business. But I was just curious because of Massimo—"

"You don't have to remind me. I know that my grandfather put his whole life into that business." And this was just one more reason why he needed to end this relationship. She was already influencing his decisions—decisions that only a couple of months ago he hadn't needed or wanted anyone's input. "No, I didn't sell the place."

"I didn't think you could part with it. It's in your blood. You'd be lost without the restaurant." A hesitant smile pulled at the edges of her lips. "Massimo will be so pleased to know the restaurant is in safe hands. It will make his birthday gift even more special."

The collage. She'd been hurt because of him—because he'd forgotten to pick up the present. Guilt ate at him. An apology teetered on the tip of his tongue, but at the last second he bit it back. Comforting her would only muddy things. He had to end things as cleanly as possible—it would hurt her less that way.

"There's something else we need to talk about." There, he'd gotten the conversation started.

Lizzie sent him a puzzled look. "But we have so much to do for the party—"

"Don't you see, we can't do this? I can't do this." He turned his back to her, unable to bear the weight of seeing the inevitable disillusionment on her face. "We were kidding ourselves to think that we could ever have something real."

"What's going on, Dante? I thought that we were getting closer. I thought—"

"You thought wrong," he ground out. He hated himself for the pain and confusion he was causing her.

"You...you're ending things because I screwed up and wrecked your car?" The horror came across in the rising tones of her voice.

"It's not that."

He turned around then and saw the shimmer of unshed tears in her eyes. It was almost his undoing. But then he recalled the paralyzing fear of thinking that something serious had happened to her. He just couldn't cave in. It would mean risking his heart and waiting for the day that his whole world would come crashing down around him.

"Then it's my past." She looked at him with disbelief

reflected in her eyes. "I should have never told you. Now you think that I'm damaged goods."

"I never thought that. Ever." He stepped closer to her. No matter what it cost him, he was unwilling to let her think such a horrible thing. "You're amazing." His fingers caressed her cheek. "Any man who is fortunate to have you in his life will be the luckiest man in the world."

She stepped back out of his reach. "You expect me to believe that when you're standing there saying you don't want to see me again."

He groaned. "I'm doing this all wrong. I'm sorry. I never wanted you to think this had anything to do with you. You're the most beautiful woman I've ever known." He stepped toward her. "You have your whole future ahead of you."

She moved back. "Save the pep talk. I've heard lines like yours before. I don't need to hear it again. I was so wrong about you."

"What's that supposed to mean?"

"It means I thought you were different from the other guys I've known. I thought that I could trust you, but obviously I was wrong."

Her words were like spears that slammed into his chest. He didn't know it was possible to feel this low. He deserved every painful word she spewed at him. And more...

To keep from reaching out to her, he stuffed his hands in his pockets. "Don't you get it? I don't do well with long-term commitments."

She waved off his words. "Save it. I don't need to hear this. I have packing to do."

There was still the surprise party to deal with and Lizzie was in charge. But after the accident, he couldn't imagine that she'd be up for any part of it. Still, he couldn't just disinvite her. "What about Massimo's party?"

Her gaze lifted to meet his. "Are you serious? You really expect me to go and pretend that everything is okay between you and me?" She shook her head, her long blond hair swishing over her shoulder. "That party is for your family—something I'll never be."

His gaze dropped to the black plush rug with a white swirl pattern. He choked down the lump in his throat. "What should I tell everyone?"

She gave him a hard, cold stare. "This one is all on you. I'm sure you'll figure something out." She strode off down the hallway. Without even bothering to turn around, she called out, "Don't worry. I'll be gone before you return to the city."

Her back was ramrod-stiff and her shoulders were rigid. He tried to console himself with the knowledge that she'd be better off without him. The fate of women who fell in love with a DeFiore was not good. Not good at all.

CHAPTER TWENTY-ONE

HE COULDN'T BRING himself to celebrate.

Dante worked his way to a corner on the patio. There was no quiet place to hide. The musicians his father hired didn't know how to keep the volume down. And the cacophony of voices and laughter grated on Dante's taut nerves.

It didn't matter who he ran into, they asked about Lizzie. It was as though he and Lizzie were expected to head for the nearest altar as soon as possible. When he explained that Lizzie was returning to the States, they all sent him an accusing look.

He should be relieved. He had his utter freedom back. No chance that he could get hurt and grow old, miserable and alone like his grandfather, father and Stefano. No taking part in the DeFiore legacy. So why did he feel so miserable?

Dante could barely hear his own thoughts. There was nothing quiet about the DeFiore family. Everyone spoke over everyone else, hands gestured for emphasis and laughter reigned supreme. Lizzie would have loved being part of such a big gathering. And she'd have fit right in.

"How's the *ristorante*?"

Dante turned to find his father standing behind him, puffing on a cigar. Dante hadn't even heard him approach.

"It's good." Now that the decision had been made, he decided to let his father in on it. "There was an offer to buy the *ristorante*. It was made by some outfit looking to expand their portfolio."

"Are you going to accept?"

It was good to talk with someone about something other than Lizzie and his failed relationship. "I thought about it. I considered selling and moving home to help with the vineyard."

His father's bushy brows rose. "You'd want to come back after you fought so hard to get out of here?"

Dante shrugged. "I thought it'd make things easier for you."

"I don't need you to make things easier for me." His father's tone was resilient. "I take it you came to your senses and turned down the offer."

Dante considered telling him that they wanted the family recipes as part of the deal but that he just couldn't go through with it. No amount of money could compensate for giving away those family secrets. Some things weren't meant to be shared. But that wasn't the real reason he'd ended up turning down the offer.

Dante nodded his head. "I almost went through with it. But in the end, I couldn't do it."

"What changed your mind?"

"Lizzie." Her name slipped quietly over his lips as the pain of loss overwhelmed him.

"You were planning to run the place with her by your side? Like your grandparents had done?"

Dante didn't trust his voice at that moment. He merely nodded.

"Then why are you here alone? Why did you let her get away?"

His father always thought he failed at things. Well, this time his father was wrong. "I didn't let her get away. I pushed her away."

"What? But why would you do that?" His father put out

his cigar in a nearby ashtray before approaching Dante. "Let's walk."

Dante really didn't want a lecture from his father, but what did it matter? He couldn't be more miserable. His father led him off toward the vines. When people wanted to be alone, the vines always offered solace.

"Son, I know you never had a chance to know your mother, but she was an amazing woman. You remind me a lot of her. I know if she were here she'd insist that I give you some advice—"

"Papa, I don't need advice. I know what I'm doing. I won't end up like you." He realized too late that he'd said too much.

"You sent Lizzie away so you wouldn't end up miserable and alone like your old man, is that it?"

Dante couldn't deny it, so he didn't say anything. He kept his head low and concentrated on the path between the vines, which was barely wide enough for them to walk side by side.

"I'll admit it," his father said. "I didn't handle your mother's death well. I never expected to be alone with two young boys to raise. I...I was scared. And...I took my anger and frustration out on you. I'm sorry. You didn't deserve it. Not at all."

What did Dante say to that? *You're right* didn't seem appropriate. *No big deal* wouldn't work either because it was a big deal—a huge deal.

"If you had to do it over again—falling in love with Mama—would you?"

"Even knowing how things would end, I'd still have pursued your mother. She was amazing. When she smiled the whole world glowed. Loving your mother was one of the best parts of my life."

"But you...you always look so sad when anyone mentions her."

"And that's where I messed up. I closed myself off

from life. I dwelled so much on my loss—my pain—that I couldn't see clearly. I missed seeing what I was doing to my family."

"Is that why you never married again?"

Papa nodded. "I was too consumed with what I'd lost to see anything in front of me." He ran a hand over his face. "I can't go back and change any of it. My only hope is that you boys don't make the same mistakes. Love is like life—it's a gift not to be squandered."

Dante studied his father's face, trying to decide if his father was being on the level with him. "Are you serious? You'd be willing to give love another try?"

"If the right woman came along. What about you? Do you love Lizzie?"

Dante's heart pounded out the answer before he could find the words. He nodded. "But how do I live knowing that something might happen to her? That someday I might be alone?"

His father gripped his shoulder. "You don't. You just have to cherish the time you have together. No one knows the future. But by running from love, you're going to end up old and alone anyway."

Dante hadn't thought of it that way. In fact, if it weren't for Lizzie, he wouldn't be having this conversation with his father. Somehow Lizzie had worked her magic and reconnected him with his family.

His father cleared his throat. "Here's something else for you to consider. You've always known you're different from me and your brother. It's your mother's genes coming out in you. I know sometimes that drove a wedge between us. But that doesn't mean that I love you any less. Sometimes being different is a good thing."

Really? And here he'd been punishing himself for being so different from his father and brother. But if he differed from them in his choice of professions, why couldn't he be different when it came to love? Maybe there was a chance his story would end differently than theirs.

"Now, what are you doing standing here talking to me?" His father gave him a pointed stare, like when he was a boy and had forgotten to do his chores. "Go after the woman you love."

Dante turned to the villa when he realized that he didn't have his car. And the next train was hours away. He didn't have time to waste if he was going to catch Lizzie and beg her forgiveness.

"Hey, Papa, can I borrow the truck?"

His father reached into his pants pocket and pulled out a key ring. "You know it's not fancy like that sports car of yours."

"That's okay. I've learned that sort of stuff isn't what makes a person happy."

Lizzie had taught him that lesson.

Now he had to track her down, even if it meant flying to New York. He'd beg her forgiveness. Whatever it took, he'd do it.

Maybe he and his father weren't all that different after all.

CHAPTER TWENTY-TWO

How could she have let herself get caught up in a dream?

That was what this whole trip had been—one amazing dream. And now Lizzie had awakened to the harsh glare of reality. The truth was no matter how much she wanted to believe that Dante was changing, he was never going to be willing to let his guard down enough to let her in—even if she'd foolishly let him into her heart.

After Dante had left, she'd spent the night lying in the dark reliving her memories of Dante—memories that she'd treasure for a lifetime. Because no matter how the fairy tale ended, it'd still been a dream come true—falling in love under the Italian sky and kissing the man of her dreams in a breathtaking vineyard.

Tears streamed down her cheeks as she called the taxi service to take her to the airport. She took one last look around the apartment, but she couldn't bring herself to walk down the hallway to the master suite. Some memories were still too raw for her to delve into.

With the front door secure, she made her way down to the restaurant. With it being Sunday, it was closed. Maybe she had time to slip inside and—what? Remember the time she'd spent there with Dante? No, that wasn't a good idea. There was only so much pain she could take.

Would that taxi ever show up?

At the sound of an approaching vehicle, she turned. She frowned when all she saw was an old truck ambling down the road. Needing something to distract her, she reached into her purse and pulled out her cell phone. She'd been putting off calling Jules for as long as possible. Her foster sister would be full of questions as soon as she learned that Lizzie was catching an earlier flight than was planned.

Her fingers hovered over the keypad. How was she going to explain this?

"Hey, are you here for the hostess position?" came a familiar voice from behind her.

Lizzie spun around to find Dante leaning against an old truck. "What are you doing here? I mean, what are you doing back so soon? Is the party over already? You did have the party, didn't you?"

She was nervously rambling and he was smiling. Smiling? Why was he smiling? The last time she saw him, he'd looked miserable.

"The party is probably still in full swing. Once my family gets started, it goes on and on."

"That's good." She didn't want to think that anything she did would ruin this special day for Massimo. "I...I'll be out of your way in just a minute."

"Don't go."

"What?" Surely she hadn't heard him correctly.

Before Dante could repeat himself, a taxi pulled over to the curb. She should feel relieved, but she didn't. Whatever Dante's reason was for returning early, it was none of her business. He'd made that abundantly clear before he left yesterday.

Lizzie turned and slung her purse over one shoulder and her carry-on over the other shoulder. She grabbed the handle of her suitcase and turned in time to see Dante leaning in the window of the taxi, handing over a wad of cash. What in the world?

As she approached them, Dante straightened and the taxi pulled out.

"Hey! Wait!" She was going to miss her flight. The last

one for the day. She turned on Dante. "What did you go and do that for?"

"We need to talk."

She frowned. She wasn't up for another battle of words. She was bruised and wounded from their last go-round. All she wanted was to be alone to lick her wounds. "There's nothing left to say."

"I'm sorry."

His words caused the breath to catch in her throat. This time she was certain about what she heard. But whether he was talking about how he'd dumped her or whether he was referring to dismissing the taxi, she wasn't sure.

"About what?"

"Let's go inside and talk." He moved to the restaurant door and unlocked it. When he held it open for her, she didn't move. "I promise that if you hear me out and you don't like what I have to say that I'll drive you to the airport myself."

She glanced at her wristwatch. "You've got five minutes."

"Fair enough."

She must be losing her grip on reality. What other reason would there be for her to agree to put herself through more heartache and pain?

Her feet felt as though they were weighed down as she walked inside the oh-so-familiar restaurant. She really was going to miss this place and the amazing people that she'd gotten to know here—most of all, she'd miss Dante.

She stopped by the hostess desk and turned to him. "What is it you want?"

"You."

"What?" Her lack of sleep was not helping her make sense of what he was telling her.

"I want you, Lizzie. I love you."

Her heart tripped over itself. She'd been waiting for so long to hear those words, but before she went flying into his arms, she needed to understand. "But what about yesterday?"

"I panicked. When I got a phone call telling me that you'd been in an accident, I overreacted. It seems like the DeFiore men are destined to grow old alone and I thought— Well, it doesn't matter. All I could think about is that if I lost you I'd be devastated and unable to go on."

Really? No one had ever cared about her that much.

"But if you felt that way, how were you able to just dump me?"

"I thought that by protecting myself that I wouldn't be hurt. But my father pointed out the fallacy of my logic—"

"Your father? You two were discussing me?" She wasn't so sure how she felt about that detail.

"Thanks to you, we had a talk that was long overdue." He looked around at the restaurant and then back at her. "You opened my eyes to a lot of things including how much I love this place...especially with you by my side."

Her heart tap-danced in her chest. "Do you really mean that?"

He peered deep into her eyes. "I love you with all my heart. And I would be honored if you'd consider staying here and running Massimo's with me."

"I couldn't think of anything I'd like more."

He stepped closer and wrapped his arms around her. "I promise no more panic attacks as long as you promise not to take up skydiving."

"Now that's a promise I can readily make." She smiled up at him as she slipped her arms up over his shoulders. "I'm scared of heights."

"So we're partners?"

She nodded. "But I think we should kiss to make it official."

"I think you're right."

His head dipped. Their lips met and the rest of the world slipped away.

At last Lizzie was home.

EPILOGUE

A month later

THE CLINK OF champagne flutes sounded in the empty dining room.

"To the most amazing man." Lizzie stared into the eyes of the only man she'd ever loved. "I love you."

"I love you, too." Dante pressed a kiss to her lips that promised more to follow. And soon.

"Can you believe we were on television? Our grand premiere." Lizzie couldn't keep a silly grin from her face.

"And you were amazing."

She waved off his over-the-top compliment. "I think those bubbles are going to your head."

"Nope. It's just you."

"Can you be serious for just a minute?"

The truth was that she had never been this deliriously happy in her entire life. Even the evenings she'd spent sitting next to Dante on the couch watching soccer...erm, football made her smile. And she never thought she'd ever appreciate sports, but Dante was opening her eyes to football and so much more.

"I can be serious. As long as it doesn't take too long." His gaze dipped to her lips.

When he started to lean forward, Lizzie held out her hands. "Dante, do you think of anything else?"

A lazy smile pulled at his lips. "Not if I can help it."

"Well, try for just a second."

His tempting lips pursed together. "What's on your mind?"

"What do you think about the television studio's offer to give us our own show?" They'd just received the call and Lizzie was too excited to trust her own reactions.

"I can think of something I'd like better."

She searched his face to see if his mind was still in the bedroom, but his expression was totally serious. "What is it?"

"How about you become my partner?"

"Well, of course I'll be your partner. That's what the studio is interested in. You and me working together—"

"No, I don't mean that." He took her hand in his and looked deep into her eyes, making her heart skip a beat. Then he dropped to his knee. "I mean I want you to be my family."

The breath hitched in her throat as tears of joy obscured the view of the man she loved with all of her heart. She blinked and the tears splashed onto her cheeks. With effort she swallowed the lump of giddy emotion in her throat.

"I can't think of anything I'd like better."

He got to his feet and encased her face in his palms. "I'm sorry I'm unprepared but I hadn't been planning to propose tonight. I've been playing it over and over in my mind. And I just couldn't wait any longer."

She stood up on her tiptoes and pressed her lips to his. Her heart thumped with excitement. She didn't know how it was possible but she'd swear with every kiss it just kept getting better and better.

When Dante pulled away, she pouted. He smiled and shook his head. "I take it that was a yes?"

"Most definitely."

"I have one more serious question."

"Well, ask it so we can get back to the good stuff."

He laughed and she grinned.

"I have an idea and I don't know how you'll feel about it, but what about having the wedding at the vineyard?"

She couldn't think of a more romantic spot on the entire earth. "I love it but..."

"But what?"

"What about Jules?" The thought of being permanently separated from her foster sister dimmed her excitement. "She's my only family—"

"Not anymore—I'll be your family, too. And Jules is always welcome here."

"But she has grad school. I won't let her give up. She's worked too hard for this. I want her to reach for her dreams."

"And she will. We'll make sure of it."

"But how?"

Dante pressed a finger to her lips. "Shh... Nonno always says, *Where there's a will, there's a way.*"

Lizzie's mind and heart were racing. The two people she loved most in this world were divided by an ocean. "I don't know."

"Look at me." Dante's gaze caught and held hers. "Do you love me?"

Without any hesitation she uttered, "With all of my heart."

"Then believe in us—in the power of our love. Believe that the future will work out for all of us. Maybe not in the way we'd expect, but sometimes the unexpected is just what people need. There's a way to make this work with Jules and we'll find it. Do you believe me?"

"I do."

He pressed his lips to hers and the worries faded away. Together, they could do anything.

* * * * *

ST PIRAN'S: ITALIAN SURGEON, FORBIDDEN BRIDE

MARGARET McDONAGH

With special thanks to:
The Medical Romance team for inviting me to be
a part of this wonderful project and my fellow authors
for their support, especially...
Jo, Lucy, Mimi, Sheila, Carol, Caroline,
Kate and Maggie Charlie & Will—for 'Charlie'...
and for making the best bears in the world!

Namlife for the information on living with HIV:
www.namlife.org

CHAPTER ONE

'YOU need Jessica Carmichael.'

He didn't *need* anyone...not any more.

Giovanni Corezzi bit back his instant denial of the suggestion made by paediatric registrar Dr Megan Phillips. It was his first day as consultant neurosurgeon at St Piran's Hospital in Cornwall and although his primary focus was always on doing his best for his patients, he also hoped to make a good impression and to form a friendly working relationship with his new colleagues.

'Jessica Carmichael?'

He frowned, disturbed at the way the unknown woman's name flowed from his tongue. As if it were a caress. And somehow important. What nonsense was he thinking? With an impatient shake of his head, he refocused on Megan.

'Jess is a hospital counsellor. She's very knowledgeable and good with patients and their relatives,' the paediatric registrar explained with obvious admiration. 'Unfortunately we don't have extra time for everyone. Jess fills that gap.'

'I'll bear it in mind,' Gio replied, knowing the involvement of a counsellor was often helpful to his patients but reluctant to bring one in now.

'It's your decision.' Megan's disappointment and disagreement were apparent. 'I think you'd find Jess useful in Cody Rowland's case.'

Gio bit back irritation as the young registrar questioned his judgement. Instead of an instant retort, however, he considered whether he had missed anything regarding the young boy admitted to his care. Three-year-old Cody had fallen from a climbing frame two weeks previously, but had not shown any symptoms at the time. Recently he had become increasingly listless, complaining of a headache, going off his food and feeling nauseous. His frightened parents had brought him to the hospital that morning.

A and E consultant Josh O'Hara had examined Cody and called the neurology team. Busy in Theatre, Gio had sent his registrar to do an assessment. The subsequent tests, including a CT scan, had revealed the presence of a chronic subdural haematoma. As the bleed had continued and the clot had increased in size, it had caused a rise in pressure and the swelling brain to press on the skull, causing bruising and a restriction in blood flow.

Cody was now on the children's ward and awaiting surgery. Unless he carried out the operation soon, Gio feared the boy's condition would deteriorate and, if the clot and pressure continued to grow, there was a possibility of irreversible brain damage.

It was after noon and his first day was proving to be a hectic one. That morning he had undertaken three minor and routine operations—as minor and routine as any brain surgery procedures could be—and his first neurological clinic was scheduled later that afternoon.

Before that, he needed to return to the operating theatre with Cody.

'I'm sure this woman is good at her job,' he commented, 'but Cody—'

'Cody might need Jess at some point. Right now I'm thinking of his parents.'

Gio hated to admit it, but she was right. He *did* have concerns about the Rowlands and that Megan had picked up on the same signs was something he should find pleasing, not irritating.

'They aren't coping well,' he conceded with frustration. 'And their anxiety is distressing Cody. I need him to be settled for surgery—and for his parents to be calm and understand why we need to operate. I wish to press on them the urgency without further panicking them. They are listening but not hearing, you know?'

'I know,' Megan agreed. 'They're in denial...Mrs Rowland particularly.'

'Exactly so. Which is understandable. I'm not unsympathetic but I don't know how much time we have to play with.'

Megan hesitated, as if unsure of her ground. 'That's why I suggested Jess. I'm sorry to keep on about her, and I'm not questioning your skills,' she added hastily as his eyebrows snapped together. 'But I know how helpful she is in these situations. Everyone in the hospital likes Jess. She's a wonderful listener...and it isn't just the patients and their relatives who benefit. The staff frequently offload their problems on her, too. She's definitely your woman.'

Gio's frown returned in earnest, both at Megan's phraseology and the implication of her words. 'I don't know...'

Was he being too hasty? It was uncharacteristic of him not to listen to the suggestions of others, even if they were his juniors. He considered his reluctance to follow Megan's advice. Was it because he didn't want his new colleagues to think he couldn't do his job? Here he was, halfway through his first day and already needing to call in someone else to help with a case! He shook his head. What mattered was the well-being of his patients, not his own status.

Checking his watch, aware that *he* was now the one wasting precious time, he wondered how long it would take for Ms Carmichael to arrive. Once she was there, he would need to bring her up to date on the case and, as yet, he had no idea how much she understood of medical issues.

'Won't she be tied up with existing appointments?' he asked Megan. 'Cody can't afford to wait much longer.'

'Jess doesn't work like that, Mr Corezzi. She's on call and responds to whichever department or ward has need of her. It's just a matter of paging her—she usually comes right away,' the paediatric registrar explained, jotting a note on the front of Cody's file.

'Call me Gio.' He made the invitation with a distracted smile as he considered his options. He needed Cody in Theatre without further delay. If this counsellor could help facilitate that, then so be it. 'All right, Megan, please call her,' he invited, decision made, adding a word of caution. 'However, if she's not here soon, we may have to move without her.'

Megan's smile was swift. 'You won't be sorry, Gio,' she assured him, and he could only hope she was right.

'I'll ensure the operating theatre and my team are

ready. And I'll arrange for the anaesthetist to assess Cody,' he informed her. 'Everything will be in place and we can move quickly—*when* we have the Rowlands' consent.'

As Megan went to the ward office to organise the page, an inexplicable shiver of apprehension and anticipation rippled down Gio's spine. He had done the right thing for Cody. So why did he feel unsettled? And why did he have the disturbing notion that in bringing Jessica Carmichael on board he would be taking on much more than he had bargained for?

'Consultants don't spend time taking histories or chatting to patients and their relatives. That's why they have registrars and juniors,' Jess protested with a mix of wry cynicism and surprise.

Megan chuckled. 'This consultant does. He's pretty amazing, Jess, and very hands on.'

The news that Mr Corezzi remained on the ward was disturbing enough, but knowing Megan was so taken with their new consultant neurosurgeon left Jess feeling more unsettled. A sense of premonition refused to be banished. On edge, she opened her notebook and balanced it on top of the other items she carried, jotting down a few pointers as her friend gave a brief summation of Cody's case.

'Mr Corezzi…Gio…will give you more detail,' Megan added, the prospect making Jess feel more nervous.

'And Cody is three,' she mused, considering how best to help. 'I'll get Charlie.'

'Who is Charlie?'

The question came from behind her and the deep, throaty voice with its distinctive Italian accent not only identified its owner but set every nerve-ending tingling. Jess knew it was his first day there, and within moments of his arrival the overactive grapevine had been buzzing about the gorgeous new consultant. Female staff the length and breadth of the hospital had been preening themselves, eager to meet him and make an impression on him.

She had not been one of them.

Jess tensed, her knuckles whitening as her fingers tightened their grip on her files. Clutching them like a protective shield, and feeling suddenly scared in a way she didn't understand, she turned around and saw Giovanni Corezzi for the first time.

Oh, my!

For once the rumourmill had been right. The new Italian surgeon *was* something special to look at and even she, who had sworn off men a long time ago, could appreciate the view. A bit like window-shopping, she thought, smothering an inappropriate smile. You could admire the goods even though you had no intention of buying. But her inner humour vanished in the face of her body's impossible-to-ignore reaction.

She hated the breathless feeling that made it difficult to fill her lungs, the ache that knotted her stomach, the too-fast beat of her heart, and jelly-like knees that felt unable to support her. The instinctive responses were unnerving and unwanted. She had not been attracted to any man for a long time—had not expected or wished to be. Not since her life had taken an abrupt change of direction four years ago, turning her world upside down and having an irrevocable impact on her future, forcing her not only to abandon her hopes and dreams but to reinvent herself to survive. The Jess Carmichael of today was a very different person from the one then…one who could no longer indulge in many things, including uncharacteristic flights of fancy over a good-looking man, even if he did stir her blood in ways it had never been stirred before.

Trying to shrug off the disturbing feelings, she allowed herself a quick inspection of the imposing man who stood before her looking relaxed and at ease. His dark hair was short, thick and well groomed. In his early thirties, and topping six feet, he had an olive-toned complexion and the kind of chiselled jawline that would make him sought after in Hollywood or gracing the pages of fashion magazines. Not that he was fashionable at the moment, dressed as he was in hospital scrubs, suggesting he had come to the ward from the operating theatre.

The shapeless trousers and short-sleeved tunic should have been unflattering but they failed to mask the strength and lean athleticism of his body, while their colour emphasised the intense blueness of his eyes. Under straight, dark brows and fringed by long, dusky lashes, they were the shade of the rarest tanzanite. They regarded her with a wariness she shared, a suspicion that had her shifting uncomfortably, and the kind of masculine interest and sensual awareness that frightened her witless.

Aware that Megan was making the introductions, Jess struggled to pull herself together.

'Ms Carmichael.'

The throaty rumble of his voice made her pulse race and ruined her attempt at sang-froid. 'Hello, Mr Corezzi.'

Jess dragged her gaze free and focused on the leanly

muscled forearms crossed over his broad chest. As he moved, she juggled the files and assorted items she carried around the hospital, anxious to avoid shaking hands. Instead, she fished out one of her cards, careful to ensure she didn't touch him. His fingers closed around the card and she couldn't help but notice that he had nice hands. Surgeon's hands...capable, cared for and with short, well-manicured nails. There was no wedding ring and no tell-tale sign to suggest he had recently worn one. His only accessory was the watch on his left wrist with its mesh strap and midnight-blue dial.

The sound of Megan's pager made Jess jump but the distraction helped cut the growing tension.

'I'm needed in A and E,' Megan told them with evident reluctance, her cheeks pale and lines of strain around her mouth.

'Are you OK?' Jess asked, knowing her friend's reluctance stemmed from some unexplained issues she had with Josh O'Hara, the charismatic consultant who had joined St Piran's trauma team in the spring.

'I'll be fine.'

The words lacked conviction and Jess was concerned. Tall and slender, Megan appeared delicate, but although she possessed an inner strength, she had seemed more fragile than usual these last few weeks. Instinct made Jess want to give her friend a hug, but she hung back, keeping the physical distance she had maintained between herself and everyone else these last four years.

'I'm here if you need me,' she offered instead, conscious of the disturbing nearness of Giovanni Corezzi, whose presence prevented her saying more.

'Thanks.' Megan squared her shoulders, determination mixing with anxiety and inner hurt that shadowed her green eyes. 'I'll see you later. Good luck with the Rowlands. And Cody's surgery.'

Alone with Giovanni Corezzi, Jess felt a return of the tension and awareness that surged between them. Determined to focus on work, and needing to put distance between herself and the disturbing new surgeon, Jess murmured an apology and escaped to the ward office to track down Charlie.

Gio released a shaky breath as the surprising Jessica Carmichael walked away. He had no idea who Charlie was, or how he was relevant to the current problem, but he had greater things to worry about. Namely Jessica and his unaccountably disturbing reaction to her.

As the staff went about their work on the busy ward, he leaned against the wall and pressed one hand to his stomach. The moment he'd seen Jessica, it had felt as if he'd been sat on by an elephant. She was younger than he'd expected, perhaps in her late twenties. Below average height, she looked smart but casual, dressed for the August heat in a multi-coloured crinkle-cotton skirt that fell to her knees and a short-sleeved green shirt, her hospital ID clipped, like his own, to the top pocket.

Her eyes were a captivating and unusual olive green, while her hair—a gift from mother nature—was a vibrant auburn, with shades from burnished chestnut, like a conker fresh from its casing, to rich copper red. The luxuriant waves were confined in a thick plait which bobbed between her shoulder blades. He longed to see it unrestrained and to run his fingers through its glory.

When Jessica emerged from the ward office, the disturbing heaviness pressed on him once more. He straightened, shocked by the slam of attraction that shot through him. The cut of her shirt highlighted firm, full breasts, while the sway of her skirt hinted at curvy hips and thighs. He found her rounded, feminine figure so much more appealing than the reed-thin bodies many women aspired to.

Gio took an involuntary step back, disturbed by the surge of desire that threatened to overwhelm him with its unexpected intensity. This was the first time he had even *noticed* a woman for a long time. He couldn't believe it had been five years— No! He slammed his brain shut on *those* thoughts. This was neither the time nor the place. But he'd allowed a crack in the internal armour encasing the memories, the pain and his heart, and panic swelled within him. He didn't want to be attracted to anyone, yet he could not deny the strength of his reaction to Jessica or the way his body was reawakening and making new desires and needs known.

Disconcerted, he met her gaze and saw her eyes widen in shock at the unmasked emotions she read in his. She kept a safe gap between them, but she was close enough for him to see her shock turn to confusion, followed by answering knowledge and then alarm. Silence stretched and the air crackled with electricity. It was clear Jessica didn't want the attraction any more than he did, but that didn't make it go away. And, perversely, her reluctance intrigued him and made him want to learn more about her.

She stepped aside to allow a nurse pushing a wheelchair to pass, her smile transforming her pretty face and trapping the air in his lungs. Cross with himself, he was about to return to the business of Cody Rowland when she shifted the things she was carrying and he noticed the teddy-bear puppet she wore on one hand.

'Meet Charlie,' she invited, holding up the plush toy, which had marbled brown fur and a friendly, mischievous face, its mouth open as if laughing. 'He helps break the ice and explain things to young children, calming their fears.'

The husky but melodic burr of her soft Scottish accent was sensual and set his heart thudding. Feeling as flustered as a teenager with his first crush, he struggled to ignore his unwanted reaction and focus on the matter at hand.

'Very clever.' Her innovative method impressed him. He reached out and gently shook the teddy bear by the paw. 'It's nice to meet you, Charlie.'

Jessica's flustered reaction confirmed his suspicion that giving him her card had been a ruse to avoid shaking hands. Was it him, or did she dislike touching other people, too? That he was immediately attuned to her unsettled him further.

'What are the priorities with Cody?' Jessica asked, moving them onto ground which, he felt sure, made her feel more comfortable. 'Have his parents signed the consent form?'

'Not yet.' Gio ran the fingers of one hand through his hair in frustration. 'The injury occurred over two weeks ago,' he explained, unsure how much Megan had told her. 'The parents are too upset to understand that while Cody may have appeared fine at first, the situation has changed.'

'And you don't want to waste more time.'

Grateful that Jessica was on his wavelength, Gio smiled. 'Exactly so.'

'He's deteriorating more quickly?' she asked, glancing at the notes.

'What was a slow bleed building a chronic subdural haematoma could be worsening,' he outlined, sharing his concerns. 'Or something more serious could be underlying it.'

Jessica nodded, making her beautiful hair gleam. 'And the longer you wait, the more chance there is of permanent brain damage.'

'I'm afraid so.'

'His parents must be very confused.' Her expression softened with understanding. 'They may feel guilty for not realising that what seemed an innocuous incident has become something so serious.'

'There is no question of blame, although such feelings are common,' he agreed, impressed by Jessica.

Her smile was rueful. 'I come across this in a wide variety of circumstances. We need to explain things to the Rowlands without frightening them further.'

'Yes...and Megan says you're the best person to help.'

A wash of colour warmed her flawless alabaster cheeks. 'I'll do what I can, of course.'

'Thank you, Jessica.'

Again her name felt right, unsettling him and curbing his amusement at her flustered reaction. Ignoring the hum of attraction between them by concentrating on work might not be effective long term, but hopefully it would get them through this encounter.

'Do you have suggestions about the Rowlands?'

Her relief was evident and she nodded again, loosening some strands of fiery hair, which tumbled around her face. As she raised her free hand, he saw that her fingers were ring free, and that she wore a narrow silver-toned watch around her wrist. She tucked the errant curls behind her ear, drawing his attention to the attractive stud earrings she wore. Set in white metal, the olive green stones matched her eyes and he made a mental note to discover the identity of the gem that so suited her.

'We need their consent so Cody can go to Theatre without delay. Then I can spend time with them and run through everything in more detail.' Even, white teeth nibbled the sensual swell of her rosy lower lip, nearly giving him heart failure. 'Do you have a rough guestimate on how long the operation might take?' she queried, snapping his attention back to business. 'The Rowlands will ask—and I need to reorganise my schedule to support them.'

Gio was encouraged by Jessica's common-sense approach, knowledge and apparent dedication to her patients. With real hope of a resolution, he gave her all the information he could.

'Can you talk with the father while I try the mother?' she asked next, walking briskly towards Cody's room.

He would happily do anything to speed things along. 'No problem.'

Following her, he admired her gently rounded, mouth-watering curves. As she stepped into Cody's room, sunlight spilling through the window made the natural red, copper and chestnut tones of her hair glow like living flames, captivating him. And, for the briefest instant, as he stood close behind her before she shifted to give him more room, he could have sworn he caught a faint, tantalising aroma of chocolate.

Fanciful notions vanished as he observed that Cody appeared more listless than when he had checked him several minutes ago. His frightened young mother sat close to him, clinging to his hand, tears spilling down her cheeks. The father, scarcely more than a boy himself, stood to one side, pale and withdrawn, at a loss to know what to do.

Jessica glanced over her shoulder and he met her gaze. The connection between them felt electric and intense, and it took a huge effort to look away. Clearing his throat, he introduced her to the Rowlands.

As Jessica began the delicate process of winning the trust of the troubled young family, Gio released another shaky breath. He was in big trouble. He had sensed Jessica would be more than he'd bargained for. Professionally. What he could never have foreseen was the impact she would have on him personally. It was unexpected, unwanted and scary. But bubbling within, as yet unacknowledged and unexplored, was growing excitement.

Even as they worked together to see Cody and his parents through the trauma that had befallen them, Gio was aware of the simmering connection between himself and Jessica. However hard they fought it, it was not going away.

All he knew for sure was that Jessica threatened to blow the ordered and lonely world he had lived in these last five years wide apart, and that her impact on his life would not leave him unscathed.

CHAPTER TWO

SHE didn't *look* any different.

Jess peered at her reflection in the mirror above the basin in the tiny bathroom next to her office. She wasn't sure what she'd expected to see, but she *felt* different. Changed somehow. And scared. Because of Giovanni Corezzi. Thinking about him made her pulse race and raised her temperature to an uncomfortable level—one she couldn't blame on the scorching August weather.

After splashing cool water on her overheated cheeks, she buried her face in the softness of her towel. Even with her eyes closed, images of St Piran's new Italian surgeon filled her mind. Unsettled by her reaction to him, she had endeavoured to keep things on a professional footing, determined to banish the disturbing feelings he roused within her.

She hadn't wanted to like him, but it had proved impossible not to. Ignoring the inexplicable and overwhelming blaze of attraction would have been easier had he been arrogant and horrible to work with, but nothing was further from the truth. He'd been compassionate and patient. As his initial suspicion had evaporated once he had witnessed her with the Rowlands, the likelihood was that she would be called to work with him again.

What was she going to do?

Jess sighed, discarding the towel and glancing at her reflection again. Less than an hour in his company had left her shaken and anxious. Megan had been right to describe him as hands on and caring. It was something Jess admired, yet it made him even more dangerous to her.

She had to find a way to limit his impact on her. He had reawakened things long forgotten, things she would sooner remained buried. She had to fight the desire he roused in her...because nothing could come of it. *Ever.* And she was leaving herself open to heartache if, even for a moment, she allowed herself to imagine anything else.

For the last four years, since the bombshell had hit her, changing her life for ever, she had turned in on herself, keeping focused on her new career and keeping people at bay. She hadn't worked so hard to reinvent herself to allow the first man to stir her long-dormant hormones into action to undo everything she had achieved. In the unlikely event she could ever trust a man again, there was no way she could allow any kind of relationship to develop. Not beyond friendship. To do so would be too great a risk. Besides, once Giovanni learned the truth she had kept secret for so long, he wouldn't want her anyway.

Quashing disobedient feelings of disappointment and regret—and, worse, a flash of self-pity—Jess hardened her battered heart. She had to keep Giovanni Corezzi at a distance and ensure any meetings with him were kept as professional and brief as possible.

Shocked how late it was, she returned to her office. She'd had to rearrange her schedule for the Rowlands, which meant she had much to catch up on and now she would have to rush if she was not to be late for an important appointment.

Five days ago, and less than three weeks after moving into the run-down cottage she had bought near Penhally village, an unseasonal storm had caused serious damage. Today the insurance company's assessor was carrying out an inspection, after which Jess hoped permission would be given for the repairs. The sooner the better… before anyone discovered the unconventional lengths she was going to to keep a roof over her head.

Smothering her guilt, she took care of a few urgent tasks before shutting down her computer. She just had time to dash across the grounds to see hospital handyman Sid Evans and collect the precious cargo he was watching for her.

'Hello, Jess, love,' the kindly man greeted her as she hurried through his open workshop door. 'Everything is ready for you.'

'Thanks, Sid.'

'Here we are, all present and correct,' he told her in his lilting Welsh accent as he handed her a basket.

'I'm sorry to rush, Sid. Thanks for your help.'

'No worries.' He smiled, but Jess could see the sadness that lurked in his eyes. Following the recent death of Winnie, Sid's beloved wife of forty years, Jess had taken time to visit with him. 'And I'm the one who's grateful. You've been wonderful, love, letting me talk about my Winnie. I'll not forget it.'

'It's been my privilege,' she replied, a lump in her throat.

Jess hurried back to the psychology unit, glad everyone had left for the day, allowing her to sneak the basket into her odd little annexe at the back of the building. Dubbed the 'cubby hole', it had been assigned to her as the only spare room available, but she couldn't have been more pleased. Apart from the office and next-door bathroom, it had an adjoining anteroom and a basic kitchen. Away from the main offices, it gave her privacy, which suited her just fine. Especially with circumstances as they were…circumstances no one else knew about and which brought another surge of guilt.

Setting down the basket, Jess checked the contents then picked up her bag and keys. The sooner she went home, the sooner she could return to St Piran's. Hopefully she would be too busy in the coming hours to think about Giovanni Corezzi.

Opening her office door, she hurried out, only to collide with something solid and warm and smelling divinely of clean male with a hint of citrus and musk. Her 'Oh' of surprise was muffled against a broad chest as she lost her balance.

'Easy there,' Giovanni's voice soothed.

His hands steadied her, closing on her bare arms above the elbows. She felt the impact of his touch in every particle of her being, the brush of his fingers on sensitive skin making her tingle. She felt as if she'd been branded. A bolt of awareness and long-suppressed need blazed through her, scaring her.

The urge to lean into him and savour the moment was very strong. It seemed for ever since she had been touched and held, even in a platonic way. Not that there was anything *platonic* about the way Giovanni made her feel! But that knowledge acted like a bucket of icy water. Panic gripped her, both at the physical contact and her overwhelming reaction to this man. The need to break the spell overrode everything else and she struggled free, her desperation causing her to push away from him with more force than she had intended.

'What are you doing here?' she challenged brusquely.

Intense blue eyes regarded her with curiosity. 'Forgive me, I didn't know this part of the hospital was out of bounds.' His tone was gently teasing, but a blush stained her cheeks in acknowledgement of her uncharacteristic rudeness.

'It's not, of course, Mr Corezzi, but—' Jess broke off. Everything about him threw her into confusion.

'Please, call me Gio. I came to update you on Cody,' he explained, his throaty voice and sexy accent sending a shiver down her spine. 'And to thank you for your help.'

Her breath locked in her lungs as he rewarded her with a full-wattage smile. 'I was just doing my job.'

'I also wish to discuss another patient soon to be admitted whom I feel will benefit from your involvement,' he continued.

'That's fine. But is it urgent? I'm in a hurry.'

Although she had softened her tone, his dark eyebrows drew together in a frown. 'It's not urgent, but I hoped you'd have a minute…'

'I'm afraid I don't.' Jess cursed her stiltedness. She seemed unable to behave normally around him. 'I'm sorry, I have to rush home. I'll talk with you later.'

Eager to make her escape without him seeing inside her office and discovering the secret she had kept hidden so far, Jess fumbled behind her for the handle and pulled the door closed with a determined snap. She turned round, removing herself from his inspection, locked her office and pocketed the key. Then, carefully skirting him, she walked briskly to the main entrance, conscious of him following her.

'Jessica...'

The way he said her name tied her insides into knots. It wasn't just his voice or pronunciation but that he alone used her full name and made it sound like a caress. Thankful she had a genuine excuse to escape, she opened the front door and stepped aside for him to exit ahead of her.

'I have to run,' she said, concerned at his reluctance to leave.

A muscle pulsed along the masculine line of his jaw, indicating his dissatisfaction. When he stepped outside, allowing her to do the same, the door swinging closed and the lock clicking into place, Jess released the breath she hadn't realised she'd been holding.

He looked down at her, a brooding expression on his far-too-handsome face. 'Later.'

It was more demand than question and it filled Jess with alarm...and a dangerous sense of excited anticipation that was the most scary of all.

'Later,' she allowed reluctantly.

As she hurried towards her car, she sensed him watching her. So much for her earlier resolution. He was going to be more difficult to avoid than she'd anticipated. And this second encounter had confirmed what a risk he posed to the carefully constructed world she had manufactured for herself. Now a sexy Italian neurosurgeon had bulldozed his way into her life and was in danger of unravelling everything she had worked so hard for.

* * *

Heavy-hearted at the way his first day at St Piran's was ending, Gio washed, disposed of his scrubs and dressed in the jeans and short-sleeved shirt he had pulled on after arriving home. He'd not long left the hospital after making a final check of his patients when the emergency call had come for him to return.

A multidisciplinary team had assembled in Theatre, but despite their best efforts their nineteen-year-old casualty had succumbed to severe chest trauma and brain damage after an alcohol-induced accident.

Gio sighed at the waste of a life. Pain stabbed inside him as his thoughts strayed to another young life that had been cut cruelly short and he closed his eyes, determined to control his emotions and push the destructive memories away. Instead, he found himself thinking of Jessica Carmichael.

His impulsive visit to her office in the psychology unit—situated in one of the buildings adjacent to the main hospital and abutting the consultants' car park— had not gone to plan. He usually got on well with people. *'You could sell sand in the desert, Cori!'* Remembering the teasing words brought both amusement and an ache to his heart. Friendliness, politeness and a touch of flattery soothed troubled waters, but it wasn't working with Jessica, who remained tense and reserved.

Their unsatisfactory encounter had disappointed and confused him. He lived for his job, trying each day to make up for the failings that had haunted him for the last five years. Which was why his immediate and intense response to Jessica had shocked him. She had affected him on a deeply personal level. And he didn't *do* personal. Not any more. His reaction—and the attraction he wished he could deny—left him disconcerted and off balance.

When she had rushed out of her office and cannoned into him, instinct had taken over and he'd caught her as she'd stumbled. He'd felt the incredible softness of her skin under his fingers, the press of her femininely curved body against him, and he'd breathed in the teasing aroma of chocolate that lingered on her hair and skin. His attraction and body's response to her had been instant and undeniable.

But it was Jessica's reactions that had left him puzzled and unsettled. Her alarm had been real, and he had not imagined the panic in her beautiful green eyes as she'd wrenched herself free. For some reason Jessica didn't like to touch or be touched and he was determined to find out what lay behind it. There were several possibilities and each one caused him concern.

Gio stepped out of the surgeons' wash room, unsure what to do next. Why had Jessica been so dismissive of him and in such a rush to leave? He was positive she had felt the same bolt of awareness that had slammed into him when they'd first met. And that it had scared her. So could it be, he wondered, heading to the paediatric intensive care unit to check on Cody, that Jessica's cool professionalism and anxiety were flight responses? Was she trying to ignore the feelings and make them go away? If so, he could tell her it didn't work.

Using his swipe card, he let himself into PICU. Aside from the noise of the various monitoring machines and ventilators, the unit was quiet and dimly lit. He nodded to the charge nurse on duty and made his way to the bay that held Cody's bed. As he approached, he heard voices, one of which was Jessica's. He halted, surprised. What was she doing back here at this time of night? Curious, he listened before making his presence known.

'And when I think what could have happened,' Elsa Rowland commented, fear and guilt lacing her voice.

'You mustn't blame yourself, Elsa,' he heard Jessica respond softly, the gentle burr of her Scottish accent so attractive to him. 'A chronic subdural haematoma builds gradually. It can be weeks, even months, before the symptoms show. You did the right thing bringing Cody to A and E as soon as you realised something was wrong.'

'Thank you.' The woman's relief was tangible. 'I know Mr Corezzi explained it all to us but I didn't take anything in. And someone told me he's new. The thought of Cody's head being cut open is frightening.'

'Of course it is. But you can trust Mr Corezzi. He might be new to St Piran's but he's a very skilled and highly respected consultant neurosurgeon and he's come to us from London with a tremendous reputation,' Jessica explained to the anxious woman, her glowing endorsement of him taking Gio by surprise.

'Cody looks so still and small. Are you sure everything is all right?' the tearful mother asked, and although Gio wanted to reassure her, he was keen to hear what Jessica would say.

'He's doing very well,' she replied, her tone conveying sympathy and authority. 'It's standard procedure for him to be in Intensive Care following the operation.'

Gio was impressed. He was also intrigued by the depth of Jessica's knowledge. She seemed too assured and informed for someone with no medical training.

'Ally's gone to get something to eat. The nurses want

us to go home, but I can't bear to be away from Cody,' Elsa fretted.

'There's a cot in a room nearby for parents to use, and I'd advise you both to get what sleep you can there. But after tonight it would be best to get back into a normal routine. You and Ally need to keep strong so you are fit and ready to take Cody home,' Jessica urged, her common-sense approach pleasing him. 'I'll see you again tomorrow, but you can ring me if you need anything.'

There was a pause in the conversation and Gio waited a moment before making a sound and entering the bay. Elsa Rowland gave him a weary smile as he greeted her, but his attention immediately strayed to Jessica. She tensed, her gaze skittering to his and away again, a delicate flush of colour staining her cheeks.

As he checked Cody, who was sleeping peacefully, and looked over his chart, Gio was attuned to Jessica. What was she doing back at the hospital? Had she misled him when she'd said she was leaving for the day? He hoped to find answers as soon as Cody's father returned and, after a few pleasantries, Gio was able to escort Jessica out.

'I was surprised to see you,' he told her once they had left the unit and were in no danger of being overheard. 'I thought you had left for the day.'

Once more a tinge of colour warmed her smooth cheeks. 'I had to rush home to meet the insurance company's assessor. I said I'd be back,' she added defensively, refusing to meet his gaze.

She *had* said that but he'd assumed she had meant the next day. Apparently unsure what to do with her hands now that she was no longer carrying the assorted paraphernalia he'd seen her with before, she pushed them into her skirt pockets.

'What about you? Why are you still here?'

Her questions cut across the electrically charged atmosphere that hummed between them.

'I was called in after a young woman was knocked down by a coach.' He gave her a brief summary of the events and the unsuccessful struggle in the operating theatre. 'Her injuries were too severe...there was nothing we could do.'

Jessica's expression softened, understanding and sympathy visible in her olive-green eyes, and in her voice when she spoke. 'What a rotten end to your first day.'

'It could have finished on a better note,' Gio admitted with a rueful shrug, running the fingers of one hand through his hair.

Leaning back against the wall, Jessica met his gaze, and he witnessed her first real smile for him. *Dio*, but she was beautiful! The heavy weight settled back on his chest, making it difficult to breathe, and he felt each rapid thud of his heart.

'If it's not too late and you still want to talk about your patient...' Jessica's words trailed off and she bit her lip, looking hesitant and unsure.

'That would be good, thank you.' He'd take any opportunity to spend time with this elusive and most puzzling woman. 'Shall we go to the canteen? I've not eaten and the now congealed ready meal waiting in my microwave holds no appeal.'

Gio thought she was going to refuse and he found himself holding his breath as he waited for her answer. That it meant so much to him and he wanted so badly to be in her company should have worried him—*would* have worried him even one day ago. But in the short hours since he had met Jessica he felt changed somehow. Where this inexplicable but intense attraction was heading he had no idea, but he was keen to find out.

'All right.'

However reluctantly given, her agreement cheered him, and as he walked by her side down the deserted hospital corridor he felt as if he was setting out on one of the most important journeys of his life…with no map to help guide him and no clue as to the final destination.

CHAPTER THREE

'THAT wretched woman!'

Jess looked up in surprise as Brianna Flannigan, a nursing sister from the neonatal intensive care and special care baby units, banged a plate down on the canteen table and sat down, joining Megan and herself.

'What woman?' Jess and Megan asked in unison, concerned that the gentle, dedicated and softly spoken Brianna was so upset.

'Rita.'

Rita was the ward clerk in NICU/SCBU and renowned for nosing into other people's business, making her opinions, and often her disapproval, known. Few people took notice of her, but none wanted to fall under her spotlight. Both Brianna and Megan had suffered when Rita had picked on them in the past, and news she was hassling Brianna again brought out Jess's protective instincts.

'I'm sorry.' She sent her friend a sympathetic smile. 'What brought this on?'

Brianna idly pushed her salad around the plate. 'Now Diego and Izzy are no longer occupying Rita, she's refocused on me,' Brianna explained, frustration and displeasure in her lilting Irish voice.

'Tell her to mind her own business…that's what I do,' Megan riposted, stirring a sugar into her mug of tea. 'Not that it stops her. She's started making comments about me again, too.'

Jess knew Rita wasn't easily diverted once she set her mind on something. She suppressed a shiver. The idea of anyone probing into her past and her secrets was too awful to contemplate.

'She's always been nosy and judgemental. I thought she'd given up on me, but now she's asking where I came from and what I did before I joined St Piran's,' Brianna continued.

Jess recognised the dark shadows in her friend's brown eyes and couldn't help but wonder what had put them there.

'She'll never change,' Megan predicted. 'If she's not prying into someone's business, she's having a go about single mothers…or teenage ones. And don't get her started on her daughter.'

'What's wrong with her daughter?' Jess queried with a frown.

Megan dunked a biscuit in her tea. 'Nothing. That's the point. Marina's been happily married for twenty years and has several children—I've treated some of them for the usual childhood accidents and illnesses. They're a great family. Noisy and loving. Maybe that's what bugs Rita. She claims Marina married beneath her and shouldn't have had such a big family,' Megan finished, brushing crumbs from her lip.

'It's true she picks on Marina,' Brianna agreed. 'She finds fault with her grandchildren, too.'

The talk made Jess even more grateful that she had managed to avoid Rita's attention and speculation.

Megan and Brianna were the closest she had to friends, yet they knew no more about her than she did about them, even after the years they had known each other. Which was probably why they got along so well. The mutual trust was there and they guarded each other's privacy, sharing an unspoken agreement not to ask personal questions, yet they could turn to one another should they need to, knowing their confidence would be respected.

'Rita's also asking questions about Gio Corezzi,' Brianna added, snapping Jess from her thoughts.

'Why would she start on him?' she asked, fighting a blush at the mention of Gio's name. 'She hasn't even met him, has she?'

Brianna nodded. 'She met him this morning. We all did. We have a baby with hydrocephalus—along with several other problems, the poor mite—and Richard Brooke called Gio up to the unit for advice,' the caring Irish woman explained, referring to the consultant who headed NICU.

'What sort of questions is Rita asking?' Jess queried, striving for casual indifference.

'She wants to know why someone who was such a wow in London would chose to "*bury himself*" in Cornwall,' Brianna told them, spearing some food with her fork. 'She saw Gio in the consultants' car park with James Alexander, chatting about cars—apparently they own the same model Aston Martin, but in different colours, so Rita's sure Gio's loaded.'

'For goodness' sake,' Megan responded, with the same disgust Jess was feeling.

'Rita asked Gio if his wife would be joining him here.' Brianna paused, and Jess steeled herself for what her friend would reveal next. 'Gio said, "Unfortunately not," and you could see the speculation in Rita's eyes until Gio added, after a deliberate pause, "She's *dead*." It was just awful. I felt terrible for him. He looked so sad. Even Rita was embarrassed, and that's saying something.'

As Brianna and Megan discussed Rita-avoidance tactics, Jess sat back and battled her emotions. Her heart squeezed with pain at the news of Gio's loss. Concerned for him, she also felt guilty for the unstoppable flicker of relief that he wasn't already taken. Not that *she* had any future with him. Or with anyone. But she couldn't help wondering what had happened…or question why he hadn't told her himself. Not that it was her business. She respected his privacy. And she hadn't told him *her* secrets.

Discovering how protective and possessive she felt of Gio was disconcerting. She knew the answer to some of Rita's questions, but she would never divulge them. Not even to Brianna and Megan. Not because they might gossip, they wouldn't, but for much more complicated reasons. She didn't want to admit to her friends, or to herself, how much she enjoyed and looked forward to Gio's company.

After Gio had returned to the hospital on the evening of his first day and had found her in PICU with the Rowlands, they had spent well over an hour in the canteen together. She'd had little time to wonder if he'd overheard any of her conversation with Cody's mother because she'd been pole-axed by the charge of electricity and blaze of sensual awareness that hit her every time she saw him. He'd looked gorgeous in jeans and a blue shirt, the shadow of stubble darkening his masculine jaw making him seem rakish and dangerous.

The canteen had been far less crowded than it was now, Jess acknowledged, shifting her chair in to allow a group of nurses to pass and access a nearby table. Gio had chosen a full meal, while she'd opted for a small bottle of mineral water and a packet of sandwiches... out of habit selecting things in disposable packaging. She hadn't budgeted for an extra snack, but as she'd not eaten anything but a banana and an apple since breakfast, she'd been hungry.

Having sunk everything she'd had into buying her cottage, she was counting every penny. The storm damage had been an unforeseen disaster but the insurance company was going to cover repairs for her roof despite the policy only being a month old. Having overstretched herself on the property, she was having to be frugal with everything else, not that she had hinted at the sorry state of her finances to Gio—or anyone else.

'Have you always worked here?' Gio had asked, turning their conversation that first night away from his patients and to work in general as he'd tucked into his dessert.

'No. I joined St Piran's when I was in the final year of my training,' she'd explained to him, amazed he'd found room for apple pie and cream after the large portion of lasagne that had preceded it. 'They asked me to stay on once I'd qualified.'

What she hadn't told him had been the extent of her relief that she'd not needed to move on again, something she had done several times since the life-changing bombshell had brought things crashing down around her. She'd carved out a niche for herself in St Piran, fulfilling a role that patients, relatives and staff all appreciated and which allowed her some welcome autonomy.

'You don't see patients in your office?' Gio had queried.

'Very rarely—although I have done so if circumstances required it,' she replied, thinking of Izzy, the young A and E doctor who, then six months pregnant, had wanted to return to work after taking leave following the traumatic time she had experienced.

It hadn't been easy, for Izzy or herself, but things had worked out well. Now Izzy had a beautiful baby girl and an amazing new man in her life in the shape of attractive Spaniard Diego, who had been a charge nurse in NICU/SCBU, and Jess wished them all the happiness in the world.

'My role is more immediate,' she had gone on to tell Gio. 'I give emergency help to those who need it, be that on the wards, in A and E, or elsewhere in the hospital.'

'Like the Rowlands.' Gio's smile had nearly stopped her heart.

'Y-yes.' Flustered, she'd tried to get a grip. 'There can be a wide variety of situations...parents making difficult decisions about treatment for their child, or a young man who has crashed his motorbike and, overnight, has gone from being fit and active to waking up in hospital to the news he'll never walk again. Or it could be an older person who's had a stroke and is unable to return to their home. Or a relative in A and E trying to come to terms with a sudden bereavement.'

Something dark and painful had flashed in Gio's intense blue eyes, alerting Jess to the possibility there had been some traumatic event in his past. She hadn't pried, and Gio had declined to refer to it, but she had wondered about his background.

'So you see people through those first stages?' he'd asked next, pushing his empty dish aside and reclaiming her attention.

'That's right. Sometimes people need a shoulder to cry on and a friend in their corner. Others need greater help and back-up. I can liaise with other departments and with agencies outside the hospital that can offer care, advice and support, like social services, or relatives who have expectations that the patient may not want,' she'd explained, finding him easy to talk to. 'My job is to support them and their rights, and to help them achieve the best solution to whatever problem they're facing. If they need ongoing counselling once they leave hospital, they are assigned to one of my colleagues through Outpatients, or to an outside support organisation.'

Gio had shaken his head. 'I hadn't realised the full extent of what you do for people. It's very impressive... *you're* very impressive. I can see why everyone here respects you so much.'

The admiration in his eyes and praise in his sexy voice had warmed her right through and brought an uncharacteristic sting of tears to her eyes. 'It's hardly brain surgery,' she'd quipped to mask her embarrassment.

Gio's husky chuckle of appreciation had tightened the knot of awareness low in her tummy, and a sudden wave of longing had stolen her breath and made her realise how alone she had been these last four years. She enjoyed a friendship with Megan and Brianna, but it didn't extended beyond work and could never fill the cold and lonely void that had grown inside her since her life had turned upside down.

'Your first day's been hectic and hasn't ended in the best of ways, but how have you found St Piran's?' Jess had asked, anxious to move the conversation away from herself.

'I would rather not have returned to Theatre for that poor girl tonight,' he'd admitted, and she had seen the lines of tiredness around his eyes. 'But I've enjoyed today and it's good to be in near the beginning of a new unit for the hospital. It was one of the reasons I took the job. I was impressed with Gordon Ainsworth, the senior neurological consultant, the state-of-the-art equipment and the plans to increase the neurosurgical services here. Being able to help shape those services and build my own team appealed to me. Of course, many people cannot understand why I would leave London to come here.'

'It's none of their business, is it? If it's what you want, that's all that matters,' she'd told him, his surprised expression suggesting her matter-of-fact support had been in short supply.

'Thank you.' His slow, intimate smile had threatened to unravel her completely. 'St Piran's offered me new challenges and fresh opportunities, as well as the chance of more rapid career progression.'

It had made sense to her. 'Better to be a big fish in a small pond?'

Again the smile with its devastating effect on her. 'But it's much more than that...more than what I might gain for myself.' He'd leaned forward and folded his arms on the table, a pout of consideration shaping his sexy mouth. 'I commit a fair bit of time and money to a charitable trust that not only funds research, equipment for hospitals in various countries and support for patients and their families with brain tumours and other neurological conditions. We also bring children in desperate need of specialist treatment to the UK.'

She hadn't been surprised to learn of this side to him. She'd seen the kind of doctor he was. Instinct had told her how important the charity work was to him, and she'd suspected there was far more to it than he had told her...reasons why the trust was so close to his heart.

'That's fantastic. And it must be so rewarding.'

'It is. That St Piran's is interested and has given permission for me to continue to bring over a number of children each year, donating the hospital facilities free of charge, was a huge factor in my decision to come here.'

Jess had been fascinated as he'd talked more about the work he'd done with the trust. Her heart had swelled with pride as she'd thought about his selflessness and determination to use his skills to help others.

'He is *very* handsome, isn't he?'

Brianna's comment impinged on Jess's consciousness and she blinked, looking up and following her friend's gaze in time to see Gio carrying a tray across the canteen and sitting at a table with Ben Carter and James Alexander. Her pulse raced at the sight of him and she had to beat back a dart of jealousy at Brianna's evident appreciation of Gio's looks.

The man in question turned his head and met her gaze. For several moments it was as if there was no one else in the canteen—the myriad conversations going on all around her faded to a background hum and everything was a blur but Gio himself. A shiver ran down her spine and a very real sense of fear clutched at her.

Less than a week and already this man had breached her defences and become all too important to her.

What was she going to do? If she allowed the friendship to develop, she knew things would end in heartbreak. Despite knowing that, and despite a desperate need to preserve all she had achieved these last four years, she wasn't sure she could give Gio up.

A sudden clatter and burst of laughter from across the room caught the attention of everyone in the canteen and snapped Gio's gaze away from Jessica. He glanced round in time to see three junior doctors trying to contain the mess from a can of fizzy drink as the liquid spewed from the top in a bubbly fountain, soaking everything and everyone within range.

'The Three Stooges,' Ben commented wryly.

James chuckled. 'Were we ever that young and foolish and confident?'

'Probably!' Ben allowed.

Gio tried not to dwell on the past. His memories were mixed, all the happy ones overshadowed by the bad ones and the blackest time of his life. Ben and James, fellow consultants with whom he had struck up an immediate rapport, began detailing the merits of the three rowdy young doctors, but Gio's attention was inexorably drawn back to Jessica. The now familiar awareness surged through him, tightening his gut and making it difficult to breathe.

Jessica was sitting with two other women. Megan Phillips, the paediatric registrar with whom he worked frequently. And Brianna Flannigan, a kind and dedicated nursing sister in NICU/PICU, whom he'd met for the first time that morning. On the surface, the three women shared many similarities and yet they were distinctly different. And it was only Jessica who made his pulse race and caused his heart, which he had believed to be in permanent cold storage, to flutter with long-forgotten excitement.

They had sat in this very canteen and talked for a long time that first night, yet he'd discovered precious little about her. He, on the other hand, had revealed far more than he'd intended.

Her understanding and support about his move to Cornwall had warmed him. Many people had appreciated his need to leave Italy for New York five years ago. Some had comprehended his decision to leave New York, and the team of the neurosurgeon who had taught him so much, to move to London. But very few had grasped why he had chosen St Piran's over the other options that had been open to him—options that would have meant more money and working at bigger hospitals.

Those things hadn't interested him, which had not surprised Jessica. St Piran's offered the opportunity of advancing to head of department within a decade, Gordon Ainsworth grooming him to take over when he retired, but it had been the administration's support of his charity work that had swayed his decision.

He'd told Jessica about the trust but *not* why it was so important to him. Not yet. That he was thinking of doing so showed how far she had burrowed under his skin. Even as warning bells rang in his head, suggesting he was getting too close too quickly, he couldn't stop himself craving her company and wanting to know more about her.

They'd seen each other often during the week, working together with a couple of new patients and a rapidly improving Cody Rowland. Their friendship grew tighter all the time but Jessica remained nervous. She'd relax for a time then something would cause her to raise her defensive wall again. Her working hours puzzled him, and the extent of her medical knowledge continued to intrigue him.

The little she had revealed about herself centred around her work at St Piran's. Listening to her describe her role, and witnessing her way with people—including the use of Charlie, the teddy-bear hand puppet, to interact with frightened children—had left him full of admiration for her devotion and skill.

'Much of my work involves supporting people who face life changes and difficult decisions caused by illness or accident. It's a huge shock to the system,' she'd told him and, for a moment her eyes had revealed such intense pain that it had taken his breath away.

He'd wanted to comfort and hug her, but he'd resisted the instinctive urge, aware of Jessica's aversion to touching and being touched...one of her mysteries he hoped to unravel. But the incident had left him in little doubt that she'd experienced some similar trauma. As had he, he allowed, with his own dart of inner pain.

'Patients and relatives often try to be strong for each other,' Jessica had continued with perceptive insight, 'when often they need to admit that they're scared and have a bloody good cry.' She'd sent him a sweet, sad smile that had ripped at his already shredded heart. 'I'm merely a vehicle, a sounding board, someone outside their normal lives on whom they can offload all the emotion.'

What toll did that take on her? Gio wondered

with concern. And who was there for her? They were questions to which he still had no answers.

Without conscious decision or prior arrangement, they'd met each evening in the canteen, lingering over something to eat, discussing work, finding all manner of common interests in books, music and politics, both of them steering clear of anything too personal.

He'd learned very quickly to tread carefully, watching for the triggers that caused her withdrawal. He liked her, enjoyed her company and was comfortable with her but also alive, aroused and challenged, feeling things he'd not experienced in the five long years since his world had come crashing down around him.

Taking things slowly was a necessity. For both of them. But every day he became more deeply involved. So much so that having to say goodnight to her and return alone to his rented house was becoming increasingly difficult.

'Oh, to be that young and free from responsibility.'

Edged with bitterness, the words were voiced by Josh O'Hara and pulled Gio from his reverie. The Irishman took the final empty chair and set his plate down on the table. Gio regarded the other man, wondering what had sparked his reaction.

'Something wrong, Josh?' Ben asked, a frown on his face.

'Bad day.' He pushed his food aside untouched. 'I've just had to DOA an eighteen-year-old...I was going to say *man*, but he was scarcely more than a boy with his whole life ahead of him.'

Gio sympathised, recalling how he'd felt a few days ago when the young woman had died in Theatre from multiple injuries. 'What happened?'

'He was an apprentice mechanic at a local garage, driving the work van and following another mechanic who was returning a customer's car after service,' Josh explained, emotion in his accented voice as he told the story. 'Some bozo going home from a liquid lunch at the golf club and driving far too fast ploughed into the van. The boy wasn't wearing his seat belt, the van had no air-bags, and he went through the windscreen. He had horrible head and facial injuries—apparently he'd been a good-looking boy, not that I could tell—and a broken neck.'

Gio exchanged glances with Ben and James, both of whom were listening with equal solemnity and empathy. 'And the drunk driver?' Ben queried, voicing the question in all their minds.

'Yeah, well, there's the rub. There's no justice in this world.' Josh gave a humourless laugh. 'The boy's colleague, who witnessed the crash, is in shock. The drunk driver hasn't got a scratch on him. The police have arrested him and I hope they throw the book at him, but whatever sentence he gets won't be enough to make up for that young life, will it?'

'No,' Gio murmured with feeling.

As his three companions discussed the case, Gio struggled to contain memories of another injustice and senseless loss of life, one he had been unable to prevent and which had plunged him into the darkest despair he had ever known. A darkness he had believed he would never escape. His gaze returned to Jessica, who, in just a few days, had brought flickerings of light and hope back into his life.

A shaft of sunshine from the window beside her made the vibrancy of her rich auburn hair gleam like pure flame. Brianna also had auburn hair but hers was a much lighter shade, lacking the coppery chestnut richness of Jessica's. Megan, whose hair was darker, was the tallest of the three, slender and fragile-looking. Brianna, an inch or two shorter, was lithe and athletic, while Jessica was shorter still and more rounded, her shapely feminine curves so appealing to him. She looked up and, as their gazes clashed once more, she sent him a tiny smile.

'From the Three Stooges to the Three Enigmas,' Ben remarked, his gaze following Gio's to Jessica's table, just as the rowdy young doctors left the canteen.

Fearing his new friend would detect his interest in Jessica, Gio dragged his gaze away and pretended not to know what Ben meant. 'Sorry?'

'Brianna, Jess and Megan,' Ben enlightened him. 'St Piran's Three Enigmas.'

'It's interesting that the three of them gravitated to each other,' James said, as he looked across at them.

Ben shrugged. 'I'm not surprised. They have so much in common. All three are intensely private and have somehow managed to elude the gossip-mongers. And all three have also ignored the attention showered on them by the majority of the single—and some not-so-single—men in the hospital. I don't think anyone knows anything more about them, or their lives outside work, than they did the day each of them began working here,' Ben finished.

'How long *has* Megan been here?' Josh asked, his apparent nonchalance only surface deep, Gio was sure.

'It must be, what…seven years? Maybe eight,' Ben pondered, and Gio noticed the set of Josh's jaw and the way he flinched, as if the time was somehow important.

Gio glanced over to Jessica's table again, his gaze resting a moment on Megan. He was just about to smile at her when he realised that she wasn't looking at him but at Josh. Pale faced and seemingly upset, Megan turned away.

Across from him Josh looked strained and affected by the silent exchange. There was a story there, Gio realised, but it was none of his business. He had enough to concern him settling into a new job, a new town, and dealing with the sudden and unexpected resurgence of his libido.

As the four of them prepared to return to their respective departments, their break over, Gio noticed activity at Jessica's table, too. She was standing up and reaching for her pager, a frown on her face as she read the message.

He wondered what had happened and who needed her now. Like a schoolboy with his first crush, he hoped he would meet up with Jessica later, craving the moments at the end of the day when he had her to himself, at least for a while.

She was becoming ever more important to him and he was both scared and excited to discover what was going to happen.

CHAPTER FOUR

As HER pager sounded, Jess rose to her feet, frowning as she read the call for her to attend A and E urgently.

'I have to go,' she explained as her friends said goodbye. 'I'll see you later.'

Jess squeezed her way between the tables, wishing she was as slender as Megan and Brianna. Before she left the canteen, she couldn't resist looking back at Gio. Her gaze clashed with his, delaying her, her footsteps slowing as if ruled by an inbuilt reluctance to leave him.

Gio waved, drawing Ben's attention as the men stood up from their table. Ben smiled at her, and she blushed, hoping he would think she was including all of them, and not that she had any special interest in Gio, as she sketched a wave in return and hurried out of the canteen.

As she made her way to A and E, her thoughts remained with Gio. Beyond the dangerous attraction, she enjoyed his company, admired him, professionally and personally, and felt good with him. If she had any sense, she'd guard her heart and keep her distance, but she feared it was already too late. She'd begun to slide down the slippery slope by foolishly convincing herself it was

OK to be friends with him...provided they both knew friendship was all it could be.

She knew Gio was curious and wanted to know more about her, but he'd been circumspect so far and she was grateful. Meeting in the canteen each evening challenged her resolve but his comments on how he hated returning to the empty house he was renting had touched a chord within her. She knew all about the loneliness found between the walls of somewhere that didn't feel like home. One more of the many things they had in common.

Arriving in A and E, Jess set thoughts of Gio aside. Ellen, a senior staff nurse in the department, greeted her and outlined the reason for the call.

'The girl came in very distressed, asking after a young man killed in a road accident,' the middle-aged woman explained, shaking her head. 'She's terribly young, Jess, but she insists she's the girlfriend. Unfortunately we're rushed off our feet and as she's not physically injured or ill, we don't have time to spend with her, but we didn't want her to leave in such a state.'

'I understand. Has she been told anything?' Jess asked, her heart going out to the unknown girl.

Ellen sighed again. 'I'm afraid one of the inexperienced clerks told her the boyfriend, a lad named Colin Maddern, had died.'

'Oh, hell.'

'Exactly.' The nurse's displeasure matched her own. 'The girl wants Colin's things. He had no one but her. And there are photographs of her in his jacket, so she's genuine. I've checked with the police and they don't need anything, so I'll arrange to have the jacket and the possessions we salvaged brought to her.' Ellen nodded in the direction of the closed door to one of the quiet rooms used for relatives. 'She's in there. She wants to see him, but...'

'You don't think it's a good idea,' Jess finished for her.

'No, I don't. The poor boy wasn't wearing a seat belt and there was no air-bag fitted. He was hit at speed, went through the windscreen and was killed. A broken neck. And his face is a mess.'

Jess struggled to keep her emotions from showing. 'And the other driver?'

'Returning home drunk after lunch at the golf club. The police have arrested him. Needless to say he's not even bruised. Josh had to deal with both of them and he's furious. It's so unfair,' Ellen finished, mirroring Jess's own sentiments and explaining the grim expression on Josh's face when he'd arrived in the canteen.

'Do we know the girl's name?' Jess queried, jotting a few notes on her pad.

'No. Other than asking for Colin—and his things— she's not said anything. She broke down after she learnt of his death.'

'Thanks, Ellen.' She would not have relished the task of delivering the news, but Jess wished the girl had learned the truth in a more gentle and caring way. 'I'll see what I can do.'

The woman smiled. 'If anyone can help her, love, it's you.'

Jess hoped so. After Ellen had gone, she drew in a breath, hoping to find the right things to say in an impossible situation. Tapping on the door, she opened it and stepped inside. A junior nurse sat awkwardly near the sobbing girl, and jumped to her feet, clearly glad to leave.

Once they were alone, Jess pulled a chair closer and sat opposite the plump form huddled on the two-seater sofa. With her face buried in her hands, a curtain of straight, corn-coloured blonde hair swung forward, hiding her face from view. A cooling cup of tea remained untouched on the table beside her.

'Hello. I'm Jess Carmichael. I've come to see if there's anything I can help you with.' Jess waited for some kind of response or acknowledgement of her presence. 'I'm very sorry to hear about the accident.'

Slowly the girl looked up, her hands dropping away from her face and falling to her lap. Jess barely managed to smother a shocked gasp as she discovered how terribly young she was...no more than sixteen. Grey eyes were awash with tears, leaving no doubt at the depth of her devastation.

'They won't let me see him,' she murmured. 'Is it because I'm not officially family?'

Jess hesitated, unsure how to explain without causing further upset. 'It's a difficult decision. I'd urge you to think carefully, because once it's done, it can't be undone. They advised you against seeing Colin because of the nature of his injuries,' she continued, deciding it was important to tell the truth, even as the words caused the girl to flinch. 'Wouldn't you rather your last memory of him was a good one? What would he want for you?'

'Colin wouldn't want me to do it,' she admitted, a frown creasing her brow.

'There's no hurry to make a decision, so have a think about it.'

'OK.'

Jess hoped she would decide not to see him. 'Is there someone I can call for you? Your parents, maybe?'

'No!' The denial was instant and accompanied by a vigorous shake of her head. 'I can't.' Taking a tissue from the box on the table, she blew her nose. 'No one knows about Colin and me.'

Jess let it go for now, not wanting to pressure the girl or distress her further, hoping instead to build rapport and a level of trust that would enable her to help if she could.

'Can you tell me your name?'

The girl fiddled nervously with the chain around her neck, suddenly clutching it before tucking it inside her blouse and doing up the top button, as if to hide it. Before Jess could consider the odd behaviour, the girl shifted nervously, her gaze darting around the room.

'Marcia Johns,' she finally offered, barely above a whisper.

'Thank you, Marcia.' Jess smiled, accepting the name, even though she was unsure at this point whether or not it was genuine. 'Would you like to talk about Colin?'

A firm nod greeted the suggestion, and although tears shimmered in her eyes, a wobbly smile curved her mouth, revealing how pretty she could be. 'Yes, please. Is that OK?'

'Of course. I'd like to hear about him. When did you meet?'

'Over a year ago when I started my summer job,' she explained. 'Colin worked nearby. He was three years older than me, and never in a million years did I imagine him noticing *me*. Tall and handsome, with dark hair and blue eyes and a gorgeous smile, he was the one all the girls wanted. I'm shy and overweight and always fade into the background,' Marcia continued, revealing low self-esteem. She shook her head, as if in wonder, and gave a little laugh. 'When Colin began spending time with me, I couldn't believe it! There were all these thin, pretty girls chasing after him but he kept saying it was me he wanted, that he saw the real me inside. That I was kind and smart and funny, and he loved me the way I was.'

What a lovely young man, Jess thought, seeing how Marcia lit up talking about him. And what a terrible tragedy that his life had been cut so short. Sensing Marcia's need to talk, she encouraged her to continue.

'We were going to get married when I finished school and got a full-time job,' she said, toying with the friendship ring that encircled the middle finger of her right hand, no doubt a gift from him, Jess thought. 'His father died when he was twelve, and his mother when he was sixteen, so Colin had to look out for himself. He was much more responsible and steady than the boys I knew at school. There was never much money, but that didn't matter. We spent all our time together, walking on the beach, having picnics, watching DVDs or listening to music at his flat, talking for hours. Talking about everything. For the first time I felt as if someone really knew me and understood me.'

'Don't you feel that at home?' Jess probed, hoping to find out more about Marcia's background.

'Not really.' She gave a casual shrug, but it obviously mattered to her. 'We're a big family. My parents are busy working and caring for us all, and my brothers and sisters are all outgoing and active, and so much more attractive than I am. They all have the family colouring. I got the eyes but my hair is dead straight and mousy blonde. I'm interested in books and music, not sports. I don't understand them and they don't understand me. I know they love me,' she added, wiping away the twin tears that tracked down her rounded cheeks. 'They just don't *see* me. Everything is so hectic and noisy. I don't think they notice whether I'm there or not.'

'But Colin noticed.'

'Yes. Yes, he did.'

Jess understood how special and important the young man must have made Marcia feel, boosting her confidence and setting her free from the shadow of her vibrant family. Marcia might be very young, but she had a sensible head on her shoulders and for her, her relationship with Colin had been a close and genuine one.

Marcia pulled her shoulder bag on to her lap and rummaged inside for a moment before producing a couple of photos and handing them across.

'Thanks.'

Jess looked down at the first picture, seeing a very handsome young man dressed in jeans and a black leather jacket, wavy black hair brushing over the collar. The blue eyes were startling, full of intelligence, humour and kindness, his smile adding to the impression of warmth and friendliness. The second picture, of Marcia and Colin together, banished any lingering doubt about the full extent of this young girl's relationship with Colin. No one seeing the two young people together could question their feelings. Their happiness and love shone out, and the expression of devotion on Colin's face as he looked at a laughing Marcia brought a lump to Jess's throat.

'They're lovely. Thank you for showing me,' she murmured, handing the pictures back.

Marcia looked at them for several moments before tucking them carefully back in her bag. She sobbed, pressing a hand to her mouth, despair in her eyes.

'What am I going to do?' Rocking back and forth, tears flowed in earnest once more. 'Colin was my whole life. I love him so much. And I need him. He can't be gone. He *can't*. It isn't fair. Oh, God... Why? *Why* has this happened? What's the point in anything if Colin isn't with me?'

As she tried to comfort the girl, Jess wished she had answers to explain the cruel and senseless loss of a life. Fresh anger built within her at the driver who had thoughtlessly climbed behind the wheel of his car, his selfish actions shattering two young lives. He should be made to see Colin's lifeless, damaged body, and witness the terrible grief Marcia was suffering. What words could she possibly offer the girl that didn't sound trite?

A knock at the door announced the arrival of Ellen and provided a welcome distraction. 'May I come in?'

As Marcia nodded and mopped her tears, Jess met the kindly nurse's gaze, seeing the sympathy and sorrow in her eyes.

'I have Colin's things for you, love,' Ellen said, setting a black leather jacket on the seat beside Marcia, the same jacket Colin had worn in the photos.

Marcia drew the jacket into her arms, closing her eyes and burying her face in the wear-worn leather. 'I saved up for ages to buy this for his birthday. It smells of him,' she whispered, clutching the familiar garment more tightly to her and rubbing one cheek against it.

A lump in her throat, Jess exchanged a glance with Ellen. Maybe having Colin's jacket would bring Marcia some comfort and familiarity in the difficult times ahead.

'Here are the photographs and the other things Colin had with him,' Ellen said, holding over a large padded envelope.

Refusing to let go of the jacket, Marcia took the envelope with her free hand. 'Thank you, it means a lot. And thanks for being so kind to me.'

'You're welcome, my love.' Suppressed emotion made Ellen's voice huskier than normal. 'I'm so sorry.'

After Ellen had left them alone once more, Jess allowed Marcia some quiet time. While she waited, she took a page from her notebook and jotted down some information for the girl to take away with her.

'I don't like to think of you going home alone, Marcia. You've had a horrible shock. Are you sure I can't call your parents? Or I could arrange for someone here to take you home,' Jess suggested, willing to drive her there herself, but Marcia was withdrawing and shaking her head.

'No. No, I don't want that.' She took another tissue and mopped her eyes. 'Thank you. I'll be all right.'

Jess didn't believe it for a moment, but she couldn't force her and she didn't want to break the tentative trust between them. All she could do was encourage Marcia to keep in touch.

'You can contact me here at any time, Marcia,' she told her, adding another telephone number to the list. 'I've also given the details for the Samaritans. If you need to talk to anyone in confidence, day or night, you can call them. I volunteer once a week, usually on Friday evenings, but you can talk freely to anyone.'

'OK.'

Jess was relieved as Marcia took the sheet of paper, looked it over, and then tucked it into her bag, suggesting she might actually use it and not toss it into the first litter bin she came across.

'I'd really like to know how you are. And if there's anything I can do...' She let the words trail off, not wanting to nag.

The sound of her pager intruded. Smothering her frustration, Jess checked the display before glancing around the room and discovering there was no telephone.

'I've taken up too much of your time,' Marcia murmured, beginning to gather her things together.

'No, no, it's fine, honestly.' Jess smiled and told a white lie. 'I'm not in a hurry. I just have to reply to this. If you don't mind waiting, I'll just pop into the next door room to use the phone. I'll be back in a jiffy.'

Jess found a phone and made the call. She doubted she'd been gone more than a minute, but by the time she returned, Marcia had gone.

'Damn it!'

Upset, she rushed down the corridor and back into the busy casualty department, asking a couple of nurses and the clerks at the desk if they had seen Marcia come though, but no one had noticed her. Not even the security guard by the main doors. It brought back Marcia's own words...she faded into the background and no one saw her.

Cursing the appalling timing of the interruption, Jess went outside, hoping to catch a glimpse of Marcia, but it was hopeless. The sense of disappointment was huge. She couldn't bear to think of Marcia alone with her grief, unable and unwilling to seek the comfort of a family who loved her but seldom had time for her.

An image of Marcia and Colin before the tragedy, so happy and in love, fixed itself in her mind. Why did awful things happen? She could make no sense of the cruelty that had befallen two lovely young people. She swallowed, blinking back tears.

'Jessica, are you all right?'

Gio's voice behind her had her spinning round in surprise. 'What are you doing here?'

'I was in A and E and saw you run outside.' The expression in his blue eyes, so warm and intimate, robbed her of breath and held her captive as he raised a hand and with exquisite gentleness removed a salty bead of moisture suspended from her lashes, his fingers brushing her cheek. His voice turned even huskier. 'I was worried about you.'

Everything in her screamed at her to lean into his touch, craving what she had denied herself for so long, but reality intruded, the instinct for self-preservation ingrained. She jerked back, feeling the colour staining her cheeks as Gio regarded her in silence, speculation, concern and a frightening resolve in his eyes.

'Tell me what's wrong,' he invited as they headed back to the hospital.

Sighing, Jess gave him a brief summary of what had happened, unable to prevent her emotion from showing. 'It was just awful.'

'I'm sorry.' He shook his head, murmuring what sounded like a curse in Italian. 'Josh was talking about the accident in the canteen.'

Back in the room where she had spoken with Marcia, Gio remained with her, increasing her sense of awareness. 'I feel as if I failed her,' she admitted.

'Of course you didn't,' he chided gently.

'I don't know.' With another sigh, she gathered up her things. 'I'm even more sure now that Marcia Johns is not her real name.'

'Definitely not.'

The edge of amusement in Gio's voice had her head snapping up. There was nothing remotely funny about the situation. But before she could remonstrate with him, he shook his head and pointed to something behind her. She turned round, noticing for the first time the information posters on one wall of the room.

The 'infomercials' were sponsored by well-known drug companies and 'Marcia' had been clever enough, despite her distress, to cobble together a false name on the spur of the moment, using parts of two words from the company name emblazoned in large letters on one of the posters. Jess cursed herself for having been so thoroughly duped. She was also disappointed that the girl had felt the need to deceive her.

'She had her reasons, and I'm sure they were personal to her and nothing to do with you.'

Jess knew Gio's words were offered by way of consolation, but they did little to ease her upset and concern. 'Marcia' would remain in her thoughts and she would worry about her unless and until she had any further news of her. She could only hope that at some point the girl would use one of the contact numbers she had given her and get in touch.

'I know how much you care,' Gio said now, scarily attuned to her thoughts. 'You would not be so good at your job if you didn't, but you cannot carry the burden of everyone's problems on your shoulders, Jessica.' He stood in front of her, tipping her chin up with one finger until her gaze met his. 'Who is there for you?'

She felt branded by the contact and once more she stepped back to break it, resisting the urge to press her free hand to the spot that still tingled from the soft touch of his fingertip. This was ridiculous! She needed to give herself a stern talking to. Squaring her shoulders, she headed for the door.

'I'm fine,' she told him, injecting as much firmness into her voice as possible.

'You are here at all hours, taking on the burden of everyone else's problems,' he continued, refusing to let it go. 'Who listens to yours?'

Frightened that his perceptiveness and caring were chipping away at the defences that had protected her these last four years, she laughed off his question and repeated the words she used as a mantra to convince others...and herself. 'I'm fine!'

He took her by surprise—again—politely opening the door for her and following her out. So grateful was she that he had let the subject drop, she was not adequately on her guard.

'Where are you going now?' he asked.

'Hmm...' Jess frowned, trying to remember what had been on her agenda before the call had come in for her to attend A and E.

'If you have a few minutes to stop off at my office, I have some things to discuss with you.'

Although she would sooner have parted company there and then so she had time to re-erect her barriers against him, she was relieved he had focused back on work matters. Cursing her weakness and the voice in her head that tormented her about her vulnerability to this man, Jess found herself assenting to his request.

'All right.'

'Thank you.'

His smile of satisfaction made her uneasy. What had she agreed to? And why did she feel he'd set her up and she'd fallen for it—as she feared she had for him—hook, line and sinker?

CHAPTER FIVE

'COME this way.'

Jess found herself ushered into Gio's office, his hand at the small of her back sending a charge of electricity zinging through her. He had a disturbing habit of touching her. As he closed the door, Jess took the opportunity to put some much-needed distance between them. The room was by no means small but, confined in it with Gio, it seemed claustrophobic and she felt an urgent need for the comfort of her own personal space.

'What I am about to reveal to you is strictly confidential, Ms Carmichael. You do realise that?' he asked, his expression sombre...but for a tell-tale glimmer of mischief in his tanzanite-blue eyes.

Jess had no idea whether he was serious, or whether he was toying with her. Why did just being in the same room with him make her feel so off kilter and peculiar? She didn't like it. What she most wanted was to escape.

'Jessica?'

She jumped, continually unnerved at the way he spoke her name, his husky, accented voice far too intimate and intoxicating. But it was the light touch of one finger on her forearm that brought her inbuilt flight response into action again as she stepped back, distracted by the way all her nerve-endings were fired into life. Startled, she met the intense blueness of his gaze, seeing the curiosity, knowledge and masculine appreciation that lurked in his eyes. She didn't want anyone interested in her or asking questions about her, least of all this man who posed a unique and definite danger.

'What's confidential?' she queried, intrigued and yet nervous.

'Apart from my secretary, no one knows about this. I'm trusting you, Jessica.'

'Yes, of course.' She agreed without hesitation. It was asked of her, in one way or another, every working day, either by a patient, relative or colleague. And very little surprised her. 'What is it?'

Gio moved to his desk and beckoned her closer. She edged forward, watching as he opened the bottom drawer of his desk, pulling it back with frustrating slowness, building her suspense as centimetre by centimetre the contents came into view.

She'd been wrong to believe he couldn't surprise her. Her eyes widened in astonishment as she found herself staring at a drawer full to the brim with…

'Chocolate!'

Gio couldn't help but laugh aloud at Jessica's stunned reaction. 'What is your poison? Plain or milk? With or without nuts?' he asked, taking a selection of bars from the drawer.

'I don't eat much chocolate.'

'But you like it,' he prompted, hearing the waver in her voice. 'You must do…given the delicious scent of your hair and your skin.'

His words brought a bloom of colour to her porcelain cheeks. But it was the longing in her eyes that betrayed her sweet tooth. And then her pink tongue-tip peeped out to moisten the sensual curve of her lips, causing his body to react in such an immediate and blatant way that he drew back in shock.

'Treat yourself,' he encouraged, thankful that she appeared unaware of his response to her and, as he waited for her to make her selection, struggled to get his mind and body back under control.

'OK.' She took a small bar of milk chocolate with a hazelnut praline centre. 'Thank you.'

'Good choice,' he murmured as she moved away.

Taking a bar of dark chocolate with almond for himself, he put the rest away and closed the drawer. Sitting down, he opened his chocolate, his gaze remaining on Jessica as she inspected the expensive high-class packaging, noting the moment realisation dawned.

'*Cioccolato Corezzi?*' She looked up, stunning green eyes wide with interest. '*You* make this chocolate?'

'My family do. My paternal grandfather began the company over fifty years ago, and Papá and Mamma have grown it from a small specialist business with one shop in Turin into what it is today—one of Italy's most famous hand-made chocolate houses.'

'You're understandably proud of them.' She smiled, snapping off a square and popping it into her mouth, nearly killing him as those mesmerising eyes closed and a blissful look transformed her face as she savoured the flavours he knew would be bursting on her tongue. 'Oh, this is *amazing*!'

'Thank you.' Her opinion was important to him and her enthusiasm made him feel warm inside.

Snapping off another square, she laughed. 'No, thank *you*!' she insisted, before popping the chocolate into her mouth to savour the taste as before.

It was the first time he'd heard her laugh. It was a warm, throaty, infectious sound and he wanted to hear it often. Frowning, he acknowledged just how involved he was becoming.

'Did you never want to follow in your parents' footsteps?' she queried after a moment, perching on the edge of his desk, stretching her skirt across the pleasing curve of womanly thighs.

'No,' he answered, his voice rough. Clearing his throat, he sat forward. 'It was never an option, and my parents knew it wouldn't have suited me. Besides, I would have eaten all the profits!'

Taking a bite of his chocolate, he enjoyed another of her throaty chuckles.

'You must have lorry loads of it delivered, judging by your drawer!'

Having her relax enough to tease him was an unexpected pleasure, as was listening to the softness of her accent. He wondered how she had come to be in Cornwall, so far from home, but he refrained from asking...for now.

'Now you know my secret,' he said, keeping his tone light and teasing. 'It's only fair you tell me one of yours, no?'

The change in her was immediate and, while he regretted her withdrawal and the loss of their rapport, he was intrigued by her reaction and eager to find out its cause. Her whole body tensed, as if she was closing in on herself. Sliding off the desk, she turned away, but not before he had seen the hurt and loneliness she worked hard to hide. Stepping across to the window, her shoulders lifted as she breathed in a slow, deep breath. Finally, she turned round, popping the last piece of chocolate in her mouth and scrunching up the wrapper.

'I'm not very interesting, and I don't really have any secrets,' she told him with a manufactured smile, not meeting his gaze.

Oh, but she most certainly did. He knew it. And he was determined to uncover them and understand what she was anxious to hide. Behind the façade she presented to the world, the real Jessica was far from fine.

'I ought to be going,' she announced, picking up the collection of items she had with her all the time in the hospital.

'What *do* you carry around in there?' he asked with a mix of interest and amusement.

Her voice sounded strained now, all traces of the fun Jessica reined in and back behind her protective wall. 'I have my notebook and diary,' she began, looking down at the pile in her arms.

Gio listened as she told him about the information sheets, details of various diseases and injuries and their treatments, names and contacts for self-help groups and a welter of other things people might need. Her mobile phone, like her pager, was either attached to her waistband or in her pocket, depending on the clothes she was wearing. He suspected Jessica used the things she carried as a barrier, a shield between herself and others. He wanted to know why. The list of questions he had about her continued to grow.

Disappointment speared inside him as Jessica moved towards the door. 'Thanks for the chocolate.'

'Any time. I'll tell my secretary you have free access

to my secret drawer.' He smiled, drinking in his fill of her while he could. 'See you later. And try not to worry about your girl.'

'I'll try. Bye.'

The door closed softly behind her. At once the room felt different...and he felt lonely without the vibrancy of her presence. *Dio*. A week ago, if anyone had told him he'd be attracted to another woman, he would have believed it impossible. But Jessica had shaken him to his foundations—and out of the darkness that had enveloped his life for the last five years.

'Megan, are you all right?'

'Yes.' It was a lie, but she managed a smile for Jess. 'I'm sorry, I was miles away.'

Her friend sent her an understanding smile. 'Josh?'

'Yes,' Megan repeated, a deep sigh escaping.

It had been a huge shock to discover that Josh had joined the St Piran's trauma team back in the spring. Megan had assumed he was still in London. Wished he *was* still in London. Working with him when she was on call to A and E from Paediatrics was difficult and she had found it harder still since little Toby's funeral.

'He wants to talk,' Megan confided, her recent confrontation with Josh in the canteen still fresh in her mind. Why did he want to rake over the past? Did he think she didn't live with it every day of her life?

'Would talking to Josh be such a bad thing?'

Megan's stomach churned in response to Jess's softly voiced question. Her friend knew there was past history with Josh, but Megan hadn't divulged any details. She had never told anyone what had happened. She felt too guilty, too confused, too stupid, too hurt.

'What's the point?' Bitterness laced her voice but she was unable to soften it. 'It's over. Done. What good would be served stirring it up eight years on?'

'Perhaps *you* need to talk as much as Josh thinks *he* does,' Jess suggested, confusing her more.

Megan frowned. 'What do you mean?'

'It's clearly still causing you heartache. Things are unresolved in your own mind.' Jess paused a moment, her dark green gaze direct. 'Forget Josh and his reasons for wanting to talk. Think about yourself. Do *you* have questions that need answering before you can put things behind you once and for all?'

Too many to count, Megan allowed silently, one hand unconsciously moving to press against the flatness of her belly, a wave of pain rolling through her at all that was lost—all that Josh had taken from her. The thought of facing him after eight years was too scary to contemplate.

'Maybe, but—' Megan broke off, uncertain and indecisive.

'But?' Jess probed gently.

'Seeing him again hurts so much and has brought back so many difficult memories.' She bit her lip, ashamed that she had been so foolish over Josh—and that part of her remained drawn to him, despite everything that had happened. 'I'm so angry with him, Jess. And with myself. Yes, there are things I want to know, but I'm not sure I can cope with what he has to say.'

'Only you can decide if finding out what you need to know will help you find peace with the past.'

Megan nodded. Her friend's words made sense. She just wasn't sure what to do. The fact that Josh now had a picture-perfect wife, aside from causing her added pain and distress, complicated things even more. Although the body language she had witnessed between him and his beautiful wife, Rebecca, suggested that things might not be right in Josh's marriage, he *was* married, so having contact with him beyond the professional was inappropriate.

'It scares me, Jess.'

Her words whispered from her as she faced the awful truth—underneath the pain, anger and betrayal, a spark of the elemental chemistry still burned. She was as vulnerable to him as she had always been.

'Emotions are complicated and the dividing line between love and hate can be wafer thin.' Jess's pager sounded and she glanced at it, a faint blush colouring her cheeks. 'Sorry, Megan, I have to go.'

'Problems?'

Jess shook her head. 'It's time for the neurosurgery case meeting. Gordon Ainsworth and, um, Gio, asked me to attend,' she explained, gathering up her things. Pausing, she smiled. 'Think things over. If you need to talk, you know it will remain confidential between us.'

'Thanks, Jess.'

'Take care, Megan. And good luck.'

Megan watched the other woman walk away, her vibrant auburn hair restrained in a plait. Recalling her friend's blush, and thinking about the electric atmosphere she had noticed whenever Jess and Gio were together, she wondered if something was brewing there. It would be wonderful to see Jess happy. She was so private, and always seemed so alone. Megan shook her head, realising how alike they were. She respected Jess, and trusted her, and she knew how lucky she was to have her to talk to.

Unfortunately, her friend couldn't tell her what to do. No one could. Decisions about Josh, and whether to face the past, were hers alone.

Gio stepped into the warmth of the August evening. Dusk was falling, and he glanced up at the darkening sky, expelling a sigh. He'd been called in earlier that Saturday evening after Josh O'Hara's concern had grown about a man who had collapsed while on an outing to the beach with his wife. Further tests, including CT and MRI scans, had revealed that the man had a tumour growing in his brain, affecting his optic nerve and sensory centre. Surgery was scheduled for Monday.

The man and his wife would benefit from Jessica's input. He'd speak with her on Monday. Which was nearly thirty-six hours away and too long to wait, especially as he hadn't seen her since the previous afternoon, when she had attended what would become a regular Friday meeting for the neurological unit. Her presence had been beneficial to the team—but distracting for him on a personal level. He shook his head. Until a few days ago he hadn't *had* a personal level.

Confused that his life had turned upside down, he walked towards the almost deserted consultants' car park. The previous night had been the first when they'd not met up for an end-of-the-day chat. Jessica had been unable to come because she volunteered for the Samaritans and spent several hours there each Friday evening. He wasn't surprised. Once more she was devoting her time to other people's problems. Was it a way of avoiding her own?

In the car, he leaned back and rested his head, reflecting on how long and lonely the weekend was becoming without Jessica. He swore softly to himself. What a sorry state he was in. Part of him rebelled. He didn't want any new woman in his life. Or so he had thought until Jessica. Now he couldn't stop thinking about her or wanting to be with her. He wanted to learn her secrets and encourage the real Jessica out from behind her defensive wall. Was he the only one to notice the loneliness and hurt that lurked in the depths of her beautiful green eyes?

Starting the engine, he reversed out of his parking space, his gaze straying to the psychology building.

'What the hell?'

He braked, letting the powerful engine idle as he observed the light that shone from Jessica's office window. The rest of the building was in darkness. Had she forgotten to switch off the light the day before? He saw a flicker of movement inside and cursed. Jessica was here? *Now?* Returning his car to its parking space, he switched off the engine, climbed out and locked the door.

As he walked towards the building he reflected on Jessica's odd behaviour and her reluctance to let him see inside her office. He'd brushed it off as a quirk, but her furtiveness made him certain that something more was going on and he couldn't let this go.

Frowning, he remembered when he'd visited her office. She'd rushed home to meet her insurance company's assessor and he'd forgotten to ask why. Was something seriously wrong?

The outer door of the psychology building was locked, but his swipe card and ID code gained him access. Relocking the door, he made his way through the darkened foyer and down the corridor to Jessica's room. It was uncharacteristic for him to be impolite but, not wanting to give her time to shut the door in his face, he checked to see if it was unlocked. It was. He gave a sharp rap and swung the door open, astonished at the scene that greeted him.

Jessica, bare-footed and dressed in a pair of cotton shorts and a sleeveless tank top, which emphasised her voluptuous curves and set his pulse racing, was sitting cross-legged on a blow-up mattress on the floor. A pillow and a few items of bed linen were folded at one end. For the first time, he saw her hair in all its heart-stopping glory as it fell around her shoulders, the curtain of copper-red and burnished chestnut curls enveloping her in a halo of fire.

But she was not alone. Her companions held him transfixed and momentarily speechless. Two small, playful kittens frolicked around her, Tabby balls of fluff on stubby legs and paws that looked too big for them. His gaze returned to Jessica. The smile had frozen on her face and panic was setting in.

Determined to discover what was going on, but not wanting to alarm her, he closed the door and crossed to her before she had time to get up. He dropped to his knees, sitting back on his heels, smiling as the kittens investigated him, sharp claws digging into his thighs as they used him as a climbing frame.

Gently, he slid a palm under each warm, rounded little body, lifting them close for a better view, seeing the similarities and differences in what were clearly siblings' faces. He loved animals, and would have surrounded himself with them, but Sofia had been allergic to several kinds of animals, making pets impossible.

Thinking of his beloved wife, taken from him so devastatingly five years before, brought the familiar pain and he closed his eyes, rubbing his face against the two fluffy animals, feeling the dual purrs vibrating against his hands.

Gio opened his eyes and focused on Jessica, who sat little more than a foot away, shocked to silence, a whole mixture of emotions chasing themselves across her expressive green eyes. Turning the kittens so they were facing her, he held them against his chest, enjoying their softness and the feel of their heartbeats.

'What are their names?'

His question apparently threw her because she stared at him for several moments as if expecting him to launch into an interrogation. She bit her lip, diverting his attention to the tempting swell of her mouth. As she sucked in a breath, his gaze rose to clash with hers once more.

'Th-that's Dickens,' she finally informed him, her voice unsteady and her hand shaking as she pointed to the kitten in his left hand, which had a dark face, pink nose and round green eyes, not unlike her own in colour.

'And this one?' he asked of the kitten in his right hand, which had slanting, almond-shaped eyes in a darker shade than its sibling's.

'Kipling.'

She looked lost and alone so he handed Dickens to her, and she clutched him close as if needing the comfort.

'They are favourite authors of yours?'

Jessica nodded, her curls swaying like dancing flames. 'Partly. But also for their characters. They're very mischievous and inquisitive. With him,' she continued, pointing to the kitten cradled in his hands, 'I kept thinking he's just so naughty, just so cute, just so everything, and so I thought of Kipling and his *Just So* stories.' She was still tense, but a smile tugged her mouth as she looked at the kitten she held. 'This one was into everything and I was always asking what the dickens he was up to. The names stuck.'

'How long have you had them?'

'About six weeks. Their mother was an unknown feral stray who had a litter in the barn on a farm near my cottage,' she told him, relaxing a little. 'Flora, who lives there, and who is a nurse at the doctors' surgery in Penhally, isn't sure what happened to the mother, but the kittens were abandoned and Flora took care of them. She couldn't keep them all and was looking for homes for the others. I took these two.'

'What happens to them during the day?' he asked, intrigued how she had organised things.

'They stay with Sid Evans—he's the hospital handyman.' Gio nodded, confirming he knew of the man. 'He lost his wife recently and I've spent some time chatting to him,' Jessica continued, although he was unsurprised to learn of her kindness. 'He was very down and told me he wasn't allowed pets at his flat. So I asked the hospital management if he could have the kittens in his work room during the day and they said yes.' A warm smile curved her mouth. 'Sid loves having them.'

'I'm sure he does.' He admired her even more for her thoughtfulness. He also suspected that Jessica had set things up so that Sid felt valued, believing he was doing her a good turn. He was sure the hospital management didn't know where the kittens spent the night. 'How long have you been camping here?'

His question, getting to the core of the issue, had her tensing up again and she ducked her head, her hair falling forward, hiding her face.

'Talk to me,' he encouraged softly. With one finger beneath her chin, he urged her to look up again. 'What's going on, Jessica?'

Very conscious of Gio's touch, Jess trembled. The pad of one finger, that was all, and yet her whole body felt alive, charged and vitally aware of him. It was so long since she'd been touched...at least before this week when Gio had done so several times, stirring up desires she'd managed to banish for the last four years. But she had to quash the yearnings Gio had reawakened because he—like everyone else—was out of bounds. Steeling herself, she drew back enough to break the physical connection, concerned how much she missed the contact.

In shock from Gio's sudden arrival, fear built now that one of her secrets, albeit the least monumental and important of them, had been discovered. She didn't want to tell him anything but how could she bluff her way out? Even if she could excuse the kittens, the damning evidence of the makeshift bed was impossible to explain away.

'Jessica?'

'I, um, recently moved into my cottage,' she began shakily, unsure how much to tell him. 'The storm ten days ago destroyed the roof, causing water damage and the electricity being shut off. I tried to say there anyway...'

'*Dio!* With no power and no roof?' he exclaimed, muttering something uncomplimentary in Italian.

Jess lowered her gaze. 'It was only one night. I was

concerned for the kittens,' she explained, failing to add that not only had it been miserable with no electricity or hot water but that she'd been spooked in the isolated cottage with no security.

'So you've been staying here since then?'

'Yes,' she admitted with reluctance.

She couldn't help but be mesmerised by the way Gio continued to stroke Dickens, his fingers sinking into the soft fur. The kitten was enjoying it if his purrs were anything to go by. It made her think dangerous and never-to-be-allowed things...like how it would feel to have Gio's fingers caress *her* body from top to toe. She had no doubt she'd be purring, too.

Looking down lest he read anything in her eyes, Jess struggled to push her wayward thoughts away because no matter how much she may crave his touch, it wasn't going to happen.

'Why here, though?' Gio's voice reclaimed her attention. 'Why not stay at a hotel...or with friends?'

She fudged an answer, mumbling about the need to keep the kittens with her and everywhere being fully booked at the height of the season, because no way was she going to tell him the truth about the sorry state of her finances or that she didn't *have* any friends. Not the kind she could stay with, anyway. To explain either would involve the impossible—revealing what she could never reveal...*why*.

Why she had crashed and burned so badly...

Why her life had changed so drastically and irrevocably four years ago...

And why she was now counting the cost in so many ways, not just financially but professionally—hence her change of career and re-training in her mid-twenties to become a counsellor—and socially—keeping people at a distance and denying herself the closeness, emotional or physical, she had once enjoyed as a normal part of life. Nothing about her life these last four years had been normal. But she'd succeeded, she was coping...or had been until Gio had arrived, bringing home all she had lost and making her yearn for things she could never have again.

'It's only for a short while.' She crossed her fingers, hoping that was true. 'The insurance company have agreed to the repairs and the builders are starting work next week. As soon as possible, I'll move back in.'

'You can't stay here and live like this until then, Jessica,' he protested, clearly upset about the situation.

'It's not so bad,' she countered, trying for a carefree smile. 'I don't have any choice.'

'Of course you do.'

His words and the determined tone of his voice made her nervous. 'What do you mean?'

'As of now, you're moving in with me.'

CHAPTER SIX

UNOBSERVED, Gio leaned against the doorjamb and watched as Jessica carried out some graceful Tai Chi movements. She was dressed in a loose T-shirt, shorts that left shapely legs bare from mid-thigh down, and a pair of trainers, her vibrant curls restrained in a ponytail. He never tired of looking at her. Taking a sip of his coffee, he waited for her to finish her routine.

It was the August bank holiday weekend and they both had two days off. Jessica had been in his house for two weeks. She'd protested, but there had never been any question in his mind about where she should stay. He couldn't let her camp in her office. She'd wanted to pay rent, he'd said no, but they'd compromised and she made a contribution towards food and supplies.

She'd also set rules. No touching. And nothing more than a platonic friendship. He'd agreed. Sort of. Temporarily. If setting them and keeping things on a friendly footing was what Jessica needed to begin with, he would play along. For now. That she'd felt the need to make rules at all proved she felt the same electric awareness he did.

He was using the time to gain Jessica's trust and continuing to get her used to his touch. He stopped the moment she withdrew or showed signs of disquiet. As the days went by, it was taking her longer to step away. He had yet to discover why she struggled so hard to deny the attraction.

Having coaxed her and the kittens home that Saturday night, the next day they had driven to her cottage. He'd grown up bilingual thanks to his parents and his American-born maternal grandmother, but, however fluent he was in English, he swore best in Italian and he'd unconsciously reverted to his native language as he surveyed the state of Jessica's home. It had been far worse than he'd imagined.

Built of stone and sitting in an isolated spot surrounded by untended land, the large cottage was single storey. The thatched roof and rotten rafters had collapsed inwards, wrecking several rooms beneath, letting in the rain and rendering the place uninhabitable. He'd seen the promise, had visualised the picture-book traditional cottage as it would be when it was finished, but that Jessica had tried to stay in what was little more than a ruin had astounded him.

Turning round, he'd seen the pained expression on Jessica's face, and realised the effect his rant was having on her. Reverting to English, he'd gentled his tone and closed the gap between them. His nature was to touch, to hug, to comfort, and it had been difficult to stop himself from drawing her into his arms.

Slowly he'd raised one hand and cupped her cheek, marvelling at the peachy softness of her skin. 'I'm sorry. I was not shouting at you, just at the state of the place and knowing someone would sell it to you in such a perilous condition.'

Some of the tension had drained from her, and for

a second she'd leaned into his touch. He'd brushed the pad of his thumb across the little hollow between her chin and her mouth, watching as her lips had parted instinctively and her eyelids lowered in response. She hadn't actually purred like one of the kittens, but her reaction had been unmistakeable. He'd so wanted to kiss her, but the moment had ended as she'd withdrawn into herself, turning her head away to break the contact.

'If the cottage had been in better condition I couldn't have afforded it,' she'd told him. 'I knew the roof was dodgy...' She'd given a wry laugh as she'd looked at the blue sky visible between what remained of the rotten rafters. 'I didn't expect it to cave in with the first storm.'

He'd never had to worry about money, and he knew how lucky he was, never taking things for granted. The business had made his family wealthy and money cushioned many blows. Except grief. Nothing eased the pain of that, but at least he'd been in a position to fund the trust in Sofia's name and help other people. He hated to think of Jessica struggling to make ends meet, and wondered why she had apparently sunk every penny she'd had into such a run-down, if potentially lovely, cottage, with no money left over to furnish it...or why she hadn't stayed in a hotel when she'd been forced to vacate it. Why had she been so insistent on buying outright rather than taking a small mortgage or personal loan to leave her some working capital?

For now Jessica and the kittens were living with him. Having been alone for five years, he'd been nervous of her moving in but it felt scarily *right*. They fitted. As this was the first time he'd been attracted to another woman, he'd struggled with feelings of disloyalty. Something

Sofia would chastise him for, having made it clear she didn't want him to remain alone.

Living with someone revealed so much about them and unearthed little ways and habits previously unsuspected and which could be irritating out of all proportion. So far he'd not discovered anything annoying about Jessica but there were several things that intrigued and amused him. One was the collection of assorted vitamin and dietary supplements she had stacked at one end of the kitchen worktop. He had no idea what they were for or why she felt she needed them. She was fastidious about washing up any of the crockery or cutlery she used, sorting them into a neat pile separate from his.

'Do you have a hygiene fetish?' he'd asked with a chuckle that first weekend, but his humour had rapidly faded given her reaction.

'No, of course not.'

The words of denial had been accompanied by a forced, hollow laugh, but it had been the unmistakeable hurt mixed with alarm and embarrassment in her eyes that had grabbed him.

'I didn't mean to upset you,' he'd apologised softly.

'You haven't.'

It had been a lie, he knew it. Just as he knew that something about what he had said or how he had said it had stung her.

The more he observed about her, including her anxiety at touching and being touched, the more he wondered if she'd experienced a bad relationship. Had someone criticised her, controlled her or, what he most feared, hurt and abused her?

Jess pivoted on one leg, turning her body in his direction, and he stifled a laugh when she spotted him, her eyes widening in surprise as she missed her step and stumbled momentarily before regaining her balance.

'Hi,' she murmured, embarrassment now predominant in her olive green eyes.

'Morning.' He straightened as she approached him warily, always keeping that extra bit of distance. 'Are you done?'

The fingers of one hand tucked stray wisps of hair back from her face. 'Just about. Why?'

'I have something to show you. Come with me.'

'Where are we going?' Jess asked as Gio drove away from the house.

'I can't tell you.'

She frowned at his unsatisfactory response. 'Why not?'

'Because then it would not be a surprise, would it?' he reasoned with calm amusement.

With no information forthcoming, Jess rested back in the luxurious seat of the sleek sports car. She hated to admit how much of a thrill she got each time she rode in it. As Gio turned out of the drive and onto the B-road that hugged the coastline on its route to St Piran, Jess glanced across the fields to the house she had been living in for the last fortnight. How could she feel so comfortable and yet scared at the same time?

The house sat atop the cliff as if carved from the bedrock and perfectly suited its Cornish name, *Ninnes*, 'the isolated place'. At first glance it suited Gio, too— wild, remote, alone.

'It's very impressive,' she'd murmured when she had first seen inside the architect-designed property. It didn't feel like a home. Clinical, cold, unlived in, it was like a set from an interior design magazine.

'Now tell me what you really think,' Gio had invited with a smile. 'It is soulless, no? A show-house, not a home,' he added, mirroring her own thoughts. 'The agent instructed to rent a place for me must have imagined someone moving from London would like it.'

'And you don't?' she'd asked, relieved this was not what he would have chosen for himself.

'No. But it gives me time to find something I *do* want and at least I have a roof over my head in the meantime.'

A laugh had burst from her at his unintentional choice of words and the expression on his face as the reason for her reaction dawned on him...she was there because she currently did *not* have a roof over hers!

Judging by the tone of his tirade when he had seen the state of her cottage, it had been worse than he'd expected. Had the property been in better condition, it would have been way beyond her budget, even with the unexpected legacy that had allowed her to step onto the housing ladder. But she had fallen in love with the place, and its parcel of neglected land that would allow her to have more animals and grow her own produce.

That Gio had seen the potential in the cottage had pleased her, and telling him about her plans for the place had diverted him from his questions about her reasons for not taking out a mortgage or personal loan. Either would have enabled her to get on with the renovations and furnishing the house straight away, but when she had looked into funding she had been asked questions about herself that she'd no wish to answer—and which may have meant she'd have been turned down anyway. She couldn't explain that to Gio without explaining *why*. And that was impossible.

So she had succumbed to Gio's arguments and the shameful temptation of moving in with him. Dickens and Kipling were in heaven. She was halfway between heaven and hell. They'd settled into a routine, their friendship becoming closer every day. Contrarily, his agreement to her rules and conditions had brought an inner stab of disappointment, though she knew friendship was all they could ever share.

Her hormones raged in protest, and she had to fight her attraction to him. Keeping people at a safe distance had become ingrained within her these last four years, but Gio was breaching her defences. He made her want things she could no longer have, reminding her of broken dreams and abandoned hopes.

'Jessica?'

'Mmm?' She blinked as Gio's voice impinged on her consciousness. 'Sorry, did you say something?'

He chuckled. 'Several times, but you are living with goblins! That is the saying, yes?' he added as she stared at him blankly.

'Sorry?' she repeated, confused for a moment before realisation dawned. 'Oh! You mean away with the fairies! No, I was just thinking.' A flush warmed her cheeks. No way could she tell him where her thoughts had really been.

'We are here,' he said now, switching off the engine.

They were at the harbourside in St Piran, Jess discovered, scrambling out of the car before Gio could come round and offer a hand to help her. The less she touched him, the better. He took some things from the car, including a picnic basket, handing her a canvas bag with towels, spare T-shirts and some sunscreen. Apprehension unsettled her. She hadn't realised this was a day's outing.

Her gaze feasted on the sight of him dressed in deck shoes and shorts that left well-defined muscular legs bare from mid-thigh downwards. His torso was encased in a white T-shirt that emphasised the tone of his skin and hugged the contours of his athletic body. Jess bit her lip to stop a sigh of appreciation from escaping

'Have you been on a boat before?' he asked, guiding her towards a jetty along which several very expensive-looking craft were moored.

'Only a car ferry.'

His throaty laugh stole her breath. 'This isn't quite the same.'

Jess gathered that as he halted by a huge, gleaming, red-and-white speedboat. 'Oh, my.'

She gazed at the boat in awe, excitement mounting as she anticipated what it would feel like to ride in the kind of jet-powered boat she'd seen offshore racing on television. The name *Lori* was written on the side and she wondered at the significance.

'My one indulgence...apart from my car,' he told her with a touch of embarrassment.

'It's beautiful.' She smiled, imagining the thrill of speeding across the waves. 'How long have you had it?'

Relaxing, as if relieved at her reaction, he smiled the rare, special smile that reached his eyes, banishing the shadows that often lurked there and trapping the breath in her lungs. 'About eighteen months. I could not get out often when I was in London and she was moored on the south coast, but I hope to use her often here.'

Gio climbed aboard with practised ease, set down the items he was carrying and turned to help her. Jess swallowed. Adopting avoidance tactics, she gave him her bags instead of her hand.

'I can manage,' she told him, cursing the way he quirked an eyebrow and watched with amusement as she scrambled inelegantly over the side.

To her surprise, the luxury powerboat had a small but fully equipped cabin below, with a tiny kitchen, a minuscule washroom and a seating area that converted into a sleeping space for three people. They'd have to be very friendly, Jess thought. After putting the picnic items in the fridge, they went back outside and Gio collected two life-jackets from a locker.

'Are these necessary?' Jess asked as he handed one to her.

'Absolutely.' He fastened his in no time. 'I would never take risks with your safety.'

She knew that. They might not have known each other long but she trusted him implicitly. It was herself she worried about, she thought wryly as she struggled with the life-jacket, huffing with frustration as it defeated her.

'Here,' Gio chuckled, closing the gap between them. 'Let me help.'

'It's OK…'

Her protest fell on deaf ears as he took over. Did he need to touch her that much? Or so slowly and intimately? And he was far too close—so close that every breath she took was fragranced with his musky male scent, weakening her resolve and tightening the aching knot in the pit of her stomach. She couldn't stop breathing so she closed her eyes and tightened her hands into fists, praying for the exquisite torture to be over and reminding herself why she couldn't succumb to temptation. He was taking longer than necessary, surely, the brush of his fingers burning her through the fabric of her T-shirt.

'All done.'

His voice sounded huskier than usual and she opened her eyes to find herself staring directly into his. A tremor ran through her at the sensual expression he made no attempt to mask. Her body craved his touch, making it difficult for her to keep her distance, to step back now as she knew she must.

As if anticipating her retreat, he released her and moved away, but not before he dropped a kiss on the tip of her nose. Confused, Jess remained motionless for several moments. The tip of her nose felt warm and tingly...nothing to do with the late August heat and everything to do with the brush of his lips on her skin.

Why had he done that?

Why had she let him?

Panic welled within her. Maybe it would be best if she got off the boat now, before she did anything even more stupid. But while she was wrestling with indecision, considering her options, Gio effectively removed them by untying the moorings and firing the boat into life.

He settled her in the padded horseshoe-shaped seat adjacent to his, then he was manipulating the controls, inching the boat into the main harbour towards the open sea. The twin engines throbbed with leashed power, straining for freedom. Despite her uncertainties, a new burst of excitement coursed through her.

'I hate to confine your incredible hair, but you might want to tie it back—or I can lend you a baseball cap,' Gio said as the harbour entrance approached.

Taking his advice, she accepted the cap he offered, pulling her untamed curls back into a ponytail before feeding it through the slot in the back of the cap. The brim helped shade her eyes from the August sunshine.

'Hold on.'

Jess felt her heart thudding with excitement as they reached open water and gained speed, going west along the coast from St Piran. The sea was calm but the bow of the boat rose up and rode the crests and troughs. Gio opened the throttle and a whoop of joy escaped her. She felt free, truly understanding how he felt and how this blew away tensions and stresses.

'This is incredible!' She laughed, raising her voice so Gio could hear her above the noise of the engines, the whoosh of the wind and the sound of the boat hitting the water. She tilted her head back and closed her eyes, savouring the sun on her skin, the occasional salty spray and the sense of speed. 'It's amazing! I love it.'

Lying face down on a towel stretched out on the sand in the secluded cove they had discovered, Jessica stretched and sighed. 'I could get used to this.'

Gio smiled. She sounded sleepy and contented following their exhilarating morning flying across the waves. They had travelled miles, moving from the bay in which St Piran stood, through Penhally Bay and past the village of Penhally itself, with its horseshoe-shaped harbour and the rocky promontory at one end, off which,

Jessica had told him, lay the wreck of an old Spanish galleon.

They had headed part of the way back before finding their cove. After a swim, they had enjoyed their picnic lunch. As Jessica relaxed, he finished his apple, his gaze straying over her deliciously curvy figure. She had pulled her shorts on over her one-piece costume but that didn't spoil his view. Everything male in him responded to her voluptuous femininity. And her hair continued to captivate him. Freed from the cap, it seemed alive in the sunlight, the strands fanning across her shoulders like tongues of fire.

Her delight at the boat made Gio glad he'd brought her. He'd had doubts. He'd never taken anyone out with him before. Time on the boat was guarded jealously. It was his escape, his retreat, his guilty pleasure, and he'd been worried...not that Jessica wouldn't enjoy it but that having anyone with him would detract from what he gained being alone on the water. The desire for Jessica's company proved how fully she had breached his defences in the weeks since they'd met. Today he'd discovered that sharing the boat with her made the experience better than before.

'Why is your boat called *Lori*?'

Jessica's softly voiced question made him tense. She was looking at him through those sexy green eyes, and he dragged his gaze free, staring out to sea. Maybe it was time to tell her about Sofia. If he wanted Jessica to trust him and share the secrets that held her back from relationships with people, then he had to trust her, too. Which meant placing his broken heart in her hands. He cleared his throat, the emotion building before he even begun to speak.

'Lori was my wife's nickname,' he began, hit by a wave of memories. 'In Italy it is common to shorten someone's surname to use as a derivative. Sofia's maiden name was Loriani...to friends she was Lori. At school everyone called us "Lori and Cori".' A smile came unbidden. 'We used the names for each other into adulthood.'

Jessica's smile was sweet, interest and understanding in her eyes. 'That's lovely. You'd known each other a long time?'

'Since we were six.'

'Six?' she exclaimed with surprise. 'Wow!'

'Sofia's *mamma*, Ginetta, came to work for my parents,' he continued. 'She lived in, originally caring for the house—and me—while my parents worked long hours with the business. Ginetta rapidly became indispensable, and she and Sofia were soon part of the family.'

Gio paused and took a drink of water. 'Sofia and I were the same age and were friends from day one. We scarcely spent a day apart. Many people believed we'd go our separate ways with time, but it never happened. It wasn't something we planned.' He frowned, trying to find the best way to explain. 'We just never wanted anyone else, you know?' Jessica nodded and turned more towards him. 'We married at eighteen. I did my medical training and Sofia trained to be a teacher. Throughout everything we remained best friends.'

'Soul mates,' Jessica added, her voice husky.

'Yes.'

Leaning back on his elbows, enjoying the feel of the sun against his skin, he found himself telling her all kinds of stories as happy memories flowed so quickly it was difficult to catch hold of them.

'We were in no hurry to start a family of our own. Being together was all we wanted. We thought we had time…but it ran out,' he added, choking on the words.

'What happened, Gio?'

Jessica's whispered query took him back into the darkness. Voice thick, he told her of the moment they had found out that Sofia was dying.

'It is ironic, no, that Sofia should be struck down by the kind of brain tumour I now operate on often?' He heard Jessica's shocked gasp, aware that she was sitting up but too lost in his thoughts to stop now. 'Sofia's tumour was inoperable. It was virulent and resistant to treatment, claiming her quickly.'

What he didn't add aloud was how guilty he felt. And that he couldn't forgive himself for being unable to save her, tormenting himself as he relived those terrible weeks…to the signs he must have missed and failing to catch the tumour early enough to make a difference. His head knew it wasn't true, Sofia's doctors had told him time and again that it wouldn't have made a difference, but still he wondered and beat himself up over his failings.

'Gio, you're not in any way to blame.' Jessica was closer, he could feel her behind him, feel the kiss of her breath against his shoulder as she spoke, her voice gentle but firm. He heard the emotion she was keeping in check as she continued. 'It is too unspeakably cruel, for Sofia and for you.'

'I wish I had her courage. She faced death with the same warmth, bravery, humour and gentleness of spirit with which she embraced life. I was at her side every second of her brief but futile fight, and I was holding her hand when she took her final breath.'

His colleagues and the staff who had cared for her had left him alone with her. For the first time in his adult life, he had wept—for Sofia and for himself. And then he had shut down a significant part of himself, closing off his heart because it was the only way he could cope with going on alone. As he had somehow emerged from the blackest of days after her loss, he had thrown himself into his work, into making himself better, and in trying to stop others dying the way Sofia had.

'Life was nothing without her. We'd been inseparable for twenty-one years. I felt lost, cast adrift,' he admitted, the emotion catching up with him.

'Gio...'

Jessica came up onto her knees behind him and wrapped him in her arms, shocking him. Full, firm breasts pressed against his back and, as she rested her head on his shoulder, he felt her tears against his skin. As he drew in another unsteady breath, it was fragranced with the subtle aroma of her chocolate-scented shampoo and body lotion. Drawing on her comfort, he raised his hands, finding hers and linking their fingers.

'You worked so you wouldn't think,' she said, her voice throaty with emotion.

'Yes.' She understood, he suspected, because she did the same, focusing on other people's problems to escape her own.

'And the trust you told me about...'

'I set it up in Sofia's name, funding research, raising money to provide scanners and equipment for hospitals around the world and providing information and support for those struck down by neurological conditions, especially tumours.'

'Sofia would be so proud of you.'

'She would also be kicking me for not getting on with life,' he added wryly.

'But you have,' Jessica protested. 'You did what you needed to do for you and you've helped countless others through very difficult times.'

Her generosity touched him. And he savoured the closeness and physical contact, hoping Jessica would not suddenly remember her no-touching rule and take flight.

He took a deep breath, feeling calmer, telling Jessica of his discovery of the album Sofia had made of their lives, packed with photos and letters and memorabilia from childhood, through their wedding and to their last days together. He treasured it. It gave him solace, made him grateful that she'd been his life, but it also made him grieve for what would never be. Sofia was the only woman he had ever loved, the only woman with whom he had ever *made* love. In the last five years his bed had felt too big and cold and lonely, but nothing and no one had ever tempted him.

Until Jessica.

As Gio fell silent, Jess thought over all he had told her, feeling devastated for him and his wife. Many times she had wondered about the woman who had claimed Gio's heart. Sofia. She envisaged a glamorous, beautiful woman with a model-like figure. Whatever she had looked like, Sofia had been lucky to win Gio's love, devotion and loyalty. And cruelly unlucky to have been taken from him at such a young age.

Gio's fidelity and love for Sofia was in stark contrast to the thoughtlessness and infidelity shown by Duncan, Jess's ex-fiancé and the man who had changed her life for ever. Discovering Duncan had been unfaithful on too many occasions to count had been hurtful and shocking enough. Being eight weeks away from the wedding she had dreamed of for so long had made it worse. The wedding had never taken place. And the dream would now never come true for her.

There were so many things Duncan had taken from her, including her trust in people. And herself. Her life had changed beyond recognition. Her fiancé—*ex-fiancé*, she corrected with the anger and bitterness that had never left her—had seen to that.

The thought of never being close to anyone again was depressing, so she kept busy and absorbed helping others so that she had no time to think of herself. So she understood Gio's need to lose himself in work after such a heart-wrenching loss. That he blamed himself was terrible, and yet driving himself as he had meant he had given hope, care and fresh chances to his patients. Patients he tried so hard to save as he had not been able to save Sofia.

Her situation was different but the outcome had been similar. A lonely life devoting herself to caring for others. Now and again, in a weak moment, a stray thought crept in. A yearning for intimacy. Not even sex…just a need to be held and cherished. As she and Gio were holding each other now.

The reality of it was a shock. She'd acted on instinct in response to his pain, forgetting the need to keep distance between them. Now, pressed against him, her arms around his shoulders and their hands locked together, she battled the awareness and desire that were coursing through her.

How she wished she could satisfy the urge to bury her face more fully into his neck and breathe in his scent...the earthy aroma of man mixed with the subtle but arousing fragrance of his soap and warm, sun-kissed skin. It was crazy! But everything in her was drawn to him on some basic level. She couldn't give in to it. To do so would involve telling him her secrets and she couldn't do that. If she did, he would run in the opposite direction, just as everyone else in her life had done when they'd found out. She was tarnished, spoiled goods, untouchable. And she would do well to remember that when she indulged in any foolish notions about Gio.

Drawing in one last breath of his intoxicating, delicious scent, her desire for him threatening to melt her bones and turn her resolve to dust, she began to withdraw.

'I'm sorry, I shouldn't have done that,' she apologised, disconcerted when he kept hold of her hands.

'I'm not sorry.' He allowed her to place only a small distance between them before shifting so he was facing her. 'Thank you.'

Jess shook her head in confusion. 'I didn't do anything.'

'Yes, you did. You listened, you understood. You cared,' he added huskily, setting her heart thudding.

Knowing she was in big trouble, Jess sucked in a ragged breath, unable to drag her gaze free from the intensity of his. 'W-what are you looking at?' she finally asked, the electric tension increasing with every passing second.

'Your eyes.'

Jess frowned. 'What's the matter with them?'

'Nothing. They're beautiful.' He smiled, seeming closer than ever. 'This is the first time I've noticed the little specks of silver-grey in them.'

'Really?' Was that her voice sounding so breathless and confused?

'Mmm.' Blue eyes darkened as they watched her. 'I've meant to ask before...what is the gemstone in your earrings? They're the same shade as your eyes.'

Again he had thrown her and she tried to focus on his question and not on the affect of his nearness. 'Olive apatite. My grandmother had a passion for gemology and she gave them to me for my twenty-first birthday,' she told him, thinking with sadness and gratitude of the woman who had died the previous winter and whose unexpected legacy had enabled her to buy her cottage.

'They're perfect for you,' Gio told her, the approval and intimacy in his voice making her tingle all over.

Jess couldn't help but shiver as Gio ran the pad of one thumb along the sensitive hollow between her chin and her lower lip. She couldn't prevent her lips parting in response. It took a concerted effort not to sway towards him. Instead, Gio moved, oh, so slowly leaning in until warm supple lips met hers. Jess jumped. One of his hands still held hers and her fingers closed reflexively on his.

He tasted of things sinful, things long denied her but which she could know again if only she let go. Could she? Dared she? What if she did? How would she put the lid back on the box again afterwards? More than anything she wanted to forget common sense.

But she couldn't.

Gathering all the strength and willpower she could

muster, she turned her head away, breaking the spell. She heard his soft sigh, his smothered exclamation of regret and frustration, but she hardened her resolve. It was for the best, she told herself over and over again, hoping that repeating the mantra often enough would make her believe it. But the thought of telling him the truth made it easier.

The truth.

Her secret.

The one that hung over her like the sword of Damocles. Nothing could happen without him knowing—and once he knew, he would reject her anyway. Like everyone else. She valued his friendship too much to risk spoiling everything by giving in to a moment of madness, one she knew had no future to it.

'Jessica...'

'Please, Gio, don't,' she begged before he could continue. 'I can't. I'm sorry.'

His disappointment was clear, but he smiled, running one finger down her cheek. 'It's OK. I'm not giving up on you but there is no hurry. When you are ready, you will tell me...whatever it is.'

Jess had no reply to that, unable to imagine a time when she could ever reveal the truth to him.

'Friends, remember?' she said now, moving away and helping him pack their things ready to return to the boat for the journey home.

She'd told Gio to remember the rules, but she had been as guilty as him of ignoring them. With the boundaries becoming more and more blurred all the time, who most needed the instruction to behave...Gio or herself?

CHAPTER SEVEN

'MEGAN?'

Josh O'Hara looked at the fragile form of the woman who had caused much of the mental and emotional turmoil that had plagued him since he'd arrived at St Piran's and discovered her here. A blast from the past. One with which he'd never come to terms.

She turned around, her gaze scanning the A and E staffroom, and a frown formed as she realised they were alone. He felt uncertain and awkward as the silence stretched between them. They had been tiptoeing around each other for weeks now. He had questions that needed answers, but attempts to confront the past had been futile...meeting with hostility and denial.

Yet despite the dark cloud that hung over them, when Megan, as registrar on call, had come to A and E from Paediatrics, they'd worked well together and been attuned to each other. Now he had a rare window of opportunity to talk to her alone.

'Have you been in Cornwall all the time?' he asked, daring to venture onto dangerous ground.

Her gaze flicked to his and away again. 'Pretty much.'

At least she'd answered rather than walking out or telling him to back off. 'How is your grandmother?'

'She died three years ago.'

'I'm sorry.' Damn it, could he say nothing right to this woman? 'I know what she meant to you.'

Her small smile was tinged with sadness. 'I owe her everything.'

She'd told him once how her parents had been killed in a road accident when she'd been four and her grandmother had raised her. She'd not been in the best of health and Megan had been caring for her while going through medical school.

With Megan in a more conciliatory mood, he risked asking more of the questions that plagued him. 'Why here, Megan?'

'My grandmother lived in Penhally when she was young and she wanted to come home before she died. It seemed as good a place as any to be,' she finished, sounding so lost and alone that his heart ached for her.

He'd forgotten her grandmother's connection with Cornwall. Or had he? Was that why, when Rebecca had suggested leaving London, Cornwall had been the first place he had thought to go? Had he, some place deep in his subconscious, made the connection with Megan?

He remained as affected by her as he'd always been. The past would never go away. Neither could he change it. But he craved answers.

'I know you don't want to talk, and I won't ask again if that's what you choose, but I need to know, Megan—' He broke off, capturing her gaze, his heart in his mouth. 'Was the baby mine?'

He saw her shock and the pain his question caused as

she reeled back, anger replacing the hurt in her eyes. 'Of *course* it was yours. Don't judge me by *your* standards. *I* didn't sleep around.'

'Why didn't you *tell* me?' he demanded, his own hurt and anger rising with the confirmation of what he had known in his heart all along.

'How could I?' she threw back at him, her voice shaky with emotion. 'When was I meant to tell you? You refused to talk to me. And what good would it have done? What would *you* have done? You'd made it clear I meant nothing to you. You wouldn't have welcomed fatherhood...you never wanted children. Just as you rejected marriage—although *that's* changed in the last eight years.'

Pain and bitterness rang in her tone. Her accusations hurt...the more so because he recognised the truth in them. He *had* behaved badly. He'd been anti-marriage— for himself—and he'd never wanted children. Something he'd made clear to Rebecca from the first, and the reason why he was refusing her latest demands for a baby.

But he didn't want to think of Rebecca now. His thoughts were in the past. He'd had a right to know eight years ago. Hadn't he? Megan's challenge rang in his ears. What *would* he have done? He wasn't sure but it would undoubtedly have been the wrong thing. Avoidance of the truth. Running away. He'd been good at that. But knowing it *had* been his lifeless son he'd once held in his arms was devastating.

'You denied me any chance of making those decisions for myself.' The depth of his emotion shocked him and his voice was choked. 'You gave me no chance to say goodbye to my son.'

'You have a nerve. What chance did *you* give *me*

when you tossed me aside?' Tears gleamed on her lashes. 'You took my baby from me, Josh. And with him any chance of me having another child.'

'God, Megan. Those weren't my decisions.' His tone softened as her pain sliced through him. She looked more fragile than ever and he fought the urge to comfort her—something he should have done eight years ago.

Eight years...

He was plunged back to that terrible night when A and E had been in chaos following a multiple crash involving a coach of schoolchildren. He'd been a junior doctor facing something far beyond his experience as the paramedics had brought in a woman in the throes of a miscarriage and haemorrhaging terribly. Discovering it was Megan had thrown him.

'The obstetrician/gynaecologist did what was necessary to save your life. There wasn't even time to transfer you to Theatre.'

The possibility of Megan dying had been real. The surgeon had pulled the tiny baby from her body and given it to him. He'd stared at the lifeless form, too premature to survive, trying to work out dates with a brain that refused to function. A nurse had taken the baby away, and he'd been drawn back into the emergency procedure, assisting as the surgeon had made the decision to take Megan's womb.

'I asked him—*begged* him—to leave you hope for the future, but he was adamant there was no other way to stop you bleeding to death. What else could I have done?' he appealed to her, his stomach churning as he relived that awful night.

'I don't know.'

Tears ran down her cheeks and his heart, for so long

encased in a protective coating of stone, threatened to break at the depth of her sorrow and pain. He'd pushed the memories into the background, unable to deal with them. Megan had been living with them every day. He felt guilty, confused...

'What did you call him?' he asked, knowing he was tormenting them both but needing to know.

'Stephen.' Her voice was rough. 'After my father.'

'Thank you for telling me.'

They stared at each other, fighting the past, the pain, the memories—and the chemistry that, eight years on and despite all that had happened, still bubbled below the surface.

The sound of his pager announcing an incoming emergency cut through the tense silence, swiftly followed by the ring of Megan's pager, bringing their conversation to an end. Although he now had confirmation about the baby, a sense of unfinished business still remained.

Eight years ago he had known that Megan was different, had sensed she was dangerous to him. And he'd been right. The night he'd let down his guard had been the most amazing of his life. He'd told Megan things he had never told anyone else, and she had touched a place inside him in a way no other woman ever had. It had scared him. And he'd done what Megan had accused him of. He'd blanked her, keeping as far from her as possible because she'd burrowed under his skin.

If only he had been mature enough to know what he knew now. That the sort of connection he had found with Megan was rare. Not just the incredible physical passion that had overwhelmed them both but the deep mental and emotional union he'd experienced with no one but her. By the time he'd realised what he could have had and all he had thrown away, it had been too late.

He'd wobbled. Briefly. Then he'd gone on, focusing on his career and rapid advancement. Four years ago he'd met Rebecca and they'd seemed to want the same things, including no children. He'd cared about her, he'd been lonely and enjoyed having her to come home to. She'd wanted the doctor husband and the lifestyle. He'd convinced himself it was for the best, not the same as he'd had with Megan but safer.

Things had been wrong long before they'd left London. Bored, Rebecca had changed the rules, deciding she wanted a child. But as Izzy had said weeks ago when her daughter had been born, a child couldn't hold a bad marriage together and shouldn't be brought into the world for the wrong reasons. He wouldn't have a baby he didn't want with a woman he didn't love and who didn't love him.

Seeing Megan again, he saw with terrible clarity what he had thrown away, and he wished with all his heart that he had done things differently when he'd had the chance. As they walked down the corridor to the main A and E department, it occurred to him that he had still not asked Megan one of the questions that had been bugging him all along.

'Why *did* you stay the night with me, Megan?'

Her sharp intake of breath was audible, but she pushed through the swing doors into the busy department, bringing further discussion to an end. As he was directed to Resus, Megan was called to a treatment cubicle and she walked away from him without a backward glance. He had no more idea what to do about her—and his feelings for her—now than he had in the past. She was an itch under his skin that wouldn't go away, affecting him in the same unique way she had done eight years ago.

'Is there anything else I can do for you?' Jess asked, sitting beside the bed of the woman with whom she had spent a considerable amount of time over the last few days.

Faye Luxton, in her early seventies, had come in for a standard knee replacement but had suffered a severe bleed in her brain during her operation and had woken in Intensive Care to find her world turned upside down. She'd been handed over into Gio's care and, just days ago, he had needed to operate on a second bleed to remove a clot and also to put a coil around a small aneurysm that had threatened to enlarge and cause even greater problems.

Unfortunately, the damage already caused could not be reversed, although the numbness and weakness down one side of her body and her difficulty speaking were improving. Faye could still have a good quality of life, but she would no longer be able to live alone or care for herself and her animals.

With no family, Faye faced the horrible necessity of selling her much-loved home and moving into an assisted-care facility. Jess had helped support her when Social Services had come to discuss the options.

Faye had faced everything with courage, but had been distressed at times as she tried to come to terms with the drastic changes in her life. Jess had done all she could, helping Faye deal with the emotional upset.

'You've done so much.' Her speech was slow and

slurred, but clearer than it had been. 'I wouldn't have coped without you.'

'I'm sure you would. You have such a strong spirit, Faye. You've been a joy to care for and a real inspiration, too,' Jess assured her.

'I agree.'

Gio's voice sent a prickle of awareness along Jess's spine and she looked round, her gaze clashing with his as he strode through the door, his senior registrar, a couple of junior doctors and the ward's charge nurse trailing in his wake. Jess was all too conscious of Gio close beside her chair, blocking her exit, his leg and hip pressing gently against her, as he greeted Faye warmly.

'I'll step out,' Jess offered, making to rise.

'Can Jess stay?' Faye asked, looking unsettled.

Gio smiled at their patient. 'Yes, of course.'

Jess subsided back onto the chair as his hand came to rest on her shoulder. Although his attention was focused on the medical team updating him on Faye's condition, his hand lingered, and Jess felt the fire in her blood as his touch warmed her through the fabric of her shirt. His fingers gave a gentle squeeze before he released her and reached out for Faye's notes.

They were halfway through September and while they'd been on their best behaviour since their bank-holiday outing in the boat, Jess was finding it difficult to ignore the electric buzz of attraction that intensified with every passing day. But she valued their friendship too much to risk losing her head and doing anything stupid.

They'd been out on the boat twice more and she loved it. Much to her amazement, Gio had also been teaching her how to drive it. The thrill had been so huge it had even managed to take her mind off his body pressed close to hers—and the divine male scent of him—as he'd helped her work the controls.

The tragedy of his wife's death still affected her and she remained shocked at the way she had acted on instinct in response to his grief. It had scared her. With Gio it was too easy to forget the hard lessons of the last four years.

Curious, Jess had steeled herself to ask Gio more about Sofia a couple of nights ago. Gio had brought out the album Sofia had made when she'd known she was dying, creating a story of their lives in words and pictures, and Jess had choked up all over again at the incredible bond they had shared and the cruel way they had been parted.

Sofia had been a surprise. Rather than being model thin and styled to perfection, she'd been small, curvy and very much the girl next door, possessing the kind of fresh-faced natural beauty that could never be faked and that shone through because of the person she was, in her laughing dark eyes, her smile and her obvious love for Gio. And his for her.

The photos of Gio and Sofia in their teens, so much together, so right for each other and so in love, had reminded Jess of Marcia and Colin—another young couple who had been ripped apart by terrible tragedy, and one she hadn't been able to get out of her mind.

'How are you feeling, Faye?' Gio asked, sitting on the edge of the bed and taking her good hand in his.

'I'm frustrated my body won't do what I want it to. I can't even tell you properly.' Faye shook her head. 'I can't imagine life away from my home and without my animals. I'm thankful for all you've done for me, but knowing things will never be the same is difficult.'

'Of course. It's hard enough to recover from surgery without having to come to terms with such unexpected changes. Things seem overwhelming, yes?' he sympathised, stealing Jess's heart as he took a pristine handkerchief from his pocket and wiped the elderly lady's tears with gentle care.

'Yes, exactly.' Faye visibly relaxed, soothed by Gio's attention. 'I'm old and set in my ways.'

Gio gallantly protested, making her smile. 'You're doing well and we will all do everything we can to ensure you regain as much strength and capability as possible.' The air locked in Jess's lungs as his gaze flicked to her. 'Jessica is here to help make the transition as trouble-free as possible.'

'I'm so worried about my animals, but Jess is marvellous,' Faye confided to Gio. 'If other arrangements can't be made to keep them together, she's promised she'll care for them herself.'

A blush warmed Jess's cheeks as Gio looked at her, his expression unreadable.

Gio talked with Faye awhile longer before rising to his feet. His entourage exited ahead of him but he lingered, and Jess excused herself from Faye, worried about his reaction to the animal thing.

'I was going to tell you, Gio. The workmen are making good progress on the cottage, and I'll arrange to have the fences dealt with. If the animals have to be moved before I'm back home, I'll ask Flora if she has room for them until I'm ready,' she rushed to reassure him. 'I don't expect you to house them or anything. I—'

Her rushed words were silenced as Gio pressed a

finger to her lips. 'Stop apologising.' Blue eyes twinkled with amusement and something else she couldn't discern but which made her warm and tingly and a little bit scared. 'I would have been surprised had you *not* offered to step in.'

'Oh...'

He glanced each way along the corridor, his tone conspiratorial as he leaned closer to her, making her quiver with awareness as his warm breath fanned her face. 'Shall I tell you a secret?'

She nodded, unable to answer, hardly able to breathe, fighting every urge within her to touch him, hug him, kiss him.

'I was going to make the same pledge to Faye myself.'

Jess blinked, his nearness robbing her of thought. 'You were?'

'I was.'

Jess felt mesmerised, her skin aflame as he ran one finger down her cheek. The suddenness of an alarm further along the corridor had her snapping back, conscious of where they were. Disconcerted by his touch, she stepped away. There was nothing she could do to escape the non-physical connection, the electrically charged one that bound her ever more tightly to him.

Gio's hand slowly dropped to his side and she swallowed as she met his gaze. He smiled, the full-on smile that stole her breath. 'I must go,' he said, glancing at his watch. 'We'll drive out to Faye's after work to talk with her neighbour and decide what is best to be done. OK?'

'OK.'

Jess watched as he strode off to join his team. How

was she going to cope when she moved back to her own cottage with the kittens? Gio had become far too important in her life.

'Stop the car!'

Gio reacted instantly to Jessica's cry, startled when she opened the door and scrambled out before they'd come to a stop. Cursing in Italian, he parked safely at the side of the road and climbed out in time to see Jessica running along the pavement and disappearing from view around a corner. Concerned, Gio jogged after her. What was earth going on?

They were in the centre of St Piran, on the way home following their visit to Faye's smallholding. Enquiries to several rescue centres had proved futile, which left them bemused and amused to find themselves foster-parents to a motley collection of animals. There were more than Gio had anticipated. He'd wanted animals, yes, but he hadn't imagined taking on so many in one go! Jessica's enthusiasm had swayed him, though.

Now, along with Dickens and Kipling, their menagerie included a donkey, two Gloucester Old Spot pigs, three sheep of mixed heritage and several assorted chickens. Faye's neighbour would care for them in the short term until the fencing at Jessica's cottage, and the necessary movement licences, were arranged. Gio didn't want to think about Jessica moving out—he had ideas but it was too soon to discuss them—but whatever happened between Jessica and himself, he intended to share the cost and responsibility for the animals.

Rounding the corner, he saw Jessica walking back towards him, her shoulders slumped, her steps reluctant as she kept pausing and looking behind her.

'What's going on?' he asked as he joined her.

She looked up, olive-green eyes despondent. 'I saw Marcia.' Again she scanned the crowds along one of St Piran's main shopping streets.

'The girl who gave you the false name after her boyfriend died?' he asked, frowning at her nod of confirmation. 'Are you still fretting about her?'

'Yes.'

She tried to carry everyone's problems on her own shoulders. 'Jessica...'

'I saw her, Gio. She looked so alone, so lost. The girl I met was prettily plump and well groomed,' she told him, clearly upset. 'She's put on weight and hasn't been taking care of herself. Her skin was grey and her hair lank and unstyled.' Again she met his gaze, and his chest tightened at the expression in her eyes. 'I can't help but worry about her.'

'You have a special empathy with people. But you can't solve everyone's problems, *fiamma*,' he advised her, the endearment—meaning flame in Italian—slipping out without conscious thought.

'I know that, but—'

As her defensive words snapped off, Gio cupped her face. 'Marcia knows where you are. If she needs you, she'll contact you in her own time. Everyone comes to terms with grief in their own way. Believe me, I know.'

Fresh tears stung Jessica's eyes as Gio's words hit home, pain for him mingling with her anxiety for Marcia. 'I'm sorry.'

'There's nothing to apologise for.' His smile was gentle, as was his touch.

Jess bit her lip, fighting the temptation, the *need*, to step closer, to press herself against him and be hugged... held in those strong arms. 'I'm OK,' she lied, stepping back and manufacturing a smile.

'Jess!' A female voice called her name and she looked round, smiling as she saw Kate Althorp approaching. 'Hello, my love.'

'Hi, Kate, how are you? And how is Jem?' She had spent many an hour talking with the older woman, especially when her son had been badly hurt in a car accident earlier in the year.

Kate's smile was free from the shadows Jess had seen there in the past. 'Jem's made a wonderful recovery. Thank you. And we're all well.'

'I'm so glad.' She was painfully conscious of Gio beside her and, when Kate looked at him expectantly, Jess had to introduce them. 'Kate, this is Gio Corezzi. He's a neurosurgeon and joined St Piran's in August,' she explained, her gaze flicking to him and away again. 'Gio, meet Kate Althorp. She's a midwife at the surgery in Penhally.'

Jess watched as the two shook hands and exchanged pleasantries, noting how Kate glowed when faced with Gio's natural charm and humour.

'What Jess has modestly left out, Gio, is how wonderful she has been to me,' Kate told him. 'She not only helped me a year ago when I had a scary brush with breast cancer, but she was an absolute rock when my son, Jem, broke his pelvis five months ago.'

'I didn't really do anything,' Jess murmured with embarrassment.

Kate waved her protest aside. 'What nonsense! I couldn't have got through it all without you, life was so difficult,' the older woman insisted, deepening Jess's blush and her discomfort. Kate smiled up at Gio. 'Jess is one in a million.'

'Yes...I know.'

Jess opened her mouth then closed it again, unsure what to say in response to Gio's husky words.

Kate chuckled, a twinkle in her brown eyes. She glanced at her watch and sighed. 'I'm afraid I have to run. There's so little time before the wedding and I have a million things to do. You are coming, aren't you, my love? I so want you to be there, it would mean so much to me. Bring Gio,' she added with a wink.

As Kate hurried off, Jess turned to walk back towards the car, but Gio surprised her, catching her hand and leading her in the opposite direction. 'This way.'

'Where are we going?' she asked, all too conscious of the way her fingers curled naturally with his.

'You're going to need a dress for the wedding and, as Kate said, there isn't much time.' He headed in the direction of one of St Piran's classy boutiques. 'We can take care of it while we are here.'

Jessica tried to dig her heels in. No way could she afford anything from that kind of shop. 'I'm not sure if I'm going to go,' she admitted, pulling on his hand.

'Not go?' He halted, an eyebrow raised in query as he looked at her. 'Why ever not?'

She attempted a careless shrug. He'd known about the wedding—the invitation had been propped on the mantelpiece in his living room for some time—but now he'd met Kate, it was more difficult to explain. It was one thing interacting with Kate at the hospital and quite another to move things into a social context. Jess didn't do social. Telling Gio that she felt too shy and nervous to go to the wedding on her own sounded far too pathetic.

'Kate wants you to be there,' he pointed out.

'Yes, but—'

'But nothing.' Gio forestalled further protests, the smile that curved his sexy mouth doing peculiar things to her insides.

'Gio,' she protested as he started them walking again.

'I'm going to buy you a frock for the wedding, to which I shall be honoured to escort you,' he informed her, shock rendering her temporarily compliant as he guided her along and halted outside the door of the boutique.

'Gio, you can't buy me a dress!'

'Of course I can!' He tweaked the tip of her nose between finger and thumb of his free hand.

Gazing at him in confusion, her skin tingling from his touch, she swallowed, all too conscious that this man was getting far too close. The walls she had constructed for her own protection felt increasingly vulnerable. And she was scared. Scared that if she continued to allow Gio to breach her defences and become more than a platonic friend, she would end up breaking her heart all over again.

And this time she might never recover.

CHAPTER EIGHT

IT WAS wonderful to see Kate so happy. Sitting with Polly d'Azzaro and a heavily pregnant Lucy Carter, in the garden of the beautiful granite-built barn a few miles outside Penhally that was now Kate's home, Jess watched the older woman mingle with her guests. She had a broad smile on her face, her brown eyes were alight with joy, and Nick, her new husband, was never far from her side.

St Mark's, Penhally's small church, had been bursting at the seams as people had come from far and wide to attend Nick and Kate's wedding. Nick's grown-up children from his first marriage had been there to support their father and give their blessing to Kate. And Kate's eleven-year-old son Jem, who had only recently discovered that Nick was his real father, had recovered well enough from his broken pelvis to proudly walk his mother down the aisle. A lump had formed in Jess's throat as Jem had stood with his half-brothers and -sister, watching his mother marry his father, publicly acknowledging him and making them one big united family at last.

Nervous about attending the party, Jess would never have come alone. Having Gio there made her feel better.

When they'd arrived at the barn, anxiety had gripped her as she'd faced the prospect of socialising with so many people. Unconsciously she'd moved closer to Gio. A moment later her right hand had been enveloped in his left one. Far from flinching away, or reminding him of the no-touching rule, her fingers had linked with his and held on tight.

Now, several hours later, after endless chat and laughter, an informal buffet, complete with hog roast and lashings of champagne, the dancing was soon to begin. Having enjoyed things more than she'd expected to—although she'd lost count of the number of times she'd explained she and Gio were just friends—the prospect of the live band and dancing into the evening was making her tense.

Jess's gaze strayed to Gio, who was deep in conversation with Polly's husband, Luca. Both Italian and with similar tragedies in their pasts, the two men had much in common. Luca was also Jess's GP.

'Gio's very handsome,' Polly commented, following the direction of her gaze.

'Mmm.' Jess hoped her murmur of agreement sounded noncommittal, even though her heart did somersaults every time she looked at him. He was always stunning but in his suit and tie he looked like a matinée idol. 'We're just friends.'

Polly's blue eyes were filled with understanding. 'That's a shame.'

'It's for the best.' Jess's words emerged as a whisper and, however much she wanted to deny it, even she could hear the regret in her voice.

'Is it?' Polly's smile was kind. As a fellow GP at Penhally surgery, Jess knew the other woman was speaking both as a doctor and a woman. 'Are you sure, Jess?'

She nodded, glancing at Polly before her gaze was drawn inexorably back to Gio. 'Yes.' Although it was getting harder and harder to believe it.

Before Polly could say any more, Nick and Kate passed on their way indoors to prepare for the first dance. Nick looked on with an indulgent and contented smile as Kate hugged Polly, whom, Jess had discovered, was Kate's god-daughter.

'We're so glad you and Gio came, Jess, and thank you so much for your lovely gift and the beautiful words in your card,' Kate told her, linking her arm through Nick's. 'You're looking gorgeous today.'

'Thank you,' Jess murmured, taken by surprise.

She was wearing the dress Gio had insisted on buying at the boutique in St Piran. Sleeveless and deceptively simple, it fell to her knees, highlighting her curves, the shades of teal and peacock green bringing out the colour of her eyes and highlighting the rich reds in her hair, now drawn back in a ponytail. She felt guilty for giving in to temptation—and Gio's persuasion—but the instant she had put the expensive dress on, she'd fallen in love with it. The desire and appreciation in Gio's eyes when he'd seen her in it had set her blood zinging in her veins.

'Enjoy yourselves,' Nick instructed with a benevolent smile before leading Kate away.

Gio and Luca returned, bringing non-alcoholic fruit punch with them, which both she and Polly accepted gratefully. She met Gio's gaze, her stomach muscles tightening at the expression in his intense blue eyes, her hand not entirely steady as she sipped the ice-cold drink.

Jess was about to tell Gio that she'd like to leave before the dancing began when Luca's twin daughters came running towards them. She'd been shocked when she'd heard how their mother had died giving birth to them. Now four and a half, they were adorable, so alike in looks but so different in character. It was the bolder, more outgoing Toni who arrived first.

'Mummy Polly?' she asked breathlessly.

'Yes, darling?'

'Rosie wants to know if she can have more cake.'

'Does she?' Jess saw Polly's lips twitch as she saw through the ruse. 'You can tell Rosie she can have a piece if she wants one.'

Toni's eyes widened and her mouth formed a silent O as she realised what had happened and tried to work out what to do about it. Gio and Luca both chuckled. Toni glanced round at her sister and then looked pleadingly up at her father, who hid his grin by taking a drink. The little girl's anxious gaze returned to Polly.

'Would *you* like another piece of cake, too, Toni?' she queried, unable to contain her amusement.

'Yes, please!' The relief on the child's face was so funny they all laughed.

'All right,' Polly agreed. 'You can both have one more *small* piece each.'

The little girl leaned in and kissed her stepmother soundly on the cheek. 'Thank you!'

As Toni ran off to join her quieter sister, Jess experienced for the first time the pressing weight of regret that she would never know the joy of motherhood. She hadn't thought of it much before. She'd never felt a maternal yearning, neither had she and Duncan ever discussed having a family.

Now, seeing the twins, she couldn't help but wonder what Gio's children would look like...although any idea of *her* ever being with him was pure fantasy. But it hit home that this was one more thing Duncan had taken away from her.

Gio was aware of the change in Jessica but was unsure of its cause. She put on a smiling face, but a light had dimmed in her eyes. He wanted to know what had happened. Unfortunately this was neither the time nor the place to ask. He was proud of her. She'd been nervous and uncomfortable about the party, even before she had clung so tenaciously to his hand when faced with the throng of guests. But she'd gradually relaxed, especially when the d'Azzaro family had taken them under their collective wings.

He'd enjoyed himself, too. Much of that had been simply being with Jessica, but he'd also been pleased to meet Luca. Discovering that Luca's life had mirrored his own in many ways had given him much to think about, especially seeing how Luca had been able to move on to find love and happiness with Polly.

'It wasn't easy,' Luca had told him. 'For so long I lived only for my girls. I'd not even looked at anyone else after Elaine died and I never expected to love again. Then I met Polly.' His smile and tone of voice had revealed his emotion more than words. 'I'm so lucky. And grateful. Don't close your heart and mind to possibilities, Gio,' he'd advised, his dark gaze straying to where Jessica and Polly had been sitting. 'You have the chance for something special. Jess deserves the best. She's not someone to be toyed with.'

The warning had been gently given, but it was a warning nonetheless. Luca and Polly not only viewed Jessica with affection, they were also protective of her. Gio wondered what his compatriot knew but was unable to reveal because of patient confidentiality.

After the live band struck up, Nick and Kate taking the first dance, most of the guests took to the floor. Jessica, however, refused all offers. It was Luca who eventually managed to get her on her feet, and Gio was shocked by the rush of envy and possessiveness that washed over him. Luca was happily married and had no designs on Jessica, but Gio hated to see her in anyone's arms but his own.

'Would you mind dancing with me, Gio?'

Polly's request took him by surprise. 'I'd be delighted,' he agreed politely, although the only person he wanted was Jessica.

'Don't worry, it won't be for long.' Polly, a pretty blonde and tiny, smiled up at him. 'Luca's giving Jess a pep talk.'

'A pep talk?' Gio frowned. What was Luca saying to her? And why?

Polly glanced across to where her husband and Jessica were dancing. 'Be ready to take over when Luca gives the signal.'

Puzzled but intrigued, Gio did as he was bidden, eager for the moment they would swap partners and he would have Jessica in his arms at last.

'It's good to see you happy.' Luca smiled, holding Jess lightly and allowing her to determine the personal space she was comfortable with. 'Gio's a nice guy.'

'We're just friends,' Jess said for the umpteenth time.

Her protest produced a teasing chuckle. 'Right!'

'We *are*.' Jess sucked in a ragged breath and tried not to keep staring at Gio. Worst of all, she struggled to banish the ridiculous jealousy that swept through her as he danced with Polly. 'I can't get involved with anyone, Luca, you know that.'

Luca's expression sobered and he steered them to a quiet corner where they wouldn't be overheard. 'I know nothing of the sort. You can have a normal relationship, Jess. I gather Gio doesn't know?'

'No.' A shiver rippled through her. 'He'd run a mile—like everyone else—if he did.' She hated the bitterness in her voice but the lessons of the last four years had been learned the hard way. 'Gio's still grieving. Even were he not, no man would want someone like me.'

'You're wrong, Jess. And you're doing Gio a big disservice,' he cautioned, his words forestalling a further protest from her. 'Give him a chance. He cares about you and knows what a wonderful woman you are. If he reacts as you fear, then he isn't worthy of you. But what if he understands? Think of all you then have to gain.'

Jess bit her lip, caught in an agony of indecision. She didn't want to lose what she already had and she didn't dare to believe she could have more.

'Don't condemn yourself to a lifetime alone. I nearly did. I was so fearful of being hurt again, but my life is so enriched thanks to Polly. Think about it,' he added, guiding her back onto the dance floor. 'It might sound like a cliché, but none of us knows what the future holds so live each day to the fullest and allow yourself to love and be loved.'

It sounded simple when Luca put it into words, but Jess knew it was anything *but* simple in reality. So distracted was she that she didn't notice Luca steering her towards Gio and Polly, but in the next moment she found herself in Gio's arms as Luca reclaimed his wife. Oh, hell! She hadn't intended dancing at all, and certainly not with Gio because of the temptation when she was near him. But she couldn't make a scene in front of everyone.

She held herself stiffly as he drew her closer, his touch, his scent, the feel of his body brushing against hers having a potent affect on her. One dance wouldn't hurt, would it? One moment out of time to enjoy being in his arms, forgetting why she had to be strong?

As she relaxed, giving up the fight, Gio drew her closer, making her even more aware of him, her body instinctively responding to his nearness. When the music ended, she sighed and made a half-hearted effort to draw away.

'Stay. Please.' The throaty warmth of his voice stripped her of any remaining willpower and common sense.

The tempo slowed and Jess found herself pressed far too intimately against him, her arms winding round him of their own volition. His fingertips brushed the bare skin between her shoulder blades, exposed by the V back of the dress, making her burn with a rush of desire. She was oblivious to everyone else, focused only on Gio, every sense heightened and attuned to him.

He bent his head, the warmth of his breath caressing her neck, the brush of his faintly stubbled jaw against her sensitive skin incredibly erotic. She'd never expected to be held again, let alone dance in public. Emotion threatened to overwhelm her and, to her horror, tears stung her eyes. She buried her face against his chest to hide them...from him and anyone else.

Revelling in this opportunity to hold Jessica properly for the first time, Gio breathed in her unique womanly scent mixed with the familiar hint of chocolate that clung to her hair and skin. Hair and skin that felt super-soft beneath his fingertips.

He was conscious of her heightened emotions, although he doubted she was aware of the way she was clinging to him. Determined not to rush or scare her, he held her, swaying to the music and waiting for her to relax, welcoming the moment she gave up whatever inner battle she was fighting and melted into him. She felt so right in his arms, her curvy body a perfect fit for his.

'Ready to go home?' he asked some considerable time later as they stepped outside to get some fresh air. He wanted her to himself, relishing these moments when he felt closer to her than ever.

She tipped her head back and looked up at the night sky. 'Yes, please.'

After saying goodbye and gathering up their belongings, they drove home in good spirits and were greeted by two sleepy kittens, who stirred long enough to be cuddled. As Jessica settled them again, he went through to the kitchen.

'Hot chocolate?' he asked, smiling at the look on her face.

'Lovely!'

'I'll make it for you the proper Italian way. None of this powdered cocoa with water in a microwave.' He gave an exaggerated shudder of disgust, making her laugh.

'And what is the proper Italian way?'

He took a large bar of *Cioccolato Corezzi's* finest dark chocolate from his stash in a kitchen drawer. 'You must begin with real chocolate. Once melted, you add a little sugar and some milk, bring it to the boil and stir. Some people make it so thick it is like a mousse and has to be eaten with a spoon,' he explained as he broke squares of chocolate and dropped them into a bowl, the satisfying snap a sign of its high quality. 'I prefer it liquid enough to drink, although I keep the teaspoon to reach the last drops!'

'It sounds sinfully delicious.'

It was Jessica who was sinfully delicious. Looking at her fired his blood and stirred his body. Waiting for the water to heat, he leaned his hip against the worktop and watched as she sat at the counter, trying to undo the barrette clasp that held her ponytail in place. Something was stuck and as she muttered to herself, making him smile, he stepped in to help.

'May I?'

Before she had the chance to refuse, he moved behind her, feeling her tense as his fingers set to work. Within moments the clip was free. Unable to resist temptation, his fingers burrowed into the fiery mass of curls that tumbled around her shoulders.

'You have beautiful hair,' he told her, hearing the roughness in his voice.

She gave a shaky laugh. 'I used to hate it.'

'No! It's amazing. Silky soft.' He leaned closer and caught the scent of her chocolatey shampoo. 'And you smell so good.'

'Gio...' Her voice sounded husky and sensual.

The sexual tension increased, electricity crackling between them. Jessica slowly slid round on the stool until she was facing him, olive-green eyes dark with awareness and unmistakeable desire.

His breath caught. 'I *have* to kiss you,' he whispered roughly.

A tremor ran through her but she didn't move away. His hands fisted in her hair as he closed the gap millimetre by millimetre, his heart thudding a rapid tattoo. Finally, their lips met. He felt heady with excitement and yet incredibly nervous as he kissed her for the first time.

They were both tentative, finding their way, learning, savouring, exploring, but the passion quickly flared out of control. Jessica's lips parted and he tilted his head, deepening the kiss. She tasted like heaven. Sweet and sensual, and so addictive. He couldn't get his fill of her. Tongues met, stroked, tempted, and he heard her soft, needy whimper as she clung to him. One hand left her hair and he wrapped his arm around her waist, drawing her into him as he stepped up between her parted thighs. She wriggled closer, pressing herself against him.

Jessica was with him, taking and giving, meeting and matching the blaze of passion that flared so intensely between them, demanding more. Gio was all too aware when instant panic set in and she began to withdraw. With a sharp cry she pulled away from him, clearly distressed.

'What is it, *fiamma?*' he asked between ragged breaths, confused and concerned as tears spilled from eyes full of torment. 'What's wrong?'

She shook her head. 'I'm sorry. So sorry. I can't do this.'

Before he could respond, she pushed away from him, slipped awkwardly off the stool and ran. He heard her footsteps on the stairs and, moments later, the sound of her bedroom door closing. What the hell had happened? Running an unsteady hand through his hair, he took a moment to gather himself together and get his body, so unused to the fiery passion that had ignited between them, back under control.

No way could he leave Jessica in such a distressed state. He wanted to know what had gone wrong, but more important was his concern for her well-being. After checking the house was secure and the kittens were settled, he finished making the hot chocolate and carried two mugs upstairs, anxious about what he might find. Taking a deep breath, he knocked on the door.

'Jessica?'

There was silence for several moments, a silence that hung so heavily around him that he could hear each beat of his heart. 'Yes?' The word was so soft that had he not been listening so intently he would not have heard her.

Cautiously, he opened the door. Dressed now in unflattering but comfortable pyjamas, Jessica was sitting in the middle of the bed, her arms wrapped around herself as she rocked slightly to and fro. She looked so lost, vulnerable and scared that his heart, which he'd thought could never feel anything again, squeezed with pain for her...and such deep affection and longing he didn't dare examine the emotions too deeply.

'May I come in?' His heart was in his mouth as he waited for her decision.

She didn't meet his gaze, but finally she nodded. He

sat on the edge of the bed, careful not to crowd her. He handed her a mug, noting that her hands were shaking as she reached for it, but she cupped it in her palms and sipped, a soft sigh escaping as she savoured the thick, chocolaty treat.

Gio followed her lead, hoping she would begin to relax. She even managed the ghost of a smile when he handed her a teaspoon so she could copy him and capture the final bits of chocolate.

'Good?' he asked, nearly having heart failure as her tongue peeped out and she licked the remains of chocolate from her lips.

'Amazing.' Her voice was still soft but sounded stronger. Popping the spoon in the empty mug, she handed it to him. 'Thank you.'

Gio set the mugs aside, feeling a growing tension now the moment had come to seek answers to some questions.

'Jessica, we need to talk.' Once more she wrapped her arms around herself, lashes lowering to hide her expression, but not before he had seen the fear in her eyes. 'I need to know. I know you guard your personal space and avoid being touched. At first I thought it was me, then I noticed it was the same with everyone. Including your clever ruse using all that stuff you carry round the hospital so you can avoid shaking hands.'

The blush that brought colour back to her too-pale cheeks was confirmation that he was right.

'My imagination is running away with itself. I'm scared to ask but...has someone hurt you in the past?' He could hardly get the words out but knew he had to. 'Were you raped or abused?'

'No.'

The denial was firm and he knew she was telling the truth. The relief was *huge*. But there was still something major and important. He knew it. She looked so alone, and the despair and hurt in her eyes tore him apart.

'May I hold you, Jessica...please?'

She raised her head and met his gaze. What she was searching for, he had no idea, but whatever it was, she apparently found it as, after the longest time, she bit her lip and nodded. The air trapped in his lungs was released in a rush of relief. He moved onto his knees and edged towards her, needing the physical contact as much as she did. When he was as close as could be, he sat back on his heels and drew her into his arms with infinite care, cradling her tense and shaking form against him.

As she gradually began to relax, she rested her head against his chest. With one hand he stroked the unrestrained glossy copper-red curls as they tumbled with abandon around her shoulders.

'Can you talk to me now?' A breath shuddered out of her in response. Her casual shrug belied the tension that poured from her and the tremble he felt ripple through her whole body. 'Jessica?'

'I don't know. I...'

The whispered words were husky with emotion and he sought to discover the cause of her hesitation and reluctance. 'What worries you, *fiamma*? Do you think I won't understand? Do you fear it will change how I think of you and feel about you?'

'I know it will,' she responded, the humourless laugh and bitter edge to her voice speaking volumes.

'Listen to me,' he instructed gently, seeking the words to reassure her. 'I don't know what experiences you've had with other people, but *nothing* you tell me will make me turn away or reject you.' Whatever route their relationship eventually took, he was unable to envisage any circumstance that would change the basic friendship and bond that had formed so quickly but so intensely between them. He dropped a kiss on the top of her head. 'Trust me. I won't let you down.'

The sincerity in Gio's voice was beyond question but Jess still hesitated. He might believe *now* that nothing would make him reject her but would he feel the same when he knew?

She recalled Luca's words. He'd advised her to give Gio a chance, pointing out that only by confiding in him would she discover the depth of his friendship and the kind of man he really was. Deep in her heart she knew. And she *so* wanted to believe. But her former friends and colleagues had turned her away and her family had disowned her.

The last few weeks with Gio had been the happiest she had known for such a long time and she was terrified that revealing the truth about herself would change for ever the nature of their friendship, maybe even end it. She didn't want to lose what she already had, but every day things were becoming more complicated because her heart and emotions were ever more entangled and it was no longer enough just to be his friend.

Those moments in the kitchen when she had allowed herself to wallow in the pleasure of being touched, followed by the most explosive and incredible kiss she had ever known, had proved that. He had breached her defences so completely and she'd been so lost in Gio and her desire for him that she'd forgotten why she shouldn't have been doing it. Reality had hit like a thunderclap and she'd run. They'd crossed the boundaries of friendship now. And in reaching for more, would she destroy what she already had?

She wouldn't know the answer unless she did as Gio asked and trusted him. Cocooned in his embrace she felt safe and protected and, for the first time in over four years, she didn't feel alone. She sucked in a deep breath, inhaling the warm musky-male scent of him that had become so familiar. And arousing. Drawing back just far enough, she looked up and met his steady, intensely blue gaze. While the arm supporting her cuddled her close, his free hand caught one of hers, raising it to his mouth and pressing a kiss to her palm before he entwined their fingers, linking them and giving her his support.

'I don't know where to start,' she admitted with a nervous laugh, feeling sick inside now the decision was made and the moment had come to share her shameful secret.

'Take your time. I'm not going anywhere,' he promised. 'Is it something that goes back to the time before you came to St Piran?'

'Yes. It started just over four years ago when I was still in Scotland,' she admitted, closing her eyes as the memories flooded back. She paused, unsure if she could continue, but Gio's support and strength gave her the courage to face what had to be faced. 'I was working in a hospital there,' she explained, ignoring for now the information about her former career. 'I was living with my fiancé, Duncan. He was my first and only proper boyfriend. I was happy. I thought I had everything I wanted, and I was busy planning the wedding, which was only eight weeks away.'

* * *

As Jessica gathered her thoughts, Gio struggled with the unreasonable jealousy that assailed him at the knowledge she had been in love and about to be married, already disliking the man she spoke of without knowing any more about him. But he hid his reaction, needing to give her all his understanding now that she had done him the honour of trusting him. He couldn't—wouldn't—let her down.

'Did Duncan work at the hospital, too?' he asked, keeping his tone neutral.

'No. He worked for a company that supplied equipment and aid for relief charities out in the field and his job took him all over the world. He was away a lot. I missed him, but I supported what he did.'

He was unsurprised by her selflessness and the sacrifices she'd no doubt made. 'It's not easy maintaining a relationship long distance.'

'No.' Another shiver ran through her and he tightened his hold, wanting to protect her from the hurt she was reliving. 'I hadn't been feeling well for a while,' she continued, and his concern for her increased. 'There was nothing specific I could put my finger on, and I put it down to the pressures of work and the excitement and lack of sleep as the wedding drew closer. Duncan had to take several trips away during those weeks and so everything fell to me. A colleague noticed how off colour I was and suggested I see a doctor. I didn't think anything of it, but because I wanted to feel right for the wedding, I made an appointment to see my GP.'

Gio felt his gut tightening with the premonition that something dark and of huge importance was about to be revealed. Looking into green eyes shadowed with fear and pain, it was the dart of shame that confused him. He raised their joined hands, pressing a kiss to her fingers.

'What happened, *fiamma*?' he prompted.

'My GP didn't think there was anything serious going on, but he organised some tests to be on the safe side. And...' She halted, her voice breaking, tears shimmering on long sooty lashes.

Gio steeled himself for whatever was to come. 'And?'

'The results came back.' A sob tore through her, ripping him to shreds. 'It t-turned out that D-Duncan hadn't been the f-faithful, loving fiancé I'd imagined,' she continued, the words stuttering through her tears. 'He'd slept with countless women during his trips abroad and thanks to him I h-have a lasting legacy. The tests, unlike Duncan, didn't lie. I...' Again she broke off, drawing in a shuddering breath, her fingers instinctively tightening on his as she raised her head, tear-washed eyes bleak. 'Gio, I was...*am*...HIV positive.'

CHAPTER NINE

'Madre del Dio.'

The words escaped on a whisper of breath when all Gio wanted to do was rage and swear at the man who had done this to Jessica. He listened as she told him how she had been diagnosed with a seroconversion illness and although it was not his branch of medicine, he knew enough to understand that this was often the first sign of illness people had after they had been infected, when the body first produced antibodies to HIV.

'I had many of the usual symptoms…a fever, aching limbs, headache and a blotchy red rash…which could have been linked to a variety of conditions,' she explained, the matter-of-fact tone of her voice belied by the shadows in her eyes. 'It was such a shock and not something I had ever anticipated.'

'Of course not. You trusted the man you were about to marry,' Gio reasoned.

She nodded, and he tightened his hold as a fresh shudder went through her. 'I must be a really bad person because I can't forgive him—not just for what he did to me but I keep thinking about the unknown number of other women out there he infected, as well, and what they might be going through. I can't even feel sorry that he was diagnosed, too,' she whispered.

'No, no, no! You are not remotely a bad person! How can you think that?' Gio swore in Italian, wishing he could let Duncan know what he thought of him. 'You are an amazing woman, Jessica. Even struggling to come to terms with what has happened to you, through no fault of your own, your thoughts are still for other people. You have the generosity of spirit to worry about the women with whom your ex-fiancé—' he stumbled over the word, choked by his anger and disgust at the man '—had been unfaithful.'

'It wasn't their fault. I've no doubt he lied to them, too.'

'And now,' he made himself ask, needing to know so much but anxious not to stress her more, 'how are you? Are you taking medication?'

'I'm OK. And I'm not taking medication yet,' she told him, and the relief was immense. 'I have regular tests to monitor my CD4 cell count, which gives an idea of the strength of my immune system. And a viral load test, which can tell how active HIV is in the body. It's only if those levels reach a certain point that medication will be necessary. It's a big step to take because once started, you can't stop. I go to London twice a year to see a specialist,' she added, surprising him.

'Why London?'

'I went there first when I left Scotland. I trust Mr Jackson. When I moved to Cornwall, he agreed to keep seeing me.' Her smile was tired but brought some life back to her eyes. 'And I have Luca and the other doctors at the Penhally surgery who take care of day-to-day things.'

Gio was relieved she had someone so good caring for her. 'Was there no one giving you support at home? What about family and friends?' he asked, taken aback by her derisive, humourless laugh. Unease curled inside him.

'I was stupidly naïve and assumed that in this day and age people would be more informed and understanding,' she began with a shiver, shifting so that she was resting against his chest. 'But they weren't. I was so shocked by the negative reactions. Some people blanked me, some were openly hostile and abusive, making a big fuss if I touched them in any way, refusing to drink from a mug or eat off a plate I might have used in the canteen. Not one so-called friend or colleague stood by me.'

As he listened to Jessica outline some of the things people had said to her and what she had put up with once her diagnosis had become known, Gio's anger rocketed. It was disgraceful that people should be so ignorant and prejudiced. And it was hardly surprising after her experiences that she'd been stripped of her confidence, her self-esteem and her trust in people.

'My family were worse.'

'What happened, *fiamma*?' he asked softly, fearing her answer.

'Shocked and upset, I went home and told them the news. My father has always been a dour, strict man with rigid opinions. He disapproved of me living with Duncan before the wedding. He said...' Her fingers tightened on his and emotion turned her voice husky as she continued. 'He said it was all I deserved for living in sin, that I had brought shame on the family, and he disowned me. He turned me out with all my belongings and told me never to contact them again. He even had me barred from visiting my grandmother, who was bedridden in a nursing home by then. She was the only one who cared. She left me the money that helped me buy my cottage, but I never had the chance to see her again before she died and tell her I loved her.'

Her words ended on a sob and the tears she had been choking back escaped. She tried to pull away from him but he drew her trembling frame more fully against him and, wrapping her protectively in his arms, he held her tight, keeping her safe as she cried out the hurt and anger. After everything Duncan had done, and the reaction of those she'd considered friends, the cruel rejection by the family meant to love and care for her must have been the ultimate betrayal and almost impossible to bear. Thinking of her alone and scared tore him apart.

He guessed she'd been bottling up the emotion for a long time and now it had been set free, like opening a dam and allowing everything backed up behind it to gush out. As he cradled her, he struggled to come to terms with the truth, the reality, the consequences...and with what her life must have been like these last four or more years.

His own eyes were moist and his heart hurt as he tried to comfort her while the storm ran its course. So many things now made sense. Her reluctance to touch and be touched, the absence of any close friendships, the lack of trust and the little habits at home like the supplements and washing her things separately. No wonder she had looked so hurt when he'd teased her about having a hygiene fetish. He smothered a groan. After all she had been through since being diagnosed, it was understandable she had developed a range of coping mechanisms.

When Jessica finally calmed, he eased back and cupped her face in his hands. Olive-green eyes were framed by tear-spiked lashes while her flawless, translucent skin was devoid of colour. Concerned for her, he dropped a light kiss on lips that still trembled.

'Don't go anywhere. I'll be back in a couple of minutes. OK?'

Her nod was weary, almost defeated. Reluctantly, he released her. He didn't want to leave her, even for a moment, but he had a few things to do. When he returned, having undressed as far as his boxer shorts, prepared his bedroom with jasmine-scented candles and turned down the bed, she was sitting motionless where he had left her, her eyes closed.

'Jessica?'

Long lashes flickered then he was staring into her eyes. She blinked, her gaze skimming over him, a flush bringing some warmth back to her pale face. Her reaction amused him, momentarily easing his concern for her.

'Hi.' He smiled as she swallowed and dragged her gaze back to his. 'Are you OK?'

She nodded, remaining silent until his next moved shocked her out of her torpor. 'Gio!' Her cry escaped as he scooped her off the bed and lifted her in his arms.

'Hold on,' he instructed.

'What are you doing?' Despite her protest, she wrapped her arms around his neck. 'Gio, I'm far too heavy.'

'Nonsense.'

He carried her from the room, only pausing long enough for her to switch out the light. Walking down the corridor, he went into his bedroom, set her gently on the bed and drew the duvet over her before walking round the other side and sliding in beside her. To his surprise and delight, she turned into his arms and burrowed into him. He stroked the glossy curls that spread across his chest, each indrawn breath fragranced with a teasing hint of her scent.

'Gio...' Her voice was soft and sleepy, and it still held the lingering legacy of the emotions that had ravaged her just a short while ago.

'Shh,' he soothed, relishing the feel of her feminine curves and the softness of her skin. 'It's very late and you've been through a lot. Sleep now. I'll keep you safe.'

It was Sunday afternoon and the closer they got to home, the more nervous Jess became. She knew what was going to happen. She wanted it. And yet she couldn't help but be as scared as she was excited. Gio, too, seemed preoccupied and edgy as the electric tension continued to build between them.

She thought back to the night before and everything that had happened after their return from the wedding and the most incredible kiss she'd ever experienced. Telling Gio how her life had been turned upside down following the HIV diagnosis had been so difficult, but he had been amazing, his supportive reaction in marked contrast to those she had encountered in the past. But now her shameful secret was out, nothing would ever be the same between them again.

Spending the night in Gio's arms had been wonderful. For the first time in a long, long while she hadn't felt alone. And she wished she could wake up with him every morning, especially if it meant experiencing the delicious caress of his hands and his lips on her bare skin.

'I want more than anything to make love to you,' he'd told her, the throaty roughness of his voice resonating along her nerve-endings. 'I have since the day I first saw you, and I've wanted you more each day since.'

'Gio,' she'd murmured in confusion, hardly daring to believe that the truth hadn't put him off. He may have held her through the night, but...

'Nothing you have told me changes anything—I only marvel more at what an incredible woman you are,' he'd continued, his words bringing a lump to her throat. 'Unfortunately, right now I have no protection.'

She had masked her disappointment. 'OK.'

'But we can improvise.' The tone of his voice and his sexy smile had sent a tremor right through her. 'We can't make love fully now but I want to bring you pleasure and show what a special and desirable woman you are.'

And bring her pleasure he had. Oh, my! A shaky little breath escaped, warmth stealing through her as her body tingled at the memory of his kisses and caresses. How delicious to wake up like that every day. But she knew it was a fantasy. She was getting too far ahead of herself.

They'd spent the day doing normal things at the house, having a late breakfast and playing with the kittens before going to see how things were progressing at her cottage. The main supporting structure had been replaced and the thatcher was well on the way to creating a beautiful new roof.

Knowing that the cottage would soon be habitable again and discovering that Gio had arranged for the fields to be cleared and the fences renewed in readiness for Faye's menagerie had brought mixed emotions. Pleasure at seeing the cottage come back to life. Surprise and gratitude at Gio's generosity. But anxiety at the knowledge she would soon have to leave his house—and him. What would happen then? Gio was adamant about sharing responsibility for the animals but how would that work? And what did it mean for them?

Next, they'd spent a couple of hours on the boat, speeding across the waves. She'd felt so close to him and, now her secret was out, she hadn't had to fight to avoid physical contact. Gio had taken every opportunity to hug and kiss her. But her nervousness had returned when they had stopped at the supermarket on the way back to the house and condoms had been added to the items in their basket.

Feeling jumpy and on edge, not at all sure what to do or say, Jess helped Gio put the shopping away and then played with Dickens and Kipling for a while before feeding them. As they curled up to sleep in a tangle of limbs, she felt even more anxious.

'I think I'll go and have a shower,' she murmured, feeling as gauche and awkward as a teenager.

Gio looked up and smiled. 'OK.'

He appeared so calm that had he not bought the condoms she would have wondered if she had dreamed everything that had happened when she had woken up that morning. And what she was anticipating would happen later. Unsettled, she went upstairs and, after undressing and tying up her wayward curls to keep her hair from getting wet, she stepped into the shower, welcoming the feel of the hot barbs on skin that still felt alive and sensitive from the caresses of Gio's hands and mouth.

Eyes closed, she tipped her head back and reached

out a hand for the chocolate-scented cleanser she loved to use, a squeal of shocked surprise escaping as, instead of encountering the plastic tube she was expecting, her fingers met male skin. Every part of her trembled as he stepped up behind her, the front of his body pressing against the back of hers, making her supremely aware of his arousal.

She heard the snap of the top on the tube she'd been reaching for and a moment later felt the touch of hands that were slick with foamy cleanser. He began at her shoulders, working slowly and sensually down her back, lingering at her rear before sweeping down her legs in long, caressing strokes that turned her knees to jelly. One arm wrapped around her waist in support, and she leaned back against him, feeling boneless and on fire as he turned his attention to the front of her.

Jess bit her lip to prevent herself crying out as he devoted time to her breasts, the exquisite torture almost too much to bear. It had been so long since she had been touched like this...and yet *never* like this because the kind of explosive passion and intense desire she shared with Gio was way beyond anything she had ever experienced before.

When she thought she would expire from the pleasure of his touch, Gio turned the cleanser over to her and allowed her the same freedom to explore and enjoy his body. She turned round on legs that felt decidedly unsteady, the blood racing through her veins as she drank in the sight of him. It was impossible not to be struck by the masculine beauty of his body, the broad shoulders and the perfectly toned muscles of his arms and torso that made her mouth water. A brush of dark hair in the middle of his chest cast a shadow on olive-toned skin, tapering to a narrow line that her gaze avidly followed down over his abdomen and navel to where it nested the potent symbol of his maleness.

She refocused on his handsome face, seeing the needy desire, which mirrored her own, in his deeply blue eyes. Feeling both shy and bold at the same time, she began her own lingering caress of his body, working the foamy, chocolate-scented suds across his skin, hearing his indrawn breath and feeling the tremor and ripple of muscle as he reacted to her touch.

With an impatient exclamation his hands closed on her upper arms, drawing her back up and into a searing kiss. She clung to him, kissing him back with equal ardour, savouring the feel of wet warm skin under her hands and the sexy, sinful taste of him in her mouth. They were both breathing heavily by the time they broke apart. Gio snapped off the water before reaching for a towel and wrapping her up in it. With evident impatience he briskly ran another towel over himself. Tossing it aside, he took her hand and led her down the corridor to his bedroom, her legs so rubbery she didn't think she could walk.

Some of her anxiety returned as she entered the room with him and saw the huge bed standing ready and waiting, the duvet turned back, the generous pillows plumped up. She knew how luxurious and incredibly sexy the gunmetal-grey sheets felt against her skin. And within moments she was experiencing them again as Gio gave her a gentle rub down with the towel before removing it and tumbling them both into bed.

Excitement and tension vied for prominence. She could feel the heat of his body even though he wasn't quite touching her. Smiling, he gently removed the pins from her hair and fanned the tresses out on the pillow.

'Do you think you are the only one who is nervous, *fiamma*?' he asked, his throaty, accented voice sounding even more sexy than usual.

Surprised, she met his gaze. 'You're nervous, too?'

Her question was met with a wry laugh. 'I listen to some of the young doctors talking in the scrub room and the canteen, discussing their conquests, and I realise what an oddity I must seem for having slept only with Sofia.'

'Then I'm odd, too, because I've only ever had one relationship before,' she told him. 'And, to me, the fact that you have never been the kind of man to sleep around is a major strength, not a weakness. You are loyal and true. And you haven't played Russian roulette with your own health or anyone else's.'

She thought of Duncan, of how he had cheated on her, and his cavalier disregard for himself, let alone her or the other women. Gio was a treasure and it was the very quality he considered an oddity that made her trust him. Had he been another Duncan, she would never be here now, on the cusp of giving herself to him in the most elemental of ways.

As if by instinct, they moved in unison to close the last of the gap between them, and the instant he touched her, the instant her lips met his, the doubts that had seemed so real for a moment dissolved into nothing. They needed no words because their bodies talked for them. Jess found she couldn't formulate a single coherent thought as Gio continued what he had begun that morning and in the shower, devoting his time and attention to her.

Every touch, every kiss, every caress of his fingers and brush of his lips and tongue built the pleasure layer by layer. She writhed against him, her body turning molten as his mouth worked down the column of her throat, setting every nerve tingling and every particle of skin on fire. He trailed down the valley between her breasts, bypassing flesh that yearned so badly for his attention and continuing down to her navel. She hadn't known she was so sensitive there but the tantalising, teasing quest of his teeth and tongue had her body arching up to meet him, seeking more.

She must have spoken the word aloud because he chuckled, the huff of warm breath against her skin a subtle and teasing caress of its own. She moaned as he finally turned his attention to her breasts, the perfect pressure of his fingers driving her crazy.

'Gio, please,' she begged, craving the touches he teasingly denied her.

Relenting, his teeth gently grazed one sensitive nipple before his tongue salved the delicious sting. Then he sent her to the stratosphere as he took the peak into the warm cavern of his mouth. When she thought she couldn't bear it a moment longer he released his prize, turned his attention to its twin and began the exquisite torment all over again.

Impatient, her eager hands traced the muscular contours of his shoulders before working down his back, urging him closer. She wanted to explore and savour him as he was doing to her, but she was so close to the edge she couldn't wait a moment longer to know the joy of being united fully with him.

He took a moment to protect them and she pleaded with him not to wait any longer as he moved to make them one. She arched up to meet him, wrapping her legs around him, gasping his name at the delicious sensations as her body welcomed his and, finally, they were one.

'Jessica...'

'Yes. Please, Gio. Don't stop.'

She had never experienced anything as magical and special as making love with Gio. It was incredible, earth-shattering and she never wanted it to end. He murmured to her in Italian as they moved together in a rhythm as old as time. She abandoned herself to him completely, as he did to her, and the mix of exquisite tenderness and fiery passion she found with him was a devastating combination.

When the inevitable moment arrived, Jess clung to him, burying her face against him, breathing in his musky scent, calling his name as they drove each other over the edge to a shattering release. As she spun out of control, she didn't care if she never came down to earth again, just so long as she was with Gio.

Gio gazed at Jessica's sleeping form, the wild fire of her hair tossed across the pillow and a couple of tell-tale little marks on her otherwise flawless, silky-smooth skin following the intensely passionate night they had shared. It had been the most incredible experience, beyond anything he had imagined. And it had scared him.

He wasn't sure at exactly which moment during their sensual night together it had happened, but he had suddenly known with surety and not much surprise that he loved her. It may have happened far more speedily but, as with Sofia, they had begun as friends first and foremost. He and Sofia had been children and their emotions had evolved slowly, whereas with Jessica the friendship and the desire had hit in tandem.

The pain of losing Sofia had nearly killed him and he'd never imagined wanting another woman again. Then he had met Jessica. He not only wanted her in every way but he liked and respected her as a person and valued the special friendship they shared. So why was he feeling so unsettled? Things had happened so fast, he had fallen so deep so quickly and he knew that if he tied himself to her and anything happened, he would never recover a second time.

Could he take the risk on Jessica's health? All he knew was that he couldn't face the prospect of burying another woman he loved. It was a possibility he couldn't ignore when making a decision that would affect both their futures.

Waking up alone had been unnerving and when she went downstairs and found Gio making coffee in the kitchen, Jess's unease increased. He greeted her with a smile, but she sensed a change in him. He was on edge, distant. And when he backed off physically, moving away when she would have stepped in for a hug, a cold chill went through her.

'What's wrong?' she asked, fear building as he failed to meet her gaze.

'Nothing. I...'

'Gio?'

He ran a hand through his hair, a characteristic sign of agitation. 'I'm just not sure what to think about this. It's all happened so quickly.'

'You regret it.' Her heart sank.

'No! Of course not. Neither of us was expecting

this. The connection was there from the first and our friendship is special and important to me,' he explained, his expression sombre, and Jess sensed a 'but' coming. 'But—' Jess allowed herself a humourless smile '—maybe we should slow things down, take some time. I'd never considered having a new relationship. I'm not sure I'm ready. Especially after what happened with Sofia.'

Everything in her screamed in protest. 'I see.'

'I need to be sure, Jessica. Not of you but of me. Losing Sofia nearly killed me and I can't go through anything like that again,' he finished, emotion heavy in his voice.

The awful thing was that she understood. She couldn't argue against his words and the chance of something happening was greater with her with the HIV hanging over her head than it was with another woman. Wrapping her arms around herself, she tried to hold everything together, to not let him see how deeply the rejection had wounded her. Because that was what it felt like. And in that moment, the truth hit home with devastating force... she loved him. In every way and with every part of her being.

Gio had said their friendship was important and apparently he considered things would go on as before, but Jess felt as if part of her was dying inside because friendship was never going to be enough now.

'I'm going to Italy at the weekend for my parents' fortieth wedding anniversary,' he reminded her, thrusting his hands into the pockets of his jeans.

Her heart breaking, Jess struggled to keep her voice as normal as possible. 'My cottage should be ready by then, so I'll move out.'

'I didn't mean that.' He frowned as if her leaving was not something he had considered.

'Living here was only meant to be temporary,' she pointed out, knowing she couldn't stay with him and not *be with* him. 'It's for the best.'

His frown deepened, confusion and disappointment mingling in his intensely blue eyes. 'If that's what you want.'

It wasn't what she wanted at all, but she didn't see how she could do anything else if what she really wanted—Gio himself—was not an option.

The next few days were like purgatory, and by the time Friday arrived, Jess was at breaking point and not at all sure how much longer she could hold on. Pretending to accept Gio's decision to return things to a platonic footing had involved the performance of her life. She hadn't been able to sleep, lying in a bed a short distance down the corridor from him, wanting more than anything to be in his arms. But it wasn't going to happen and the sooner she faced that and rebuilt her battered defences, the better it would be.

He went to Italy on the Friday and, after the loneliest night in the house without him, Jess tried to hold back the tears as she packed her things into her car and then put Dickens and Kipling into their basket for the short journey to her cottage. The kittens would miss Gio almost as much as she would, she reflected sadly. He'd been so good with them. She choked back the emotion as she recalled the way he had lain on the floor, chuckling as the two growing kittens had romped over him. And the time she'd come in late one Friday night after her session of volunteering at the Samaritans to find Gio lying asleep on the sofa, the kittens curled up on his chest in a tangle.

Feeling numb inside, she secured the house and drove away from it, wondering if it was for the last time. However much she hurt, she couldn't blame Gio. She knew how devastating Sofia's death had been and it was understandable that he was wary of embarking on another relationship, especially with someone like her. She was well at the moment, and she would do all she could to stay that way. As Luca and her specialist, Mr Jackson, frequently told her, there was no reason why she couldn't live into old age with very few problems at all. But anyone would be wary of taking on that uncertainty, especially someone who had experienced what Gio had.

No, Gio was not to blame. It was her own fault. She'd hoped for too much...had dared to dream and to believe in the impossible. Now she had to pick up the pieces because fairy-tale, happy-ever-after endings didn't happen to people like her.

'Why did you stay the night with me?'

It was one of the things Megan had most dreaded Josh ever asking and it had played over and over in her head since the day in A and E when they had done the unthinkable and faced their past.

Aside from not wanting to acknowledge the truth to herself, she certainly didn't want to tell *Josh* the answer to his question. To admit that she had been drawn to him from the first moment she had seen him and that, despite his reputation, she had yearned for him for years like some lovestruck teenager was beyond embarrassing.

Between medical school and caring for her grandmother, she'd had no time for a social life, so going to a party on New Year's Eve had been a real treat. Wearing an exquisite dress, her hair and make-up done, she'd felt like Cinderella. Only she'd been granted a bit longer before the spell had been broken...not at midnight, for her, but lunchtime the following day.

For the first time, Josh had approached her. Given his undivided attention, she'd melted like an ice cube under the noon sun. He'd made her feel special. Surprisingly, they had talked and talked, and she'd found him so much *more* than she had ever expected. He'd been funny, he'd listened as if what she'd had to say had mattered, he'd sympathised about her grandmother, and he had confided in her, too. The night had ended in the inevitable way, the sexual chemistry and tension between them impossible to resist.

Megan closed her eyes and tried to push away the painful memories. She had believed in her heart that what they had shared had been more than one night. Much more. Or she never would have gone home with Josh in the first place. They'd connected. On every level. She hadn't imagined it. And it *hadn't* just been the sex, amazing as that had been. She knew Josh had been spooked by their closeness as he'd freely admitted that he'd revealed things to her that he'd never told to anyone else. He'd told her she was different. He'd been so genuine. And she'd believed him. Had *wanted* to believe him. So badly.

They had finally, reluctantly, parted but only after Josh had made love to her one last time and had made her promise to meet him that evening. It had been noon when she had rushed home to her grandmother feeling a mix of guilt and euphoria. The hours with Josh had been the most amazing of her life and she hadn't been able to wait to see him again. So when he had stood her up, failing to meet at the agreed time and place, she had been confused and upset.

When she had finally seen him several worrying days later, he had blanked her completely, laughing with his friends, ignoring her as if their night had never happened. She'd been devastated. Even now she could remember how she had felt...used, cheap, stupid, incredibly naïve and very, very hurt.

Megan shivered in reaction as the memories of that lonely, frightening time and what had followed over the next months flowed through her. Ashamed, she had withdrawn and hidden herself away. And then she had discovered that she was pregnant. And *so* scared.

Weeks later she'd experienced a searing pain and had remembered nothing until she had woken up in hospital to learn that Josh had been part of the team who had not only taken away her baby but had performed a hysterectomy, depriving her of ever becoming a mother. She'd been devastated, the sense of loss and grief overwhelming.

Eight years on, listening to his explanation and seeing his own emotion had given her much to think about. The hurt remained, both at his rejection and at the loss of her baby. But while there was much she was still angry with him about, she no longer blamed him for the miscarriage or the lengths taken to save her life.

Despite their past and all that lay between them—including the very real presence of his wife—the chemistry remained. When they worked together in A and E, they often knew what the other was thinking or doing without the need for words.

She knew he was out of bounds. She knew what had happened the last time the chemistry had led her astray. And she couldn't forget the way Josh had rejected and betrayed her. So discovering that she was still vulnerable to him, still drawn to him and still unable to get him out of her mind, frightened her.

If she showed the slightest weakness she feared what might happen. And only heartache would lie ahead. She had learned her lesson the hard way the last time round. So why did she have the terrible feeling that history was going to repeat itself?

CHAPTER TEN

LATE on Sunday afternoon Jess walked along the surfing beach east of Penhally's harbour, lost in thought. It had been another beautiful day, but the air was cooling as the sun began its slow descent towards the horizon. Pushing her hands into the pockets of the floaty skirt that fell to her knees, Jess sighed. There was no escaping her thoughts. Thoughts that were stuck in one place and refused to budge. With Gio.

He would be back tonight and tomorrow she would see him at work. She wasn't sure how to continue pretending that nothing had happened or behave normally, accepting they could only ever be friends. *Could* she be friends when she wanted so much more? It was a question that had pounded in her head all week and she still didn't know the answer. All she did know was that she had missed him terribly and faced with a choice of never seeing him again, then, as sad and pathetic as it sounded, any part of Gio was better than no Gio at all. Even if she was dying inside. Because she had fallen in love with a man who had experienced such heartache that he couldn't take a risk on someone whose future could be as uncertain as hers.

As she neared the end of the promontory on which

the lighthouse, coastguard office and St Mark's church stood, she heard shouting and laughter, and looked up to see a couple of teenagers messing about on the rocks. She was about to turn round and retrace her steps back along the beach when the tone of the teenage voices changed and she watched in horror as one of the boys lost his footing and crashed face down amongst the rocks.

Jess ran towards the scene of the accident, as did a few other people who were further away on the beach and up on the promontory. The teenager's friend was now silent and standing motionless in shock and terror as he gazed down at his stricken comrade. Reaching the rocky outcrop, and glad she was wearing trainers, Jess began to climb.

The lower rocks were slippery, and several times she lost her own footing, resulting in umpteen cuts and bruises, but she kept going as rapidly as she could, fearing what she would find when she reached the boy. Moving towards him, she misjudged a step and fell heavily. Pain seared through her foot, leg and side, and she felt the hot stickiness of blood flowing down her calf. Ignoring it, she limped and scrambled awkwardly the rest of the way to the boy.

His injuries were worse than she'd feared. Frightened eyes stared up at her, and she struggled to mask her shock so as not to distress him further. His face had borne the brunt of his fall and, along with a lot of bleeding and considerable soft-tissue damage, she could tell that his jaw, nose and one cheekbone were all broken.

Instinct took over as she did a quick assessment. There were no other apparent injuries but that hardly mattered because there was one serious, immediate and life-threatening problem...the boy was finding it increasingly impossible to breathe.

'Has anyone called an ambulance?' she shouted to the small crowd that was gathering on the rocks above her.

'Yes,' someone called. 'ETA at least twelve minutes.'

Jess swore. They couldn't wait that long. 'I need a sharp knife—preferably a scalpel. And something like a small piece of tube, or a drinking straw. Anything narrow and hollow. He can't breathe and I have to help him,' she shouted up.

'The lighthouse and coastguard station both have full first-aid kits. I'll get one of those,' the man called down to her.

'Please hurry! There isn't much time.'

Hoping the man understood the urgency, and that the kit would contain the things she needed, Jess returned her attention to the boy and tried to talk soothingly to him as she continued her assessment. With all the blood, fragments of bone and the rapidly swelling tissues around his face, there was no way she could clear or maintain an airway. It was no surprise when he began to panic as he failed to draw oxygen into his lungs and started to lose consciousness.

It seemed an eternity before the man reappeared above her and began the dangerous climb down. His exclamation of shock when he saw the boy was understandable but Jess didn't have time to do anything but take the first-aid kit from him. She winced at the shaft of pain in her side as she dragged the heavy bag close, but she pushed her own discomfort aside and opened the kit, giving heartfelt thanks that it was an extensive and well-stocked one.

Gathering together the things she needed, she told her unknown companion what she was doing. 'I have to create an opening in his throat so he can breathe. We can't wait for the ambulance. What's your name?'

'Charlie.'

'I'm Jess. I...' She paused and sucked in a breath. 'I'm a doctor,' she told him, speaking aloud the words she had not used for four years. 'Have you got a mobile phone, Charlie?'

'Yes, right here.'

'Phone 999 and tell them we need the air ambulance, too,' she requested, knowing that if what she attempted was successful, the boy would need to get to hospital as fast as possible.

As Charlie made the call, Jess focused on the task ahead. Nervousness gripped her. Shutting out the comments from the small crowds on the rocks above her and the beach below, she steadied herself and called on all her former training. She was scared, but she'd done this a few times before. She could do it now. She had to if the boy wasn't to suffocate before the ambulance arrived. Closing her eyes, she did a quick mental run-through of the emergency procedure she had never expected to be called on to perform again.

After using an antiseptic wipe on the boy's throat, she draped some gauze around the site and then she took out the sterile, single-use blade that was in the kit. She had no local anaesthetic available, but with his consciousness level low he probably didn't need it. Unsure how aware he was, she told him what she needed to do, talking through it as much to steady herself as him.

With the fingers of one hand she felt for the correct spot on the throat and, with her other hand, made a small vertical incision through the skin. Identifying the cricothyroid membrane, she made a horizontal cut through it, careful to ensure that she didn't damage the cartilage. With no proper tracheal spreader available she had to improvise again, and she used the handle of a small knife she found in the kit, inserting it into the incision and turning it so that it created a small passage. Already there was a life-saving flow of air in and out as the boy's lungs inflated and reinflated.

'Could you cut me some strips of tape, Charlie?'

As he obliged, Jess cut a piece of plastic tube to the right length and, with great care so as not to damage any cartilage or the vocal cords, angled it and slid it into the makeshift passageway. It was a temporary measure but it would keep the boy alive and his airway open until the paramedics arrived. Taking the strips Charlie handed her, she secured the tube in place.

'Well done, Jess!' Charlie praised when she had finished, giving a thumbs-up to the crowd on the promontory and beach, who broke into spontaneous applause.

Jess sat back and let out a shaky breath. 'Thanks.'

It had only taken two or three minutes to complete the procedure and yet she felt weary and quite unsteady. Taking the boy's hand, she continued to monitor his breathing, relieved that he was awake. She gently wiped away the blood from around his eyes—brown eyes that were now open again and staring at her with a mix of relief and fright and pain.

'The ambulance will be here very soon,' she reassured him, rewarded when his fingers tightened on hers.

He was going to need an excellent maxillofacial surgeon for reconstruction, Jess reflected, her thoughts interrupted by the sound of an approaching siren, and relief flowed through her as the ambulance arrived. Charlie moved the first-aid kit out of the way, then showed the paramedics the best way down the rocks. Jess recognised both men, who greeted her by name, their surprise evident as she debriefed them and they realised the role she had played in events.

Things passed in a blur after that. Charlie left, but Jess remained where she was, answering the occasional question but mostly watching the paramedics work. It wasn't long before they were joined by the medics from the air ambulance and she had to give her debrief over again. Once the boy was stabilised, volunteers were needed to help extricate the stretcher from the difficult location, but before long he was off the rocks and on his way to St Piran's in the helicopter.

'Now, then, Jess, our heroine of the day, what about you?' Stuart asked, squatting down in front of her while Mark cleared up their things and invited the more nosy and persistent onlookers to disperse.

'Me?' Jess frowned. 'I'm fine.'

He chuckled. 'I hardly think so, love. You're pale as a ghost and your leg is a mess,' he pointed out.

'I'd forgotten all about it,' she admitted, so focused had she been on what she needed to do.

'You were a bit busy, weren't you?' His grin was infectious. 'Are you hurt anywhere else?'

'Just some cuts and bruises. I bashed my side and twisted my foot when I fell. It's nothing. I'll clean up at home,' she assured him, anxiety setting in at the prospect of either Stuart or Mark treating her.

Pulling on a fresh pair of protective gloves, Stuart sat back and looked at her. 'That's a deep cut, Jess. You've lost a fair bit of blood and it's going to need stitching. And that's without getting the other things checked out.'

Her anxiety increasing, Jess bit her lip. She wished she could dismiss her injuries and refuse treatment, but looking at her leg she could see that the wound was bad and not something she would advise anyone else to try and take care of alone. As the adrenalin that had sustained her while waiting for the ambulance wore off, her foot and her ribs were also becoming increasingly painful and she feared she might have broken at least one bone. All of which meant she was going to have to tell Stuart the truth.

Fighting back an uncharacteristic welling up of tears, she sucked in a ragged breath. 'Stuart, I...' She hesitated, frightened what would happen when he knew.

'What's wrong, Jess?' he prompted, his concern evident.

'You need to double-glove,' she told him, her voice unsteady, her lashes lowering so that she wouldn't see the expression on his face. 'I'm HIV positive.'

A few seconds of silence followed and she felt sick as she waited for the inevitable reaction to her admission. An errant tear escaped and landed on her cheek. It was Stuart's hand that reached out to wipe it away and she glanced up, wide-eyed with surprise to see nothing but understanding and compassion in the forty-year-old father-of-three's hazel eyes.

'Don't you worry, Jess, love. We'll take good care of you.'

His kindness and easy acceptance, so at odds with

her earlier experiences—apart from Gio, of course—brought a fresh welling up of emotion. As Stuart set about dressing her leg, Jess struggled to push thoughts of Gio to the back of her mind. She wished more than anything that he was there with her now. But he wasn't. She was on her own. Just as she had been these last four years.

Before she knew it, they were setting off on the thirty-minute drive from Penhally to St Piran, arriving a long time after the air ambulance had deposited their casualty. Stuart and Mark were wonderful, as was Ben Carter, into whose experienced, caring and understanding hands they delivered her.

Supportive and reassuring, Ben guarded her confidentiality and refused to make an issue of her status. By the time she had been X-rayed—thankfully there proved to be no breaks—and returned to A and E to have the deep cut on her leg stitched, her other cuts and grazes cleaned and a supportive bandage put on her swollen, painful foot, she was feeling tired and woozy. The antibiotics and pain medication she'd been given didn't help.

Dismissing the nurse who had waited with her, Ben drew up a chair, sat down and sent her a warm smile. 'I know you wanted news. The boy's name is Will. He's in Theatre and has the best of chances, thanks to you. You saved his life today, Jess. Care to tell me how you did it?' he asked, signing off her notes and closing the file.

Her defences lowered by all that had happened, not just with Will and her own injury but the deep pain of Gio's rejection and withdrawal, she found herself pouring the whole story out to Ben.

'Surgery's loss is St Piran's gain,' he told her a while later when her flow of words had ended.

'Thank you.'

'Does Gio know? Do you want me to call him?'

The two questions brought a fresh threat of tears. 'Yes, he knows,' she admitted, trying to steady her voice before she continued, forcing out the words. 'But don't call him. He's in Italy. And we're just friends.'

'Friends?' Ben raised a sceptical eyebrow.

'You heard about his wife?' she asked. When Ben nodded, she continued. 'He's not ready for a new relationship. Even if he was, it's too much for him to take on someone like me.'

'I wouldn't give up on him too quickly, Jess.'

She appreciated Ben's kindness but she had little hope left in fairy-tales. Resting her head back, feeling very tired, she sighed. 'Can I go home?'

'Not for a while, especially as you'll be on your own once you get there,' he added brushing aside her half-hearted protest.

A knock on the door curbed further conversation and senior staff nurse Ellen came in. Although she smiled, it was clear that something was bothering her and, before she closed the door, Jess heard the sound of some sort of commotion going on somewhere in the department.

'I'm sorry to interrupt,' Ellen apologised. 'Ben, we have a problem out here. Can you come?'

'Yes, of course. Rest here for a while and try not to worry about anything, Jess. I'll be back shortly to see you,' he promised, giving her hand a squeeze before pushing back the chair and rising to his feet.

'Thanks, Ben.'

'Is there anything I can get for you, love?' Ellen

asked, taking a moment to fuss with the sheet and pillows and make sure she was comfortable.

Feeling tired and washed out, Jess managed a smile. 'No, thanks. I'm fine.'

As they left the room, leaving her alone, Jess closed her eyes. It was one thing to tell her not to worry, but she was finding it impossible when her thoughts were fixed firmly on Gio. Despite thinking she could never trust a man again, in such a short time she had fallen irrevocably in love. But he couldn't feel the same about her and now, when she most needed his arms around her, he wasn't there. Ben had told her not to give up, but why would Gio want someone who was living with a condition that could change at any moment and drastically reduce her life expectancy, causing him to lose someone else?

She'd taken a huge risk, opening her heart and allowing Gio into her life, and all too briefly she'd experienced a piece of heaven before it had been ripped away from her again. She had no idea what the future held in store. After years of uncertainty, she had found a place where she felt at home and could settle. Was that now all to change because of Gio?

As much as he'd enjoyed his couple of days back home in Italy, and especially celebrating his parents' fortieth wedding anniversary, Gio continued to feel edgy and unsettled. For once it was nothing to do with returning to a place that reminded him of Sofia. His disquiet was all due to Jessica. Within hours he would be flying back to the UK and driving to the house he had shared with her in St Piran these last weeks. Knowing that she wouldn't be there made that return a dismal prospect.

'Something is troubling you, *figlio*.'

Gio looked up as his father joined him on the terrace and he gave a wry smile, unsurprised by the older man's insight. 'I'm fine, *Papà*.'

'Tell me about his woman.'

'What woman?' Gio prevaricated, shifting uncomfortably.

'You said you might be bringing a friend this weekend,' he reminded, 'but you came alone.'

'I might have meant a male friend.'

His father chuckled. 'You might. But you didn't. My guess is that you were referring to the woman who has been staying with you. The woman responsible for bringing you back to life these last weeks, bringing laughter and happiness back to your eyes.'

Gio sighed, somewhat stunned by his father's words. And by the realisation, the truth, of how much Jessica had changed him in the short time he had known her. He leaned against the railing and gazed out at the familiar Piedmont countryside. It was home—and yet now his heart felt as if it belonged elsewhere.

'Gio?'

Turning round, he pulled up a chair next to his father. 'I think I've made a big mistake, *Papà*.'

It had not been his intention to unburden himself, but now he found himself telling his father all about Jessica—and his dilemma.

'*Figlio*, you have never lacked courage. Do not start doubting yourself and your feelings now,' his father advised when he had finally run out of words.

'What do you mean?' Gio asked with a frown, running the fingers of one hand through his hair.

'Tell me,' his father asked, leaning forward and

resting his elbows on his knees, his gaze direct, 'would you have forgone the life you had with Sofia if you had known in advance that you would lose her when you did?'

A flash of anger flared within him at the question. 'Of course not!'

'That is what I thought.' His father smiled and although his tone gentled, his words lost none of their impact. 'Yet now you risk throwing away this second chance for love and happiness because you fear that you will one day lose Jessica, too.'

'*Papà*...'

His father gestured with one hand to silence him. 'Jessica is clearly a very special woman and she has become very important to you. You love her, I can see it in your eyes and hear it in your voice when you speak of her, and yet you're holding back. I know the pain and heartache you suffered when Sofia died. We all miss her. What you had together was so rare and so special. Few of us are blessed with that kind of happiness *once* in a lifetime, let alone *twice*,' the older man pointed out with a shake of his head.

In the brief pause that followed, the words sank in and Gio reflected on just how lucky he had been. He looked up as his father rested a hand on his shoulder and continued.

'We are all going to die at some time. What is important is what we do with the time we have. You have made us so proud, *figlio*, not only with your career and the work you do in Sofia's name but also because of the person you are. From all you have told me of her, your Jessica is a rare woman, and not one who would ever now trust herself to a man lightly. Yet she has trusted herself to *you*. Are you going to let her down? Are you going to let fear turn you away from love and the many years you could have together?'

The questions hit him full force, shocking him, but his father had not yet finished with him.

'Sofia would be so angry with you, Gio. She wanted you to live, to be happy, to love. Now you have found someone worthy of you, someone who has brought so much to your life. Don't throw that away, *figlio*,' he pleaded softly. 'You have our blessing, and Ginetta's, too,' he added, referring to Sofia's mother, who remained part of their family. 'You deserve new love and happiness. So does Jessica. Follow your heart…go back to the place that has become your home and show the woman who has given you so much the kind of man I know you to be.'

Hours later everything his father said still resonated in his head. It was early on Monday morning but he had given up trying to sleep. He had driven past Jessica's cottage before coming home from the airport but her car had not been there and it was clear no one was in. When he had also been unable to reach her by phone, unease had set in. Where was she?

Now he stared out of the window, seeing nothing but the darkness. There was also darkness inside himself. The house had felt cold and stark and lonely without Jessica, as he had feared it would. And so had he. All the joy and fun and warmth had left it with her departure. A departure he could blame on no one but himself.

He pressed one palm to the hollow ache in his chest. He had been so blind, so stupid. How could he have ever believed that he could live for the rest of his life in a vacuum? He hadn't been living at all, only existing. It was Jessica who had brought meaning back to his world again and had made him want to embrace life in every way.

Leaning his forehead against the coolness of the glass, he reflected on his mistakes. He had coaxed and cajoled Jessica into trusting him, caring for him, opening up to him. He'd taken what she had given him without properly considering just what it must have taken for her to trust, and exactly what that trust meant. She had shown such courage, while he had got cold feet. In doing so he had behaved as abominably as her ex-fiancé, her family and her former friends and colleagues had. How must Jessica be feeling now? *He* felt lower than low when he forced himself to consider what his withdrawal, his insistence that they could have nothing but friendship, must have done to her.

Dio!

How was he going to put things right?

Because he could see now with startling clarity that all his father had said was true. And he thought of Luca, who had been through a similar kind of loss as his own and who'd had the courage to let love back into his life again. He was a doctor, Gio chided himself. He knew that Jessica could fall ill tomorrow—but equally she could live a long and normal lifespan, keeping fit and well. Given the right care and precautions, even having a healthy child free of HIV was not the impossibility she believed it to be. Whatever she wished, he would support her all the way.

No one knew what the future held in store, just as his father and Luca had said. And facing the rest of his life alone was no longer the answer he had once thought. He could not guard himself from hurt without denying himself all the joys. And he knew now, after such a short time without Jessica, that he didn't want to waste any more time alone. Whether they had five years or fifty years, he wanted to share every moment with her. If she would forgive him and allow him a second chance.

Jessica had trusted him in the most elemental way and he had let her down. The knowledge cut him to the quick. In the face of her bravery he had been nothing but a coward. Were he to be lucky enough to win her back, he would spend the rest of their lives together proving to her that she was loved and cherished. Going downstairs, he made coffee and stepped outside into the coolness of the pre-dawn air, lost in his thoughts.

Along with the album Sofia had made of their lives had been a final letter for him. He carried it with him always, with her photo, next to his heart. He knew it word for word as she told him how much she loved him, that every moment had been worth it because they had been together, how she respected him and supported him.

'You must go on with your career, Cori, and with your life. Grieve for me, but not for too long. We have been so blessed and had so much more in twenty-two years than many people have in a whole lifetime. I know you, *amore mio*. And I beg you to move on, not to stay alone and sad for the rest of your life. I want you to be happy, fulfilled, cared for. You have so much love to give. Open your heart, Cori. For me. I will always be with you and will always love you. Look up at the night sky and the brightest star will be me smiling down on you, wishing you the best of everything and for a special woman to love you as I love you.'

His throat tight with emotion, he turned his gaze up to

the sky, finding the brightest star. He thought of Sofia's words, of her wish for him, her blessing, and realised he was letting her down by refusing to accept all life had to offer him. Had their places been reversed, he would have wanted the same for her...that she would find someone to care for her, who would make her happy. And his courageous, spirited Sofia would grieve, would never forget, but would face life with her customary bravery. Just as Jessica was doing in her own way, making a whole new life for herself after being so badly betrayed and left to cope with the devastation alone. He owed it to Sofia, to Jessica and to himself to step back into life.

He looked back at the star, opening his heart, knowing Sofia would always be there, that he would never forget and would always love her, but that there was room and a special place for Jessica, too. It was time. For a moment it seemed as if the star glowed even brighter, filling him with a sense of peace. As dawn broke, the stars fading as the sky slowly lightened, bringing a rosy glow to the magnificent Cornish coastline, Gio knew what he had to do.

CHAPTER ELEVEN

'OH, MY God.' Jess felt her whole world shattering into tiny pieces as she stared in horrified disbelief at the local newspaper. This couldn't be happening. 'How? Why?'

Ben sat solemn-faced beside her, appearing tired and drawn, as if he hadn't slept in the hours since she'd last seen him. 'I'm sorry, Jess. We tried to stop it.'

Fighting back tears and a terrible sense of doom, she re-examined the lurid headline emblazoned in large letters across the front page...

HOSPITAL HEROINE HAS HIV!

The night was a blur. She'd fallen asleep in A and E, knocked out by the medication and emotional exhaustion. 'We don't normally have staff sleeping in the department overnight but we made an exception for you,' Josh had teased her when he'd checked her over before the night shift ended.

When Ben had come back on duty, she'd discovered that the disturbance he'd been called to had been caused by Kennie Vernon, a reporter on the *St Piran Gazette*, known as 'Vermin' for his unpleasant methods and his motto of never allowing the truth to spoil a good story.

She'd met him once when he'd delved unsuccessfully into the background of a patient in her care, and he'd left an unfavourable impression. Short and stout, his greasy black hair worn in a narrow ponytail, he had a goatee beard, beady brown eyes and a shifty nature.

'One of the bystanders in Penhally overheard you telling the paramedics about the HIV and informed Kennie. The bastard ran with that angle of the story.' Ben's anger and disgust were evident. 'He came poking around A and E. I threw him out. You were sleeping, so Josh and I decided to keep you here. We didn't want you going home alone or risk you running into Kennie.'

Jess wrapped her arms around herself, unable to stop shaking. 'What am I going to do?'

'You told me about the appalling way you were treated when you were first diagnosed, but that isn't going to happen here,' he reassured her, but she lacked belief.

'Right.'

Ben took her hand. 'You'll be surprised, Jess. I'm not, because I know you are loved and respected. There may be one or two idiots, but ninety-nine percent of the hospital are supporting you. We've had endless calls sending you good wishes and they're continuing to come in.'

Jess didn't know what to say.

'We took the liberty of making some arrangements on your behalf,' he continued, and nervousness fluttered in her stomach.

'What arrangements?'

'Flora wanted to help. She said she held a spare key for your cottage in case of an emergency?' Jess nodded, trying to take everything in. 'Knowing you'd worry, she's picked up your kittens and will look after them for as long as you need.'

'Thank you,' she murmured, surprised but relieved.

'Your car remains where you left it in Penhally, so you'll need a lift to pick it up, but Megan met Flora at your cottage and collected some things you might need.'

Fresh tears pricked her eyes. For someone who seldom cried, she could have filled a swimming pool this last week. She didn't ask, but the person she most wanted to know about, and to see, was Gio. He'd be back from Italy. He might even be in the hospital, she realised, glancing at her watch, shocked by the time. What would he think? She felt sick with worry.

When Ben left, Jess gingerly slipped out of bed, thankful for the adjacent shower room that meant she didn't have to wander down the corridor in the unflattering hospital gown she was wearing. After a wash, she sat on the bed, feeling emotionally and physically battered as she wondered what to do.

'Where is she?'

Jess heard Megan's anxious question from outside and someone's voice mumble in reply. She barely had a moment to compose herself before her friend rushed in, her face pale and tears spiking her eyelashes. Without uttering a word, Megan dropped a carrier bag on the bed and wrapped her in a hug.

'You silly, silly girl,' she admonished, halfway between a laugh and a sob. 'Oh, how I wish I'd known. I can't bear to think of you going through this alone.'

Megan's acceptance and support was overwhelming. Jess began to explain, her voice shaky and whisper soft, when Brianna arrived. She looked as worried and upset as Megan. And, like Megan, Brianna's first instinct was to hug her.

With her friends giving the caring support she had never expected to know, Jess told them what she had told Gio—about Duncan, her diagnosis, the prejudice, ignorance and discrimination she'd encountered, and being disowned by her family. They were all crying by the time she had finished.

'I'd have been scared witless doing an emergency cricothyroidotomy,' Megan admitted when the talk moved on to the incident on the rocks and Jess's former career. 'I'm in awe at what you did.'

Brianna hugged her again. 'We all are. You're amazing, Jess. How far through your training were you?'

'I'd qualified and had begun a trauma rotation when I was diagnosed. I wanted to be a surgeon but was advised to find another career.'

'That's awful,' Brianna stated.

'It is,' Megan agreed. 'But it explains why you're so knowledgeable and able to explain things to patients when we don't have time. Do you miss it?'

'At first I was devastated. I attended an HIV support group and someone there suggested I think about counselling,' she told them, sharing things she'd told no one but Gio. 'I could continue helping people but without physical contact. I enjoy what I do and wouldn't change it now.'

'What about Gio?' Megan asked softly.

'He wants friendship, that's all.' It didn't become any easier with repetition. 'I understand why after he lost his wife. And it isn't as if I have anything to offer him.'

'Stuff and nonsense!' Brianna exclaimed, her Irish accent stronger than usual.

It hurt too much to talk about Gio so Jess changed the subject and reflected on the damage the newspaper article might have caused. The nightmare was real, the secret she had guarded was now public knowledge, and she feared the consequences. She was mulling over what to do when Ben returned.

'I'd rather you had a couple of days off and rested that leg, but sitting at home alone won't be good for you.' He frowned, deep in thought. 'We can look out for you here at the hospital. Just be sensible and don't over-stretch your side. And keep your foot up as much as possible. I've brought you some pain medication. Come and see us if you're not feeling well or you have problems with the wound.'

Jess took the tablets and smiled. 'OK. Thanks, Ben, you've been wonderful. How's Lucy?'

'About to pop!' he said, making them laugh. 'She's fed up and excited. We can't wait for the baby to arrive.'

Jess noticed Megan's and Brianna's smiles dimmed and both had pain in their eyes. She suspected her friends carried secrets and had been hurt in the past, and she wished there was something she could do to help them.

After Ben had given her a hug and final instructions, he returned to work. Megan and Brianna had to do the same but, before leaving, they arranged to meet up for lunch. Before heading to her office and what could be an uncomfortable chat with her boss, Jess changed into the clothes Megan had collected for her and went up to the ward to check on Will, anxious to know how he was. She felt nervous and unsure of the reception she would receive from colleagues and patients.

* * *

Driving to the hospital, Gio joined the queue at the traffic lights, his gaze straying to the pavement outside the newsagent's shop. His heart threatened to stop as he noted the headline on the local paper. Pasted onto a sandwich board for all to see, it shrieked out at him...

HOSPITAL HEROINE HAS HIV!

He swore furiously in Italian. There was little doubt to whom the headline referred. What the hell had been going on while he'd been in Italy? Anxious for Jessica and desperate to find out what lay behind the headline, he waited in frustration as the lights changed and the traffic moved forward then made his way as fast as he could to the hospital.

Dread clutched at him as he parked his car and hurried inside. One of the first people he saw was Ben, who gave him a brief résumé of events and then showed him the newspaper. While he felt deep concern for her well-being and fury at the thoughtless reporter, he was also full of pride at the way Jessica had saved the young man's life.

'Thank you for taking such good care of her,' he said now, shaking Ben's hand. 'Where is she?'

'She left here about five minutes ago and was going to visit Will in Intensive Care before going to her office.'

'Thanks,' he repeated.

Ben nodded, holding his gaze. 'Jess needs you, Gio,' his friend told him, and he knew he deserved the hint of chastisement that had laced the words.

'I need her, too,' he confided, earning himself a smile. 'I won't let her down again.'

Determined, he set off to find her.

* * *

'May I sit down?' Josh asked, taking advantage of the rare opportunity of finding Megan sitting alone in the canteen.

'OK.'

The agreement was grudging, but at least she *had* agreed and hadn't told him to go away. He set down his mug of coffee and pulled up a chair.

She looked at him, a small frown on her face. 'You look tired.'

'Is that a polite way of saying rough?' he teased with a wry smile, running the palm of one hand across his stubbled jaw, intrigued by the flush that brought a wash of colour to her pale cheeks.

'No, I didn't mean that.'

'I've just pulled an extra couple of night shifts and needed the caffeine fix before going home for some sleep. I'm back on days tomorrow,' he explained, savouring the hot, reviving drink.

What he didn't tell her was that he'd been doing extra shifts to avoid having to go home. Things were becoming more and more untenable with Rebecca and he didn't know what to do about it. They had grown further apart than ever. He had tried to encourage her to get out of the house, to take up some kind of voluntary work or hobby if she didn't want to get a job. Anything to give her something else to focus on instead of sitting at home working out ways to try and persuade him to change his mind about having a baby.

He wasn't going to change his mind. Ever. What he hadn't told Rebecca was that he had once teetered on the brink of fatherhood—unknowingly and no more willingly as that may have been at the time. He took another drink, his gaze fixed on Megan. Since talking to her and hearing once and for all that her baby had been his, he'd been able to think of little else.

Hearing in words the reality that he had held his tiny, lifeless son in his hands had hit him far harder than he had ever expected. And it had only made him more certain that having a baby with Rebecca was the wrong thing to do in so many ways, for him, for her and, most importantly of all, for any resulting child.

Setting down his mug, he folded his arms and leaned on the table, watching as Megan spread honey on a granary roll. 'How's Jess?'

'A bit sore. Very upset about the newspaper report. That beastly man,' she growled, echoing his feelings and those of everyone he knew.

'Poor Jess. No one needs that kind of thing.' He shook his head. 'I think people are more stunned at discovering she's a qualified doctor and saved that boy's life than anything else.'

Megan licked sticky honey off her finger, a simple gesture but one that nearly stopped his heart and brought a wave of all-too-familiar desire—the same desire he had always felt for her and her alone.

'Megan...'

'Don't, Josh, please. I—' Her words snapped off, her expression changing as she looked beyond him. He sensed her complete withdrawal, but before he could ask what was wrong, she spoke again. 'Your wife is here.'

He swore under his breath, looking round and seeing Rebecca standing just inside the entrance of the canteen. As always she looked picture perfect. Expensively dressed, polished, outwardly beautiful...and completely out of place.

'Megan,' he began again, returning his attention

to her, not at all sure what he wanted to say, still so confused and churned up inside, knowing only that he resented Rebecca's intrusion.

'Just go, Josh.'

After a moment of indecision he rose to his feet, spurred into action as Rebecca spotted him and began to close the distance between them. After an inadequate word of farewell, he left Megan and worked his way between the tables towards Rebecca and the exit.

'What are you doing here?' he asked, taking her arm to steer her out of the canteen, irritation shooting through him, compounded by the tiredness of two long night shifts.

She made her customary pout. 'You said the garage wouldn't have your car ready until this afternoon, so I thought I'd surprise you and pick you up.'

'I told you there was no need.'

They walked in silence towards the exit. A silence that spoke volumes about the physical, mental and emotional distance between them. They had nothing to speak about, nothing left in common. They didn't talk any more. He wondered if they ever had. One thing was certain…he could never share with her the jumble of emotions that continued to rage within him about Megan and about Stephen, their lost son.

'You! Ms Carmichael. Or Dr Carmichael…whatever your name is!'

Leaving Intensive Care after visiting Will, who was making good progress, and having been thanked by his grateful parents who had seen the newspaper report but were just relieved that their son was alive, Jess halted.

Her stomach churned as she turned to face the man whose angry voice had bellowed her name.

She'd been overwhelmed by the support she'd received from colleagues, many of whom had made a point of stopping her on her walk from A and E to Intensive Care. Now she was forced to encounter someone who sounded far from friendly.

The man was short and stocky with a ruddy complexion and a receding hairline. His heavy footsteps pounded on the floor as he strode determinedly towards her. Nervous, Jess heard the familiar ping that announced the arrival of one of the lifts, accompanied by the soft whooshing sound as the door opened. Unfortunately the lift was too far away for her to use it as an escape route.

'It's outrageous that you are allowed to walk around this hospital so close to vulnerable patients,' the man stated loudly, making her cringe with embarrassment. 'I don't want you anywhere near my wife.'

As the man continued his tirade, his language becoming ever more abusive, Jess was very aware that they were drawing a crowd. People walking the corridors stopped to see what was going on, while others emerged from nearby wards and offices. No one intervened. She was on her own.

Alarmed and humiliated, Jess stepped back, only to find her path blocked as she came up against something solid and strong and warm. Before she could even draw breath and absorb the fact that Gio was really here, one of his arms wrapped around her, across the front of her shoulders, drawing her against his familiar frame, making her feel protected.

'That is enough, sir.' Gio didn't raise his voice and

yet his words rang with such authority and steely command that her detractor at once fell silent. 'You have no business abusing any member of hospital staff at any time, and even less so when your information is wrong and you are speaking from ignorance.'

'But—'

'But nothing. Jessica is a highly valued and respected colleague. Her status is no one's business but her own and she poses absolutely no danger to anyone else,' he stated firmly, his hold on her tightening as she relaxed into him, drawing on his strength. 'Yesterday she saved the life of a young man who would have died had she not been there. For her courage and her selflessness she deserves gratitude and praise, not the ill-informed comments and judgemental attitudes of people who do not know what they are talking about.'

Jess remained speechless with amazement as Gio launched into his defence of her, declaring his support of and belief in her. But even when the man who had challenged her had been silenced and walked away by Security, she discovered that Gio had more to say, uncaring of their audience of colleagues, patients and visitors who remained.

'I am so proud of you, Jessica, and so sorry that I was not here for you when you needed me,' he declared, gently turning her round and cupping her face in his hands. She stared into intense blue eyes, every part of her shaking. 'I love you. I want to marry you and spend the rest of my life with you...if you will have me and forgive me for being so stupid this week and letting you down.'

Jess barely heard the gasps of delight and whispered comments from the people around them. All she could see, all she could hear, all she cared about was Gio, the man who had changed her life in such a short time, who believed in her and accepted her and who had just announced his love for her to the world.

'If I'll have you?'

She didn't know whether to laugh or to cry! So she did both. At the same time. He was everything she wanted. All she wanted. After the last few days of pain and uncertainty, thinking she could never have more than his friendship, she could hardly dare to believe this was true. For now, a wave of love and joy swamped the doubts that still lingered within her. Uncaring of where they were, of her painful side and throbbing leg—even of providing more gossip fodder for nosy Rita—she wrapped her arms around his neck, welcoming the instant response as his own arms enclosed her and held her close.

'I love you, too,' she managed through her tears.

As he swept her off her feet and into a passionate kiss, she dimly heard the whistles and whoops, the calls of congratulations and the spontaneous round of applause. She kissed him back with equal fervour and with all the emotion, love and thankfulness that swelled her heart.

After what had seemed the longest of days, and when he finally had Jessica to himself, Gio could not banish the flicker of unease that nagged at him. Concerned for her well-being and her injuries, he had brought her home to her cottage and insisted she rest while he cooked them a meal. She had eaten it, but she had grown quieter and quieter as the evening progressed. Now, as she paced the living room, her limp evident, he could bear the suspense no more.

As she passed within reach of his armchair, he caught her hand and drew her down to sit on his lap. A deep sigh escaped her and although she didn't pull away from him, she was far from relaxed.

'What is wrong, *fiamma*?' he asked, scared that she was having doubts and changing her mind. 'You are so restless. Talk to me.'

'I can't thank you enough for what you did today. It was horrible and I didn't know what to do.' For a moment she hesitated, her gaze averted, then she sighed again and looked at him, revealing the shadows in her olive-green eyes. 'Then you were there and made everything right.'

So why did he suddenly feel that things were now wrong? His heart lurched in fear. 'Jessica...'

'I won't hold you to it. I'll understand if it was something you said on the spur of the moment because of the circumstances,' she told him in a rush, her voice shaky.

'You won't hold me to what?' he asked, genuinely puzzled.

Long lashes lowered to mask her expression and her voice dropped to a whisper. 'Marrying me. You don't have to.'

'You don't want me to?'

'Yes. No. Not if you don't want to.'

She frowned in confusion and he felt bad for teasing her, but now he could see to the root of her worries, it felt as if a huge weight had lifted from his shoulders. He understood her doubts. He deserved them after the way he had behaved. But this, he hoped, he could deal with.

'Look at me.' He cupped her face with one hand,

drawing her gaze to his. 'It is true I had not planned on asking you to marry me in such a way, with so many people listening. But at the time a public declaration seemed right.' Uncertainty remained in her eyes. 'Can you pass me my jacket?'

'OK.'

He held her steady as, her frown deepening, she reached out to retrieve the jacket of his suit, which he had discarded and left draped over the arm of the adjacent sofa.

'Thank you.' With his free hand he checked the pockets until he found what he needed. 'The timing and the setting may have been unplanned, but I meant every word I said.'

He heard her indrawn gasp of surprise and she looked at him with a mix of warring emotions in her eyes. 'Gio?'

'I'm not surprised you doubted me. I deserve that after the terrible way I behaved last week,' he told her, pressing a finger to her lips to silence her protests. 'It needs to be said, *fiamma*. I was wrong. I knew how badly other people had treated you and yet I allowed my own momentary fears to rise up and my withdrawal, timed with my trip to Italy, must have felt like another rejection of you. I am so sorry.'

'Don't.' She caught his hand, their fingers instinctively linking together. 'I understand. And I don't blame you.'

'You should.'

She shook her head, her loose hair shimmering and dancing like living fire. 'No. You went through so much with Sofia. I knew you were scared of going through anything like that again. And, let's face it, the odds could be less good with me.'

'I do not care about odds, Jessica, I care about *you*,' he insisted. 'I never imagined that I could fall in love again, that I would ever know happiness and peace again, but my life changed for the better the moment I met you. Thanks to you I stopped existing and started living again.'

'Gio,' she whispered, her eyes bright with unshed tears.

'Please, I need to say this.' He drew her hand to his mouth and kissed it. 'I hate that I hurt you, that my withdrawal left you so lonely and uncertain. You deserved so much more from me and, if you will let me, I'll spend the rest of our lives proving to you how much I love you and that I'll never let you down again.' He paused a moment, sucking in an unsteady breath, his heart thudding against his ribs. 'I came back from Italy knowing what an idiot I had been and knowing what I wanted and needed to do. Events overtook us, and my plans went awry.'

Eyes wide with disbelief and hope, she bit her lip, her fingers clinging to his. 'What plans?' she managed, and he could feel the tremble running through her.

'My plans to be with you alone, like this, to beg your forgiveness and to ask you properly to be my wife.' Holding her gaze, he released her hand and reached into his pocket once more, drawing out the box. 'I bought this in Italy. For you. I meant all I said this morning, I just meant to say it in private! So the timing may have been wrong, but the question was heartfelt and genuine, not something I made up on the spot.' He placed the little box in her hand. 'Jessica, I love you. I want to spend the rest of my life cherishing you, being your friend and your lover. Please, will you make me the happiest and luckiest of men and marry me?'

'Yes. Yes, yes, yes!'

Jess felt as if her heart had swollen so full of love and joy that it would surely stop beating. All day doubts had nagged at her, but now her fears had been allayed as Gio had laid his own heart on the line for her. Again. Her vision blurred by tears, her fingers shaking so badly she could hardly make them work properly, she did as he encouraged and opened the jeweller's box.

'Oh, my,' she gasped. 'Gio!'

'You like it?' he asked nervously, and she laughed through her tears that he could doubt it.

She gazed down at the gorgeous ring. Set in platinum were three stunning olive apatite stones that exactly matched those in the earrings her grandmother had given her and which she wore every day. The three stones were set on a slight angle with the shoulders of the ring overlapping each side, each sparkling with a row of tiny diamonds. It was the most divine ring she had ever seen. She didn't dare imagine how much it had cost but it was not the monetary value that mattered, it was that Gio had chosen something so special, with such care, knowing what it would mean to her and giving it to her with love.

'It's beautiful,' she murmured huskily as he took it from the box and set it on her finger. 'Perfect. Thank you.'

'You are perfect and beautiful.'

He cupped her face, bestowing on her the gentlest and most exquisite of kisses. Jess sank into him, wrapping her arms around him, wondering how she had ever been lucky enough to know such happiness. As the passion flared between them, healing the past, uniting them heart and soul and full of promise for the future, she gave thanks for this very special man.

'I love your home,' Gio told her softly as they lay in bed later that night, replete after the physical expression of their love and togetherness. 'I feel at peace here,' he continued, filling her already overflowing heart with new joy as his feelings mirrored her own. 'Any day the fences will be ready and our menagerie will come home.'

'I thought maybe you'd arranged for that to be done so I'd leave your house and move back here,' she admitted softly.

'No!' He sounded so shocked she couldn't help but laugh, secure now in his feelings and her own. 'That was not why at all,' he insisted. 'It was to make you happy but also, selfishly, because I wanted to come here and to care for the animals with you. Can this *be* our home, *fiamma*? Can we bring this beautiful shell back to life together and make it ours for ever?'

'Yes, please!'

Snuggling into his embrace, she smiled into the darkness, knowing that they shared the same vision, not just for this place that would be their home but for their future. However long they were blessed with they would share together. And with the friends and colleagues who had shown them so much support and understanding.

It was not just the cottage that had been a shell that would be brought back to life. She and Gio had been shells, too. They had each been alone, rocked and ravaged by the events that had turned their lives upside down. But fate had brought them together…two people who had needed each other so much. They had found their place. Had found each other. And together they had found the sunshine, new hope and a fresh joy of living.

Safe in Gio's arms, Jess felt truly at peace, secure in a love, a friendship and a happiness that neither of them had ever expected to know again. They had been granted second chances and they had found their rightful place in this special part of Cornwall.

It had been a difficult journey but, finally, she was where she was meant to be…with Gio.

LET'S TALK
Romance

For exclusive extracts, competitions
and special offers, find us online:

- facebook.com/millsandboon
- @millsandboonuk
- @millsandboon

Or get in touch on 0844 844 1351*

For all the latest titles coming soon, visit
millsandboon.co.uk/nextmonth

*Calls cost 7p per minute plus your phone company's price per minute access charge

Want even more ROMANCE?

Join our bookclub today!

'Mills & Boon books, the perfect way to escape for an hour or so.'

Miss W. Dyer

'Excellent service, promptly delivered and very good subscription choices.'

Miss A. Pearson

'You get fantastic special offers and the chance to get books before they hit the shops'

Mrs V. Hall

Visit millsandbook.co.uk/Bookclub
and save on brand new books.

MILLS & BOON